Born in Paris in 1947, Christian Jacq first visited Egypt when he was seventeen, went on to study Egyptology and archaeology at the Sorbonne, and is now one of the world's leading Egyptologists. He is the author of the internationally bestselling RAMSES series, THE STONE OF LIGHT series and the stand-alone novel, THE BLACK PHARAOH. Christian Jacq lives in Switzerland.

Also by Christian Jacq

Master Hiram and King Solomon

Christian Jacq

Translated by Marcia de Brito

POCKET
BOOKS

LONDON · SYDNEY · NEW YORK · TOKYO · TORONTO

First published in Great Britain by Pocket Books, 2003
An imprint of Simon & Schuster UK Ltd
A Viacom Company

3 5 7 9 10 8 6 4

Simon & Schuster UK Ltd
Africa House
64–78 Kingsway
London WC2B 6AH
www.simonsays.co.uk

Simon & Schuster Australia
Sydney

A CIP catalogue record for this book is available from
the British Library

ISBN 0-671-02857-X

Typeset by SX Composing DTP, Rayleigh, Essex
Printed and bound in Great Britain by
Cox & Wyman Ltd, Reading, Berkshire

Master Hiram
and King
Solomon

First Part

I will make Wisdom my life companion.
She will be my counsellor on happy days,
The consolation in my worries and sorrows.
Thanks to her, I will gain fame with the crowds,
And though still young, honour with the elders.
Who, more than Wisdom, is the builder of the Universe?

Book of Wisdom, 8, 9–10 8, 6

Wisdom educates her children
And takes care of those who seek her out.
Those who love her love life itself,
Those who seek her from the morrow
Will be filled with joy.
The one who possesses her will inherit glory.

Ecclesiastes, 4, 11–13

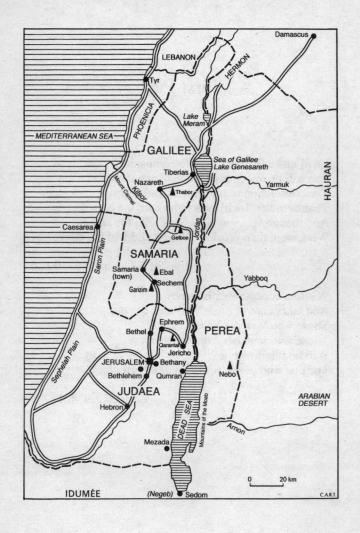

1

Solomon caressed the Ark of the covenant lovingly. He alone among King David's children was able to make such a gesture without being struck down by the mysterious energy emanating from the sanctuary containing the Tablets of the Law.

For a few days longer, the Ark would remain in Silo, in the very heart of Judah, the province of the King. It was here that Abraham had venerated the true God, the one and only God who had changed humanity's destiny by choosing Israel as the Promised Land. Silo had been the first of David's capitals, before he settled in Jerusalem. The old monarch had demanded that the Ark should periodically travel to remind the Hebrews that they were still nomads seeking for the Lord.

Solomon had been put in charge of protecting the most precious tabernacle of all. At the head of an escort made up of elite soldiers, he had left Jerusalem, stopping at the Machpelah cavern where the patriarchs rested. He walked among the vines laden with grapes, contemplating the terraces that assailed the dry and rocky hills. In Judah, there was nothing to hinder gazing off into the distance. The horizon was a fawn colour, inhabited by an unflagging sun. The steps of the travellers raised a red dust that settled on the lemons hanging on the trees by the road.

The expedition was headed for Silo. The small city, built on the territory of the tribe of Ephraim, was proud to have welcomed the Ark when the famous battle against the Philistines took place. Yahweh's sanctuary had been taken to the heart of the fray. It had confirmed God's presence and had granted Israel victory, in a great cacophony of howls of pain and cries of joy.

The wailing and shouting haunted Solomon. War, violence, blood . . . Were his people condemned to suffer such calamities? Would Yamweh always be a vengeful God, avid for confrontation?

In his heart Solomon, a young prince of mesmerising beauty, harboured strange, anguishing thoughts. At the time of his birth, the seers had predicted his high forehead would harbour Wisdom, his face would not bear a wrinkle and his features would not age. From the time of his adolescence, Solomon had shown a serene power and a natural authority that subjugated those who came into contact with him.

Who would have imagined the intensity of his inner turmoil, like a ship that had lost its rudder? Solomon could no longer sleep. He was losing his innate love of study and poetry. Even prayer did not bring him solace.

The third watch was coming to an end. After the one when the stars lit the sky, there came the midnight vigil and then the last through to dawn. Solomon had stayed near the Ark, begging the Lord to finally grant Israel peace. Why did the villagers tremble with fear? Why were so many of them struck down by the sword? Why were their houses pillaged and burned? Why should every breathing living creature be put to death? Why did the clans of Israel continue to decimate each other and fight with their neighbours?

Solomon had asked these questions a hundred times.

But God remained silent.

The moment the sun pierced the early morning mist with its first rays, the son of David dared put his hand on the Ark.

The source of energy from which Israel drew its strength was contained in a casket in acacia wood, a cubit and a half high and two cubits and a half long. Covered in the purest gold, inside and out, it was protected by Cherubim wings on which Yahweh sat, invisible, the rider of the clouds. Using these as his chariot, He crossed the universe up to the Garden of Eden whose doors were guarded by winged lions with human heads, symbols of a courage that no weakness could ever corrupt.

Solomon was tempted to open up the reliquary and take out the two stone plaques on which the ten divine commandments had been engraved. The Sinai pact by which Israel had become Yahweh's faithful servant. But that privilege was reserved for the King. Only David was capable of reading the original message by contemplating the word of the celestial Master.

Solomon spread out a precious fabric made with the skin of a she-goat. He then protected the gilded acacia bars with ram skins dyed red so that the Ark would be invisible to its bearers.

The son of David went out of the tent that sheltered the Ark. The light of day had invaded the green prairie that spread at the foot of the hill; the camp had been set up at the summit. Solomon had the feeling that the world belonged to him. Chasing away that mad thought, he raised his eyes to the nascent sun. Dazzled, he dreamed of disappearing in a blaze of light.

Would the Hebrews[1] be condemned to roam the earth forever? Beyond the cultivated land was the desert. That desert separated Israel from Egypt, the hated civilisation Solomon had secretly admired since childhood. Weren't the teachings of the Egyptian sages more profound and subtle? Was not Egypt the only power that enjoyed the delights of peace and wealth? The son of David had suppressed his predilection for the empire of the Pharaohs. He had shared his secret with no one, and kept it above all from his father who might have gone as far as to banish him. Like him, Solomon was a man of the desert, of infinite spaces, a seeker of the absolute. He knew

---

[1] in the time of Solomon, the term 'Jew' did not exist. 'Israelites' or 'Hebrews' was the terminology in use.

that God only revealed Himself in silence and in solitude. But Solomon could not accept that Israel bury itself in sterile memories. To establish a long-lasting peace, the Hebrews needed a powerful State and a capital as brilliant as Thebes in Egypt.

That was just wishful thinking.

Arms crossed, his eyes fixed on a small village that was awaking, the son of David thought he heard a cry of pain. Was he having one of those nightmares that the demons of the night so often inflicted?

He heard men's voices and what sounded like a fight.

Solomon went up to the edge of the rocky plateau. On a platform, about ten metres away down the slope, two soldiers from his personal guard were fighting, wielding staffs with incredible violence. Sweating profusely despite the chill of the morning air, wearing only loincloths, they were fighting to the death. Their comrades watched this scene with excitement, egging on the two champions.

The pair added curses to the physical combat, hoping to wear down the other's resistance. 'I will throw your flesh to the birds of the sky and beasts of the field!' cried the shorter one, with stout legs and a broad torso. He lifted his stick very high, drew a strange curve, bringing it down on the skull of the soldier who had challenged him, forcing him to respond with arms. The blow was decisive. The vanquished fell, his face covered in blood.

The drama has been played out so quickly that Solomon had not had time to intervene. The victor shrieked with joy, throwing his staff down on the corpse of the vanquished soldier.

'Let this dog rot among the vultures!' he cursed. 'The birds of prey and the rodents will be his gravediggers. May his bones become refuse blown to the winds!'

Suddenly, one of the soldiers saw Solomon. He tapped on his neighbour's shoulder who in turn warned his comrades. In a few seconds there was total silence.

'Let that man come up and see me,' ordered the son of David, pointing at the sad hero.

The man looked around, frightened. No one came to this rescue. He obeyed and hesitantly trod the steep path to the brow of the hill. To come before Solomon was more worrying than fighting a colossus to the death. He knew that the son of David detested violence.

'Sire,' he said, kneeling down, 'I did not betray the Law. I was challenged, and responded according to custom.'

Solomon knew only too well the Hebrews' love of combat and duels. A large audience was guaranteed. David's exploit in killing Goliath with a sling had popularised its use. Every year several young people died, their forehead crushed by a projectile.

'Why did you kill your adversary?' asked Solomon.

The question took the soldier by surprise.

'I did not have a choice, Sire. Did the angel not fight with Jacob before naming him Israel? We are warriors. In combat, we might fight to the death!'

The victor was excited. He did not feel the slightest remorse. He would do the same tomorrow, if similar circumstances were to present themselves. If Solomon punished him, he would provoke indignation and displeasure among the soldiers who were members of his guard.

'Go away,' he ordered.

Smiling, the killer left. He planned to celebrate his victory with his mates and would not forget to thank Yahweh for making his arm powerful.

After having asked his head guard to come and watch over the Ark with an escort, Solomon went down the hill. He sat on a rock and buried his head in his hands.

Peace was but a dream. A mirage that he wanted to believe in to give his life meaning. He must face reality. He would be confined to being an elegant prince, harbouring his boredom in the royal palace and composing poems that courtiers would be forced to admire.

The crystal-clear sound of a bell rang through the morning air.

Solomon was startled.

David had forbidden the use of that instrument since the bell the angels had given him had fallen silent. When the King presided over his court, it rang in the presence of the innocent and was quiet when the guilty party took the stand. Thus, divine justice presided as the absolute mistress over the whole of Israel. But David had sinned and the bell had been silent, forcing the sovereign to exercise his own judgement, and risk erring.

David no longer presided over the court. The old sovereign waited, hoping in desperation that the bell would again sound out, his bell . . . But was that what Solomon was hearing? He stood up and walked towards a grotto from where the ringing seemed to come. He entered into that obscure, dank world. The sound grew louder.

The sound was transformed into a powerful voice, very deep, too deep to be human. A profound serenity invaded the heart of the son of David. He knew that that invisible presence was that of God.

Solomon listened with his whole being. Kneeling down, he murmured a prayer: 'From you Almighty Power among all powers, I ask for neither fortune nor long life. But grant me the intelligence needed to find the path to peace and the discernment to distinguish good from evil.'

An intense light filled the grotto, forcing Solomon to close his eyes. The deep voice, that had emitted only vibrations, fell silent.

When the son of David left the grotto, the sun was already high in the sky. The soldiers of the guard were agitated and ran around shouting. Their chief ran towards his master.

'Sire! We have searched for you high and low. A messenger has come from Jerusalem. You must go home immediately. Your father is dying.'

2

Jerusalem stood on the hill of Zion. The city looked like a fortress rendered invincible by its fortified walls and gates. Nevertheless, David had conquered it, launching an assault on the high ramparts after organising the siege. The King had won his most decisive victory, gaining Israel its new capital.

Flanked on three sides by austere valleys, Jerusalem was surrounded by steep ravines where wadis filled with storm water had dug out sinuous veins. The fortress was protected by the topography of the surrounding landscape. David had not judged it necessary to add new fortifications, except on the northern wing. On the Offel promontory, seven hundred metres high, stood David's Zion.

Solomon entered Jerusalem by one of the fortified gates that was always guarded by armed soldiers. The capital of Israel gave him more anguish than joy. Why did the city present such a grim façade? Why did it cover its charms under a closed, aggressive mask? The palaces of the rich, situated in the upper part of the city, added a far too discreet note of gaiety to that troubled universe.

Usually so animated and so noisy, Jerusalem was wrapped in a veil of silence. Standing on a chariot pulled by two horses, Solomon responded to the salute of the guard responsible for the post set above the main entrance. At that point, the fortified wall was three times as thick as those of the rest of the fortification. Contrary to the usual practice, the soldiers were not letting the flocks of sheep, returning to the farms in the lower quarters, come through the city centre. Nervous, Solomon went directly to his father's palace, urging the horses forward. Streets and alleys were deserted. The inhabitants had closed their wooden shutters over the narrow apertures that let light into their houses. The news had spread throughout every neighbourhood in the city, causing despair among the people. With David's demise, a troubled period would begin during which the ambitious would fight it out for power and domination. The populace would suffer the consequences of these bloody confrontations. Already mothers were thinking of hiding their infants. Many men were intending to take refuge in the countryside, fearing the coming of savage hordes wanting to impose their favourite contender by the sword.

The palace of the King was just a house, though larger and more solidly built than the others. Built out of limestone, it had thick walls and was built on rock, the most solid of foundations. Neither tempest nor rain would carry away the residence of the sovereign, even if his son wished it richer and more sumptuous. The limestone mortar used to bond the stones was as solid as the building itself. There were no gifted architects in Israel, none capable of erecting a large palace that could rival the Pharaoh's in beauty.

David had allowed himself just one luxury: the floors of the main rooms were made of polished stones and there was a magnificent cedar floor in the bedroom. The poor had to make do with beaten earth. To atone for his sins, the monarch would have preferred to emulate them, but his wife, Bathsheba, had objected. Solomon disliked the place. He felt it cold and inhospitable. But just when he had decided to speak to his father about the matter, hoping to convince him to build an abode worthy of his rank, destiny had dealt a heavy blow. Was David not an immortal? Had his chanting not once gladdened God's heart?

Solomon had never even conceived that one day David, the supreme authority incarnate, might no longer be there.

However he was not unaware of David's shortcomings. He had not managed to reinstate peace, nor make Israel a unified nation, powerful enough to keep its enemies at bay. Obsessed by his past mistakes, he had withdrawn into himself and his suffering, more concerned with himself than with his people. But these reproaches counted little beside the love Solomon felt for his father. He would have given his life to preserve David's own. Never had he challenged an order issued by the King, even when he did not agree with what was being requested.

It was Nathan, Solomon's private tutor, who welcomed him on the threshold of the royal apartments. He had been the young man's spiritual guide, more so than David. Estimating that his disciple was beloved of God and that wisdom had branded him with its seal, he devoted most of his time to Solomon, initiating him in the meaning of the sacred texts and the practice of occult sciences.

Solomon was an eager pupil, the more he learned the more he wanted to discover. The frivolous side of existence held no interest for him. To work under the direction of his private tutor seemed to him the ideal life.

Nathan, a tall, elderly man with a white beard, was dressed in a long white robe with a square neckline. He did not wear any jewellery, no outer sign of his position at court, but his striking bearing betrayed his high rank. His mood was always constant and his face never betrayed emotion.

Nevertheless, he now looked tired. The tutor's subtle smile, sure of himself and of his wisdom, had been replaced by a grave, disturbed expression. Solomon took his arm.

'My father, how is he?'

'He is very ill. That is why I sent for you.'

'The Ark is now back in Jerusalem. Its presence will save him.'

'May God heed your words.'

For a moment, the voice he had heard in the grotto filled Solomon's head. He managed to control himself and not show any outward disquiet.

9

'May I see him?'

'Your mother awaits you,' replied Nathan.

The tutor showed Solomon into a small room with bare walls. Bathsheba was sitting on a low stool, with her eyes closed; she seemed asleep. As soon as her son entered, she stood up and embraced him.

'Solomon, you've come, at last.'

'I was not able to return sooner, Mother.'

'I am not rebuking you. I was so afraid . . .'

'Why?'

'Evil is all around us, my son. Israel is in danger. David has not yet died, but already there are those who are coveting the throne.'

Hailed by the people as the noble lady, she had preserved, although beyond her sixtieth year, exceptionally noble appearance. She was tall, thin and with such fine features that the King had been seduced, even to the point of displeasing Yahweh. She reigned over a court that her husband had neglected.

'What do you expect of me, Mother? You know full well that I will protect you against any aggressor, even if they be pretenders to the throne.'

Bathsheba moved away from her son. She found it difficult to hide her distress.

'I love David and David loves me . . . How will I be able to . . .'

'The time for tender feeling is past,' declared Nathan. 'The King is dying. If you do not act quickly, Israel itself will perish.'

Fighting back her tears, Bathsheba left the small room and went into the chamber where the King was dying.

Solomon tried in vain to understand the meaning of these strange events.

'What is happening, Nathan?'

The private tutor became very stern in his demeanour.

'The time has come to reveal to you the secret that I have

shared with your mother for a very long time. It concerns the future of the country.'

A terrible cold invaded Solomon's bones, so glacial that he almost cried out in pain.

'How does it relate to me?'

'It concerns only you, Solomon. David promised his wife that he would choose you as his successor.'

'Me?'

Solomon lost his voice. To become Israel's sovereign, to sit on David's throne, to be in charge, guiding the people on the path of wisdom, never would he be able to fulfil such a daunting task.

'Who imagined this folly?'

'The one who knows you best: your tutor. From a tender age, I beheld in you the greatness of Kings. I confided in your mother. She has come to the same conclusion.'

'What about my father . . .?'

'David recognised the pertinence of our understanding. He gave his word. Today, he will make it official. Follow me.'

Solomon did not protest. Stunned by the news, he let his tutor guide him.

The two men went into the monarch's chamber.

David had his eyes fixed on the flame of a torch. His body was covered with a woollen stole. The cedar floor screeched under Solomon's steps. He took his place by his mother, at the head of the bed.

The face of the dying man was marked by suffering. All trace of grace had vanished. There was but the weight of seventy years spent loving, praying and fighting.

'King of Israel,' said Bathsheba, in a trembling voice, 'you swore to me, your faithful servant, that your son Solomon would reign in your stead. Israel has its eyes on you. The country waits for you to announce the name of your successor.'

'Nathan must leave the room,' ordered David.

The tutor obeyed.

The old King sat up, as if he regained by some miracle his past vigour.

'I swore by Almighty God who delivered me from all distress, what I pledged I will abide by. Come forth, my son, give me your hand.'

Solomon obeyed, moved by the firmness in his father's tone of voice.

He was convinced that David would overcome this illness and live to govern his people for many years to come.

The son placed his right hand in his father's, who held it tight.

'I bestow royalty on you, Solomon, that which God entrusted in me and that which I proved myself unworthy of. Death is the rope that is being cut by His hand, the picket that is wrenched, the tent blown away by the desert wind. My soul is ready to cross the sky to stand before my judge. I have fought wars and won. May those times be gone forever. You who bear the name of Solomon, that means "peace be with you", go forth and make peace reign on this earth. Make it the bond between Israel and the heavens. My crown is tainted with blood. Severed heads lie by my throne. That is why I have been unable to build God's House. Fulfil this task, my son. Seek wisdom ceaselessly, the primordial wisdom that existed before all time, before the birth of the sea, of the rivers and of the springs, before the mountains stood on high, before day was differentiated from night, before light emerged from chaos, and the skies were firmly established. It is with wisdom that God measures the universe and it is with wisdom that he created the earth, it is thanks to wisdom that he carved the paths that the stars travel, without it you will build nothing.'

The hand of David trembled. His eyes rolled upwards. Solomon helped him to lie down. Death assailed him again.

'Bathsheba,' asked the King with shallow breath, 'call the crown's council at once . . . I want to speak to its members. My son will remain by my side.'

David's wife soon rounded up the dignitaries that composed the council: Nathan, the tutor, Sadoq, the High Priest, and Banaias, the commander of the Army. The latter was a colossus, whose impressive muscles contrasted with the leanness of the High Priest. Each knew that Banaias had become the most powerful man in Israel. Without his support, the future King would be but a helpless puppet. The commander of the army rarely spoke. He had served David with the utmost fidelity. But no one knew what he thought about the succession to the throne.

David asked Solomon to help him sit up straight, despite the sharp pain he felt in that position. He wanted to speak out as a monarch and not as a dying man.

'Members of my council,' he announced with an energy that was almost fierce, 'I am about to reveal my ultimate decision. Solomon is the new King of Israel. Whoever dares to claim this title and does not swear allegiance to him will be put to death.' Sadoq was the first to nod his head, then it was Nathan's turn. Banaias, dressed in silver armour plating, seemed to give the matter some thought. Bathsheba's throat felt dry. If the head of the army had chosen another pretender to the throne, his spear would soon pierce hearts of those close to David.

'The will of the King is God's will,' said Banaias with a hoarse voice. 'Let Solomon command and I shall obey.'

David smiled. His face found once again the enticing charm no one resisted. The wizard shunned the hideous mask that awaited him.

'Please leave now. You, Solomon, stay.'

As soon as they were alone, the King pushed his son away curtly. Taken aback by this change of attitude, Solomon saw his father's gaze lit by an ardent flame, almost juvenile, possessed fleetingly by the angel of folly.

'I devote my last moments to you, my son . . . promise that you will obey me.'

'I am your faithful servant . . .'

'No, Solomon! You are the King now. Your only master is God. But I, your father, have a request to make.'

The son of David knelt down and took the dying man's hands in his. David's breath grew shorter and shorter.

'Speak and I will fulfil your desire.'

'Bless you, Solomon . . . You can grant me the peace I need so. You know that Joab, that infamous traitor, killed people whom I loved, among them a nephew of mine. Avenge me, Solomon! Apply the law: an eye for an eye, a tooth for a tooth, a life for a life. Do away with that murderer. As King, you are the supreme judge. You will act according to what you deem wise . . . but for the love of me, for the love of your royal station, do not let Joab descend in peace into death's oblivion, despite his white hair.'

David's voice broke. His trunk fell forwards. God had just taken back the poet whose voice was as sweet as honey.

3

Around the arena, the spectators screamed. They cheered on their champion, the most courageous man in Israel, Banaias. At the bottom of the empty tank, slipping on a puddle of oil, he confronted a lion captured in the mountains. During the period of mourning between the death of David and the crowning of Solomon, the commander of the army thought it appropriate to distract the people. He was keen on proving to them that their security was ensured by a brave warrior, stronger than a beast. Ever since he had terrorised an Egyptian giant by grabbing the spear with which he had been threatened and breaking his opponent's skull with a wooden club, Banaias had acquired extreme confidence in his own powers. With bloodied hands, the Israelite had felt no pain. Drunk with victory he had felt invincible.

Incapable of finding a staying point, the lion, furious, attacked when he was off guard. Banaias, used to training on this kind of surface, avoided the claws and caught the beast, grabbing the back of his neck, using his hands like a vice with fingers as hard as stones. The cry of victory mingled with the howls of the dying animal. He was acclaimed by the crowd. He had just enough time to wash and dress to go to the palace where he had been summoned by Solomon. On the road to the palace, he was greeted by numerous citizens.

Solomon received Banaias in an office that was austere. The two men remained standing. The military chief felt that the son of David, dressed in a blue seamless tunic, was no longer just an elegant prince, whose sole occupation was writing poetry. The gravity of his expression, even for a young man, betrayed the intensity of his concerns.

'Have you decided to serve me as you served my father, Banaias?'

'I belong to a family of soldiers, your Majesty. I was born at the far end of the desert, where one learns to fight and defend one's life.'

Solomon, with his deep blue eyes, gazed at the soldier for a long time. The latter was completely subdued.

'I name you Supreme Chief of my army,' declared the son of David, 'and Head of my private guard. We will consort with each other often. Do not go far from the court. I may, at any moment, need your services.'

Banaias was filled with immense pride. David had certainly recognised his valour, but Solomon went much further.

'By the sacred name of Yahweh, I swear that I shall remain faithful to my master both in war and in peace.'

Solomon disguised his joy. He had just won the first victory of his reign. But how could he taste true happiness, when he was haunted by his dying father's terrible request?

'I need to consult you, Banaias.'

The recently appointed head of the army uttered a kind of grunt.

'I know how to fight, my lord, but not how to counsel a King.'

Solomon took the commander's arm and led him out of his office. They crossed a corridor and went on to a terrace with a view over the houses of the city's wealthy citizens. The white walls shone under the sun. At the end of this eventful day, the town remained agitated. Would it soon have a King capable of governing?

'Which are the crimes condemned by God, Banaias? To revolt against Him, to be an idolater, to utter blasphemies, not celebrate Easter, not respect the Sabbath, not circumcise one's male child, to indulge in black magic . . . But to follow the orders of the King, is that a crime?'

'Of course not!' protested the commander of the army.

'If you believe so, Banaias, find Joab, David's enemy.'

'And when I have found him . . .?'

'May your arm carry out my sentence: death.'

'Before tomorrow's sun is risen, Sire, your wish will be satisfied.'

Banaias left. Solomon felt like screaming in despair. He had no choice. How could he not fulfil David's last wish?

The future King of Israel dined with his mother, but did not touch any of the delicacies. He sent the musicians away and ordered that the greatest silence should reign in the palace.

'Why are you so tormented? God's will was that you should be David's successor. Any rebellion is in vain. Respect his wishes and you will experience peaceful days. Allow me . . . allow me to make a request.'

Solomon awoke from his apathy. His mother adopted the attitude of a servant before her master. She no longer looked upon him as her child, but as her King. A world had crumbled. Another universe had now opened whose laws he had yet to discover.

'Speak, Mother.'

'Adonias, a courtier, has asked to marry one of David's concubines. He implores your consent.'

Solomon, livid, stood up.

With the back of his hand, he knocked a cup of wine. Never had Bathsheba seen her son succumb to such a suppressed rage.

'Mother, are you conscious of the meaning of this request? My father's concubines are now mine! What Adonias is claiming is the throne itself.'

Solomon was not mistaken. The request of the courtier concealed an attempted coup d'état. Bathsheba had made an unforgivable mistake.

'Whoever is guilty of proclaiming himself King in lieu of the King himself, is condemning himself to oblivion.'

17

When Banaias came back to the palace, Solomon was contemplating the Pole Star. Gazing into the axis of the world, and seeing an invisible thread linking heaven and earth, he had tried to forget human affairs, to replenish himself with the energy of celestial light which extended into the infinite.

Banaias stayed in the shadows. Solomon did not turn around.

'I have failed, Sire,' he murmured in his coarse voice.

'Have you disobeyed me?'

'When Joab was told of my arrival, he took refuge by an altar in the countryside. It is a sacred site. He put himself out of my sword's reach. We must wait . . .'

'No one can raise a hand against a man who seeks refuge in God's house,' admitted Solomon, 'except if he is a criminal. Is this not the case, Banaias? Joab killed David's nephew. He had his friends murdered. Do you believe that he deserves your indulgence? Do you really think that God will provide him protection?'

When Solomon raised his eyes towards the Pole Star again, Banaias' horse was already heading out of one of Jerusalem's fortified gates.

According to the mourning custom, Solomon had not washed or shaved and wore but old clothes.

As a cortege of women mourners expressed their sorrow loudly, the son of David approached his father's corpse, lying on a wooden sledge in the middle of the small esplanade in front of the palace. The mortal remains had been washed with fragrant oils and perfumed with myrrh and aloe wood.

A purple robe covered the corpse. On his right was the harp he used to accompany his singing; on his left the sword with which he had fought. On David's brow a diadem shone.

Solomon kissed his father on the temple. It was the last kiss, the embrace of filial love that would endure beyond death. Thus, the soul of yesterday's sovereign migrated to the soul of the future King.

Bathsheba led the cortege, followed by mourners who chanted monotonously accompanied by a flute playing a lugubrious tune. The widow was the living symbol of Eve who, after having introduced the human race to death, had to open the path to the other world.

The more the procession progressed, the more the women's wailing grew louder, as they covered their heads with dust and cried out in despair. Bathsheba, whose majestic stance impressed the crowd that gathered on the path leading to the tomb, did not take the road normally followed by funerals, which went to the valley of Jasaphat, more than fifty cubits from town; instead she headed for the highest wall of the fortified town.

A deep tomb with a flattened vault had been carved halfway down a declivity and access was by a ramp. Inside the stones were roughly hewn. Solomon, Banaias and Sadoq, the High Priest, slid the body down. The son of David went alone into the tomb and meditated a long time beside the corpse, sitting on a small limestone stool. Near the head, a bouquet of aromatic plants gave off a sweet perfume evoking the paradise David was being offered. As soon as Solomon left his father's last abode, Banaias blocked the opening with a large stone that the masons adjusted, concealing it. The memory of the centuries would forget, flesh and bones would decompose, but David would remain present in his capital's fortified walls, ready to protect it from darkness.

During the meal that gathered together Solomon, Bathsheba and the members of the crown's council, the only food was mourning bread blessed by the High Priest. Each guest was given a glass of wine.

While serving Solomon, Banaias whispered in his ear:

'The deed is done, Sire. The criminal has been punished.'

The commander of the army had wrenched Joab from the holy altar, although he in turn had clung on until his fingers bled. Then he cut his throat. Afterwards, he had gone to Adonias' house and had inflicted the same fate on him for the

19

high treason of plotting against the King. Thus the orders of David's widow were obeyed. Now, the dead monarch could rest in peace.

The ritual wine burned Solomon's throat.

Tomorrow, he would be crowned.

4

The mule with its beautiful light grey coat trotted at a steady pace along the road to Gihon, where the main spring used by the inhabitants of Jerusalem was situated and the sanctuary of the Ark had been built.

On its back, Solomon, magnificent in his tunic embroidered with gold thread, prepared for the crowning ceremony that would make him, in the eyes of his people, the new King of Israel.

Under a mild sun, the route was quickly travelled. Solomon communed with the animal, feeling the rhythm of its cadence, forgetting everything but the present moment.

Before the Ark were the High Priest, Sadoq, and Nathan, the tutor. They wore beige robes. Sadoq had had to renounce the luxurious garments attributed to his function, for on coronation day, only the King's appearance was to disclose the wealth of his attributes.

Solomon dismounted the mule and patted its neck. Then he took nine steps, stopping between Sadoq and Nathan, before the disclosed Ark. A row of soldiers held the courtiers back at a distance.

What was to take place in Gihon was only to be contemplated by God and his closest servants.

Sadoq and Nathan raised above Solomon's head a horn full of oil and poured the contents slowly down the back of the sovereign's head.

21

'The spirit descends into you,' revealed the High Priest. 'It renders your person sacred. Divine grace will henceforth inspire your heart. Your past is erased. You are now Israel's Messiah, its saviour and its King.'

Nathan gave Solomon a gold sceptre and crowned him with a gold diadem.

After greeting the two Cherubim who guarded the Ark of the Covenant, the High Priest opened it. He removed the Tablets of the Law, engraved by God's hand, and raised them before Solomon, who set eyes on them for the first time.

'Eternal is the Law of the Eternal One!' proclaimed Sadoq.

Solomon, now crowned, wore David's bracelets on his wrists, and sat on his throne. He read Yahweh's decree that recognised him as King and sealed with him a pact that only death or unworthiness could destroy.

The doors of the room were opened.

The trumpets rang. The people, jubilant at having escaped civil war, gathered at the bottom of the hill, shouting in unison: 'Hail King Solomon!'

The feat that followed would dissipate any remaining anxieties.

Solomon was getting used to the throne made of ivory and gold with its back set off by bull's heads. Two sculpted lion's bodies were the armrests. The King had spontaneously adopted a position that allowed him to fill the illustrious seat with dignity.

Dignitaries and courtiers paid homage to Solomon while wine flowed freely in the streets of Jerusalem. Each noticed the surprisingly dignified countenance of such a young man, seemingly fearless in the face of his new position.

Two death sentences, one pronounced by his father and the other by his mother. Two executions carried out before Solomon's reign started. The ritual of the coronation had obliterated that past. But how would he banish those acts from his memory? Would they not gnaw at his conscience day after day?

Solomon had moved into the palace he disliked. Disquieting shadows flickered along the walls. Prior to that moment, the son of David had uttered no criticism of the way Israel had been governed. Silence was his law. The post that Yahweh had entrusted him with required lucidity, even if the price was an inner torment whose gravity only he would know about.

Who had been the famous King Saul? A peasant who ate the fruit of his fields, himself driving his flock, willingly sleeping under the stars, considering Israel a simple fertile field. The outer world held no interest for him. Other peoples were just looters dreaming of despoiling him.

Who had David been, if not a shepherd in love with country dances and rustic games, an insatiable lover who had preserved the Hebrew's traditional way of life, forgetting that the universe was changing around him?

Like his predecessors, David had considered his country to be a small island that had sprung up in the middle of a hostile sea.

To build a new palace: that would be Solomon's first task. The King of Israel could not live in an abode so modest that it hardly differentiated him from the wealthiest of his courtiers. It was necessary to bestow on royalty the magnificence it deserved. The head of the Hebrew State could no longer be compared to the chieftain of a clan.

Solomon sat on the steps that led to the royal chapel, so poor and so denuded that God himself must have little pleasure living there. But David had obstinately refused to build another sanctuary. The Ark of the Covenant benefited from safe shelter, why build something grander? The King avoided the shadow of a service tree in bloom, where bad genii were fond of finding shelter. He had to think about organising his government, and appoint responsible men to govern at his side. Those with broad vision and whose ambitions would be for Israel rather than for themselves. What Solomon conceived frightened him. Would he dare carry out his projects? Would he not have to face such violent opposition that he would be obliged to renounce?

His mother, Bathsheba, sat by his side, wearing no ornaments, as a sign of mourning.

'You have avoided the evil shadow, my son. Your reign should be an enlightened one. Do not forget that human beings, even if they are your subjects, prefer darkness.'

'You are sat on my right side. You who are the great lady of Israel will continue to exert influence at my court.'

'No, my son. That is the very subject I wanted to talk to you about without delay. I will be content to have the honours, but you are not to share your power as sovereign. You are to take decisions, no one else. My advice would just be inopportune. I have made a grave mistake. I belong to a past era, the era of David, which deep in your heart you judge most severely.'

Solomon did not protest.

'Up to now,' she continued, 'I thought I understood reality. Deprived of David's presence, I need to rest. Let me retire into the palace's silence.'

Solomon did not want to constrain Bathsheba to review a position she had weighed carefully.

She opened her right hand. It contained a gold ring, which she slipped on to the little finger of her son's left hand.

'A golden apple embedded on a chiselled silver surface,' said Bathsheba, 'such is the word of a sage. Does it not have the perfection of this ring that belonged to David and before him to our father, Adam? Take good care of it, Solomon. When you turn it on your finger, you will understand the message the wind brings, from beyond mountain summits. Your spirit will fly over those paradises where eternal harvests grow, where pearls are born of vine branches. You will speak the language of the birds, perceive people's intentions, subdue their spirit. Wild animals will lie at your feet and lick your sandals. That ring is the ring of power. It will serve you as long as you obey God. Your thoughts will extend from one end of the earth to the other and reach up to heaven. But, if you leave the path of wisdom, you will become the most miserable of creatures. That is the fate of Kings.'

Solomon looked closely at the strange object. It was characterised by a star-shaped seal inside which were engraved the four letters that spelt the secret name of Yahweh. The son of David would have liked to obtain more explanations from his mother, but she was already standing, ready to return to her apartments.

Nathan copied out onto quality papyrus a very ancient text whose original had crumbled into dust. It was about the Hebrews' departure from Egypt. He was not surprised to see Solomon come into the library.

'I was waiting for your visit, Highness.'

'Why, Nathan?'

'Because your work started at the very moment you were anointed. You have ambitious plans and will waste no time putting them into practice.'

'Which plans?' asked the King, intrigued.

Nathan moved several papyrus rolls that cluttered a shelf. He uncovered a huge ruby which he presented to Solomon.

'This precious stone was entrusted to me by David on the day after his enthronement. It is the secret of Kings. According to the first prophets, it was the leader of the angels who gave it to Moses at the top of Mount Sinai. It is the token of the Alliance. Due to its presence, the breath of every human being celebrates God. The monarch who possesses it reigns over the creatures of the air, those that live in water and on the earth. Should he desire their support, it is enough for him to lift this stone towards the clouds and to call them.'

Solomon put out his hand and closed it over the ruby.

'This celestial stone . . . is it not the foundation on which the temple of God should be built?'

Nathan seemed to ignore the question.

25

'We have often spoken about it, tutor. I should like to abandon the chapel and build a new sanctuary. My father rejected the idea violently. You approved.'

'That is true,' admitted Nathan.

'Multiple temples throughout the country . . . it's not enough.'

'Quite right,' acknowledged the tutor.

Solomon was astonished. Nathan smiled.

'I had great influence over your father. I refuse to exercise it over you. I was the one who stopped David starting major building work in Jerusalem.'

'For what reason?'

'Because David's building would have come crushing down, due to his sins.'

The King did not have time to meditate on his tutor's words. Just as he was leaving Nathan's library, Banaias came looking for him. The head of the army seemed very agitated.

'Sire . . . the three sons of a clan chief ask for your arbitrage! If their quarrel is not resolved, they threaten to launch their troops against each other!'

The danger was real. If Solomon failed in his attempt at reconciliation, there would be dozens of dead. And he would have to send his own troops to crush the rebels.

'Call a meeting with them on the forecourt. I will pronounce my judgement there.'

Banaias was overwhelmed with apprehension. A judgement! David would not have dared use that procedure. He would have tried to appease the quarrellers and, if he failed, he would have led a war party against them.

The courtiers had assembled to witness the judgement. Many had bet on the King's failure, which would condemn him to renouncing the throne. Dormant, disappointed ambitions were reawakened.

Solomon sat on a folding stool, at the centre of the square, facing three young men who carried in their arms an old man with a black beard.

'What do you want?' asked the King.

'What is my due,' answered the eldest of the three brothers. 'My father, on his dying bed, revealed that only one of us was his true son and left him all he owned. He expired before pointing out who his heir was. I know I am his son. These two impostors are contesting my rights.'

'No one can know the secrets of the dead,' stated the youngest. 'Let us share the inheritance.'

'I refuse,' said the third brother. 'My father's wishes must be respected.'

'Hand over your father's corpse to Banaias,' ordered Solomon. 'He will bind it to a pillar, at the end of the square. To each one, he will give a bow and arrow. You will aim at the corpse. The best archer will be the heir.'

A murmur arose from the crowd. The three plaintiffs were forced to accept.

The eldest was promptest. As soon as Banaias stood out of the way, he aimed and fired. The projectile perforated the hand. The youngest, pleased with this mediocre result, took his time in aiming. The arrow bore into the forehead of the dead man. His aim had been perfect. The third brother stretched the bow, pointing at the heart. Furious, he threw his weapon to the ground.

'This is shameful,' he protested. 'I will not be my father's assassin, even if he is already but a corpse. I prefer to be poor.'

As he was leaving the square hurriedly, Solomon called him back.

'Stay here and be the worthy heir of a clan chieftain. Only you can be his true son.'

'Hail King Solomon,' shouted Banaias.

Soon a hundred other voices followed suit.

5

The master of the palace, in charge of organising court life, was at the end of his tether. For the fourth consecutive day, he refused to open the sovereign's door to the courtiers requiring an audience. The protests grew more and more numerous and acerbic. But the master of the palace, a jovial and portly character, remained adamant. Carrying the key to the main door on his shoulder and bearing the royal seal, each morning he conversed with the sovereign who indicated to him the names of the people he agreed to see. The high dignitary patiently held his counsel on the threshold during the time these audiences lasted. The day was long and fastidious. But the function aroused so much envy that its holder bore the inconvenience gladly.

Solomon had disrupted his habits by shutting himself up in his study where the master of the palace brought him the lists of civil servants who made up the ranks of the country's administration. Solomon studied them with great care.

What else could this attitude mean but profound upheavals? The master of the palace himself had no illusions any more. The new King had made up his mind that he would change the hierarchy. An old farmer with sunburnt skin, who owed his good fortune to David, was to be master of protocol to the King, telling him what was happening in the country was well as organising the official ceremonies. But he was worried about his future, as Solomon's silence did not bode well.

Master Hiram and King Solomon

As the sunset cast its last rays over Jerusalem, Solomon called the master of the palace and the harbinger. Ill at ease, the two dignitaries presented themselves together before the monarch, around whom were strewn several unrolled papyri. The face of the King did not betray fatigue.

'The civil servants appointed by my father,' announced Solomon, 'will stay at their posts. The administration of this palace is correct. I will add twelve prefects who will, alternatively, supply the royal household. Each day, they will supply barley and straw for the horses as well as flour. They will take ten fattened ox and twenty pasture cattle and a hundred sheep to the abattoirs. My cooks will see to the allotting of the food equitably. You, the master of protocol, will render these decisions public tomorrow morning.'

The dignitary, very pleased with himself, bid goodbye. He was to keep his post.

Worried, the master of the palace dared ask a question.

'Sire, who will you see tomorrow?'

'Only one person: Elihap.'

'I fear that your wish . . .'

'It is not a wish,' Solomon corrected him, 'it is an order. Elihap is part of the staff of this palace. He serves the King of Israel.'

'Well, Elihap is of Egyptian origin and . . .'

'Go on.'

'Your father probably did not know this and employed him because he spoke several languages.'

'That is rather a quality.'

'No doubt, Sire, but Elihap has made a grave mistake.'

'And what could that be?'

'When his father died, a little before David's death, he wanted to bury him according to Egyptian rites. We protested and . . .'

'You even threatened him,' added the King.

'No doubt, he misinterpreted our warning.'

'Where is he now?'

'Elihap has ran away,' revealed the master of the palace.

'He is in hiding. You and the harbinger will have to find him before dawn.'

'Majesty . . .'

Solomon's look did not encourage any argument.

Elihap was ushered into Solomon's office a little after dawn. It was a tired man who knelt before Solomon. Nevertheless, despite his rags, a pride showed through that adversity had not tamed. Bald, about fifty years old, tall, with black piercing eyes, Elihap did not tremble before the monarch who was about to proffer sentence.

'Does Jerusalem really reign over Israel?' asked Solomon.

The question astonished Elihap.

It was addressing his old capacity as secretary of the palace.

'No, Majesty. The provinces enjoy a positive autonomy with regard to the capital.'

'How are the taxes determined?'

'Either in coins or in labour carried out on the building sites ordered by the King.'

'How many of those are there?'

'Very few. Two or three in the provinces. One in Jerusalem for the restoration of the southern fortified wall.'

'Sit down at this desk, Elihap.'

With a manifest joy, the Egyptian drew out his writing reed and a little jar full of black ink.

He adopted with ease the posture of the scribe, bust straight and legs crossed before him.

'You are now my secretary and my trustworthy adjutant,' indicated Solomon. 'You will draw up decrees. Let's start with the one that defines your duties. You will write the internal and external correspondence of the palace, you will collect and register the sum of the contributions, and you will direct the Chancery.'

Elihap wrote with a sure and quick hand.

'Who is your God?' enquired Solomon.

The Egyptian rested his writing reed on the writing board. The trap lay open before him and he did not try to avoid it.

'I worship the God Apis. It is the meaning of my name, "Apis is my Lord". In him the supreme God is incarnate.'

By pronouncing these words, Elihap was condemning himself. In the land of but one true God, jealous of his supremacy, he did not have the right to profess such beliefs. But the Egyptian no longer wanted to live as a recluse and deny the path his heart followed.

'What is the nature of that supreme God?' asked the King.

'He is Light itself,' answered the secretary. 'The bull Apis is the earthly symbol of his power. That is why the Pharaoh wears on his headdress a bull's tail.'

'The God of Israel is also Light itself. Follow your faith and its teachings, Elihap, but know how to silence your tongue. Take up your writing reed. We have a lot of work to do.'

The olive and fig trees protected the Valley of Kidron from the ardent heat of the sun. The place was sweet and peaceful. The noise from the capital crashed on to the slopes of the surrounding hills. Nevertheless few people ventured into these secluded places. A cemetery had been built there where famous heroes rested in peace, such as Absalom.

King Solomon prayed to the Lord by Nathan's tomb.

The tutor had died in his sleep in the night of a full moon. His face conveyed perfect serenity, the semblance of a servant who had known how not to be subservient. With his disappearance Solomon's adolescence was gone forever. From now on, he would no longer have anyone to confide in, no friend to talk to, no one with whom he could share his doubts and his anguishes. Nathan had educated him, brought him up to be King, without inculcating in him the vanity of believing that one day he would preside over the fate of Israel. He had effaced himself behind his teaching in order to broaden the consciousness of his pupil further. He had devoted his life to bringing Solomon up, far away from court rumours and intrigues.

The King had dug his tutor's grave with his bare hand. He had rejected the presence of the mourners to be able to commune, in the perfumed silence of the Valley of Kidron, with the soul of the man who had guided him to become his true self.

Solomon did not know if he would prove worthy of Nathan's hopes. As he was alone, abandoned by those close to him, obliged to reign without sharing his power, he would try to fortify his people and his country to the glory of the Almighty. On Nathan's tomb he took that oath.

6

Had David not proclaimed: 'I will create Jerusalem for my joy, and its inhabitants for my exhilaration'? Had he not named the town, ordering his subjects to live in it to gain their salvation? Had he not settled in that town to make of it the Holy City, the centre of revelation? David had lived in it because it was situated on the border between the two Kingdoms of Judah and Israel, asserting its vocation for conciliation. Was it not written that, at the end of time, Jerusalem would welcome the elect within its walls covered in gold and its streets paved with rubies?

That admirable destiny, which Solomon wanted to render palpable during his reign, was potentially in peril due to a grave occurrence. The throne room had been invaded by the town's rich citizens speaking in the name of the fifteen thousand souls who inhabited the capital.

'The situation is desperate, Sire,' declared the master of protocol, who had been assailed with complaints. 'The upper part of town has no water. The only spring, that of Gihon, has been polluted and will not be operational for another month. As for the lower part of town, the poorer quarters will soon suffer penury. There may be a rebellion brewing.'

David had also been confronted with the capital's insufficient water supply. He had suppressed any attempt at riots by harsh measures.

But Solomon said, 'I will not send soldiers to repress the

33

inhabitants of Jerusalem. They are in the right: this situation is intolerable.'

Sitting at the foot of the throne, Elihap, the Egyptian secretary who was now officially ensconced in his new post, noted the details of this unusual interview.

'I entrust Banaias with a peaceful mission,' announced Solomon. 'The men who are assigned to labour the construction sites in the provinces will form teams of water carriers to bring to Jerusalem the water from springs situated about one hour's walk from here. As soon as Gihon has regained its purity, conduits will be dug and water will be stored in reservoirs.'

The master of protocol, speaking in the name of one of the old notables, put forward an objection.

'It will take many months, Sire, to carry out your plans.'

'A little less than a year, considering the insufficient teams of men we can count on.'

'The cisterns are empty,' recalled the master of the palace, 'what will happen to us in the coming days?'

'Today it will rain, grant God and your King your trust.'

Solomon stood up. The audience had ended.

Jerusalem awaited anxiously.

A vast blue sky unfolded its intense light above the city. The elders knew enough about nature's signs to know that no rain would fall for a long time yet. Solomon had been wrong to have defied the god of clouds. The son of David was just a braggart who would come to regret being so pretentious.

In the middle of the day, Solomon climbed to the summit of his palace. From the highest watchtower, occupied permanently by an archer whom he dismissed, he addressed the firmament and implored it to grant the water that would bring deliverance.

'You who reign in the Light,' murmured the King, 'pray listen to my prayer. If your skies remain locked and deprive us of rain, how will your country survive? Grant me my wish. Do not spread misery throughout your city. Let rain fall on the land that your people have inherited from you.'

Solomon thrice turned over the ring he wore on the little finger of his left hand. He called on the spirits of the wind and ordered them to engender a storm. When the first black cloud appeared from behind the Northern mountains, with a pregnant belly like that which graced elephants in fairy tales, Solomon thanked the Lord.

The potter, alerted by his apprentices, hurriedly left his house made of beaten earth. He girded his loins with a cloth and contemplated the unbelievable spectacle.

Solomon, his secretary Elihap, Banaias, the head of the army, and a squad of soldiers had just turned up before his workshop, in the heart of a small village in Judah that had never before had the honour of welcoming a King.

Since Solomon had obtained sufficient water to fill the cisterns of Jerusalem, his reputation had spread out to all provinces. Even if the priests uttered reservations, citing a happy coincidence, the humbler folk proclaimed their belief in a new prosperous era that would transform Israel into that paradise Moses had dreamed of.

The King stopped by the potter's wheel. How could he not think of God's work creating humanity when looking at that tool, perfect among all instruments, drawing from the clay the living forms that he moulded with his hands and his spirits. In Egypt, it was the ram god who created the world on his potter's wheel. The Hebrews had preserved that symbolic trade, their artisans had learned their craft in the land of the Pharaohs. Solomon dreamed of the universe that he wanted to deliver from chaos. Do we not owe to the potter the most humble of daily receptacles, as well as the most refined vases, the small jugs as well as the large jars from keeping the grain, the lamps and even the toys? Solomon would imitate the artisan. He would give his people material riches. But this would only endure on condition that the wealth emanate from spiritual abundance. That is why the King tried to commence a new era by assembling, far from their estates, the chieftains of the twelve tribes of Israel, those of Ruben, Simeon, Levi, Juda, Zabulon, Issachar, Dan, Gad, Aser, Naphtali, Joseph and Benjamin. Those powerful, rich men, great landlords, had competed in elegance to meet their King in that place unworthy of their rank. Their private hairdressers, using gold or ivory combs, had composed refined hairstyles with floating curls or with long oiled locks falling on their backs. The belts that held at the waist brightly coloured tunics were ornamented with diamonds and rubies. Beside the chieftains, Solomon looked almost like a commoner.

He bid them sit down on the straw mats that Banaias had unrolled at the foot of a large fig tree. His guests, intrigued, wondered about the meaning of this strange summons. Solomon offered them a plate of cucumbers, onions and lettuce. Some ate wholeheartedly. Others were wary. Kings had often used poison as a weapon to get rid of their enemies. Rumour had it that Solomon wanted to reign as an absolute monarch.

'I planted some vines,' said the King, 'created gardens and orchards, built ponds to water plantations. I have given you servants, herds of oxen and sheep. You benefit from a well-being which was unknown not long ago. Why should you mistrust me?'

'You have made us rich,' recognised the chieftain of the Dan tribe, 'but is it not a trap to numb our vigilance? You are not the kind of man who would bestow gifts without asking for something in return.'

'You speak truthfully,' admitted Solomon. 'No one is contesting your rights. Without you, the provinces would be neglected. But you owe allegiance to the King.'

'Who would dream of rebelling against you?' asked the chieftain of the Levi tribe, indignant. 'I would fight whoever dared do so!'

His peers nodded approvingly, some more willingly than others.

'I know that your allegiance to me is assured, but that is not enough.'

The chieftains looked at one another, taken aback.

'As long as you are rivals, Israel will remain a weak State. Your only possibility to preserve what you have acquired is to side with me. I will make a real capital of Jerusalem and of our people, the most powerful and glorious. I need your absolute obedience. You will continue to lead your clans, but you will be my loyal vassals. If I need soldiers, you will send them to me, putting the country's best interest before yours. If I ask for new taxes you will collect them for me and you will keep a share, to each of my desires you will reply with diligence. Do it for Israel, not for me. I want your reply here and now.'

Solomon had expressed himself in a very soft tone of voice, friendly, but the force of his proposition was nevertheless implicit. The chieftains gathered together behind the potter's house, where the King had settled to await their decision.

The artisan was decorating a wine jug. Despite the monarch's presence, he carried on with his work.

'What do you expect from your King, potter?'

'The happiness of my children.'

'What does that depend on?'

'On peace, Sire. It is the mother of all joys. The glory born of war is the undoing of humble people. But what King remembers that?'

'Solomon will not forget it.'

The deliberation lasted for three hours.

Three hours during which the King watched the potter's wheel turn with a music he found quite enchanting. These moments would either be unforgettable or the final upheaval in the existence of Israel . . . The vision of those deft hands freed the spirit of the King from anguish and darkness. He felt elated, indifferent to his fate.

It was the chieftain of the Dan tribe who, in the name of the eleven other families, presented to Solomon the result of their meeting.

37

'I was the last to be convinced,' he confessed. 'But unanimity has been reached. We accept.'

'Without a great vision, the people do not have an ideal to live for. Happy is the one who perceives the King's mind, for he envisions the far distant future.'

The chieftain of the Dan tribe scrutinised Solomon's soul. He saw no tyrant's vanity, just the will of a King.

7

Solomon had unified Israel. Jerusalem, David's religious centre, had become the political capital of a Kingdom whose young sovereign, to whom magic powers were attributed, was the uncontested master.

The chieftains of the tribes congratulated themselves on their choice. Once the spectre of a civil war was overcome, internal conflicts ended. Each thought only of living a happier life and rendering the land more fertile or the workshop busier. The rich grew richer, the poor became less poor and the High Priest reminded people of how Nathan had foreseen the wisdom inscribed on Solomon's semblance. The King worked without respite. The palace, so gloomy and so cold in David's time, now resembled a beehive in perpetual activity. Elihap registering successive royal decrees which, little by little, modified the administration and made it efficient. In less than two years of reign, Solomon had learned all there was to learn about Israel. From the highest echelons of state to the smallest local administrations, there was nothing he did not know about his country. The private secretary had proved his remarkable competence by keeping his files organised and up to date. In these, precise information had accumulated down the months.

The first stage of Solomon's work was coming to an end.

Now he must tackle the second. To build, to transform soldiers into artisans, to close the barracks and open building sites. Persuading Banaias that it was all for the good of the country proved indispensable. Israel would keep an elite corps, able to defend the crown, but would reduce its military contingent.

Various royal decrees were ready when the head of the army was called. The face of the colossus, ordinarily so blank, expressed desperation. Solomon knew immediately that something serious had happened. Banaias was unable to speak. He gave the King a wooden tablet inscribed with a text written by the Governor of Damascus. It was in Aramaic, Solomon read it twice.

'What . . . is your decision, Sire?'

'First of all, I have to think, then we shall decide together.'

The head of the army left.

Elihap felt it was necessary to break the King's inner dialogue.

'Has one of the tribes committed a belligerent act, Majesty?'

'It's disastrous, Elihap. An Aramæan general, a veritable devil, has attacked the village of Damascus; he refused to submit to my authority and decimated our garrison which occupied the oasis and supervised the road from Palestine and Phoenicia. This rebel has proclaimed the independence of his Kingdom of Damascus.'

The secretary understood Solomon's disappointment. The coup had ruined his projects. Damascus had never been lost in David's time.

'So, that means war, Majesty.'

'No, Elihap. I refuse to go to war. If I try to reconquer Damascus, I will have to fight Syria's allies. The infernal cycle will start again.'

'Then you will be covered in shame. People will say you are weak. All your work will have been in vain.'

'A day . . . I need one day. Bring me a detailed map of the country.'

Where was wisdom hiding? Was it concealed in such a deep

abyss that it was necessary to go down it on a rope woven in light by angels, longer than time itself? Should one shut oneself in a cage of clarity and plunge into the unfathomable chasm whose final depths could not be reached in twelve times thirty days and twelve times thirty nights? Only God had travelled the path of wisdom and knew the place where it rested.

To study Israel's map was for Solomon unexpectedly enlightening. What he had imagined was but a pretentious utopia. To decrease David's army would have put the country in peril. The capture of Damascus was divine warning that set the King back on the right path.

Solomon convoked Banaias and Elihap. That small war council would be enough.

'Damascus is lost,' he reckoned. 'It is only a worthless oasis. This reversal of fate will soon be forgotten. Specially considering the territories we control are more numerous than in my father's time. That Aramæan devil will haunt my sleep for a long time. Nevertheless he has clarified an important point, we need to reinforce our defence corps. We will start by fortifying Palmyra, then we will reorganise the army. When it is sufficiently large it will impress the enemy and we will no longer have to wage war.'

Banaias did not understand his King's speech. Why should soldiers be deprived of fighting? But he trusted Solomon's judgement.

Some large sheep weighing more than ten kilos passed in front of Solomon's litter set down under a shaded bower. In this autumn landscape, Jerusalem's countryside was delightful to see. The warmth at noon was welcome after the briskness of the morning air. After several weeks of labour, the King was enjoying a few hours' rest away from the palace.

'We have a great King,' proclaimed the Hebrews louder and more frequently.

But Solomon was conscious of reigning over a small

Christian Jacq

country that was nothing beside the great Egyptian nation. Israel . . . the forest, the plain and the desert, a sky of fire, rocks burned by the sun, rivers making their way between banks that were in turn arid and grassy. Only one hour's walk separated dried, barren landscapes from verdant stretches of field. A gift from God, a holy land that stretched from Dan to Beersheba, from the mountain chain of the Hedron between Lebanon, Syria and Israel to the steppes of the Moab. A people that the King had defended against internal strife and that he had to preserve from external peril.

After finishing the construction of a pipeline network that brought water to Jerusalem, Solomon was now concerned about the state of the circulation routes. The great road leading to the capital had been paved with basalt stones. The other routes, now secure for merchants, had been essential for the establishment of sustained trading between the provinces, as well as the passage of the army chariots whose sight had so impressed foreign spies.

Having quelled internal conflicts, Solomon had quietly reorganised his army, dividing his 30,000 soldiers into units containing fifty, one hundred and one thousand men directed by officers. The wars waged by David against the Philistines, Edomites, Ammonites, Moabites, and the Aramæans had led to the formation of an Israeli empire which, although it could not be compared with the Pharaoh's, had, nevertheless, a certain coherence. When speaking to the different regiments, Solomon had warned them that he would not pursue a policy of territorial expansion, but simply one of defence of the country that was Yahweh's sanctuary. That was why the most powerful army Israel had ever had was busy building or consolidating citadels, after having destroyed the oldest. The work was often rough, but had the advantage of being robust. In all the strategic points of the Kingdom, fortresses were now guarding the frontiers, secure at last.

Solomon's private secretary had written a text that had been widely circulated: 'The King has endowed Israel with riches, chariots and soldiers; he has erected citadels on the plains and on the hills. On their walls he has had figures of angels and heroes sculpted, with bodies made of bronze and escorted with precious stones. All the roads lead to Jerusalem, our protective mother.'

If Solomon could rest without fear in a peaceful country-side, it was thanks to his government policies. The Hebrews discovered with delight the happiness of living in safety, far from pillaging brigands and bloody conflicts between factions. Mothers could let their children play freely in the gardens and the fields. Peasants returned home singing, no longer afraid of being attacked at every bend in the road. Already, people were murmuring that Solomon's century would be comparable to none other, that a whole generation would not know what war was about. A miracle that had never occurred since kings reigned over Israel.

Solomon hoped for much more. He wanted a consolidated peace for many centuries to come.

His success would depend on the first battle that he would fight at Megiddo, the most recent of the rebuilt fortresses against which an assault was being prepared by rebellious Bedouins. Without taking into consideration his counsellors' advice, the King had decided to command his troops himself. There was no other way of determining if the type of defences he had ordered built were sufficient to dissuade the enemy.

A breath of hot air caressed the back of the King's neck. The summit of the mountains was slowly being tinted with ochre. In a stream, some adolescents were bathing. A farmer drove his donkey to the market, laden with baskets overflowing with grapes, but the time to go into combat was approaching.

Solomon had mobilised the whole of the royal guard, composed mostly of foreign mercenaries. The only soldiers left in Jerusalem would be the veterans, led by Israeli officers to ensure the protection of the palace during the monarch's absence. The elite corps would conquer Megiddo under his direct command.

Solomon went to the stables. The entrance was through a large courtyard paved with limestone with a stone cistern that contained more than ten thousand litres of water. Since his last visit a month before, the works had progressed. Each stable, divided into five units, had an independent access. The whole compound could be reached by a broad paved road, which made it easy for the horses' provisions to be brought, as well as facilitating the cleansing of the stables. Each beast was attached to a pillar marked with a number. Between these there were angels made of plaster. The airing and the lighting were ensured by regulated apertures on the roof.

'Who is responsible for these buildings?' asked Solomon.

The secretary consulted the register he always kept with him.

'Jeroboam, Majesty.'

Two guards went to fetch a red-haired man, around thirty years old. With his forehead marked with a scar due to a horse's shoe, a flattened nose, an angular chin with a dimple, Jeroboam was an athlete with a physique that was almost as impressive as Banaias'. Barefoot, his loincloth stained with the clay that he used to seal the joints between the limestone paving stones, he trembled with emotion as he approached the King.

'Where were you born?'

'In the Ephraim mountains, Sire. My father is dead, my mother stayed in our village.'

'What is your title?'

'Inspector of Works. I was trained in an agricultural militia, then with the team who restored Jerusalem's fortifications. After that, I was requisitioned to serve in the stables. I gave a few ideas and they were judged good. For the last two months, I have been putting them into practice.'

Solomon evaluated the man: lively, authoritarian and ambitious.

'I name you Head of all workmen from the tribes of Ephraim and Levi. When you have finished these stables, you will present me with the projects that you have in mind.'

A broad smile lit up the face of the red-haired colossus. A fantastic career was opening up before him.

Solomon studied closely the walls of the Megiddo fortress as rebuilt by soldiers who had had to become masons. Helped by a few specialists, they had replaced bricks by rocks, correctly cut and adjusted. The whole seemed solidly built.

Elihap, standing alongside the sovereign, observed the flat open country from whence would come the Bedouin attack. Troubled by vertigo, he felt ill at ease on the summit of this tower buffeted by violent winds. Banaias waited for the King's command to throw his bravest men into battle.

Solomon, with a gold diadem adorning his black hair, a sceptre in right hand, was the first to notice a cloud of dust that announced the arrival of the adversary.

The Hebrews stretched their bows.

'Guards, get away from those walls,' ordered Solomon. 'Let them come close.'

The commander of the garrison would not have given those orders. Moreover, the King did not have a reputation as a warrior.

The Bedouin horsemen, screaming, launched their arrows against the fortified walls. As the Hebrews did not counter-attack they were persuaded their number was negligible.

'Remove the steel bars that lock the main doors,' demanded the monarch.

'Majesty!'

The commander made no further objections. His attitude was in itself an insult to the royal person. But why was Solomon taking such a risk? Why was he leaving himself open to enemy blows? The Bedouins effortlessly forced their way through the now unguarded main entrance. Certain that they had won an easy victory, they shouted with joy. But that first enclosure led on to another that was not so high, but wider. On the ramparts, Hebrew archers popped out and let fly their arrows, piercing the breastplates of the disoriented Bedouins, trapped in a narrow space with their horses kicking out madly.

In the enemy ranks there were no survivors. Not a single Hebrew was wounded. The trap Solomon had set had worked perfectly. The Megiddo victory would be recounted by the court's poets and the glory of the King of Israel would travel the universe, striking fear into his enemy's hearts.

8

The report drawn up by Elihap left no doubt; the weapon of the future was the three-man chariot. The three would ride, the archer, the conductor and his assistant, who would protect his comrades with the help of a large shield. The best horses were to be found on Egyptian stud farms. Egyptian arsenals manufactured the best chariots. One Egyptian horse was worth one hundred and fifty cycles (shekels). An Egyptian war chariot was worth six hundred cycles. To ensure Israel's safety, Solomon needed at least four thousand horses and three thousand chariots.

'Take a papyrus,' the King ordered his secretary.

Elihap put aside the seals and tablets that littered his desk and considered a papyrus manufactured in a provincial town using plants that lived in marshes along the River Jordan before choosing one that came from Memphis, the large commercial town situated in lower Egypt.

'I do not have a papyrus that is more beautiful. I was keeping it for a special occasion. Would you rather have a wooden or a wax tablet?'

'The text that I have to dictate is too long, Elihap. When one is writing to the Pharaoh of Egypt one must not economise on respectful compliments.'

Solomon saw an intense emotion in his secretary's eyes. Elihap mixed some charcoal, a little gum diluted in water to obtain quality black ink. He cleaned the royal seal that he would later stamp on the bottom of the missive.

'Your hand seems to hesitate,' said Solomon.

'To write to the Pharaoh . . . is this not an enterprise that is bound to fail?'

'He is the only one who can sell us the horses and chariots we need. He will certainly refuse my first proposition. I do hope this will kindle a desire to make a counter-proposal.'

'Why would he wish to reinforce your army?'

'Because he knows I want peace. Even though it is strong, the country that Pharaoh Siamun governs is not as secure as it seems. Would it not be in its interest to refuse war?'

The secretary nodded in agreement. In fact, Siamun's power was contested by Thebes' High Priest, who had a strong following in southern Egypt, where the religious traditions were still vigorous. That was why the Pharaoh had set up his capital in Tanis, in the delta not far from Egypt's northeastern frontier.

'What do you know about him?'

'He is a secretive man who fulfils his duty with great rigour. Like most of his predecessors, he works tirelessly and is up to date on every governmental issue.'

'Does he have a belligerent temperament?'

'How can a Pharaoh not dream of grandiose feats? Egypt no longer possesses the splendour it enjoyed in Ramses' time, but it remains ambitious. Siamun must long to conquer Asia again. The road to his victories will have to cross Israel. That is why I fear that your letter might seem but amusing to him.'

Elihap had spoken unequivocally. Solomon appreciated his sincerity.

'I share your opinion, my secretary, but I love impossible challenges. The name of that Pharaoh resembles mine too closely for our destinies not to cross. As he is "the beloved of Maat", the goddess who incarnates the order of the world and truth itself, he will understand my intentions. Let us get down to work, Elihap. Let's begin with: "From King Solomon to his brother the Egyptian Pharaoh . . ."'

The precious missive had been entrusted to the royal post for over a month. Solomon, whose sleep was becoming lighter and lighter, could barely conceal his irritation. He shortened his audiences and took time for long meditations in the palace's chapel. He knew that the Hebrews detested Egypt, a country where, according to legend, they had been reduced to slavery. But they also knew that the Pharaonic monarchy, which established a solid link between heaven and earth, was an extraordinary model. It placed on the throne a being inspired by divinity. Only a king who was heir to that tradition could lead his people to the path of wisdom and happiness. Therefore Solomon, overcoming sentimental reactions and past rancour, had fashioned the Hebrew State and its administration after the Pharaonic example.

Solomon was convinced that he was not betraying his people. He nevertheless still hoped for a sign from Yahweh that would comfort him in his choice: to become Israel's Pharaoh. A reply from the Lord of the Clouds reached him one night as he was passing an old man in charge of sweeping the steps leading to the throne. A question came into the King's mind. A question that he felt he must ask this modest servant.

'You, what do you think of Egypt?'

The sweeper thought it over.

'I have lived there. So has my father and his father too. And so did our ancestors. They all said the same thing: it is an idyllic country. One eats well there and no one experiences deprivation. We were happy there. We love Egypt as much as we hate it. It is too powerful a neighbour for Israel . . . Therefore, it's natural that hate should speak louder than love. It is stupid, my King, but that's human nature for you, no one will change it.'

'Is the highest mountain not the one worth climbing? Wisdom has spoken through you. Leave your broom and hire a younger man to take your place. The palace will see that you lack nothing in your old age.'

*

'Here's the Pharaoh's answer, at last,' announced Elihap.

'Read it to me,' demanded Solomon.

'It is not a papyrus, Majesty. But some news brought by Banaias. The Egyptian army has vanquished the Philistines, taken the town of Gezer and is now heading to Israel's frontier.'

Solomon shook with silent anger. Not only had he failed, but he had also provoked a violent backlash on the part of his most formidable adversary. Israel's very existence was in danger.

'Let all my regiments assemble. We will not die without fighting.'

Full of eagerness, Banaias walked in front of the Israeli troops. Solomon's prestige was so great, his fortresses offered such exemplary safety, that victory over the Egyptians seemed certain. Solomon was not as optimistic. The Egyptian army was not as naïve as the Bedouins. If its vanguard let itself be trapped in the successive enclosures, the same would not be true of the core of the army. By vanquishing the Philistines at Gezer, Siamun, the Pharaoh, had proved his qualities as a good strategist. To invade Israel would cost him many lives. But he had the advantage of having more men and being better armed.

Despite the trust they placed in their King, the Hebrew soldiers shuddered when they saw the Egyptians deployed across a broad front. Ahead of the foot soldiers, there were dozens of chariots pulled by two horses. Each soldier had heard about the precision of Egyptian archers, who were reputed to decimate their adversaries. Banaias himself lost some of his nerve.

At the top of the fortified tower, where Solomon had taken up his post, with his secretary and the army's general, there reigned an anguished silence. The fight would be one against six, to ceaselessly throw back the ladders that the assailants would set against the citadel's walls, and prevent them from setting foot inside. How long could they resist?

A chariot came forward, advancing slowly towards Israeli positions. This was unusual behaviour. The chariot stopped at a safe distance. From it a head officer stepped down and ostentatiously threw down his sword and his shield. Then he walked in the desert and stood still about one hundred metres from the border.

'Sire, just give me the go-ahead to slit his throat.'

'Wait here for my orders.'

The King had the door of the fortress opened. He went towards the Egyptian officer. Soon, the two men were face to face.

'May the gods be with you,' said the Egyptian. 'I am the head commander of the Pharaoh's armies, whose vanguard lies before you.'

'May Yahweh grant his blessing to the Master of Egypt. Why do you approach my country's frontier so closely?'

'Sire, did you not send a letter to the Pharaoh? Did you not request that he send you horses and chariots?'

'I ask for nothing. I desire to buy them from him. His price will be mine.'

'My master wants to know the secret of your heart, King of Israel. Do you desire war or peace?'

'A King only reveals himself to another King,' said Solomon.

The Egyptian general bowed.

'The truth speaks from your mouth. The Pharaoh will see you at once, if you so desire.'

'So be it.'

Under the bewildered eyes of the Hebrews, their sovereign climbed into the Egyptian dignitary's chariot.

Solomon was not unaware of the inherent danger. If the Pharaoh took him hostage, he would capture Israel without even a blow. But never had an Egyptian King acted dishonourably. He was the Son of Maat, Goddess of Cosmic Order, who hated lies and cowardice.

The desert wind whipped Solomon's face. The general had

launched his horses into a gallop, avoiding with skill the piles of rocks that would have made the vehicle capsize.

A few minutes later, he pulled up before a white tent, whose entrance was guarded by two foot soldiers armed with spears. At his guide's invitation, Solomon entered the Pharaoh's abode.

The latter, dressed with a loincloth embroidered with gold thread and wearing a broad necklace of chalcedony, approached his guest.

'I am happy to welcome my Brother,' said Siamun warmly. 'The wisdom of Solomon is already famous.'

'Reputation is often illusory. My Brother the Pharaoh belongs to a more illustrious lineage than mine, has wisdom not been its nourishment for centuries?'

Siamun smiled.

'May my table always be laid with such food! Would my Brother do me the honour of accepting a glass of white wine from the Delta?'

'Its reputation is too solid to be illusory. Who would refuse such a pleasure?'

The two monarchs sat facing each other on chairs made of cedarwood. The Pharaoh served his guest himself. If he had dispensed with all the servants, thought Solomon, it was because not only did he intend to honour him in a remarkable manner, but he also wanted to speak with Solomon in the greatest secrecy.

'Israel is a flourishing state,' said the Pharaoh.

'God so desires,' replied Solomon. 'My country is young, it lacks experience. If it did not possess a good model, what hope could it possibly have.'

'Which is that model?'

'Is there a more accomplished one than Egypt?'

'Nevertheless,' objected the Pharaoh, 'our two peoples do not appreciate each other.'

'The Hebrews love and hate Egypt with equal passion,' explained Solomon. 'It is up to their King to make the beam on the weighing scales tilt one way or the other. I have chosen mine and will not waver.'

Siamun was an aristocratic man, with fine features and brown eyes that were perpetually animated. He did not seem endowed with great physical strength, but Solomon was not deceived by appearances.

Siamun was not a hesitant leader, but a true statesman. His sense of diplomacy masked an iron will that must overcome the slightest obstacle.

'I vanquished the Philistines at Gezer,' remembered Egypt's master. 'It was an important victory, but not a decisive one. The Philistines are mighty warriors, who will fight until their people are extinct. Many Egyptians will lose their lives. I am responsible for their existence. What they expect of me is to be able to live happily and not lose their lives in combat.'

The two monarchs savoured white wine from the Delta. A remarkable vintage that enchanted the palate.

Solomon was beginning to understand his host's strategy.

'The letter of the King of Israel is very strange,' continued the Pharaoh. 'Why should my Brother wish to acquire so many horses and chariots, if not to prepare to wage war against Egypt?'

'It is precisely to avoid it,' rectified Solomon. 'Israel is in danger. If its army is strong, its neighbours will think of peace and not war.'

'A vision worthy of Egypt, my Brother, my glorious ancestors thought likewise. My military demonstration against the Philistines had no other intention but that of setting an example. Should I lead my troops against my enemies or should I wait and see?'

'Would you perchance be in need of assistance?' asked Solomon solemnly.

The King of Israel was aware of the incongruous nature of that question. He was going beyond the limit of good manners. The Pharaoh's reaction would depend on his sincerity.

Siamun poured some more wine.

'Yes, my Brother, I need you. If Egypt and Israel conclude an alliance, death and distress will retreat. The Philistines will be contained between the two countries and forced to surrender their arms. Peace will reign as far as the sweet Northern wind blows.'

To accept the Pharaoh's proposal meant a complete reversal of Israel's foreign policy, to impose on the Hebrews the acknowledgement of this envied and hated neighbour as a privileged friend. The Egyptians would then become Israel's protectors.

Solomon was staking his throne.

Silent, the King of Egypt demanded an answer.

'The situation is not that simple,' judged the King of Israel. 'My country, even with chariots and horses, will not have Egypt's power. What my Brother proposes means such an upheaval . . .'

Siamun looked at Solomon attentively.

'Of course, the King of Israel expects guarantees from Egypt's Pharaoh.'

'Indeed,' replied Solomon, 'otherwise the King of Israel would be very naïve and the Pharaoh would despise him.'

'Would the truth not be the most important of guarantees? Israel wants to live in peace, Egypt also. We fear an attack from Libya. Sooner or later its jackals will be let loose on us. We must also protect our Asian borders. It is not by setting up against Israel that I can adopt the policy that I deem to be the best. Are these explanations sufficient for you?'

'Thank you. I appreciate your position, but . . .'

'But more is needed to satisfy Solomon!' replied the Pharaoh, losing his temper. 'Is he in a position to make demands?'

Solomon looked into his host's eyes.

'It is up to my Brother to judge,' he announced calmly.

'I want peace,' stated the Egyptian monarch. 'I desire passionately that we may build it together. The guarantees that my Brother wishes for will be granted.'

9

A little before dawn, Solomon left David's palace. That morning, the protocol would not be respected. The protocol master would have to adapt to the circumstances. The King needed to reflect in peace, away from the palace.

Dressed in a white tunic, Solomon drove his chariot himself. He took the direction of Ein Atan, a secluded place where a summer palace had been built surrounded by a park in which a healing spring welled. During this season, the abode was deserted. The sun was rising when Solomon entered the domain. Abandoning his chariot, he walked up to the top of the rocky promontory that rose above the spring. In the old days, the peasants offered sacrifices to Yahweh there. The King, with ancestral gestures, picked some wild flowers and made a bouquet that he elevated to the heavens. Thus the Almighty would inhale the immaterial perfume of his creation. The spring was vigorous, silver drops sprang up in the sunlight. Following one of the beams with his eyes, Solomon heard God's voice.

'I order that you build a temple on top of my holy mountain. Wisdom will guide your labour. It will stay by your side as it did with me when I created the world. It is through wisdom, and only through wisdom, that the paths of those who are on earth are drawn with rectitude.'

Solomon remembered the legend that his tutor had told him many times. In the origins of time, the skies had opened. From them came a large stone that fell on the sea. On that solid surface the earth was created. God had stretched his gardener's line over the void and organised chaos with a level. The architect of the world had separated light from darkness.

To build a temple . . . Solomon's vocation was taking shape. The call that he had felt in his deepest self for all these years was finally gaining form, to erect the future edifice in honour of Yahweh. To be a great King he must become a builder. Solomon thought of the Step-pyramid built by the Pharaoh Zoser: by opening a gigantic building site he had once and for all unified his country. Israel needed a temple. A magnificent sanctuary built to the glory of the one and only God. A sacred abode that would be the sun of the Kingdom.

Inebriated with joy, Solomon ran to his chariot and sped back to Jerusalem.

The soldiers of the monarch's private guard were in a state of alert. No one knew where Solomon had gone. The master of the palace had clumsily tried to hide Solomon's disappearance, which caused scandal among the courtiers. The palace's esplanade was full of priests and dignitaries who demanded explanations. Some were ready to call the King a weakling, a firefly or a volatile spirit.

When Solomon reappeared, resplendent in his white robes, the rumours were silenced. His subjects were struck dumb and, with eyes fixed on him, they stood very still. Each waited for the mysterious absence to be explained.

Elihap, with a papyrus roll folded in his hand, walked towards the King, pushing the courtiers out of his way, and bowed before him, presenting the precious object.

'Here is what your tutor, the prophet Nathan, had asked me to give you.'

'Why choose this moment to hand it to me?'

'God inspired Nathan. David's testament had to be given to you only on a day when you had left the palace at dawn and come back alone on your chariot, when the sun made the purity of your robes shine with light. Thus spoke the prophet.'

Elihap's declaration struck the audience with terror. Solomon could no longer be considered just a man. Was he not like those angels who had assumed a human semblance to fulfil heaven's will on earth?

When Solomon proceeded into David's residence, he still did not know that his prestige was now immense and that no one would have dreamed of contesting his authority. He had but one desire: to read the text that had been hidden from him for so long.

The King unrolled the papyrus on the paving stones in the throne room. It was indeed his father's handwriting.

'I live in a modest palace, and the Ark of Yahweh is placed under a simple tent. I wanted to build a noble abode for the one and only God, but the prophet Nathan always opposed this project vehemently. If I had tried to carry out my project, Yahweh would have struck me down. Therefore, during my reign, God was content with travelling from place to place, whereas I was occupied shedding a great deal of blood on earth. But I prepared the path for the future. A huge treasure is hidden in the palace's cellars. It will serve my son Solomon, to build the temple that my heart desired and that my eyes will never see. I have assembled materials, gold bars, bronze and iron. I have built an altar where the future sanctuary will stand. I bought the land that now belongs to the Crown. My son, when you read these lines, show yourself worthy of the tasks you have inherited. At long last, you can share my secret.'

Solomon called his secretary.

'This text is incomplete,' said the King. 'It comes with an oral teaching and you are the only one who could have received it.'

'It's true, Sire. That is why I left the palace waiting to see what kind of King you intended to become.'

'Are you conscious of how impudent you are being?'

'Indeed, master. Would you have behaved otherwise?'

Solomon could never easily circumvent the Egyptian scribe. But he appreciated his lack of subservience and his straightforwardness. Nathan, the prophet, had not been mistaken in trusting him and in letting the young King reveal his intentions.

'Where is the altar that will be the temple's foundation stone?'

'You will encounter numerous enemies,' prophesied Elihap. 'To build a temple like the one you intend to erect is contrary to nomadic habits, deeply rooted in Israel's soul.'

'That is exact,' admitted Solomon, 'but my father has entrusted me with a mission and I will see that it is fulfilled. This country needs a temple, the most magnificent there is.'

'The altar is situated on the rock of Jerusalem, Sire, on the Northern peak of the mountain. The place has been prohibited for years. It is almost inaccessible due to the ravine that separates it from the nearest houses.'

'The old grounds where the wheat was thrashed, where Noah offered a sacrifice, where Jacob saw a staircase linking the earth to heaven . . . Is that the place, Elihap?'

'Yes, Sire. Nathan thought that that rock was the primordial stone around which the world was created. At its centre, the spring of paradise flows. It goes up to the sun and come down as rain on the earth. That rain whose master you have become.'

'The primordial stone . . . Don't the Egyptians claim to possess it as well, at Heliopolis?'

'As many sacred sites, as many centres of the world, Sire,' answered the secretary, 'it is up to you to build the one that will belong to your people.'

Solomon left David's palace. Helped by two soldiers who fixed up two ropes that functioned as a crossing, he walked over the precipice and spent the rest of the day through to sunset on the majestic rock where his temple would rise.

From the top of Jerusalem's mountains, he rediscovered his capital and his country. To the North there was Samaria and Galilee. To the East was Jordan, the Dead Sea and the desert.

Judah stood to the South. To the West, the plains ended on the Mediterranean coast.

Solomon contemplated the land he ruled, with its hills, its river, its seas, and the tribes he had brought together. No one, since David had consecrated an altar on this rock, which occupied the whole of the summit of the mountain, had contemplated Israel from such a height and from such a distance.

David had chosen the site well. It had the necessary power, sufficient beauty and mystery for God's abode. Soon the Ark of the Covenant would no longer be itinerant. It would not be long now before the Hebrews would be able to see the sanctuary that would anchor them forever in the love of the Almighty.

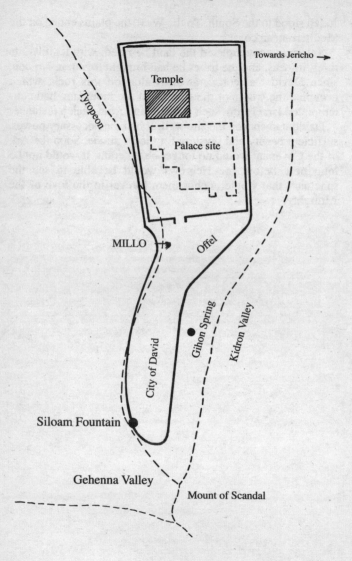

Towards Jericho →

Tyropeon

Temple

Palace site

MILLO

Offel

Gihon Spring

Kidron Valley

City of David

Siloam Fountain

Gehenna Valley

Mount of Scandal

10

The day after the first autumn Sabbath was marked by a succession of unforeseen audiences. Solomon, who was expecting a message from the Pharaoh and who still believed in his word, was feeling melancholy. He studied the plan left by David for the future temple of Jerusalem, but he found it imperfect. His father had only planned for a larger chapel without architectural genius.

Where was he going to find a Master Mason? The Hebrews had learned how to pave roads, how to build or consolidate the walls of fortresses, but they did not know the secret art of erecting the eternal stones destined for the sanctuary.

With the arrival of Jeroboam, carrier of a message important enough to justify interrupting the King's meditation, the latter was filled with renewed hope. Could it be that that young Master Mason was the architect that Israel needed?

The red-haired athlete, with a nude torso, his hips covered in a leather apron, was very excited. When the King bade him speak, he expressed himself with volubility.

'Master, the stables are finished! Your horses will be happy there. The teams in charge of feeding and cleaning them will have a room to circulate. Nothing similar exists elsewhere!'

'You can be proud of your work, Jeroboam.'

'My King, I have other projects! I will fulfil them if I can have a sufficient number of workmen.'

'I'm listening,' said Solomon.

Did Jeroboam wish to see Jerusalem crowned with a temple? Did he perceive the future of the country? If so, he would become the Master Mason in charge of working side by side with the King.

'I want to build the new palace of the King of Israel,' declared Jeroboam with assurance. 'The people whisper that David's palace is unworthy of Solomon. I will use bricks and wood on several floors, with an immense terrace and . . .'

'Do you think that that is the first building we should construct?'

'Yes, my Lord!'

'Is there not another more urgent?'

'Of course not!'

'Think about it.'

With tight lips and an anxious gaze, Jeroboam looked in vain for the reply Solomon desired. The King was patient, but what he read in the soul of his Master Mason dissuaded him from offering him anything but his present task.

'Abandon the idea of that palace, Jeroboam. We will soon be needing larger stables. Choose a plot of land close to Jerusalem, prepare the plans and organise the building site. You will work under the orders of the master of the palace.'

Upset, Jeroboam took his leave.

He had just left the audience room when the master of the palace came in as troubled as his predecessor.

'Majesty, we are heading to disaster!'

'Why is that?'

'Your secretary, Elihap, has diverted numerous contributions that should have been handed to me for the upkeep of the court. I ask that he be severely castigated.'

'In that case, it is the King who must be punished, for Elihap has acted under my orders.'

Panicked, the master of the palace stepped back.

'Forgive me, Majesty . . . I did not know . . . but how can I continue to . . .'

'I was expecting your intervention much earlier. It proves that you do not examine your accounts very often. Use your intelligence. The money amassed by Elihap will serve to build the temple. The expenses of the court will be reduced to a minimum without its grandeur being altered.'

Happy to escape a terrible fate, the dignitary dashed to his office. On the way out he bumped into the former High Priest, Abiathar, who asked to see Solomon urgently.

Abiathar, appointed by David, was the only descendant left of an illustrious family of priests who had lived in Shilo, the most famous holy place before Jerusalem became the capital of Israel. He had escaped the massacre of David's partisans organised by Saul. It was he who had managed to rescue the Ark and the High Priest's ritual vestments.

Informed of the old man's presence, Solomon came to meet him and, offering him his arm, led him to one of the sheltered terraces. Abiathar had trouble walking.

'You are a young man, Solomon. As for me, I am almost deceased.'

'You were my father's friend,' said the sovereign, 'you shared his trials. May God bless you.'

'I am the guardian of the tradition, Solomon. If I come out of my usual reserve, it is to forewarn you. Your father never intended to build a temple. That edifice would be a sacrilege. The Ark should not be confined to Jerusalem, but it must continue to travel the provinces. Do not profane the custom of our people. Banish from town the foreigners, whose number seems to grow ceaselessly. Get rid of that Egyptian, Elihap, who is a bad counsellor.'

'Would the building of a temple disgruntle the clergy?'

The old man, Abiathar, sat down on one of the terrace's low walls, with his back in the sun.

'The clergy won't stand for it, I can assure you! Your father divided it into twenty-four classes that share religious duties. A temple would oblige them to regroup in Jerusalem and leave their provinces! Nothing must change. The strength of Israel lies in her past and to want to destroy it would be betraying the divine will.'

Solomon admired the rock that dominated Jerusalem.

'You, Abiathar, are you familiar with that will?'

'I know how to make the oracles speak!'

'It is one of the faults that I reproach in you. A High Priest should be attentive to ritual and not magic. Your successor, Sadoq, is not so imprudent.'

Abiathar was surprised by the vigorous tone.

'There are more serious questions: I know that you supported my enemy Adonias, whose execution I deplored. It was, unfortunately, indispensable.'

The old man tottered. Solomon stopped him falling.

'You deserve death, but considering your advanced years I am content with sending you to a village to the north of Jerusalem, from whence you will not leave. If you disobey, do not expect clemency.'

The former High Priest stood up without help.

Looking like a lost child, he observed a monarch radiant with youth, intent on sweeping away yesterday's world, reducing it to nothing, as if he actually burned it to the ground.

Nevertheless, Solomon had not been at all aggressive. His countenance had remained calm and smiling, as if he had sung a poem about the autumn's muted colours.

'Has Sadoq, my successor . . . not tried to convince the King that he was misguided?'

'Sadoq is himself an old man,' reminded Solomon. 'He is prudent. If he came to oppose the monarch that he himself crowned, how would he be judged by God? The priests do not matter, it is up to the King to lead his people towards the light. Is that not the teaching you received from your father?'

Abiathar lowered his head.

Solomon watched him leave the terrace, knowing that he would never see the old man again.

11

After having awoken the divine light in the Holy of Holies of the temple of Tanis, Pharaoh Siamun collected himself. Only the light hidden in the mystery of that place where the Egyptian King alone was allowed to enter could inspire him on this day when he had to take a very important decision.

Preceded by his sandal carrier, he crossed the great open-air courtyard. The sky was clouded and the air was heavy with sea odours that came from the Mediterranean. A chariot took Siamun from the temple to the palace. He was once again delighted to admire the beauty of Tanis, surrounded by trees and gardens. The architects had been inspired by Thebes, the magnificent, to recreate in the North a town full of majestic villas where it was pleasant to live.

When the Pharaoh entered the council room, Amon's High Priest, the first ritual master and the first general stood up to greet Egypt's monarch. The latter sat on a throne made of wood decorated with gold, whose back was ornamented by a crowning scene.

'My friends,' he announced, 'I have learned from a secure source that King Solomon has decided to build a huge temple on the rock of Jerusalem.'

'How absurd,' said the High Priest. 'Israel is not a poor country, but Solomon does not have the funds necessary to carry out such a project.'

'Make no mistake. David accumulated riches that his son will make use of.'

'Why does he want to imitate us? The Hebrews are nomads,' reminded the ritual master. 'They do not need a large sanctuary to shelter their God.'

'Solomon has understood that he should become a builder to make a great nation out of Israel,' said the Pharaoh. 'We will support him.'

'The general did not try to disguise his reticence.

'Your Majesty was very generous to sell chariots and horses to Solomon. Why help him further?'

'So that he may consolidate peace,' answered Siamun. 'The temple of Jerusalem will deter the waging of war. If the King of Israel concentrates all his efforts on building, our two countries will commune through their gods. But Solomon is as prudent as he is wily. He will only accept an allegiance treaty if we give him a guarantee of our good faith.'

'Which, Majesty?' asked the High Priest.

'Solomon is familiar with our traditions. He knows that only a marriage can seal a peace treaty.'

Siamun's three counsellors were aghast. What the Pharaoh was implying was unthinkable.

'The Pharaoh cannot be thinking of giving the hand of his daughter to a Hebrew?'

'It is the only way of convincing Solomon that we hate war as much as he does. Like you, I know very well that never before has a Pharaoh's daughter married a foreigner. But we must be realistic. Egypt is becoming weaker. It would not bear the burden of several conflicts. Our alliance with Israel will guarantee our safety in the Northeast. We will then be able to concentrate on protecting our Western borders.'

The Pharaoh's analysis was correct. The general could find no objections.

'Israel has neither stone, wood, nor the gold needed to build a great temple,' estimated the ritual master. 'Will the Pharaoh supply all these?'

'That would be a mistake,' judged Siamun. 'It would make Solomon too dependent on Egypt. He would not accept. We will act in an indirect way. Solomon will have to address the King of Tyre.'

'He cannot refuse us anything,' admitted the general.

'Apart from being a reliable ally against the nomads' raids, Israel will be an important economic ally,' said the Pharaoh. 'It will give us access to the commercial roads that we do not control.'

On consideration, the alliance with Solomon, after a proper examination, presented only advantages. Nevertheless, the Pharaoh was still worried.

'Are there any further obstacles?' asked the High Priest.

'A major obstacle,' answered Siamun. 'We have to become acquainted with the secrets that Solomon will ensconce in his temple.'

'We need an Egyptian who will accept to convert to Yahweh's religion,' reasoned the ritual master.

'That, Majesty, you cannot demand.'

'I will not become the culprit of such a villainous act,' promised the Pharaoh. 'There is another tangible element that Solomon will require, a human one: the Master Mason who is able to build his temple. The architect who will erect Yahweh's sanctuary will be an Egyptian.'

An unusual agitation reigned over the House of Life at the temple of Tanis. Normally, the site was devoted to silence, study and meditation. Those who were learning hieroglyphs and those who composed the rituals came to work there. Architects, sculptors, doctors, important administrators had spent some time in the workshops of the House of Life learning their profession.

The initiates who stayed permanently in that place where the wisdom of the ancestors was conveyed were few. The outer world held few attractions for them. They had chosen to consecrate their life to God and no longer dealt with human affairs. Therefore, they were surprised by the arrival at nightfall of the ruler of Egypt, the Pharaoh in person.

The King had been the pupil of the sage who directed the House of Life. The latter ushered the sovereign into a room with columns whose circumference was furnished with stone benches. About ten adepts were sitting there.

'If I requested this meeting, it is because I need to consult you. Israel has become a great nation. It is governed by Solomon, an exceptional monarch. He wants to build a temple in honour of Yahweh. No Hebrew architect is able to carry out such a task.'

It matters little,' judged an adept. 'Israel is our enemy.'

'It used to be,' rectified the Pharaoh. 'Solomon wants to end the hostilities that divide our nations.'

'Beware of the Hebrews,' recommended another adept. 'They are not to be trusted.'

'Solomon wants peace. Let us help him.'

'In what way?'

'By sending him an architect who will be capable of building Yahweh's temple,' answered the Pharaoh.

'That is impossible. Our secrets must remain in Egypt.'

'Nothing will be revealed,' stated Siamun. 'They will remain concealed in the construction. The form will be that chosen by Solomon.'

The master of the House of Life addressed the Pharaoh.

'As your decision has been taken, Majesty, which one of us have you chosen?'

Siamun, used to controlling his emotions, was forced to take a deep breath.

'Horemheb, son of Horus.'

The eyes focussed on an adept around thirty years old, with a wide forehead and a muscular build. He was twelve when he had become an apprentice and had spent his adolescence on the building sites in Karnak. Horemheb had become a Master Mason three years before. He had chosen to delve deeper into his art by studying the treaties written by Imhotep, the greatest of architects, preserved in the House of Life.

Horemheb did not give vent to his feelings. He made no comment.

'I realise the weight of the sacrifice that I am imposing on you,' said Siamun. 'Leaving Egypt is a trial that few of us can face, no matter how wise. If you believe that my decision is unjust, you must refuse.'

Horemheb bowed before the Pharaoh,

The master of the House of Life stood up.

'The King and I have talked for a long while before adopting our present position. Perhaps we are mistaken. It is possible that Solomon and the Hebrews are hiding their passion for war. Our architect may not be successful but if he succeeds in building this temple in Jerusalem, the wisdom of our ancestors will be conveyed to another nation that will, in turn, convey it to future generations. This enterprise will be the responsibility of one man. Let him meditate and prepare himself. Let us leave him alone.'

Siamun left the council room last. He turned around to Horemheb, who stood very still.

'Tonight,' he announced, 'we leave for Memphis.'

In the moonlight night, King Cheops's pyramid emerged as a huge mountain whose white limestone facing shone in the darkness.

Siamun and the Master Mason went inside after having gone through the silent alleys of the high temple. Horemheb knew the plan of that prodigious building that no builder would ever equal. The Pharaoh ordered him to descend into the subterranean room and fetch the ritual objects that had been deposited there many centuries before.

The Master Mason crouched and slipped into the narrow granite conduit that led into the earth's entrails.

When he came back up carrying his precious burden, the Pharaoh embraced him.

'From now on, your name will be Hiram.'

12

Nagsara, the Pharaoh's daughter, was terrified. She was seventeen and had never left Egypt or the royal court, where she had lived in comfortable luxury, far from the outer world and its ugly reality. As she was not destined to reign, Nagsara had enjoyed the culture that was the privilege of Egyptian noblewomen. Poetry, dance, music, participation in the rites of the goddess Hathor, service in the temple, country walks and promenades on the banks of the Nile, sumptuous banquets had been her lot. The adolescence of the Pharaoh's daughter had taken place in a whirl of pleasures and festivities. When she deemed the right time had come, she would betroth the man she had fallen in love with and would give him two children, a boy and a girl. Then happy days would follow one another, flowing with the seasons, under the protection of the divine sun.

The young princess's dreams of happiness had been brutally broken when her father had summoned her to the palace in the most official manner, in the presence of his counsellors. He had informed her of his decision. In order to serve Egypt's interests, Nagsara would leave for Jerusalem where she would become Solomon's wife, thus sealing the pact that would initiate an era of peace and friendship.

Very disturbed, the young woman lacked even the strength to remind her father that such a practice was contrary to tradition and that she would be the first Pharaoh's daughter ever given to a foreigner in marriage.

Nagsara cried for an entire day. She thought of throwing herself into the void from the top of the palace. But no human being had the right to end their own life, or they would risk annihilating their soul and not gaining entrance to the realm beyond.

To the time of departure, Nagsara had lived in a fog, like the mist that invaded the streets of Tanis on winter mornings and only dissipated when the sun triumphantly broke through the clouds. But the heart of the Pharaoh's daughter, in the grip of a glacial night, had lost the path to the light.

She who was usually so joyful now looked sad and tired. She languished and had let herself be dressed and made up without reacting. Her hairdresser cried. Of course, she had embellished Nagsara's still childish features, but had not managed to make them cheerful. The braided wig, perfumed with jasmine, was a work of art. The princess's black eyes, her lips painted red, her cheeks lightly tinted with an orange blush and her long eyelashes gave her enormous charm. But what was the use of rendering seductive a woman condemned to the most terrible fate, to live in exile?

Since her departure from Tanis, Nagsara had closed her eyes, hoping that this fake somnolence would take her into the world of the gods. When she opened them again, it was to discover the road paved with basalt leading to Jerusalem on which her chariot rode, pulled by plumed horses. It was followed by a convoy of vehicles full of presents for Solomon. The princess was protected by an elite corps and accompanied with many servants in charge of fulfilling her slightest desires. But what could a Pharaoh's daughter promised to a foreigner King wish for, when she feared him more than a nocturnal demon?

In this beginning of winter, the sky was of a troubling greyness. The cortege had faced the rain and the wind, leaving behind the light dawns and the golden sunsets of Egypt.

A smell of fish hit Nagsara's nostrils, it was market day in

Israel's capital. The alleys smelt foul. They were so narrow that the chariot had difficulty making its way. Nagsara cried out with fright when about ten beggars, excited and shouting to one another, hung on to the wooden grill that served as a carriage window. In rags, shouting insults, with dirty hands, they wanted to touch the beautiful Egyptian girl who had travelled from a legendary country. The archers rebuffed them brutally. They bolted, stepping on a leper who had not been able to get out of the way quick enough. Among the rich houses covered with roof tiles and those of the poor with reeds on the roof and made of beaten earth, the soldiers tried in vain to restore some order. The excitement reached its peak and the crowd drummed up a noisy gaiety, stupefied to see that the rumours were true after all: a Pharaoh's daughter was coming to offer herself to the King of Israel!

There were no wide avenues as in Thebes or Memphis, but a succession of small entangled arteries, some of which had steps to facilitate the climbing of the asses carrying victuals. Nagsara had the feeling of entering a closed world, where she would be forever captive.

Gone were the gardens preceding the abode of Egyptian nobles; faded were the blooming trees and bushes; lost were constructions in wood, covered in foliage under which people relaxed in the shade.

The progression of the chariot was interrupted by some geese and chicken that had fled from a farm situated in the centre of the capital. The incident did not make Nagsara smile, but a familiar perfume calmed her nerves for a few moments: emanating from a giant jasmine bush that graced the walls of a small courtyard where copper utensils were piled up. In this season, it was a miracle. The young woman loved that smell that reminded her of her childhood games near the palace's pond. But a few yards further on that wonderful scent was overcome by the pestilent smell of black smoke. Housewives were burning detritus and excrement; others were cooking meat or fish. The brutality of Jerusalem's odours had quickly dissipated a dreamy moment.

Suddenly, Nagsara bit her wrist, almost drawing blood. Then she realised she was behaving foolishly, in a manner unworthy of her rank. That a Pharaoh's daughter should present herself to the King of Israel in this miserable state appalled her. The jumble of houses, the lack of space should not make her forget that she was entering into the capital of a powerful state, governed by a monarch whose fame was on the rise. In this region, Nagsara represented Egypt. She was the heir and the symbol of her country's nobility.

The cortege was forced to halt near a coppersmith's workshop. The artisans had taken up much of the road with their tools. With hammers, they beat the metal-plate into cauldrons. Responding to the solders' shouts they reluctantly made way for the chariot. A water carrier approached the vehicle.

'Drink, princess! See how fresh the water is!'

Nagsara accepted. In exchange, she handed the merchant a silver bowl.

The water carrier showed off his magnificent trophy and praised the goodness of the Egyptian who brought riches to the common people. Nagsara had just conquered the heart of one of Jerusalem's neighbourhoods. Despite the despair that gnawed away within her, she had decided not to behave like some languishing little girl.

Soon, she would come before Solomon, whose beauty and intelligence had been extolled. She decided she must not disappoint him.

After two hours of patient, dedicated effort, the servants of the High Priest Sadoq finished dressing their master in his attire for the ritual. The corners of his beard had been left untrimmed in accordance with the custom. Sadoq was coiffed with a turban made of a purple sash topped by a golden tiara on which an inscription proclaimed: 'Glory to Yahweh'. On his linen tunic, a purple surplice was placed, ornamented with pomegranates between which hung small bells of gold. Their shrill sound chased away the evil spirits. On top of this, he wore but a single item, the ephod. Woven in golden and crimson thread, it was fixed on the shoulders of the High Priest with gold clasps studded with two onyx stones.

The famous breast ornament with the twelve precious stones was attached to the ephod. Among the gems, which symbolised the twelve tribes of Israel, were topaz, emeralds, sapphires, jaspers, amethysts, agates, carbuncular gemstone and sardonyx. Joined to this ornament was a small bag containing two dice. By throwing them, the High Priest revealed the Numbers used by God to build the world.

Sadoq, who was a thin man, gained when dressed in this fashion an admiration that was heavily tinged with fear. Preceded by two priests, he was introduced into the throne room where Solomon awaited him.

'Why did you request an audience, Sadoq? Were you not meant to be supervising preparations for my wedding?'

Haughty, the High Priest replied in a cutting tone.

'This union displeases Yahweh, Majesty. Why not choose a spouse from among your concubines? This Egyptian girl does not partake of our faith. She will make a bad Queen and will draw misfortune on Israel. Renounce this marriage and do not anger your people. It is God that speaks through me.'

Solomon's eyes shone. As anger welled up within him, he felt like striking this insolent priest who owed him absolute obedience. But the King of the Hebrews had to control himself under all circumstances.

'If I disregard your words, Sadoq, what then happens?'

'I would refuse to celebrate this heretical marriage, Majesty. I would go before the people and discard my ceremonial habits, I would explain to them that Yahweh's High Priest is thus placing a curse on the King and his Egyptian bride.'

Sadoq, a sardonic smile crossing his lips, felt triumphant.

Solomon thought he had named an obedient puppet who would carry out his orders without question. He realised that the High Priest had real power. Sadoq was counting on becoming a notable figure, almost the King's equal. Solomon would then be forced to consult him before taking any decision.

Sadoq was astonished that Solomon remained so calm. He had hoped for a violent reaction that he would have taken advantage of, by discrediting it and saying the monarch was still too young. But the latter, either out of weakness or reasonableness, did not even try to put up a fight.

'Take the dice that you are carrying, Sadoq.'

'The dice, but . . .'

'Before throwing them on the paving stones of this room, prove to me that you are speaking in the name of God by announcing the Numbers that will be revealed.'

'That is a legend, Sire, nothing more, and . . .'

'The Five and the Seven, Sadoq. The Five the number of man and the Seven the number of Woman. If my forecast is correct, God will bless my wedding with the daughter of the King of Egypt. Throw the dice, High Priest.'

After first hesitating, Sadoq withdrew the dice from the leather pouch. He held them in his right hand and then threw them. They rolled for a long time, resonating on the stones.

Solomon stood still.

Sadoq advanced, with the gold bells on his ceremonial habit tinkling his progress. Their metallic ring seemed demonic to him when he saw the numbers that chance had thrown up – five and seven.

13

Nagsara, a Pharaoh's daughter, was sure she would be received with the honours due to her high rank. The least of which would be the presence of her future spouse, King Solomon.

When the chariot stopped before a grey building adjoining the palace, a portly man carrying a key and bearing a seal on his shoulder helped her descend. 'I am the master of the palace,' he declared, adding pleasantly, 'Welcome to Israel.'

Nagsara was indignant.

'Where is the King?'

'He will soon be here. The preparations for the marriage have delayed him.'

'This is a grave insult! I am not his servant.'

The master of the palace was impressed by the virulence of this woman, who was quite short and of rather mediocre beauty. As he expected, the presence of a daughter of Pharaoh at Israel's court was already likely to result in conflict and scandal.

'Please follow me, Majesty. My duty is to show you to the quarters where you will live.' Nagsara looked around. The Egyptian soldiers were but few. Solomon's guard would easily suppress any outbreak of rebellion. The Pharaoh's daughter had no immediate means of reacting to the humiliation she was being put through.

Therefore, she followed the master of the palace. Her

disappointment was tremendous. The abode with rugged walls to which he showed the princess was less luxurious than the most modest houses in Thebes.

There was no interior garden, no water ponds, no colonnaded rooms. The rooms were square, devoid of elegance, without decoration, unworthy of a royal princess. Nagsara was feeling the anger well up in her chest when she heard laughter. Two young women, dressed in short dresses, drew back a curtain, left the room they were in and ran past the Egyptian. A third, older woman followed them. Ironic, she stared at Nagsara like a curious animal, then retired into another room from whence came spicy perfumes.

'Who are they?'

'Solomon's other spouses,' answered the master of the palace. 'They used to belong to his father, David. There are about twenty of them . . . Moabites, Edomites, Sidonites, and even Hitites. The one who observed you closely is an Ammonite. She comes from the city of Ammon which controls the route going from Jerusalem to Damascus. It is an important strategic position. Therefore, this secondary wife holds a prominent place among the concubines. Unfortunately for her, her age . . . Solomon needs a new Queen, very young . . .'

'And I would be the one who . . .'

Nagsara did not dare finish her sentence. Had that monstrous King decided to take her for his slave, to submit her to his lowest instincts? The Pharaoh had planned a diplomatic marriage that would mean living as a recluse. That miserable fate now seemed sweet to Nagsara, compared to what she foresaw.

'I refuse to become your King's bitch,' she announced to the master of the palace. 'If he touches me, it will be war. Never will my father accept that I be treated in this way. I will not live here, in the company of those horrible women.'

'Majesty . . .'

'I forbid you to address me. Solomon is an unworthy being.

In Egypt, you would be less than a fisherman from the Delta. I will never leave this chariot.'

Nagsara walked to the vehicle. She took but a few steps. On the threshold of the building stood Solomon, who had witnessed the arrival of the Pharaoh's daughter.

He smiled, unruffled. Nagsara looked at him. The blue eyes of the King of Israel were the eyes of an enchanter. They ravished the soul. A strange maturity was perceptible beneath the youth of his features.

'Forgive my lateness,' he begged in a warm voice. 'Lack of courtesy is unacceptable in a King. I could explain to you that I had to confront a High Priest who opposes our marriage, but would I be convincing?'

'A great King does not depend on any of his subjects,' replied Nagsara, 'least of all a priest.'

She had intended to be acid, but her eyes betrayed her words. In reality, she found it difficult to remain indifferent to the fascination that took hold of her. Solomon was not a brutal beast, but a man endowed with extraordinary beauty.

'You're right,' recognised the monarch. 'This place is not worthy of your noble rank. But Jerusalem does not compare with Tanis or Thebes. I have the intention of turning my capital into a magnificent city. Would you grant me a little patience? Special apartments have been reserved for you, in order to avoid contact with the concubines.'

Nagsara would have liked to protest, to state forcefully that those arrangements were not satisfactory, that she was the trustee of a peace treaty, but the words did not breach the barrier of her lips.

'Take some rest, Nagsara, and prepare for the great banquet where we shall celebrate our union.'

Nathan, the tutor, had taught Solomon the secret of the ivory produced by the elephant, of the honey that the bee prepared, of the pearl that was manufactured by the oyster, of the viper's venom. He had taught him the meaning of the hawk's flight, the art of picking fruit, the name of the stars to which he blew kisses to thank them for shining. To the sun he offered holy oil and to the moon, perfume. He had thrown precious stones in the sea so that the brilliance of the waves should increasingly shine forth. Nathan had also showed Solomon how to drive away ghosts and demons by striking the skins of wild beasts with hazel sticks. From the master, the disciple had received the knowledge of the rooster announcing the birth of light, that of the swallow, messenger of the rains that bring life, the capacity of the owl for seeing in the dark, that of the passage of the crane pinpointing the seasons. Solomon had partaken of the mystery of the eagle capable of looking straight at the sun.

When these sciences had penetrated his spirit and been incorporated into the young man's blood, Nathan had conveyed to him the capacity of knowing the future. Astrology, the art of Kings, practised since time immemorial, was not the kind of sinister divination that was the sad prerogative of fallen angels.

Solomon drew a zodiac on the sand. Observing the nocturnal sky, he located the planets and inscribed their positions in the signs. Only the King had the right to know the future, not for himself, but for the benefit of the community of human beings under his protection. Solomon read the astrological theme of that day, on which the arrival of a Pharaoh's daughter in Jerusalem had occurred, thus initiating a new era that neither David nor his predecessors had imagined. Then he sought to see into the far distant future, asking the skies about the far distant morrows.

The answers were ambiguous. Never had they seemed so complicated, forming an inextricable network like the streets of Jerusalem. Did they bode well or did they announce misfortune? Did they foretell success or failure? If the zodiac and the planets refused to speak, was it not up to Solomon to take the initiative and not be afraid of facing any danger?

Effacing the drawing, the King of Israel had the feeling of depriving himself of a precious tool. Like the sailor who sails deep into a tempest, he could only rely on his intuition to avoid sandbanks.

Solomon had left the land of illusion. His marriage would disturb the soul of his country. By throwing the dice, he played the game of the Lord of the Clouds. But would a mere man, even though a King, know the laws that govern the universe.

14

'The Hebrews stink,' said the princess Nagsara to her hair-dresser. 'Burn some incense and myrrh. I demand that this miserable house be constantly perfumed.'

The female servants of the Pharaoh's daughter had been working without respite since the early hours of the morning to adorn their mistress, preparing her for the evening's banquet during which the State marriage would be celebrated. Using a gold comb, the hairdresser had arranged Nagsara's fine hair. She contemplated herself ceaselessly in a copper mirror with a perfectly polished surface.

Despite the subtle advice given by the master of the palace, Nagsara had refused to make the slightest concession to Jewish custom. She would dress as an Egyptian and would appear as a splendid Queen issued from the oldest and most respected of civilisations. Therefore, prior to leaving her apartments to go to the palace, Nagsara had her head coiffed with a cone of perfumed incense that would melt into her wig as the evening progressed. As a precaution, she placed in her sandal a tiny skin vaporiser. A slight pressure from the toe would liberate delicate scents. Nervous, the princess verified her hair once again and found it insufficiently curly. Her makeup no longer pleased her. Hairdresser and beautician went back to work, manipulating spatulas, combs and spoons. They refined the design of the lips, and underlined the line of her eyebrows with a blue-black paste. The eyelashes were tinted blue, the nails of hands and feet painted red.

Satisfied at last, Nagsara accepted the fine linen dress that had been offered by the women weavers from Tanis before she left Egypt. Because of the coolness of the evening, she threw a woollen stole on her shoulders.

Solomon had sent her soldiers from his personal guard commanded by Banaias, and a chariot in gilded wood with a comfortable seat, covered by a canopy. Inside the palace, the King had ordered two walls to be pulled down, creating a large space where some low tables had been installed.

The King welcomed each one of his guests, gave them the kiss of peace and washed their feet. They sat at the place indicated by the master of the palace, some with folded legs on cushions, others on wooden seats. In the middle of the room, the table of honour stood isolated and magnificent. Its gold decorations shimmered in the torches' light.

Cooks, cupbearers, bakers had worked with their best skill so that this banquet was evoked as the most sumptuous in the history of Israel. On coloured tablecloths were laid out silver cups and dishes, spoons made of ivory and wood. In the terracotta dishes were capers, mint, rosemary, garlic, onions, coriander and saffron. No one dared touch these starters, all eyes were fixed on the entrance of the reception room. Nagsara, daughter of the Pharaoh Siamun, made her entrance. The future Queen of Israel, in the magnificence of her linen dress and gold jewellery, made the dresses of the courtiers' wives look plain. It was the legendary beauty of Egypt that now penetrated Jerusalem, brutally reducing it to a small provincial town.

In this woman, who already provoked jealousy and envy, Solomon saw only a peace that would spare the lives of thousands. Nagsara perceived the coldness of the one who would be her spouse. The King of Israel looked at her in her red and blue dress, embroidered with gold thread, without tenderness. His thoughts sailed towards the alliance between two countries and did not dwell on the love of a young princess.

'Would the powerful King of Israel deign to hear my country's voice?' she asked sweetly. 'The chants and the dances will remind me of the land where I was born. They will dissipate my pain and make me forget that I have left my family for good and will disseminate joy in the hearts of those present.'

In came the harp, lute and tambourine players, followed by dancers dressed with a simple loincloth made of vegetal fibre that floated upwards with each movement they made. They danced following the mesmerising rhythm of the orchestra. The guests, dazzled by so much daring, stared at the small breasts and the agile legs. Their ears were seduced by a soft music, while Solomon, taking the hand of the princess in his, invited her to sit beside him.

'I will build you a lovely house in the enclosure of the temple,' he murmured.

'When will it be completed?'

Solomon did not reply, pretending to admire the dancers' movements. Nagsara, furious with herself, bit her lips. Her stupid question had importuned the man she now wanted to conquer. Her father, Siamun the Pharaoh, against whom she had felt such rebellion, had not reserved such a terrible fate for her. She might yet thank him for allowing her to become the wife of such a seductive monarch. Could it be love, this ecstasy that took hold of her and made her have eyes only for Solomon?

A fatted calf was served, as well as pigeons, partridges and quails roasted on a wood fire, and, the most exquisite delicacy, a lamb cooked in a vine stock fire. Even more delicate, grasshoppers boiled in water and salt. The cooks had removed the legs and the head after having dried them in the sun, others had been candied in honey. The cupbearers ceaselessly poured a vermilion-coloured wine.

At the end of the last wake, the master of the palace demanded silence. Solomon took Nagsara's right hand. The master of protocol proclaimed their marriage, sealing the peace and friendship treaty that united Egypt and Israel, sealing their allegiance against any aggressor. Acclamations greeted the event. Then the banquet feast started again, noisier and more unrestrained than before.

Solomon had taken his hand away. This surprised Nagsara.

'Are we not husband and wife, Sire?'

'The law of Kings so ordains. But how could I force you to love me?'

'Never has an Egyptian woman lived under restraint.'

Nagsara immediately regretted her bold words. She was behaving like a wild, indomitable being, whereas she wished to manifest her trust. What bad spirit forced her to betray herself in this way?

Solomon took his wife's hand in his once again. The sweet contact of his fingers made Nagsara quiver.

'You are now Queen of Israel, remember that the breath of our existence is but a cloud of smoke that disperses in the sky. When it disappears, our body is reduced to ashes, our spirit fades away like a breath of light air. Our lives will pass like the trail of a cloud, like the invisible trace of a shadow. Our thoughts will have been but sparkles flashing in tune with our heartbeat. Enjoy the moment and think of nothing else. What do poverty and old age matter? Here on earth they are but illusion. The vermilion wine that I am offering you is the messenger of the sun that matured it, let it glide down your veins, may it be the light enlightening your gestures.'

Nagsara accepted the cup that Solomon was offering her. After having drunk with delight, she presented it to him. When he took it to his lips, she felt their communion was complete. With a slight pressure of her foot, she liberated the perfume hidden in her sandal. It formed an invisible screen between the couple and their guests.

Nagsara was alone, cruelly disappointed. At the end of the banquet, her servants had accompanied her back to her rooms. Solomon had remained in the company of his guests. No doubt he had finished the night in bed with one of his numerous concubines. Their nascent love had been scorned. Not only would she stifle the feeling in her heart, but furthermore she would reject that monster with all her might if he tried to come near her.

When the hairdresser announced the King of Israel, Nagsara, refuting all protocol, refused to see him.

Solomon forced entrance into his wife's rooms.

Furious, she stood up to him.

'Leave my house immediately,' she ordered.

'It is also my house,' stated Solomon calmly, holding Nagsara by the wrists while she tried in vain to strike him.

'Please leave!'

'I accept, sweet wife, but not without you. I have so many marvels to show you. Our chariot is ready, I will drive it myself.'

'I want to stay here.'

Nagsara's hostility was abating. The contact with Solomon enchanted her. She could hardly resist the strange warmth that invaded her being.

'Leave me alone,' she begged.

'Why are you rejecting me?'

'Because I detest you!'

Nagsara wretched herself away from Solomon's grip.

'You have insulted and ridiculed me! You are treating me like one of those concubine bitches! Incarcerating me in this place and abandoning me.'

The King seemed surprised.

'I do not understand, Nagsara. What grievous fault have I committed?'

The princess turned away, sulking.

'Your absence . . . tonight.'

'Is that what this is about . . . Protocol . . . beautiful Nagsara . . . nothing but protocol. I did not have a choice. My thoughts were with you. How can you doubt that?'

Any final resistance from the Egyptian melted. She took Solomon's arm.

'But . . . I am hardly dressed. I . . .'

'The Queen of Israel is beautiful as she is. Let us not waste any more time.'

Nagsara entered the chariot beside her spouse. When he held her by the waist, she stiffened. His victory had been too easy. He manipulated her like one of those rag dolls that children love. Solomon did not force her, content to tie her in so that she did not fall.

The couple crossed short plains dotted with woods that dissimulated peaceful villages. Between the small valley covered with mulberry bushes and the hills with peach trees, there were numerous vines. Solomon stopped at the foot of the terraces that held the earth, preventing a landslide. He took Nagsara to a lake dominated by a wooded hill. On the bank, some fishermen were repairing their nets, handling the needle with dexterity. On the ground copper fish hooks were strewn. The casting net with ballast sinkers was large and the most adroit knew how to throw it with just one gesture from wide boats made to withstand the current. The men sang. They had had a good fishing trip and were sorting out the impure fish, those without fins or scales. Their boss offered the royal couple a pike that was grilling on the wood fire. Nagsara rejected this food that the King ate happily.

Then they left, crossing a scented scrubland with broom and acanthus. Some birds flew around the wild mustard branches, whose grain the cooks mashed to obtain mustard. Letting her hand hang loose on the chariot's side, Nagsara was prickled by a giant nettle. Solomon kissed the burn at length.

At the sight of the Sea of Galilee the young bride forgot her pain. It was only a small lake in the shape of a harp. A good swimmer would cross it in less than an hour, but its beauty was such that even the most indifferent eyes lit up at the sight. Those waters, of a sapphire blue, were furrowed with small fishing boats. The fishermen lived in the small white houses built among the jasmine and the pink oleander that ornamented the banks. The soft green hills protected them from the winds that, on that lovely day, made the flowers dance.

'Here,' revealed Solomon, 'nothing has changed since the beginning of the world. Only peace reigns. It is after seeing this tranquil sea with eternal colours that I desired that peace should always prevail between my people and yours.'

Nagsara stopped fighting with herself.

She was feeling emotions similar to those that had welled up in the gardens of Faiyum by the stretches of water where beautiful princes with perfect bodies swam.

She rested her head on Solomon's shoulder. Feeling her abandonment, he kept very still for a long time before taking her in his arms and offering her a first kiss.

Nagsara's gaze had changed. Her eyes cried and laughed simultaneously. The past died inside her, effaced by the breeze that wrinkled the River Jordan, towards which the King was leading her. He guided his spouse along a narrow path that rose over some marshes, before climbing between the basalt rocks and entering into a landscape made of steep banks and thick bushes.

Nagsara dared not question Solomon as to the finality of their escapade. She enjoyed being guided by the man who had mesmerised her.

Falling from a high cliff on a small island inhabited by ibis, a cascade filled the light air with its crystal chime. The world became a limpid dream, sweeter than honey. Pink oleanders blocked the way. Solomon pushed aside the branches to reveal a curious pond whose waters remained agitated. From a hillock, a seagull took flight. Nagsara stepped back when she trod on soft and humid earth whence grew papyri and rushes, but a warm liquid caressed her feet.

'Hot springs,' explained Solomon. 'The most secret in Israel. Come and bathe in them, they will take away your tiredness.'

The King took off the princess's dress before taking off his own clothes. Then, his lips joined with hers, he took her in his arms, and delved into the depths of the springs. Tinted with the gold of sunset, their bodies massaged by a delicious bubbling, the King and Queen loved each other enveloped by the delirium of their desire.

15

The dream endured. Nagsara did not leave Solomon's side. He had forgotten his concubines. The new Queen of Israel had conquered the court by her imposing presence and elegance, although the jealousy of the noble ladies towards a foreigner did not cease. The King, attentive to his young wife's impulses, had abandoned current affairs, leaving them to his secretary and the master of the palace.

There was no love lost between the two men. They set traps for each other, so much so that open conflict erupted, demanding Solomon's intervention.

When the latter sat on his throne, after a new amorous day spent at the hot springs, he refused to listen to the two dignitaries' recriminations. Something became clear to him: a great King might have been capable of a brilliant diplomatic coup, but he had forgotten his duties to busy himself with the games of love.

Solomon sent the master of the palace away, and kept his secretary by his side.

'Have you finished the inventory of the riches accumulated by my father, Elihap?'

'Yes, Sire.'

'Are they sufficient to finance the building of a great temple?'

'Certainly not.'

'Is there a Hebrew architect capable of drawing up new plans and of organising the work site?'

'You know very well, master, that there is no such person. We lack quality materials and cedarwood. Our carpenters and our masons are not numerous enough and lack the experience necessary. Renounce the idea of this temple. To fail in this enterprise would tarnish the glory that you enjoy thanks to your alliance with Egypt.'

Renounce . . . Solomon hated the word. By forgetting the temple, he would lose all dignity. Nagsara's lovely body, the pride of having married a Pharaoh's daughter, had made him neglect his duties. How had David's son been able to behave in such a despicable way?

The temple: that sacred building that would guarantee the union between Israel and God, the bond between the earth and the heavens. Only the temple would ensure the treaty with Egypt lasted. It would be the peaceful enclave that no barbarian would dare destroy. Solomon would not be content with human happiness.

To renounce . . . that would be to destroy himself, to accept a horrible death that would eat up his heart. But how could he carry out this project, if not by making Israel richer, by transforming a small country into a commercial power and finding elsewhere the necessary men and materials?

Solomon would accept that impossible challenge, even if he had less of a chance than David against Goliath.

'The precious materials that my father kept hidden, who did he buy them from?'

'From the King of Tyre,' answered Elihap.

'Prepare a ship for me. I am leaving for Tyre tomorrow.'

By going impetuously to that nautical city, the economic capital of ancient Phoenicia, situated west of Lake Merom and south of Byblos, Solomon did not respect the usual protocol that demanded that two Kings exchange letters and ambassadors before meeting.

A prudent and wily man, about sixty years old, the King of Tyre was known as an uncompromising negotiator. The prosperity of his city rested on commercial and skilful exploitation of the natural riches of the region it controlled.

Tyre was protected by a kind goddess, the heir of the smiling Egyptian Hathor, who watched over sailors and their ships. The captain who offered her a sacrifice before sailing was insured against the wrath of the sea and guaranteed to safely reach his port of destiny. Although his mother was from Israel, from the tribe of Nephtali, the King of Tyre had refused to convert to Yahweh's religion, judging it intolerant and belligerent. He had consented to sell some cedarwood to David, to build a temple. But that unrealistic project had quickly been abandoned. Solomon had been in no hurry to reactivate relations with Phoenicia. After his allegiance with Egypt, was he planning to invade a region that was so near Israel?

When the arrival of Solomon was announced, the King of Tyre found that Siamun's general, who had just left his palace, was right when he predicted a visit from the Hebrew monarch. Egypt had ensured the Phoenician's behaviour, by guaranteeing protection in exchange for absolute obedience. What was requested of the King of Tyre did not soil his honour. Therefore, he would conform to the instructions received, so as not to displease the Empire that stood on banks of the Nile.

Solomon presented himself alone, with no war vessel, no armed forces, without a retinue of servants. Shrewd move, thought the Phoenician. Thus, he put himself under the protection of his host who should, therefore, look after him as an honoured guest.

Would the Hebrew honour the flattering reputation that preceded him? Did the poet not say that he knew the language of the cedars and the hyssops, that of the birds in the heavens and of the animals in the fields, of the creatures that crawled on the ground and those who swam in the waters? Was this not exaggerating the wisdom of such a young monarch?

The palace of the King of Tyre was built with thick blocks of stone on a promontory that dominated the port where numerous trade ships were anchored. Large openings allowed the rays of the sun to enter and illumine rooms paved with coloured mosaics. The military presence in the palace was discreet. Tyre presented itself as a town open to all, with no partisan spirit, where every nation had the right to trade. Each was keen on preserving Tyre and its fleet, to let goods such as iron, silver, tin and lead circulate freely, allowing for fruitful transactions. The Phoenician port no doubt enriched Kings, even when they were enemies. The Phoenician sailors were exceptionally good and in demand from the most illustrious navies. But Solomon, with ambitions as vast as the ocean, had decided to change that situation to the benefit of his small country.

Solomon was accompanied only by his secretary, who stood behind him carrying a writing tablet and reed pen. The King of Tyre welcomed Solomon on the most pleasant terrace of his palace, lit by a soft winter sun. He offered the visitors palm wine and crystallised fruit.

Solomon's charm had an immediate effect on the monarch, though he was used to welcoming princes and Kings. To admirable features and a bearing of astonishing serenity were added a steady voice. It must be difficult to resist such an enchanter. All this made the Phoenician even more suspicious. With a sovereign of that calibre, would Israel not try and establish its supremacy over other States in the region?

'I am only the grandson of peasants,' declared Solomon. 'Israel is a country of rural folk who know nothing of the dangers of the sea. My subjects are poor, yours are rich. Is Tyre not at the height of its glory?'

The Phoenician listened to the compliments half-heartedly.

'After the apogee, is there not the decay? I had a good relationship with David, your father. After his victories over the Philistines and the Moabites, he treated me like an ally. Is that also your intention?'

'Does my coming not reveal that?'

'Your Empire has become larger since you ascended to the

throne of Israel. It extends from Jordan to the sea, and to the West it reaches the fringes of the Egyptian Delta. The peace and prosperity of Tyre will depend on your policy.'

The Phoenician was afraid that he had been too frontal. Would that defiance provoke an angry reaction?

Solomon smiled.

'Your words fill me with joy,' he said. 'Israel's happiness depends on yours. It is on a durable and stable peace that our friendship will be based.'

The King of Tyre hesitated.

'I would like to test your wisdom.'

'As you will.'

'There is a living being who cannot move,' indicated the Phoenician. 'When it dies, it can finally mutate. What do you think it is?'

Solomon thought about it and with a gesture that went unnoticed, he swivelled the gold ring he wore on his annular finger.

'The tree,' he answered, 'when living it cannot move, when it is chopped by the woodcutter it dies, but it becomes a ship that sails on water.'

The King of Tyre acknowledged his defeat.

'Thank you for your teaching,' said Solomon. 'By alluding to your maritime power, you have put your finger on Israel's weakness. That is why I need your help.'

While the secretary noted down the conversation between the two monarchs, the Phoenician accepted being won over by his peer. He trusted his desire for peace was genuine.

'Rumour has it that you intend to build a large temple in Jerusalem.'

'That is indeed my desire,' admitted Solomon. 'My father failed to do so, but I will succeed. I have the intention of buying a great quantity of material from you, especially metals, cedar and cypress wood.'

'What do you propose in exchange?'

'Cereals, wine, fruit, aromatic herbs and honey.'

'I would also need wheat and oil,' demanded the King of Tyre.

'I would add the agricultural production of twenty Galilean villages.'

The Phoenician was very pleased. The transaction was in his favour.

'Where shall I deliver all of this to you? You do not have a port. The roads are not easy to travel.'

'In a year from now, there will be a port,' stated Solomon. 'I will give you a share of the benefits it will bring, on condition . . .'

'What condition?'

'Send me teams of masons and carpenters. The best artisans of the Orient have worked in Tyre. The Hebrews do not know the secret techniques required to build the temple that I have in mind.'

'What advantages will that bring me?'

'Gold,' answered Solomon.

'Gold? That means that you will demand still more from me.'

'You will make me a partner in your maritime traffic. Thanks to my alliance with Tyre, I will guarantee its vessels complete safety. We will all benefit from this agreement. Phoenicia cannot live in isolation.'

The King of Tyre reflected, but only for a short time.

The latent menace contained in Solomon's speech was far from imaginary. The solution he proposed was as reasonable as it was inevitable.

'It's a deal, King of Israel. Your reputation is well deserved. But there is just one more thing . . . What Master Mason have you chosen to build your sanctuary?'

Solomon seemed embarrassed.

'I am looking for one,' he confessed, 'but no Hebrew seems qualified to fulfil such a demanding task.'

'Have you examined the walls of my palace? The work was not easy to carry out. I entrusted the task to a young architect who carried it out admirably. He will soon be leaving Tyre.'

'What is his name?'

'Master Hiram.'

'Please send him to me.'

'I will try . . .'

'Why such reticence?'

'Because Master Hiram is an independent spirit, with a rather difficult character, whose presence is sought in various capitals. He only directs large sites where his art can be expressed.'

Solomon was intrigued.

'Would Jerusalem be a large enough city for him to express his genius?'

'I don't know,' replied the King of Tyre.

'Please try to persuade him. I would like to meet the man.'

Once Solomon and his secretary had left, the King of Tyre had a tablet engraved addressed to Egypt's Pharaoh. He had kept his promise and was claiming his reward for having caught a fish named Solomon.

16

Nagsara was anointing her face with a refreshing cream made from privet leaves. She had painted her nails a gold colour and spent hours priming herself for a King she hardly saw any more. Solomon's passion had faded when he returned from Tyre. Nagsara had tried in vain to seduce him. Her spouse had, without informing her, left Jerusalem to go and live in a humble dwelling on the site of Ezion-Geber, at the extremity of the Elamitic Gulf, on the banks of the Red Sea.

'You wanted to see me, Majesty?' asked the master of the palace, worried.

'Where is my husband?'

'At Ezion-Geber.'

'For how long? His absence is becoming exasperating.'

'The King is building a port,' explained the master of the palace, fearing a new fit of rage. 'What would you like for supper?'

'I am not hungry!' shouted Nagsara.

The master of the Palace exited discreetly. The Queen fell on her bed sobbing.

In her distress, Nagsara swore to find the means of attracting Solomon's attention and to keep him by her side.

The gale that blew in from Africa buffeted the port of Ezion-Geber violently, preventing the large ships from entering port and forcing them to anchor further out. Solomon's fine hair flew about in the fierce gusts that whipped up the high waves.

The King of Israel was pleased with the ongoing work carried out by the teams of artisans placed under the direction of Jeroboam, who was happy to have the chance to again prove his competence. On approximately seven hundred hectares, a town had quickly been erected. Admittedly, the materials used had been of mediocre quality. The houses lacked charm and comfort, but the people of Israel had, at long last, an important port. Nevertheless, Solomon was under no illusion. The Hebrews were afraid of the sea. They loved to feel terra firma under their feet. Never would they rival Phoenician sailors. Never would they control Western or Eastern maritime routes. That was not the intended goal. Going through the fortified gates of Ezion-Geber, protected by eight-metre-high walls, the caravans started a series of round trips that would benefit Israel's economy. Soon, the materials bought from the King of Tyre would be unloaded. Ezion-Geber, a stop on the African, Arabian and Indian itineraries, would attract numerous ships that would pay mooring fees.

This measure would not suffice to finance the construction of the temple. Between his index and his thumb, Solomon caressed a gold nugget the size of an olive stone. There were plenty more, as large as a medlar pip or even as big as a big walnut in the land of Ofir, which the Egyptians named Punt and the Africans, Sheba (south-east Sudan). Their mountains were made of gold and the dust of silver. Their populace wore golden bracelets and necklaces of such purity that it was not necessary to refine it in a crucible. The Queen of Sheba, Balkis, was the richest woman in the world. She exploited mines of red gold, exempt from any traces of silver, as well as mines of beryls and emeralds.

The people of Sheba, renowned for their peaceful characters, also sold opium and spices. Their leader was usually a woman, the subject of a powerful God.

Solomon needed the gold from Sheba in order to pay the

King of Tyre and build the temple of Jerusalem. But this wondrous land could only be reached by sea. That was why the King of Israel had created a port, had ordered the building of trading vessels and obliged a corps of infantry soldiers to become sailors.

Solomon's fleet, carrying oil, wine and wheat, was ready to leave for Sheba. When it returned with the red gold, the young monarch would know that his great project could be carried out.

Elihap interrupted Solomon's meditation. The secretary, who disliked wind, was forced to raise his voice.

'Forgive me, Majesty . . . but the master of the palace requests your immediate return to Jerusalem.'

'What is happening?'

'A riot,' confessed the secretary, 'The people are rebelling.'

Jars of wine lay thrown on woven wool materials. The butchers raised their knives and lacerated the fabrics; pieces of meat lay on the floor, crushed by an unruly crowd of textile workers who rushed to Jerusalem's upper neighbourhood. Beggars took advantage of the confusion to pillage the stalls of the fishmongers and steal fruit in the market. The shoemakers threw shoes at the soldiers of the guard who, under the command of general Banaias, forbade access to the alley leading to the palace. Women and children had taken refuge inside their homes.

The furious crowds had screamed their way across the enclosed rose garden dating from the time of the prophets. The frightened asses cavorted around, spilling their burden. There wasn't an alley that had not been invaded by a wild crowd shouting insults about David and his lineage.

In the absence of the King, action failed Banaias.

Should he order the archers to fire and start a civil war? To see order thus shattered threw him into despair. No, he would not surrender the royal house to these villains. Better to die fighting.

Suddenly, the leaders looked back. An unexpected event had just happened and its impact disturbed the rioters' rank. From the low quarters of the town up to the vicinity of the palace the shouting ceased. Then, a heavy silence fell.

Solomon, alone and unaccompanied by a guard, had come through the large entrance gate and calmly made his way through the large crowd of the rebels. Many of the inhabitants of the capitals were seeing the King up close for the very first time. None of them dared touch him, afraid of being struck down. Solomon's face did not betray any fear. He seemed as serene as if he were taking a walk in the scrubland.

Solomon addressed one of the most excited agitators of the rebellion, a tanner with worn hands.

'What is the reason for this tumult?'

The tanner knelt.

'Sire . . . It is the Egyptian woman . . .'

'Why do you blame the Queen of Israel?'

'She is worshipping the serpent of evil, the one who banished us from paradise!'

'Who says so?'

'It is the truth, Sire! You who are our King do not tolerate such an offence to Yahweh!'

'Go back to work. I reign by God's will. It is from Him that I have obtained my power. Never will I betray Him.'

The tanner kissed the hem of the sovereign's robe. Getting up, he shouted with all his might: 'Hail Solomon!'

The acclamation was replaced by the crowd.

One hour later, the usual transactions were back in full swing in the marketplace.

Nagsara, made up in the inimitable art of Egyptian women, defied her spouse.

'Is Israel incapable of admitting other cults? Would Yahweh be so jealous and so stupid?'

'Do you not know that the serpent, to my people's eyes, is the symbol of evil?'

'Your people are ignorant. In Egypt, the cobra I worship[1] protects the harvests. By rendering homage to it, I am requesting prosperity for Israel.'

Solomon, indifferent to the seductive looks that the Pharaoh's daughter was giving him, remained severe.

'You are a cultured woman, Nagsara. You have certainly heard the tale of the serpent who abused Adam and Eve's trust. By offering a public sacrifice to your sacred cobra, you have endangered my throne.'

'Yes, I have provoked Jerusalem. It was the only way to make you return from that forsaken port on the Red Sea. Condemn me. Punish me. But at least look my way.'

Solomon took the Queen in his arms, making her lie down beside him on a bed of cushions.

'You are being unfair, Nagsara. The role of a King is demanding. God has entrusted the task of building Israel to me. Should it not be my first concern?'

'The young Egyptian put her head on Solomon's shoulder.

'I accept being placed second. But I want to be loved, Sire. The fire that you have lit in my veins can only be quenched by your presence. Thanks to you, my pain becomes joy. I love you, my master.'

Solomon, with a skilful hand, unfastened Nagsara's dress, letting it slide down. She closed her eyes, inebriated with rapture.

The swallows danced in the evening light. Their flight was so quick that Solomon's eyes could not follow.

The King of Israel remembered the legend according to which those birds were the immortal souls of Egypt's Pharaohs returning to the light from whence they had come.

He felt very distant from them in these moments of solitude.

---

[1] Serpent goddess Renenutet, sovereign of silence and guardian of prosperity. The word 'Eve' derived from an Egyptian term meaning 'sovereign' and was written graphically representing a serpent.

Solomon had put an end to the scandal provoked by Nagsara. The people continued to grant him their trust, despite the fact he allowed the Queen to continue practising her faith. From now on, she would celebrate her cult in a secluded place, situated high above the town, protected from the glances of curious onlookers. The fact that everyone knew about it did not matter. The important thing, from the point of view of the cast of priests, was that it was not done before the eyes of the populace.

Nagsara experienced perfect happiness. She had been listening to the more sensual concubines and offered herself to her spouse with complete surrender. But how could Solomon enjoy a body with abandon, even if perfectly beautiful, when his spirit was in the grip of unbearable worries?

Since David and Nathan had disappeared, Bathsheba lived as a silent recluse. Nagsara was imprisoned by her selfishness. Solomon found that he had no one to confide in any more at a time when he faced terrible failures, when the great project of his reign had been shattered against the wall of an implacable reality.

His ships had not reached Sheba. The Egyptian navy, considering that territory their private enclave, had peacefully but determinedly turned them back. How could Solomon protest, considering he had tried to trick the vigilance of the Pharaoh's fleet? A hasty, badly planned expedition . . . Solomon had overestimated his soldiers' capacity.

The gold from Sheba would not come. The King of Israel would lose face before the King of Tyre. The temple would never be built.

Solomon had lost his wager with God.

SECOND PART

You ordered that I build a temple on Your holy
    mountain,
An altar in the town where You Lord mounted your
    tent,
In the image of the sacred tent that You prepared from
    the beginning of time.
With You is the Wisdom that knows Your works.
And that was present when You created the world.

Book of Wisdom, 9,8–9

17

Coming from Tyre, Master Hiram followed the mountain ridge path. It was the end of the winter and he had taken care to schedule his departure for the end of the twenty-ninth day of February, when the crescent of the new moon had appeared in the sky. On the mountain top, lights shone warning all and sundry of the change of the month, facilitating the journey of a voyager.

The rain fell heavy and cold, as was usual for that time of the year. Most routes were deserted, having been transformed into muddy paths by violent showers. *Before the birth of spring*, according to a proverb, *the ox shivers at dawn but looks for the shade of the fig trees at noon*. The freshness of the night had forced Master Hiram to take a heavy woollen coat that he wrapped around himself to sleep under the stars. He had made it himself, by sewing two thick blankets and making a hole for the head. On the wide belt worn over his hips he had slipped some silver coins.

Beside him trotted a light grey donkey, a hardy beast that did not balk at any effort. On his back, two goatskins, one containing pure water and the other water mixed with vinegar, a pair of sandals, some clothes and a dry pumpkin that served as a goblet to draw water. Capable of walking more than forty kilometres per day, the quadruped had grown fond of his companion.

Hiram had crossed with some difficulty the snow mountains

of Mount Carmel, where the prophet Elias had taken refuge. Luckily, the donkey knew every inch of the terrain of the straight mountain neck linking North and South Palestine. This allowed the master to leave the land under Phoenician rule and enter the Kingdom of Israel.

The Master Mason had taken a tortuous trail above the fortress that guarded the place. Covering the donkey's hooves with rags, Hiram had not attracted the attention of the watchmen. Now, he had only to tread from crest to crest, going up and down all the time, over Thabor, Gelboe, Ebal and Garizim. It was true that the highest hill was not even twelve hundred metres high, but the route was tough on the legs.

Hiram admired the centenary oak trunks whose crests stood twenty metres from the ground and whose plantation was attributed to Abraham. Further on, he encountered a forest of terebinths with innumerable, interlocked branches. Soon they would exude powerful scents, purifying the throat and lungs.

So as to avoid any encounters, the Master Mason had chosen the time of year when the caravan drivers were gathered in camps under canvas until the snow had melted from the mountain tops. Hiram was wary of going into Samaria, where there were still bands of robbers. The most pious Hebrews considered the region a breeding ground for heretics. Far away, westwards, towards the Saron Plain, orchards preceded the dunes signalling the coast. The traveller thought with nostalgia of the Egyptian desert, where he had learned the secrets of his profession at the side of demanding teachers who took him from temple to temple, from one eternal abode to the next. But Hiram did not have the right or the leisure to dwell on his past. His mission was far more important than his person.

Harassed, he crossed the River Yabboq, a branch of the Jordan, and reached a rest house, a large building protected by an enclosure. Passing under a wood portico that was partially destroyed, he discovered a muddy courtyard full of beasts of burden. A wing was taken up with straw mattresses for passing guests.

The innkeeper greeted Hiram with suspicion.

'Where are you coming from, friend?'

'Never mind that. I would like something to eat.'

The Master Mason gave him a silver coin. The innkeeper put it inside his belt and nodded towards the guests' table.

Hiram dined in the company of two men who were as silent as he. They shared some cumin bread, fennel soup and drank some macerated rue tea, known for its digestive properties.

A dishevelled woman burst into the dark room, which was lit only by a smoky torch. She rushed at one of the lodgers, trying to pluck his eyes out. The victim screamed, his face full of blood. His companion came to his rescue, but the woman, bellowing insults, was out of control. She grabbed him by the testicles and pulled violently. The second boarder rolled on the ground. The man with the wounded face struck the woman with a blow on the back of her neck.

The scene had taken but a few seconds. Hiram tried in vain to get up. The knife that the innkeeper pointed at his throat stopped him from budging.

'It's a family business. Do not meddle with it, my friend, otherwise your trip will be over here and now.'

The woman was dragged outside by her two opponents.

'What is the meaning of such violence?'

'Those two nice young lads are her husband and her lover. The idiot has just realised that they got on like a house on fire and that they made fun of her behind her back. The whole of Samaria has known about it for a long time. She should have laughed it off. She will be harshly punished for her despicable misdeed. The law requires that my friends cut off her hand, for it has become impure. The spilling of blood must be avenged.'

Horrible screams were proof that the punishment had been carried out there and then.

'Why such violence?' repeated Hiram to himself.

*

The Master Mason had refused to spend the night in that inn, preferring to continue on his way towards Jerusalem. Putting his feet in the donkey's hoof tracks, Hiram descended a steep slope that led down to a fertile plateau from which one could make out the capital of Israel in the far distance, dominated by bare rock. A flock of sheep barred the Master Mason's way. The animals were numerous and undisciplined, excited by their first outing after wintering in the mountain sheepfolds. Some sheep had one leg tied to their tails, to stop them running away and getting lost. They rivalled each other in their bleating, making the donkey nervous.

For the second time in less than a day, the Master Mason felt a weapon at his throat. A long straight dagger whose blade pierced his flesh, drawing a drop of blood.

'I am also holding a iron-tipped bludgeon. If you try to defend yourself, I will be forced to kill you.'

Hiram took deep breaths to calm down, reducing his heartbeat, according to the practice taught by the medicine men in the Egyptian House of Life.

'Keep very still, my prince, that's fine, very well . . . You're certainly rich, whereas I am poor. Very poor. A simple shepherd who slaves away all year round. So, naturally, I am also a bandit! Surely, you will not hold that against me!'

The shepherd slipped his hand into Hiram's belt and removed the silver coins.

'Fantastic, my prince! A real fortune! When I saw you I had a good feeling. With this I will at last leave poverty behind. Because of the hyenas and the jackals, I lose a lot of sheep. My existence is hell. At night, the cold bites into my flesh. My colleagues pillage my belongings. What when the animals are sick! And the births! And the shearing!'

Hiram tried to make a gesture. The blade went slightly deeper.

'Quiet, my prince. I have wanted to cut up a rich person for a long time. I who am called Caleb, the dog! I have tried to attack some caravans on the road that goes from Jerusalem to

Jericho. But Solomon's police have become efficient. Even the traders who paid me to rob their competitors have forgotten me. The prey is becoming rarer these days. You are a gift from heaven.'

The donkey brayed very loudly, scaring the sheep. For a moment, Caleb was distracted. That slight error was enough for Hiram to throw himself backwards and thrust his elbow deep into his aggressor, thereby disarming him. The Master Mason was expecting the robber to put up more of a fight. But Caleb was but an old man, incapable of a struggle.

He crawled up to a small, stone wall, chucking a rock in the direction of Hiram, who avoided it easily.

'I am a poor man!' cried Caleb. 'Do not hurt me.'

Like a real believer he banged his chest and kept his eyes cast down.

'Israel is our God!' he exclaimed. 'God is the Eternal One! You will love Him with all your heart, with all your soul and with your whole spirit. Let God's commandment be engraved in you, especially the most important among them: Thou shalt not kill!'

'I will respect it,' stated Hiram. 'Every man worthy of that name is a sacred being.'

Caleb stood up and knelt before the Master Mason.

'Blessed be the womb that carried you,' he exulted, 'blessed the saints who nurtured you. May God's peace be with you. You are more glorious than the wind, more luminous than the sun!'

Hiram's face remained inscrutable. Caleb was almost certain that he had escaped death, but he still feared that his arm would be severed. The traveller did not seem inclined to be merciful.

The Master Mason removed from his wrist a bracelet ornamented with a fine gold strip on which his name was inscribed in Phoenician.

'Take this, Caleb, and take it to King Solomon. Tell him that I will wait for him three days and three nights at the bottom of the Ghor, near the well of the cobra. If he does not come, I will leave Israel forever.'

The shepherd kissed the feet of the one he had not succeeded in relieving of his money. He received the precious object.

'Keep the silver coins,' said the Master Mason. 'But do not even dream of stealing the small gold plaque and forgetting your mission, otherwise I will hunt you down wherever you flee and I will not spare you a second time.'

Caleb stopped his protestations of respect and stood up. As he was leaving, Hiram noticed that he limped. The sheep followed the shepherd, bleating and bumping into each other.

When the road was free, Hiram freed his donkey. The ass accepted a caress and took the road that he felt was best. Hiram set off in the direction of the Ghor, the most sinister of Israel's sites.

18

A horned viper slithered along a metre away from Hiram and slid under a bush. The Master Mason stood very still. For three nights and three days he was of an almost mineral immobility, indifferent to the lizards and serpents that visited the bottom of the Ghor, hostile to any human presence. A narrow and deep depression, the Ghor was an anguishing furrow in Israel's flesh, dug at the bottom of Mount Hermon up to Edom where the Bedouins, who were enemies of Israel and Egypt, loitered. In summer, the heat was unbearable, with the cold bitterly harsh during the winter. According to ancient texts, that was the place where the cities of Sodom and Gomorrah had been built, accursed by God. The prophets claimed that when the new deluge came, furious waters would engulf the Ghor basin to efface all of humanity's crimes.

Hiram sat beneath a date palm, his back on the rugged trunk in front of the cobra well, which had been dry a long time. The palms, towering about twenty metres above the ground, offered some shade when the sun became too hot. The Master Mason loved this violent and arid landscape where nothing interfered with meditation. The most venomous insects caused less devastation than men. Not to importune them was enough to protect oneself.

Hiram was used to periods of isolation. They were imposed on all Master Masons by the House of Life before they started to draw up the plan for a new building.

He needed to focus and find his centre by assembling the energies dispersed by daily life. In this way, he found the soul that primordial work was endowed with.

Those efforts were nothing compared to exile. Hiram had spent a few weeks in foreign countries. He had been to Syria, Tyre and Nubia, to finish work on certain sites and study temples. Never had he considered leaving Egypt for good. He had hoped to spend the rest of his career in Karnak, where the sanctuaries were always being embellished, forming a gigantic complex in perpetual growth.

Why had Siamun chosen him? Why had he sent him to this hostile land where his task was to simultaneously help a King and fight against him? Through the Pharaoh's person, destiny was subjecting him to merciless trials. Far from Egypt, Tanis and Karnak, separated from his loved ones, Hiram was condemned to succeed in secret. All he could hope for was that Solomon did not come to the meeting.

The third day was coming to an end. The fair ethereal light of a day that announced the coming spring started to dwindle. The King of Israel had not accepted the Master Mason's invitation. There could be no other explanation. The cripple was too afraid not to have delivered the message.

When Hiram stood up, having made up his mind to climb the steep slope, about one kilometre long, that would lead him outside the Ghor, a shadow fell beside his.

'Welcome to my country, Master Hiram,' said Solomon. 'This place is not the most auspicious for a meeting.'

'I love the silence.'

'This is where the magicians who know the plants that heal and those that kill come. Would you be one of them?'

'My kingdom is that of stone and wood,' answered Hiram. 'I know how to mix iron and copper ore, not poisons.'

The Master Mason turned around.

His surprise was such that he barely suppressed an exclamation.

For a moment, he thought that Solomon was the Pharaoh

Siamun's double. Dressed in a crimson robe, bare-headed, the King of Israel closely resembled the young Pharaoh who had been one of the most brilliant pupils of the House of Life. But the light was fading, Hiram had had an illusion. The Ghor induced mirages.

'Where did you come from, Master Hiram?'

'From Tyre. Its King informed me you were looking for an architect.'

Solomon was impressed by this man whose gaze was fiery, with a tall forehead and broad shoulders. His black hair and thick eyebrows and an aquiline nose gave the face a severe expression. Robust, sure of his power, Master Hiram did not belong to the race of slaves and servants. Whereas Solomon was seductive and charming, Hiram was distant, almost haughty. No one at Jerusalem's court had such a striking personality as this architect that came from Tyre.

Solomon felt admiration intermingled with fear, as if this man was announcing simultaneously his salvation and his perdition.

Hiram was intrigued by Solomon. The King of Israel had a Pharaoh's bearing. He did not resemble those tyrants and clan chieftains who used their power to satisfy their passions at the expense of their country and their people.

Solomon was not in the habit of answering the call of an inferior, even though he may be a famous architect. For two days he had asked for an enquiry to be conducted on Hiram's past. Elihap, his secretary, had told him that the Master Mason was the son of a widow of the Dan tribe and of a man from Tyre. He was known as a rather fierce and solitary being, indifferent to honours and praise, capable of solving great technical problems and of mastering the most rebellious materials. Hiram was not chosen. He made his own choice.

'What science do you practise, Master Hiram?'

'The Art of Planning.'

'What is its application?'

'Cutting, assembling and lifting stones, so as to put them

into place without alterations and in a way that makes the building last in time.'

The art of planning. Who had not heard of that mysterious science without which, throughout the centuries, no edifice could have been built? The Hebrew artisans did not know its secrets.

'Would you accept revealing that art to me?'

'No, Sire. Either you employ me giving me full powers on my work site or I leave.'

'That is not very diplomatic language, Master Hiram.'

'I am not a diplomat and have no intention of becoming one.'

'To make concessions, is that not the beginning of wisdom?'

'It is not how I see Wisdom, King of Israel. Is Wisdom not God's creation? It is eternal and existed well before the earth was created. Is it not the fountain of all human knowledge?'

A raucous growl interrupted the dialogue.

Crouching on a rock, ten metres above both men, a leopard was preparing to leap on the two, who were easy prey. High on his legs, weighing more than eighty-four kilos, the magnificent feline was a veritable acrobat that jumped from slope to slope with the agility of a wild goat. Reaching in a few seconds the speed of a furious wind, he would never return from hunting without a prey.

His black and yellow eyes contemplated his future victims.

'One of us will not survive,' declared Solomon, with a steady voice. 'Would you know how to defend the life of a King?'

'I will defend mine first,' answered Hiram. 'I am not your servant.'

'From this moment on, you are. I hire your services as Master Mason and entrust you with the construction of a large temple in Jerusalem. Your life for mine, such is now your duty if circumstances require it.'

Hiram placed himself slowly in front of Solomon. The leopard sat upright and growled once again, revealing his fangs.

The King of Israel turned the ring that Bathsheba had given him. Then passed his index finger on the letters composing the name of Yahweh.

Crazed, the leopard uttered a cry of pain. With his right front paw, he tried to push away an invisible adversary that was biting his flank. Irritated, he pounced on a pile of stones, lost his balance and disappeared into some prickly bushes.

'God is watching over us.'

'Your reputation is well deserved,' observed the architect.

'It is God who led you to the bottom of this abyss. It is He who requested that I choose you. You are no longer your own man, Master Hiram.'

19

Hiram entered the chariot that Solomon was driving, escorted by about ten men under general Banaias' command. He had begged Solomon in vain not to venture alone into the depths of the Ghor.

When he saw the King appear in the company of a foreigner, a profane thought came into his mind. Was Solomon perhaps an angel who was manipulating destiny? Had he brought back a demon with multiple powers from the depth of the cobra well, one that he would use to increase his powers?

Banaias felt a disquieting sensation upon seeing Hiram. The man that Solomon had gone to fetch in a region forbidden to believers was endowed with a dangerous power, analogous to that of a wild beast. The general was afraid. How could he admit that to the King? Banaias, a hero in Israel, capable of killing a lion with his bare hands, did not have the right to succumb to fear. Deeply troubled, he promised himself to watch the actions of that disturbing character who had obtained the King's favour much too rapidly.

In the distance Jerusalem was discernible, blue and grey, under a menacing sky.

'That is my capital,' announced Solomon to Hiram. 'Contemplate it, Master Mason. It will be the site of your glory or of your misfortune. I will not accept failure.'

'You hired me by shrewd means,' estimated Hiram, 'but you will not compel me to labour.'

'I have no such intention. Look at that city . . . It is a diamond born of the highlands of Judea, the sacred land where nomadic and sedentary people come together, the privileged place where the routes that go from the Mediterranean Sea to the provinces of the East, to Phoenicia and Egypt cross. Jerusalem is the heart of a star whose branches irrigate the Holy Land. It still looks like a fortress. Tomorrow, thanks to you, it will be the jewel casket of the temple of temples.'

Hiram thought of Karnak where he had known the joy of learning and the happiness of creating. If he started to build the sanctuary of the King of Israel, how many years would he have to stay away from Egypt? Would he live long enough to see it again? Already exile weighed too heavily on him, despite his having left his homeland only a short while ago.

Black clouds were gathering above the capital. A glacial shower fell on the royal cortege. Hiram's face was hit by the hailstones. He remained as undisturbed as Solomon.

After having entered the enclosure, the chariot stopped in a small square.

'I shall leave you here, Master Hiram. General Banaias will take you to your house. Have a rest. Soon, we will meet again.'

The architect did not bow. Banaias was shocked by this defiance to the King of Israel's authority. Why did Solomon accept it?

The general guided Hiram without saying a word up to a house made of bricks situated in an alley leading to the upper part of the city.

A short inspection told the Master Mason much. Too much hay in the bricks and these had not been well baked. And yet the construction was remarkable compared to the miserable shelters made of cobs in the lower part of town and the interior was quite pleasant: a central court lit by apertures on the ceiling and around it several small rooms. A living room, an office, two bedrooms, a kitchen, a water room and latrines. The structure, which was too light, would not withstand the test of time. The walls were covered by a mere coat of plaster.

But the disposition derived from Egyptian architecture preserved a cool temperature in summer and retained heat in winter.

The stormy sky made the inside of the house quite dark. Hiram could smell the characteristic odour of olive oil that the terracotta lamp exuded. It was placed in a niche on the wall, with a linen wick that burned day and night. He verified that the reservoir was full and, holding the lamp by its handle, he explored his domain, as Banaias stood at the threshold. In the living room, a chest that was divided into two compartments, one for fabrics and clothes and the other for provisions. That sole piece of furniture, pushed to the centre of the room, would serve as a table on special occasions. Most of the time, it was the custom to eat on the floor. In one of the rooms there was a bed resting on feet; in the other about a dozen cushions, a pile of blankets and a wooden headrest where the sleeper, as was the custom in Egypt, rested the back of his neck. As for the mats, they would be useful to sleep on the terrace in the summer. The kitchen was equipped with a charcoal brazier, an undeniable sign of wealth. There were several stoves. Clean and tidy, they were fed with stubble. Outside, near the staircase that led to the roof, there was an oven heated with peat for roasting meat.

Solomon proved thus his esteem for the Master Mason. No doubt he had dislodged a notable to house Hiram in such a comfortable way. But an essential detail bothered the architect. He examined the entrance door carefully, making it swivel on its hinges, and manoeuvred the lock.

'I need a key,' he said to Banaias.

'A key? But why . . .?'

'This house will be my workshop. It will contain my plans and my drawings. It must be hermetically closed and watched day and night.'

'These demands . . .'

'These demands must be met without delay, otherwise I shall leave Jerusalem.'

Banaias took his sword out of its sheath. Hiram's cool look made his blood run cold. There was magical power in the eyes of this foreigner. A sorcery that did not need a weapon to kill.

The general put away his weapon and took from his belt a heavy key that he handed to the architect.

'The law demands that I be its sole guardian.'

'Your general law is not mine.'

Banaias blushed with anger.

'Beware, foreigner, Israel does not like arrogant folk.'

'As for me, I detest nosy people and liars. No one, not even you, may enter this house.'

Hiram banged the door and locked it with the key from the inside. That that roughneck, narrow-minded soldier should become an enemy was a matter of indifference to him. By his behaviour, the Master Mason would force Solomon to trust him completely or send him away.

The Master Mason settled in the office. He found it pleasant. It reminded him of the monks' cells that gave on to the sacred lake of Karnak. The papyri that lay there did not have the beautiful golden hue of the ones made in Egypt, but their texture seemed correct. The pens made of reeds had to be sharpened to draw perfect lines.

A noise coming from the kitchen caught Hiram's attention.

There he found a young woman, about fifteen years old, frightened like a young deer from Samaria.

'How did you get in?'

She crouched and showed a tiny low door that would let a thin person through. Hiram understood why Banaias had not hesitated too long in handing him a key that would prove useless. The first task the Master Mason would carry out would be to close every access except that leading on to the street.

'What are you doing here?'

'I am your servant, master, and your neighbour. I am the one who will provide the oil and watch the lamp's flame. They told me that if I let it go out, I shall die in childbirth. I will

119

make your bread, knead the dough and cook food in the oven, I . . . '

Someone was banging at the door with double knocks.

Hiram opened.

In came Caleb the cripple, brandishing his iron-tipped bludgeon.

'I thought so, I knew it!' he cried. 'That she-devil must leave immediately!'

Swiftly and violently, Caleb grabbed the young girl's arm and threw her out.

'Do not interfere, my prince! I am here to help you. Jerusalem is a city full of dangers. The first among them are the women! Their meanness is worse than combat wounds. There are no snakes whose venom is more venomous. I would rather live with a dragon or a lion than with a woman, hold a scorpion in my hand rather than hold that malefic body. That girl would have been your perdition. You saved my life, now I come to your rescue!'

'Thank you, Caleb, but who will be my servant?'

'Me, my prince! No one holds a broom better. No one bakes bread as tasty as mine. The dough I knead on the bread table and cook on the fire, I make it round, a circle that has to be broken and not cut. A woman would not have taught you that. Would she have told you that raw meat has to be placed on a piece of bread and never on a hot stone? Would she have indicated to you that one does not pick up crumbs whose size is smaller than an olive? Women mislead. I am an honest man. I will guide you in the streets of Jerusalem. I have many friends here.'

'I would like to shave and to have a wash.'

Caleb smiled broadly.

'Without me, that's impossible! Despite Solomon's water pipes, water is still rare. Only the King and the rich have water at home. I will go and get it for you from the fountain, in large jars as often as you wish. The rest, I will take care of as well.'

*

Caleb fetched a tub that he filled with warm water, a pumice stone, some natron and a soap made from a soda base. He also brought him a sponge, a brush, rosemary to perfume the bath and aniseed to clean his teeth. That was indeed a luxurious treatment. The devoted servant shaved Hiram carefully. His blade did not scratch the skin at all. It glided delicately on a throat that it would gladly have cut a few hours before.

The dinner was excellent. Caleb had prepared a dish of lentils with onions, aubergines and green peppers. Starving, the crippled devoured a watercress salad afterwards.

'I have the best suppliers,' he explained. 'They cultivate small gardens in the lower part of town, sheltered from the winds.'

Caleb cried out in pain and put his hand on his cheek.

'This wretched tooth again . . . It's making my head throb. This can't go on. It must be pulled out, but the blacksmith is expensive. If you had a silver coin . . .'

'Aren't there any doctors?' asked Hiram, astonished.

'Plucking teeth out is the blacksmith's work.'

The dentists of the Saïs in Lower Egypt would not have appreciated this custom, for they extracted teeth without making the patient suffer and covered the wound with a vegetable substance to avoid infection.

'I will go with you,' said Hiram.

'Me? Don't bother, my master. The silver coin will suffice.'

The Master Mason was already opening the door. The cripple understood that once his master had made up his mind, no one could dissuade him.

20

Sitting near the anvil, the blacksmith with his skin reddened by the flames of the hearth was just about to finish beating the blade of a plough. Coming close, Caleb the cripple tried to speak to him in a low voice. But Hiram cut in first.

'My servant is in pain due to a bad tooth. It needs to be plucked.'

Caleb stepped back. The blacksmith abandoned his work and fetched a pair of tongs that he reddened on the fire.

'I am no longer in pain,' declared Caleb.

'Pay the practitioner,' ordered Hiram.

'My prince, he does not deserve that much . . .'

The blacksmith grabbed the cripple by the back of his neck, as if he was catching a cat. He laid him down on the floor of beaten earth and opened his mouth.

'It's no good,' he estimated. 'These teeth are rotten. They will fall out of their own accord.'

Caleb rolled over, happy to escape his torturer.

'How many blacksmiths are there in Jerusalem?' asked Hiram.

'About ten.'

'What task do they carry out?'

'They manufacture tools for the peasants.'

'Is there no State forge?'

'None.'

Duly informed and rather astonished, Hiram took an alley

that went up to the palace. He walked quickly, Caleb had trouble keeping up. The Master Mason stopped before a half-naked one-legged man, slumped against the wall of a decrepit house.

'Some bread, Sire . . . I have not eaten for three days . . .'

Caleb kicked the wretch in the ribs.

'Let us go further, my prince,' he said to Hiram. 'Do not let these beggars bother you. There are hundreds of them, flea-ridden, lame creatures, who soil our beautiful city.'

Hiram gave a bronze coin to the one-legged man. The latter grabbed it from him, scratching his hand in doing so. Out of dark corners there immediately emerged dozens of dirty and smelly creatures who rushed towards the wealthy foreigner, trying to steal his money. A furious battle took place. Caleb forced Hiram to distance himself.

'Do not stay here, come along, my prince, you might be hurt.'

Troubled, Hiram ignored other beggars, other extended hands, other grim looks. He walked straight to the royal palace and encountered Solomon's guard.

Presenting himself as the architect employed by the monarch, he asked for an audience.

Caleb had vanished. The sight of the uniforms, of the lances and of the swords frightened him out of his wits. Some of the soldiers might have recognised him as a caravan looter whose head had been claimed by numerous merchants.

Hiram did not have to wait long. The master of the palace came for him and introduced him into a room heated by two braziers where Solomon was reading, sitting on a wood chair in a seat made of a brown fabric. The King of Israel was studying some proverbs that he intended to assemble in a book.

'Your rest must have been short, Master Hiram. Take a stool.'

'I prefer to stand, Majesty. What I have seen in the streets of Jerusalem does not encourage me to remain here any longer.'

Solomon rolled the papyrus.

'Those unfortunates who suffer hunger and thirst . . . Do you think that that spectacle gladdens my heart? Do you think I could be indifferent to that misery?'

In Egypt, thought Hiram, no feast was celebrated if there remained one poor person in a village. The families helped each other out. And everyone could address the Pharaoh, trustee of his people's happiness. The ideal proclaimed by the nobility was to nourish the hungry, quench the thirsty and dress the naked.

Solomon stood up.

'Let me govern my people and busy yourself with your new tasks, on condition that you are truly worthy of these, Master Hiram. Look at this ivory rod, stuck between two stones. The palace of David was built around it, upon the instructions of a prophet. The one who knows how to seize it will be the next Master Mason. His hand will remain intact, if not it will burn. Do you accept this trial?'

Hiram approached the rod. Was it his desire to fail? Was he not ready to offer a part of his body to return to Egypt without delay? If he was deemed unworthy by Solomon, he would have no choice but to go back to his country.

Hiram gripped the ivory rod.

He immediately felt a deep sensation of heat, almost unbearable. An immense hope filled his heart. The suffering seemed negligible. Even if his skin should remain glued to this emblem of the Hebrews' power, even if he should lose the use of his hand, he needed to withstand it. His failure would announce his imminent happiness.

Solomon saw a wave of pain cross the architect's eyes. A smell of burning flesh invaded the nostrils, but the Master Mason did not let go.

Suddenly, an intense cold followed the burn. Hiram moved away from the stick, looking at the palm of his hand in astonishment.

'It is God's prerogative to hide things,' said Solomon. 'It is that of Kings to reveal them. This trial reveals you to yourself, Master Hiram. How can you still doubt your destiny?'

The monarch lit a bronze lamp with seven holes. Its handle, finely chiselled, represented a Judean leopard. The perfume of olive oil pervaded the room. The magnificent object, one of the few beautiful items in the palace, had belonged to Nathan.

Solomon thus rendered homage to the tutor who had enlightened him. The King took Hiram by his shoulders, embraced him, kissing him on both cheeks as if he were his equal. The Master Mason ought to have knelt and kissed the hands and the feet of the monarch. He was content to accept the demonstration of his esteem.

'You are the one I have been waiting for since the first day of my reign,' confided Solomon. 'You are the one who will build the temple of peace. May each instant of your life be henceforth oriented towards this sole aim.'

'You are stealing that very life from me, Sire.'

Hiram did not believe in Solomon's sincerity. His demonstration of affection was just meant to mollify a difficult character. The only glory that the architect would serve was that of the most ambitious of Kings.

'The celestial signs have appointed you, Master Hiram. You are predestined. It is not chance that guided your footsteps to Jerusalem. Your task is supernatural. Never forget that.'

Solomon opened a chest made of acacia wood. He took from it a long crimson coat and put it on the architect's shoulders.

'Here is the habit of your function, Master Hiram. You will wear it on the day that your task is completed.'

'I prefer the leather loincloth. If I sold this coat, how many poor would I be able to feed?'

The insult was like a whipping. Solomon remained calm.

'If the temple is not built, poverty will increase. Men are not only nourished by the material world. To a people, one must offer a spiritual centre. It will be the only sacred place where the Divine is ever-present. Only God can guide a country towards a joy beyond time, a joy that is the key to every man's happiness. To sell the habit symbolising your function would be to sin against the spirit. I would rather you find the means of obtaining the gold that I lack to finance the works.'

'Are you not rich, Majesty?'

Solomon looked at his Master Mason, regal in his crimson robe.

'Not sufficiently wealthy, Master Hiram. I can start the work but I do not have the means to conclude it. A more cautious King would show more patience. But I feel that the time is ripe, that the whole of Israel must unite to seek its grandeur.'

Solomon was neither exalted nor utopian in his purposes. The passion for creation enlightened his voice. Indeed, his God was not Hiram's, but this venture was beginning to seduce the Master Mason.

'Why not ask the Queen of Sheba for gold,' he suggested. 'Her country runs with it, but she does not have wheat.'

Solomon sat down, engrossed in his thoughts.

'It's useless. That kingdom is inaccessible to Israel.'

'Not to me, Majesty.'

Solomon looked at Hiram, staggered.

'What do you mean?'

'I spent some time in that country and I have worked there. One of the Queen's architects is a friend of mine. Our corporation does not have many members. Deep bonds unite us. We have sworn to help each other in difficult situations. If I ask him to intervene with the Queen to set up a bond of trade, he will do so.'

'What about the Queen?'

'I cannot promise anything.'

Solomon was incredulous.

'Tell me about Sheba.'

'It is the island where the sun is born, the primordial hillock on which the Phoenix landed, a burning pyre of incense, myrrh and olibanum. In its forests there are cheetahs, the rhinoceros, panthers and giraffes. The inhabitants tame baboons. The mountains are sculpted with deep galleries where gold and silver abound. Flocks graze on their slopes. There are no poor. Everyone owns gold plates. The feet of chairs are made of silver. The Queen is not avaricious. She pays generously for the food her people need. But she chooses the countries that supply these goods carefully. It is said that her beauty is legendary, worthy of a goddess.'

'Have you ever met her?'

'No. When I was staying in Sheba, I was but a young architect, undeserving of being received by the Queen. I saw her pass in her litter covered in red gold, but I could only make out her tiara.'

Solomon hesitated in becoming indebted to Hiram. To ask for his help meant forgetting his royal station and admitting that the architect mastered a universe that the King of Israel had no power over. But the temple of God was certainly more important than a monarch's pride.

'I do not like people who boast, Master Hiram. If you are capable of so doing, have the gold of Sheba sent to us.'

21

For more than two weeks, Hiram improved the house that Solomon had assigned to him. He consolidated the walls, obliterated the small door that gave access to the kitchen from outside and reinforced the lock. He worked slowly, as if time was irrelevant.

After his encounter with Solomon, the Master Mason had been received by the King's secretary. Together, they had composed a letter addressed to the architect who lived in Sheba. Elihap had taken care of the formal protocol letter and Hiram wrote a coded message with signs that were undecipherable to profane eyes. Solomon's work sites depended on the result of this initiative.

Caleb took care of his bad teeth that often forced him to rest. Nevertheless, he prepared the meals, keeping up a good appetite despite his dental condition. The cripple slept in the house, crouching in front of Hiram's bedroom. Never had he enjoyed such a pleasant roof over his head, sheltered from the wind and rain. Caleb wished wholeheartedly that Hiram should remain as long as possible in Jerusalem. Every day, he thanked Yahweh to have allowed him to find a generous master who was not very demanding.

One tempestuous night, when the pelting rain filled the wadi that created ravines in the mountains, Hiram heard a strange noise. Caleb, as usual, was sleeping soundly. The Master Mason left his office where he was drawing some geometric grids[1] and walked to the door. The soldier employed by Banaias to stand guard had had to leave his post and shelter under a nearby porch.

Someone was trying to break into Master Hiram's house.

Hiram opened the door suddenly.

Before him was a wet, famished dog, a cross between a wolf and a jackal. His brown eyes implored without shyness or subservience.

'Come,' said Master Hiram.

The erring dog put his front paws on the threshold and sniffed the air of the house. Judging it to his taste, he looked sideways at the Master Mason and prudently made his way into the inner courtyard.

When he uttered yaps of contentment and licked Hiram's hand, Caleb woke up. He was furious at the sight of the animal.

'Chase him away, my prince! It is one of those monsters that devour garbage!'

Hiram prevented Caleb from hitting the animal.

'He is staying with us,' he decided. 'His name will be Anup.'

Anup, the diminutive of Anubis, the jackal of the desert that lurked in the dark night to purify the earth of the remains of the dead. Anubis, who mummified the deceased, transforming corpses into resurrected bodies. Was it not the spirit of Anubis that came to Hiram in the guise of a dog, offering him the presence of Egypt and reminding him that, at the end of his earthly path, the beautiful routes to the beyond would commence?

Nagsara left her apartments unaccompanied, taking with her a box filled with glowing coals and a cup full of fresh incense. She took an old sentry path whose stones, covered with moss, would soon be loosened by weeds. The slightest slip would

---

[1] A type of plan used by Egyptian geometers. The working drawings are like grids where the proportions are inscribed.

condemn the imprudent walker to fall down a very steep slope and break their neck. The moon, piercing the clouds, lit the path taken by the Queen of Israel.

Nagsara was not afraid and her foot was steady. She took the path leading to the summit of a rocky peak facing the one where Solomon had decided to build the temple. It was the end of the night and Jerusalem was plunged in darkness. In Tanis, the Egyptian capital where the princess had lived, lamps remained lit on the roof of the sanctuaries where the astrologers worked.

This torpor suited the Queen's intentions. With each moon quarter, she celebrated a ritual cult to Hathor, far from the heinous glances of the priests who had sworn her ruin. Nagsara knew she was loved by the majority of the people, proud of their King's magnificent marriage, and hated by the ecclesiastic class. The latter could not accept that Solomon's wife had kept her faith in foreign deities whose existence was denied by Yahweh.

Nagsara was indifferent to that opinion. Her heart suffered due to Solomon's indifference. Time did not attenuate the violent feeling that she bore this King whose mere presence mesmerised her. Solomon did not love her. He had enjoyed her as he would a concubine. If he still showed her some respect, it was because of her diplomatic role. The passionate, abandoned woman, he no longer saw. His spirit was taken by this accursed temple, that building still engulfed in the void.

The Egyptian reached the narrow platform. In the centre was a roughly hewn altar. The wind blew fiercely. But at the heart of the cold, the first scents of spring filled the air.

Nagsara took her coat off. Underneath she wore the traditional habit of the priestesses of the goddess Hathor, a white tunic with straps, leaving the breasts uncovered. It fitted most becomingly the slender body of the young woman who opened the box. The incandescent coals gave out a street light that only the sky and the goddess's eyes would see. On the modest brazier, the Queen spread some grains of incense. The perfumes dispersed too quickly in the nocturnal air, but they reminded Nagsara of the sacred feasts in Tanis, during which the Pharaoh ascended towards the hidden God, Amun, the subtle essence of all things.

The moon shone with unusual splendour, proving the presence of the mistress of the sky in the centre of her court of stars.

'Please listen to my plea, Hathor,' begged Nagsara. 'May your magic take hold of Solomon's soul. Let his eyes contemplate me and hold him to me. Please heed the supplications of your faithful servant. May your light pierce the darkness, and give me back my love of life! May Solomon become my docile slave, let his thoughts belong to me!'

The blood of the dawn spread to the East. For Nagsara, there was hope once again.

The ears of barley ripened. In the middle of March, the rains were just a disagreeable memory. The fields whitened. The gladioli unfolded their red robes on the hills, rivalling in splendour the thousands of red anemones that ornamented the fields. Winter was ending, giving way to the dozens of species of narcissus, hyacinths and tulips. In the forest, Hiram had walked on carpets of crocuses of such bright yellow that they seemed made of sunshine. The time for peasant songs was back. It was the season of the cooing of the turtledoves, of the first fruit from the fig trees, of flowering vines among which the foxes hunted.

Once the rainy season had ended, the Master Mason took daily walks in the countryside; he observed the trees attentively, the tall juniper trees, the pistachio trees, the stocky almond trees, the holm oaks, the sycamores with tasty berries, the pomegranate trees whose fruit symbolise the multiplicity of divine riches and the unending gifts of love. He stopped before the olive trees with silvery leaves, carefully tended by the landowners. Those trees yielded the precious oil used for the preparation of dishes, for medicines and toiletry products.

It burned in the lamps and was made sacred by priests. But it was their wood that interested the architect, a robust material that would supply him with trunks measuring ten metres in height, five hundred years old. The tree evoked a peaceful joy that made it ideal for sculpting statues whose beauty might equal Egyptian works of art. Hiram marked with chalk the olive trees he had chosen. The second indigenous tree that he selected was the massive cypress, whose fibres would make fine-quality floors.

'Why do you work so relentlessly,' complained Caleb, 'if you don't even know for sure if the working site will be opened? The temple is a mirage, a mad King's dream. These walks are exhausting. Don't you like our beautiful house in Jerusalem?'

Hiram did not reply and continued to choose his tree trunks. Anup never left his master. The dog leapt at his side, preventing the cripple from coming too near his owner. It mistrusted Caleb, who did not dare hit him, fearing to displease the Master Mason.

At last, the morning that Caleb had awaited with such expectation finally arrived.

When Hiram crossed the threshold to go for another of his walks, he collided with a flow of men and women advancing on Jerusalem. It was composed of Hebrews coming from the provinces, but also of Babylonian merchants and Asian traders. Rich and poor mingled in a similar exaltation.

'What is happening?'

'It is Easter. The whole of Israel is celebrating. The faithful will eat and drink to the glory of God. We are all believers today.'

The crowd going up to the palace was so dense that Hiram desisted, for he would not be able to reach the town's lower quarters. Many of them shouted 'Pesah! Pesah!', evoking the miracle of the crossing that marked the exodus of the Hebrews from Egypt. Do they realise, thought Hiram, that they are pronouncing an Egyptian word, and that they are unknowingly rendering homage to a land they detest?

Labourers and bakers walked together, the former present-ing the first ears of wheat, the latter the unleavened bread. Butchers were guiding hundreds of sheep that would be sacrificed and feed thousands of guests who participated in the vast Easter banquet where, for a few hours, the wealthy and the beggars would sit side by side.

Passing before the Master Mason's house, a priest splashed its door with the blood of the beast he had just slaughtered. The hot and sticky liquid hit Hiram's face and chest.

The architect went inside and washed. Caleb had disap-peared. The cripple did not want to miss the handing-out of wine, bread, and meat. There was only the dog left, who hated the crowd as much as his master. The latter was working on the plan that had begun to take shape. He was inspired by the outline of the ancient design of the temple of Edfu in Upper Egypt, created by Imhotep and stored in the archives of the House of Life.

Knocking and shrieking at the door interrupted Hiram's reflection. As soon as he opened it, Caleb, with an armful of victuals, dashed into the house.

'You must participate in the Easter celebrations! I've brought you some lamb roasted in bay leaves and basil, unleavened bread dipped in a pepper sauce and some Samarian wine . . . very good wine, some . . .'

The cripple collapsed, blind drunk.

Hiram left him to recover.

The alleys were now empty. He went out with the dog, walking among the fallen bodies. The feast had taken its toll with many who would only regain consciousness after several hours of comatose sleep.

Anup barked, warning his master of an imminent danger.

About a hundred metres away, Banaias appeared at the head of a troop of soldiers. The general's crude features had a self-satisfied look that did not bode well.

Hiram stood still. The dog pressed against his leg. The

sword by his side, Banaias addressed the foreigner with his raucous voice.

'King Solomon demands that you come before him, immediately, Master Hiram.'

22

Solomon received Hiram in the audience room where he welcomed foreign dignitaries. Sitting on his throne, the monarch had a severe, almost hostile, look on his face.

The architect, without showing any sign of submission, stood at a good distance.

'Who are you in reality?'

'An artisan who became an expert at his profession.'

'How can I possibly believe you after what has just happened? How could a simple artisan succeed in making the Queen of Sheba write me a letter announcing the remittance of a shipment of red gold?'

'This is what comes of having friends, Majesty. Our brotherhood is more powerful than you can imagine. The Queen of Sheba wants a splendid palace and a perfectly formed temple. Therefore, she covers her Master Mason with honours, and he is like a brother to me. My friend, who is also the Queen's Prime Minister, has heeded my request and interceded on my behalf with the Queen.'

Hiram's explanations were convincing, although they were stated with an irony that wounded Solomon. Israeli diplomacy had been unable to bend the Queen of Sheba. The maritime expedition organised by the King had ended in pitiful failure. And lo and behold, now this foreigner who had just arrived in Jerusalem gave the whole country a lesson in efficiency.

'I must be grateful to you, Master Hiram. Do you wish to hold a key post as head of my diplomacy?'

'A Master Mason does not leave his brotherhood, Majesty.'

Solomon stood up and came face to face with Hiram. He stopped a metre from him, looking him in the eye.

'Not even to become King?'

Hiram held the King's gaze.

'Not even to become King.'

'What do you desire, Master Hiram?'

'To start work. Tomorrow, I will depart for the port of Ezion-Geber.'

'To what end?'

'To organise the work site according to my plan. Didn't our agreement foresee that?'

'Go, Master Hiram, and take action.'

Once the architect had left, Solomon reread the letter from the richest woman in the world. She would send no less than twenty-three tons of gold to Phoenician sailors who would escort the shipment to Israel. With an acute sense of international relations, the Queen of Sheba had avoided requisitioning the Egyptian fleet.

Thinking about it, this collusion with the Phoenicians proved the intervention of the King of Tyre. Hiram had boasted. It had not been him and his colleagues that had changed the Queen's mind, but the wily monarch of the merchant town. To make Solomon wealthy would allow him to pocket a good part of that gold in exchange for construction materials for the temple. Apart from that, was the King of Israel not bound to use Phoenician ships to deliver wheat to Sheba?

A crafty negotiator, avid for material goods, the King of Tyre thought he had had the better of Solomon. A pretentious Master Mason who ascribed to himself powers he did not have. Neither realised Solomon's real motives. They did not understand that the construction of the temple would change the course of time and the people's mentality.

*

Hiram stayed at Ezion-Geber for several months. Caleb, the cripple, had remained behind to look after the house, where he spent most of his time sleeping. The architect had taken his dog and his plans. Before developing them, he needed some copper, which would be used for the manufacture of tools, such as chisels for the stonecutters.

Five hundred hectares of available land gave the Master Mason an unexpected field to carry out trial runs. With Solomon's agreement, he requisitioned several hundred infantrymen who could not get used to the idea of becoming sailors. The architect divided them into small teams. They built some smelting furnaces, some foundries, smitheries, and a refinery for metals. The wood that came from Edom was used as fuel.

Thus, the merchant port was converted into an industrial city.

Hiram did not wear any jewellery characterising his function. The orders were given publicly by Elihap, the secretary of the King, who was held up as the true initiator of the enterprise. The high dignitary came and went non-stop between Jerusalem and Ezion-Geber, supervising the invested sums and the regular development of the works.

Hiram was in charge of organising all the workshops. He rectified the workmen's movements, guided the labour, helped the less adroit and dismissed the incompetent. The workers both loved and feared this strange foreman, who spoke little and seemed indefatigable.

The treatment of the copper ore produced excellent results. A great many tools were stored in barracks and a large portion of the production was exported.

Until this first day of autumn, Elihap and Hiram had never spoken in private. That evening, as the sun set the calm waters of the Red Sea on fire, the two men left the last furnace, just recently completed. It would be fully operational from the following day onwards.

They walked on a vast, deserted beach, up to a sandy promontory from where they contemplated the quiet drama of the sunset. Hiram's skin was burned in several places. Sitting down, he felt as if he was enjoying the first hour of rest for many lunar months. He did not give in, judging it a dangerous illusion. Despite the mesmerising beauty of a landscape that reminded him of the Egyptian Delta, and notwithstanding the serene light that prepared the way for the enlightenment that occurred in the next world, Hiram decided to remain as vigilant as the wild beast being chased by the hunter.

The man who stood by his side wrung his hands nervously as if to ward off evil.

'This masquerade has finally come to an end,' said Elihap. 'Therefore authorise my return to Jerusalem, and I will no longer have to convey your orders.'

'Have we not achieved the desired result? Ezion-Geber produces a great deal of copper, and of excellent quality. Israel now has an industrial centre which it sorely needed. This success is largely due to you, Elihap.'

'Solomon is not fooled. And, furthermore, he is not pleased.'

'Why?'

'Because he does not value this industry and the riches it produces. The King has but one idea: to build the temple. He feels you are wasting time.'

'He gave me his agreement for the building of these furnaces. Here, I started to become acquainted with the people of Israel. I have seen them at work on a different chore, a new kind of activity for most of the workers. I have tried to give them the sense of an accomplished task, even though it is a rough one. Rest assured, I have not wasted a second. Tomorrow, we have to open a larger work site. If I had not prepared a first team of artisans, I would be doomed to failure.'

Emerging from the golden waters, a dolphin leapt out of the water, announcing the playful bounds of a leaping school celebrating the end of the day. It was said that whoever followed a dolphin rescuing shipwrecked sailors was in no danger of drowning in the ocean of the next world. Hiram had often watched the arrival of that friend of man in the Delta's tributaries. One would often head up the Nile as far as Memphis, to the great joy of the children from whom the dolphin accepted food and caresses.

A friend . . . the Master Mason had to forego that notion of finding him among the men who surrounded him.

'Leave Israel,' Elihap demanded cuttingly.

Hiram did not reply.

Elihap, the Egyptian introduced originally by the Pharaoh into the court of Israel to spy on it, had fulfilled his mission beyond the call of duty. He had to be Hiram's assistant or risk losing his life, but he was unaware of the Master Mason's true identity and his Egyptian origin. He could have been a trustworthy ally in whom Hiram could confide.

'Leave Israel,' repeated Solomon's secretary. 'No one accepts you at court. Misfortune awaits you in this country. Go back to Tyre, take up your nomadic existence once again, go construct buildings elsewhere.'

'Would you be hostile to the birth of a great temple in Jerusalem?'

'It is a folly,' stated Elihap. 'It will ruin Israel and it will be Solomon's disgrace. When the disaster becomes noticed, you will be the first to be accused. I do not want your death or the decline of this country. Even though I was born in Egypt, and although I still believe in the God Apis who protects me, I have become a Hebrew. These people are mine now. I am Solomon's servant. If he does not succumb to vanity and if he forgets this temple, he will be a good King.'

'If I leave, Solomon will choose another Master Mason.'

'No,' said Elihap, 'the King is persuaded that you have been appointed by God. If you renounce, he will admit his error and abandon his disastrous project.'

The solar disc was disappearing over the horizon. The school of dolphins was reaching the far ocean. Lighting up the night, the fire of the furnaces made of Ezion-Geber a huge glimmering table.

'What if you are mistaken?' suggested Hiram. 'If Solomon's temple was to be the key to Israel's happiness?'

'I am not mistaken. This people is a mosaic of tribes who need to confront each other ceaselessly, under the protection of a God that they believe is unique. Solomon is too great for this country. He thinks and acts like a Pharaoh. But Israel is not Egypt. That the King should want a relative peace is a good thing. That he should try to create a temple and an empire, that is courting certain failure and the end of the Hebrew nation. A misfortune that would leave you the prime culprit. Solomon is awaiting you in Jerusalem, as soon as your work here is terminated. If only you had never come!'

Elihap went away, a dark silhouette in the falling darkness.

Elected by God, predestined . . . Who could succumb to such vanity? This was just nonsense for naïve children. But Hiram loved challenges. Egypt had been built as a gigantic challenge to the invisible world. Solomon was neither his brother nor his friend. Nevertheless, the game of chess that he was playing with destiny had begun to interest the Master Mason. To serve a monarch with the stature of a Pharaoh, even if in a foreign land, was a duty which he equated to that of light breaking through clouds.

Hiram left Ezion-Geber in the middle of the autumn, a little after the beginning of holy year celebrated at the equinox, during the feast of the harvest. The sun was becoming mild. The days, now free of the scorching midsummer heat, went by in golden slumber perfumed by nostalgic fragrances. Nature prepared for rest. The sea, sometimes turbulent, dressed in blue and green and sang distant litanies dating back to the origins of the world. The architect contemplated it for a whole morning as if he would never see it again.

With a small bundle on his shoulder, holding a walking stick, dressed in a worker's loincloth, he left the town without greeting anyone. Anup trotted by his side. Ezion-Geber had become a prosperous town where merchants and exporters had known how to take power. Numerous young people had become copper artisans. Hiram knew them by name. Tomorrow, when he needed them, they would not let him down.

The walker had just reached the slope of the first hill when a cloud of dust announced the arrival of a horseman.

Anup barked.

Hiram stopped with his hands crossed, leaning over his rod.

The man made his horse rear up, menacing the Master Mason.

'Are you the one called Master Hiram?'

'I am he.'

The horseman with red hair and of stocky build pulled on the reins angrily to subjugate a rebellious mount.

'My name is Jeroboam. Solomon put me in charge of building his stables. All the work sites of the kingdom will be under my orders.'

'With the exception of mine,' rectified Hiram.

'There will be no exceptions,' declared Jeroboam. 'Either you submit to my authority or you go back to Tyre.'

'I recognise no authority other than that of the King of Israel. You want to be in charge, but are you familiar with the Art of Planning?'

The red-haired colossus lost his temper.

'Your secrets are just mirages, Master Hiram. Do not defy me and get out of my way, otherwise . . .'

'Otherwise?'

The horse reared up again.

Turning around, Jeroboam left at a gallop.

23

The night sky was tinted white and red. A reddish moon attracted the disquieted gaze of the inhabitants of Jerusalem. Was it a bad omen? Was it possible that that sinister glimmer revealed Yahweh's anger? Yet, peace reigned in Israel. The country was becoming wealthy. It was respected by its neighbours. Solomon's glory grew incessantly. But there was that woman, that Egyptian who continued to render homage and offer sacrifice to her false gods. If she had not been the wife of the King, an avenging hand would have, long ago, put an end to her days.

Nagsara prayed to Hathor more and more often. In her bedroom, she agitated the sistrum, a musical instrument with a metallic sound dear to the goddess's heart. Those efforts were not in vain. Solomon had spent a night with her and showed a renewed ardour, a passion that she had thought was forever spent. Nagsara had made no demands. Mute, she had been content with giving her husband pleasure, just like any other concubine. The King, who had feared a flow of protests, if not insults, had appreciated his wife's restrained behaviour. In order to be pleasurable, the games of love could not accommodate cantankerous attitudes.

Solomon knew that Nagsara practised magic in order to reign over his feelings. He had often ordered Elihap to follow her and observe the rites she devoted herself to. The King of Israel did not underestimate his wife's talents. When she communed with Hathor, he took care of turning the ring with Yahweh's seal towards the earth. Thus, he deviated the spells of the Egyptian and these were diffused into the earth.

Why was Hiram taking so long in Ezion-Geber? To produce copper was an important task, but the port was too distant from Jerusalem. When would the architect deliver an initial plan? When would he finally prepare the opening of the work site on which Israel's future depended? Solomon had considered hiring another architect. Hiram was too retiring, too mysterious, but he was familiar with the Art of Planning that so few builders knew. Who could replace him?

Nevertheless, Solomon was losing patience. This night would be the last; from tomorrow the King would ask Jeroboam to start recruiting workers. The King had received the red gold from Sheba, he could now pay hundreds of artisans and order the best materials. To remain inactive any longer would be an unforgivable mistake. Solomon wondered if Hiram was disappointed or bitter when he had left Israel.

The King stood beneath the rock where he intended to build his temple. He gazed upwards to its peak, a spur that dominated the hill of Offel. This rocky elevation, at about eight hundred metres of altitude, jutted out, crowning Jerusalem, guiding the town upwards in the direction of the sky. David had fortified his capital. Solomon would make it a holy place. He would carve this rock on three sides, to the west, to the north and to the south. He would flatten the upper platform, building the constructions oriented to the East.

'Your Majesty, don't you think that it would be necessary first of all to link David's city to the rock by earth embankment? This would make the builder's task easier.'

Solomon had recognised the voice of Master Hiram.

'Did you follow me?'

'I knew you would come here.'

'Can you also read my thoughts?'

'I am just an architect. Not a seer.'

'Why such strange behaviour, Master Hiram?'

'Why don't you ask the magic stone you wear on your left hand. Does it not give you a power over the elements?'

'Enough of your impertinence,' replied Solomon, irritated. 'Your success at Ezion-Geber is the work of an engineer, not of a Master Mason. I require an explanation.'

Hiram looked at the moon. Ancient Egyptians texts sung that the hare of Osiris, holder of the secrets of resurrection, was hiding in that planet. By her crescent movement and subsequent waning, the sun of the night taught the observer the art of metaphor. The bluish light illumined Jerusalem's rock, attenuating its roughness. Did it hold the promise of a future sanctuary in its radiance?

'Do you know the traditions of Sheba, Majesty?'

Solomon feared some kind of blackmail. Hiram was finally going to remove his mask.

'The natives of Sheba worship the sun,' continued the Master Mason. 'It is in its light that they find wisdom and happiness. In return, that golden planet plants a bottomless reserve of gold in the heart of their mountains.'

'They are infidels, they reject the only God.'

'Is his name not Elohim, in your sacred books? Does that word not mean "the gods" in the plural?'

'Would you be an expert in theology, Master Hiram? Do you know that our God's name is also Yahweh? "The One Who Is" and that his ineffable name is revealed only to the King of Israel.'

'What I do know, Majesty, is that the cult of that divinity requires little sacrifice and does not demand the presence of a temple. You have decided to change that situation. You desire to end the mediocrity of your rituals, to give them the splendour worthy of a great realm.'

Solomon did not deny it. What the Egyptians had accomplished, he would also achieve. Yahweh could no longer reside in miserable places. He who was the Almighty, the Unique, should benefit from a greater glory than Amun at Karnak.

'Will you let me know what you require, at long last, Master Hiram?'

The architect crouched and touched the base of the rock.

'This rock is fine. It is hot and fraternal. It will make a good support for magnificent buildings. But it would be necessary to add to it the magic protection of the natives of Sheba to make it unalterable. They possessed a gold cup and a sceptre that were given to me by the master who taught me the Art of Planning. Their presence, at the heart of the rock, will guarantee the solidity of the work.'

Solomon reflected. Would such objects displease Yahweh? Would they betray Israel's faith?

'Would this perhaps represent blackmail, Master Hiram?'

'A project such as this does not depend on human enterprise only. If the heavens are not invoked to concur with its success, failure is assured.'

'This cup and sceptre, are they devoid of all inscription?'

'They are made of pure gold,' answered Master Hiram, 'gold born of the sacred fire of the sacred mountains of Sheba. The architect who places them in his foundations is endowing the site with a light that will shine forever.'

'If I accept your proposition? When will you open the path?'

The Master Mason seemed upset.

'I have been threatened. I have been ordered to leave Israel.'

'Who dared issue such an order?'

'I am not an informer, Majesty.'

Solomon was not disturbed. He did not believe Hiram. This man from Tyre was inventing a fable to defy him again.

'It's up to you,' said the King. 'Do not expect any further concessions from me. Today, you are free to leave Israel. In three days, I shall expect your definite answer. Then, you will be unable to go back on your word. May the night bring you good counsel.'

Hiram stayed beneath the rock until dawn. If he invoked a

refusal on Solomon's part to justify his return to Egypt and his peers, no one would doubt his word. But could a Master Mason lie and not be a broken man in his own eyes?

While feeling the rocks with his fingertips, Hiram had sensed that it revealed that it was one of those exceptional places where the Divine incarnates in matter. Solomon had chosen well. It was in this place, and nowhere else, that a great temple had to be built. The King possessed the kind of will that could overcome misfortune, anchoring the vision of man in eternity. That the future sanctuary was Solomon's destiny, Hiram no longer doubted. But would he foster his own distress by enduring an exile that would be as harsh as a death warrant?

With a heavy soul, Hiram decided to go home, walking through deserted alleys where the last vestiges of the dark of the night fought with the nascent daylight. Anup was at his side.

Hiram went in. A strong smell of incense and olive oil pervaded the house. Several lamps lit the rooms. A dozen priests prayed on their knees. One of them, seeing Hiram, stood up.

'I am Sadoq, Yahweh's High Priest,' he declared emphatically. 'Are you Master Hiram?'

The architect went in. The interior had been devastated, the floor dug up and the desk forced open. The walls had been whitewashed. The chests emptied and the bed broken.

'This place had to be purified,' said Sadoq. 'It was infested with evil spirits. Only a true believer will live here, henceforth.'

Standing very straight, the High Priest was exultant. His black beard with its uncut corners made his face take on the forbearing look of the judges in the next world. But his eyes had a crazed brilliance and they betrayed the feverish state of a jealous man, avid for revenge.

'Never return to this house, do not expect to find another abode in Jerusalem, you have practised black magic. We have proof.'

With a wave of his hand, Sadoq called one of his acolytes. The latter brought a terracotta figure representing a naked woman with monstrous hips and breasts.

'This diabolic image was hidden in your writing reeds' case. If you were not Solomon's protégé, I would have demanded stoning.'

'What has happened to my servant, Caleb?'

'There was no one in this devil's den.'

Hiram, with a brief look, realised that the little he owned had been destroyed.

He walked towards the door, under Sadoq's ironic gaze.

On the verge of leaving the defiled house, he turned round.

'Rest assured, High Priest, I will not live in this hateful town. But do not dare to accuse me of witchcraft again lest that lie turn against you.'

Sadoq did not heed that warning. His victory was total. Hiram was leaving, the temple would never be built. Everyone would know that Yahweh banished the foreign Master Mason and that He did not wish the city of David to be changed.

Troubled, Solomon consulted the secret books whose sole guardian he was as King of Israel. They taught how Man could take his place on the celestial throne if he followed the path of life and not that of death. They spoke of the soul, of God and of the elements. But they did not reply to the question that had been haunting him for so many days: should he really entrust Master Hiram with the building of the temple? Did the fascination that he felt for that man not veil reality? Was this foreigner not just a nomad, a rebel, who bragged about mastering a science he did not really possess?

The King had never been prey to such a distressing anguish.

When Nagsara dared enter the library as he consulted some rolls of papyri that no lay person could decipher, his initial reaction was to rebuke her vehemently. But the Queen, clad only in a transparent veil, had known how to be seductive.

'Do you not know, wife, that this place is out of bounds to you?'

The hint of a smile hovered over Nagsara's fevered red lips. She contemplated Solomon with a passion that was hardly disguised. It moved the King. The Egyptian, coiffed with the perfumed wig so dear to the high-class women of Tanis, undid the clasps that held her dress at the shoulders.

'A library is hardly the place for love . . .'

Solomon's objection was lost in a kiss that was both sweet and passionate.

The King no longer resisted the naked body pressed against his own. For a few moments of intense pleasure, she made him forget Hiram.

'You have considerable powers, my wife.'

'They are yours. You have only to ask.'

A Pharaoh's daughter . . . had she not been educated by priests who possessed books of magic spells, that all other nations envied?

'Would you know how to consult the oracles?'

'I observed my father in the covered rooms of the Temple of Tanis. He taught me to wash my mouth and purify it with natron before praying to the gods. I possess the art of banishing headaches, by placing a flame on the head of a bronze serpent.'

'Would you accept to consult the invisible?'

Nagsara was resplendent with happiness. She would, at last, prove to Solomon that he could not reduce her to an object for pleasure.

'What is the question you wish to ask?'

'I want a name. That of the best architect for the temple.'

Still naked, Nagsara took one of the lamps to the northern angle of the room. She extinguished the others and bent over the weak glow, almost burning her face. The words she pronounced protected her.

'Flame who knows yesterday, today and tomorrow, you have to answer me! If you should remain mute, the sky and the earth would vanish! If you should remain silent, the offerings would no longer ascend to the heavens! If you should remain speechless, the sun would no longer rise, rivers would dry up and women would be sterile! I, who am a daughter of fire, I have the right to ask you questions.'

Nagsara put her right index on her forehead and grasped the flame with her left. The flesh did not sizzle. With her nail, she drew hieroglyphs on the lamp's handle. The Queen closed her eyes.

'Come nearer, Solomon.'

The King obeyed.

'Lie on your back.'

He saw undulations on the library's ceiling. The walls started to dance madly.

'Question the lamp, Solomon.'

The King did not recognise his own voice, such was its gravity.

'Who should be the temple's architect?'

The flame grew, invading the room, attacking the papyrus rolls, setting Solomon and Nagsara ablaze. But the King felt no pain. He accepted this igniting phenomenon as a blessing. He was travelling on a river of blood that pierced high mountains.

Calm was brutally restored.

Nagsara, lying on her side, was asleep.

With the flame of the lamp, Solomon lit the others once again. His disappointment was cruel. The invisible had refused to speak.

It was impossible to wake the Egyptian, who was breathing normally. The King took the Queen in his arms.

On the young woman's white throat was an inscription in Hebrew script. It was easily read.

In the flesh of the Queen of Israel a name was engraved: Hiram.

24

The flock of sheep scattered as Hiram approached. He recognised the cripple's poor shack. Caleb was on the step, stirring a soup flavoured with pot herbs.

'My prince! You managed to escape their grasp?'

Behind the house was a large heap of wool, of a better quality than the spring's. It would serve to make winter coats.

'I ran when I saw those violent fanatical priests. They do not hesitate to stone whoever gets in their way.'

'Without Solomon's consent?'

'The King cannot supervise everything . . .'

'Why did you not try to warn me?'

'There was no time, my prince.'

Caleb wondered if the architect wasn't a fiercer adversary than Yahweh's worshippers.

'I did betray you, somewhat,' he admitted, 'but I had no choice. To come back and hide out here was my only alternative. Jerusalem is no longer a safe place when the priests are on the march.'

Anup, who had followed Hiram at a certain distance to protect him from any pursuer, approached his master. Noticing Caleb, he growled.

'This wretched dog again . . . Where do you intend to go, my prince?'

Hiram went beyond the sheepfold and descended a grassy slope that ended in an abandoned field where there were some fig trees with thick foliage. They provided an abundance of tasty, sweet autumnal figs. Those trees were not cut like parasols, but developed freely according to the seasons.

The Master Mason sat in the shade of an elderly, isolated fig tree. Anup settled at his feet. That is where, under the tree most common to the land of Israel, Hiram would make his decision. Often, near the temple of Karnak, he had known contemplative moments under the foliage of a sycamore or a tamarisk on the edge of the desert. His thoughts had drowned in the silence, his dreams had evaporated in the light. When he was a child, Hiram used to climb up to the highest branches and watch the peasants pass, pushing their donkeys laden down with bundles. They made their way along the red soil paths, heading to the fields while humming an ancient song that dated back to the times of the pyramid builders. When he saw a brotherhood of scribes carrying their reed pens and palettes, the young Hiram had desired to understand and know everything. Knowledge had dazzled and inebriated more than the beer served at feasts. He never stopped questioning his parents on the characteristics of the animals, the plants, the flood of the Nile, the strength of the winds, the reading of hieroglyphs. The day he became convinced they were incapable of answering his questions, the young fourteen-year-old left his village with only a sack on his shoulder. Accepted on board a merchant ship, he reached Thebes. His goal was to reach the place where knowledge was taught, the temple where only scribes were admitted.

He had been quickly disillusioned. Although the great court was open to nobility during festive occasions, the covered rooms where the teaching took place remained hermetically closed.

Hiram had left town and meditated for a long time sitting under the gentle shade of a tamarisk. Watching the sun's course and the unfolding of the day's colours, from dawn through to the gold of the sunset, he had established the rules of his existence: to fulfil his desires to the end, not to renounce whatever the pretext, always to assume responsibility for his failure and not blame others or external events. Equipped with these assets, he had practised many professions – vegetable merchant, sandal mender, fish sorter, basket weaver, pot maker – before being noticed by a cavalry instructor. After learning to care for horses, he had learned to mount them and drive a chariot. Then it was time to decide if he was to become a soldier or a scribe.

To his surprise, hesitation had seized hold of him. Was military life not more brilliant, more exciting, a source of prestige and riches? After another meditation session under a tamarisk, before the desert where the eternal abode rose, Hiram had decided to follow the path of the temple. In his eyes, that stone being, immense and mysterious, was life itself.

Then came the happiest period of his life. A time when his studies were directed by severe masters, demanding but endowed with that knowledge that Hiram's heart had long yearned for. To learn was the most delicious of pleasures, to work was a passion, to discover was a boundless joy. The young scribe chose to specialise in architecture. He handled all the tools, from the carpenter's adze to the chisel of the stonemason. Hiram became acquainted with the comradeship of the work sites where the labour of the spirit and of the hand became but one. He was initiated into the realities of stone, taming granite, sandstone, alabaster and limestone blocks, so as to be able to select, simply by touching with the palm of his hand, blocks of stone worthy of forming part of the fabric of a building.

Then, there were the trips both in Egypt and abroad, the encounters with other architects, other techniques, other belief systems. Hiram kept quiet and listened. During that period, he had sojourned in Sheba where Egyptian influence, though very strong, was not accompanied by colonisation. Far from his country and suffering from his exile, even if only temporary, Hiram had become the friend of a Master Mason close to the Queen of Sheba. At the top of one of the gold mountains, Hiram had received the revelation of the Art of Planning.

He excavated the soil with the help of a pointed stone with slow, precise and efficient gestures.

The gold cup and the sceptre came out of the loosened earth where Hiram had taken the precaution to hide them before going to live in Jerusalem. How could he confess to Solomon that these symbols had been offered to the Pharaoh Cheops by the first Queen of Sheba, when the large pyramid had been built? The Queen, venerating the sun like the Pharaoh, had thought it beneficial to tie herself magically to the construction of that wonder of the universe. Therefore, she had gone on a pilgrimage to Memphis when, on a winter night when the Pole Star shone, surrounded by its court of indefatigable celestial bodies, she had deposited in the lower chamber of the great pyramid the sceptre of Sheba, and, under the Sphinx a cup containing the dew of the first morning of the world.

These were objects that Siamun the Pharaoh had entrusted to Hiram before he departed from Egypt to go to Israel. The Master Mason was to place them in the foundations of Solomon's temple, so that they be erected founded on ancient Wisdom. Solomon had agreed to this.

If Hiram carried out this ritual, if he thus summoned the temple into existence, he would no longer be able to abandon the Work. By giving birth to a sanctuary, the architect consecrated his life to it.

Hiram had done everything to provoke Solomon's rage. The King of Israel had stayed true to his choice. Like the Master Mason, he followed the voice of his heart and did not balk before obstacles that were apparently insurmountable.

If Hiram accepted the role of Solomon's Master Mason, if he fulfilled the very role that Siamun the Pharaoh had entrusted him with, he would know the most absolute solitude. Who could he turn to for advice? To whom could he entrust his doubts, his questions? The Karnak masters were far away, in the luminous serenity of the temple in Upper Egypt. Forced to keep his origins secret, to hide his true name, to withstand the rigours of exile, would Hiram be capable of bearing such a weight for a period of years? Nothing had prepared him for this tragedy. Educated in a community of priests, initiated into his profession of the brotherhood of artisans, the architect loved the occasional rough fraternity that presided over the daily tasks of the House of Life. He would also have to renounce that joy. Hiram would have to reign over a race of Hebrew artisans without giving his friendship to anyone.

In the shade of the fig tree, under the tender autumnal sun, in the calm of the Judean countryside, Hiram felt like renouncing.

The gap was too great between the future of an Egyptian Master Mason destined to a peaceful old age, and that of Solomon's architect confronted with an impossible challenge. How could he deprive himself of the beauty of the black, fertile earth on the banks of the Nile, of the exaltation of the desert, of the complicity of the northern wind?

Had he not attained his goal, to become one of the Pharaoh's architects, to work beside his companions in the harmony of the House of Life, daily embellishing eternal stones, indifferent to human tribulations? He harboured no other ambition in his soul. Why did the gods force him to forsake happiness by serving the King of a foreign land and building a sanctuary in honour of a divinity that did not speak to his heart?

To renounce would be to acknowledge weakness. To see Egypt once again, to once again experience the breeze that swelled the ships' sails, required a sacrifice. Hiram was ready to bear such humiliation in the face of his peers.

But before Solomon, he refuted it.

After having distrusted the King and come almost to detest him, Hiram shared his passion. Like himself, Solomon was alone. Alone, he defied a whole people, the case of priests, the courtiers, custom itself. Alone he wanted to build a masterpiece and risk losing his throne.

Solomon was the last person in whom Hiram could confide.

But he incarnated that passionate will that had animated a young Egyptian once, avid for knowledge. An impossible fraternity was born between the two men.

Angry, Hiram felt like throwing away the sceptre and the cup.

Lit by the late afternoon sun, they shone with a reddish glow, and attracted Caleb's attention. The cripple approached, hesitating to touch them. Hiram's look was sufficiently forbidding to discourage him.

The Master Mason stared at the gold from Sheba with fervour, attempting to decipher his future in its reflection.

A disquieting flame haunted his deep blue eyes.

When the last rays tinted the fig tree leaves with an orange hue, Hiram stood up. No one would ever say that an Egyptian master had fled before a task to be accomplished.

He would build the temple, even though it was Solomon's.

Saturn, enthroned in the middle of the sky, would ensure the building solid and durable. Solomon, coming from the palace, and Hiram from the countryside, arrived at the same instant at the foot of the rock.

The Master Mason presented the sceptre and the cup to the King. The red gold was impregnated by silver moonlight. Using a boring tool with a spiral cutting head, Hiram pierced the rock and dug a cavity where he deposited the precious objects. Then he sealed it hermetically, using mortar whose traces he then effaced. With the exception of Solomon and the Master Mason, no one would know that the embryo of the temple of Yahweh was the sun of Sheba. Apart from Hiram, no one would know that Egypt was the mother of the greatest sanctuary of Israel, that the hidden God of the pyramids were resuscitated in Yahweh.

Solomon could hardly contain his emotion. According to the ancient magic texts he had consulted, the place chosen by Hiram's hand corresponded to the door of a secret world. Behind it was a path leading to an abyss full of water that occupied the centre of the earth. It was there that the spirits of the dead gathered so that that which is in the world above should match what is below.

The King thus obtained the absolute certitude that the oracle consulted by Nagsara had not lied. Who else but the architect elected by the invisible would have vanquished chance? Who else would have made the right gesture at the right moment?

Solomon gyrated on his finger the ruby given to him by Nathan. He addressed a mute prayer to the spirits of fire, water and earth, so that they participate in the creation of the edifice, as they did in that of every living being. He asked them to be the guardians of the sanctuary's threshold and to surround it with a permanent presence.

Hiram observed the summit of the rock where his destiny would be played out. Solomon savoured the happiness of a birth. In this fourth year of his reign, the construction of the temple had begun.

25

Solomon's rage was so terrible that Elihap, who thought he had his master's complete trust, feared for his life. Never had the King of Israel given in to that distress of the soul that the sages condemned. The monarch continuously invoked Yahweh as being the avenging God and promised to punish those responsible for Hiram's disappearance.

'There is no culprit,' protested the secretary timidly when the King seemed to have become calm.

'Hiram cannot be found and no one is responsible? Are you mocking me?'

'Following your orders, I have sent Banaias and the elite corps to look for him. They have sought him out in the houses, the cellars, the workshops, and the warehouses. No sign of Hiram.'

'What about his own house?'

'Empty.'

'Did you question his neighbours?'

Elihap hesitated.

'Speak,' ordered Solomon.

'They saw priests come in, then take out some objects.'

The glacial tone of Solomon's voice was even more alarming.

'Let the High Priest come to see me at once.'

Elihap ran to summon Sadoq.

Solomon paced in his office with its narrow windows. What

was happening in his capital? He had been waiting three days for Hiram to come. The architect had shown no trace of life since the secret ceremony of the foundation of the temple. The hypothesis of a rushed departure was absurd. By that ritual act, Hiram had given his word that he would see Solomon's enterprise to its conclusion. The latter knew men well enough to know that the Master Mason would not betray his oath.

If he did not come to the palace, that was because someone was preventing him. In what way and who? Unless one imagined the worse . . .

Solomon received the High Priest, Sadoq, as soon as he asked for an audience.

In one of the angles of the room, Elihap, holding a tablet, prepared to note the purpose of the interview.

The King did not observe the usual rules of courtesy.

'Why did your priests invade the house of the Master Mason?'

Sadoq, dressed in a splendid purple robe, smiled with disdain.

'That Hiram is an impious man, Majesty, he practises black magic.'

'What proof do you have?'

'The King will be content with my word. Is it not preferable to forget this sinister business? It was essential to remove a dangerous man who would have soiled the glory of Israel.'

Solomon grew pale.

'What have you done to him?'

'Nothing, Majesty. That necromancer is a coward. My warning was enough to make him run away.'

'If you are lying, High Priest, you will regret it.'

Sadoq, certain of his self-righteousness, bowed. The King would quickly forget. The obsession that troubled his spirit would vanish. Hiram and the temple would be but a bad dream.

Solomon descended to the small garden created by his wife at the extremity of one of the palace's wings. He needed to breathe, to escape the anguish that held him in its grip. To oppose the High Priest would be to foster an underground rebellion that would endanger his power. The inquest into Hiram's disappearance brought no results. Was God bent on thwarting the King's plans?

Nagsara, sitting on richly coloured cushions between two dwarf cypresses, played a portable harp that rested on her left shoulder. Since the event of the oracle, the King had shared her bed every night. The spells of the goddess Hathor had brought her husband back.

Nagsara's love grew deeper every day. Solomon had every quality she could wish for. Beauty and intelligence were perfectly matched in this monarch vowed by his genius for the highest fate. Nagsara was proud to be his wife. She would know how to be his devoted servant, happy to live in the shadow of a monarch blessed by the gods.

The annoyance stamped on his semblance disturbed her. She stopped playing and knelt before him.

'Could I relieve your pain, Sire?'

'Is your magic able to find a man who is believed lost?'

'Perhaps, by consulting the flame . . . but the exercise is difficult. It often fails.'

Nagsara took Solomon into the bedroom and made it dark.

'Do you have an object that belongs to him?'

'No.'

'In that case, fill your spirit with his features. Visualise him as if he was before you and, above all, do not lose him from your sight even for a moment.'

Nagsara lit a lamp. She stared at it until she was dazzled, almost blinded.

'Speak, gold goddess, lift the veil that weighs on my eyes. Do not make my King languish, do not torture him by your silence. Reveal to him the place where hides the man he is looking for, delineate its contours in the flame.'

Nagsara lifted her hands in supplication, before fainting. She would not tell Solomon that these voyages peopled with

159

immaterial forces took many years from her existence. Was there greater happiness than to sacrifice them to the one she loved?

A strange shape showed in the flame that gained an unreal whiteness. It was composed of intertwined spirals. Then, the scenario became simpler, letting a kind of rocky cavern appear.

'A grotto,' recognised Solomon.

Anup barked warning to Hiram and Caleb that an intruder was approaching. The cripple rushed and grabbed a metal stake determinedly.

'I warned you, my prince! They will not leave us alone.'

The architect continued to polish the rock.

'Are you here, Master Hiram?' asked the raucous voice of General Banaias.

The architect came out of the grotto that he was converting into living quarters aside Caleb's. Dug into the flank of a hill, outside the town, it was a dry and healthy environment. The cripple had brought blankets, tools and food. Hiram had taught him to handle scissors and polishers. Caleb's hand soon tired. He preferred to exercise his talent as a cook and as a sleeper.

Hiram came out of the grotto. The light blinded him for a few moments.

Banaias, who had followed Solomon's instructions and explored the grottoes of the region, was pleased to have found the architect. Although he detested that foreigner he owed the King complete obedience.

The Master Mason was escorted to the palace under guard. Solomon welcomed him with enthusiasm.

'Why were you hiding?'

'I was making my new home habitable. No one will be able to blame me for monopolising a house in Jerusalem. No priest will accuse you of giving me shelter. Is that not a wise move?'

Solomon had difficulty accepting his power being diminished by a cast, even if untouchable. But Hiram was right. By living outside the capital, he remained a foreigner and did not upset Sadoq.

'This grotto is unworthy of you.'

'To be at the heart of the stone does not bother me.'

'Why did you not warn me?'

'I will do my job. Don't expect administrative reports on my whereabouts. My word has been given. I will impose one last condition: that the building of the temple be accompanied by that of a palace. If the grotto suits me, the poor residence of King David is truly unworthy of Solomon.'

No adulation was meant by Hiram's declarations; he wanted to expand the initial project further. Did great monarchs not adjoin their temporal palace to the divine abode? Should the palace not be part of the temple, reminding the King that he was God's premier priest?

'Will you convey your plans to me?'

'No,' said Hiram. 'They must remain secret. The Art of Planning is a science reserved for architects.'

'David would not have permitted such insolence.'

'But you are Solomon and I am a foreigner. We do not belong to the same race, nor do we have the same religion. But we are partners in this creation. I pledge my word that I will build and to put my science at your service. You will see that I have the means to complete this endeavour.'

'So be it. How long do you think the completion of the project will take?'

'At least seven years.'

'Here is my own plan. You will be the only one to know it.'

The two men spent the day locked in the King's office, where Elihap, his secretary, was not admitted.

Solomon had decided to orient the extent of Israel's society to the building of the temple. By a decree that the prefects of the various regions would enforce, labourers and cattle breeders would be at the service of the artisans employed in the temple's work site. Food products would be primarily delivered to them. The workers of Ezion-Geber would leave the port without delay, so as to form an initial artisan work-force. Ten thousand Hebrews would go to Lebanon where they would receive the wood shipments cut by the King of Tyre's woodcutters. At the end of a month's work, during which they would carry out the dangerous and difficult transportation, Solomon would grant them two months' rest.

The monarch had calculated the minimum number of workers: eighty thousand quarry men, seventy thousand carriers, thirty thousand artisans working on the site perma-nently. He demanded that, in the course of one year, each citizen of Israel should participate in one way or another in the great Project. The temple would be the creation of an entire people.

This radical change in the economy implied new taxes and the organisation of obligatory chores that would be imposed as a national duty. If this caused a popular rebellion, it was a risk that the King was prepared to take. Solomon was sure he would be able to contain it.

Hiram stated his requirements. The fabric manufacturers and the clothes makers were to produce thousands of aprons made of raw wool that the artisans would wrap around their midriff. For the foremen, the tanners would prepare red leather aprons, for the fellow workers and the apprentices white ones. The builders would be supplied with straw mats, sieves, stakes, mallets, hoes, levers, brick moulds, axes, adzes, saws and chisels. The copper scissors would come from the Ezion-Geber warehouses. Hiram would himself choose the quarry workers who would extract with picks the great blocks of basalt and limestone. He would instruct the stonecutters who up until then had manufactured millstones or presses. The best among them, handling the polisher with skill, had built the rich mansions of Jerusalem. But none had had the mysteries of the Art of Planning unveiled. Of the woodcutters who worked independently in the villages, Hiram would make carpenters capable of producing long wooden beams and erecting complex wooden structures. Then he would have to train the masons who would no longer be content to erect farm walls, but who would learn how to handle the floor lines, the levellers and the plumb lines to go from the linear plan to volume. They would be helped by Phoenician specialists from the coast and requisitioned by Solomon.

The King and the Master Mason were conscious of the immensity of their enterprise. The temple would revolutionise the country and the surrounding regions. It would efface the past and anchor the future in the glory of God.

'The work sites are your sole responsibility, Master Hiram. As for the rotation of chores, it will be organised by the best Hebrew architect.'

Hiram approved the decision. It was not up to him to deal with the recruiting and organisation of the artisans.

'Who is he?'

'The one who built my stables, Jeroboam.'

26

The appearance of the plots of land preceding Jerusalem's fortifications had changed radically. The peasants who tended small gardens had been evicted. They praised Solomon for having allotted farms and fields to them somewhere in the countryside nearby. With the help of the woodcutters, Hiram had erected a high fence that hid the temple's work site from the lay population. Only one entrance, guarded night and day, gave access to it. Each worker received a password personally from Hiram.

Inside, the Master Mason had had several brick buildings erected: a tool warehouse, dormitory, refectory, stores containing food and clothes. The most important among them was the Planning Workshop where Hiram spent most of his time. Two pine chests, one containing fragments of limestone on which he executed some preparatory drawings, the other papyrus rolls where the definitive plans would be drawn. The architect himself sewed the papyrus sheets that he rolled around a cylinder, to obtain a papyrus that measured more than one hundred and fifty metres. Unrolled on the floor, it would contain the structures of the Work. Since the actual beginning of the labour, Hiram had rarely returned to the grotto where he felt so at home. His dog, Anup, greeted him and cried when he left. Caleb, the cripple, was beginning to lose his good cheer. Of course, to have shelter and food, to be free of need at last, was an appreciable advantage. But he missed the beautiful house they had left behind in Jerusalem and all its comfort. To have to feed the dog and watch his health was not something he relished. But he feared Hiram's anger if he was negligent.

The Master Mason worked whole nights, drawing a hundred sketches to keep just one or two. He found once again the inexhaustible energy that presided over creativity. Hiram identified with the future temple and prepared its genesis as if it were a human being. A strange fever had taken hold of him, obliterating any sign of tiredness.

The pupil of the Karnak masters measured the difficulty of his task: to build a sanctuary where Yahweh would be worshipped, but whose architecture and symbolism would be an extension of that found in Egyptian temples. To transcribe without betraying, to transmit without revealing, to incarnate heaven on earth . . . It was a very ambitious project and the responsibility was crushing.

Another working night was coming to an end. This time, exhaustion took hold of Hiram's hand. He put down his reed pen, cleaned the little jars that contained the black and red ink, rolled a papyrus and piled up the sketches after having numbered them.

When leaving the Planning Workshop, he contemplated the work site: the various buildings were almost finished. The workers were asleep. Hiram had known how to infuse them with enthusiasm and give them the feeling that they were part of an exceptional venture. In that protected enclosure, there reigned a secret harmony that those rough men learned hour after hour while working together.

The Master Mason passed the post where the changing of the guard had just occurred. He walked in the direction of the rock's base, looking up once again to its summit. The Work had to start at the top, even through this undertaking seemed impossible.

The gallop of a horse broke the light air of the dawn.

Jeroboam stopped a metre away from the architect and jumped off his horse. The red-haired colossus was furious.

'The King entrusted me with the responsibility of recruitment. I am a faithful servant. I shall obey, but I refuse your orders.'

'Impossible,' said Hiram. 'The recruitment is not an arbitrary decision. It is part of the plan of the project. Solomon cannot have told you otherwise. You will report to me every day on this matter. I want to know the exact number of men employed and the nature of their task. A single failure to abide by this rule and you will be dismissed.'

Jeroboam, impressed by the severity of Hiram's words, understood that the Master Mason was speaking in an official capacity that he would be unwise to challenge. Simple threats would have no effect.

'You are an authoritarian, Master Hiram.'

'My function so demands. Are you really willing to serve my person, with the fidelity demanded by the King?'

'You can rest assured of that,' said Jeroboam, whose eyes full of hatred contradicted his words.

For a moment, Solomon wondered if his Master Mason was not becoming mad. The project that he was presenting, to be carried out at the top of the rock, defied reason.

'Are you sure you are not courting disaster?'

'My calculations cannot mislead me. We will be able to change the Mello ravine and to close the rift that separates David's city from the site where the temple shall be built. Thus a gentle slope will be created which will facilitate the transportation of materials and will allow the lower quarter of the town to communicate with the capital's new centre.'

The King examined the plan that the architect drew in the sand. The vision was as simple as it was grandiose. It imposed itself as self-evident. As Solomon had intuited, by its very presence the temple would create a new Jerusalem, the celestial town promised to the just in the Scriptures.

Hiram thought of the huge works that had been the prelude of the pyramids at Giza: the selection of various hectares of elevated terrain, the opening of huge quarries, the flattening and levelling of a plateau, the placement of access ramps and the perfecting of leverage techniques whose secret had not been divulged, the rigorous organisation of a work site where a great number of artisans and a smaller number of geometers and stonecutters worked. To link, by means of a landfill, a rocky spur to an inhabited hill seemed to Hiram a venture that was almost facile compared to the prodigious works he had undertaken in the past.

'Are you not risking the life of your workers?'

The Master Mason rolled his eyes upwards, exasperated.

'Do not ever suspect me of such a disgraceful attitude. If there was ever that possibility, I would immediately take leave of my post. The security of the men who work under my direction is the first of my concerns. If any accident should be my responsibility, dismiss me at once.'

Solomon regretted upsetting Hiram.

The following hour, the Master Mason gathered the hundreds of workmen who had already arrived on the work site. Their annexes extended around the original heart of the work site, at the centre of which was the Planning Workshop. Some were experienced, whereas for others it was their first job. Hiram put them under the orders of the technicians he had trained at Ezion-Geber. It was too soon to divide them according to the ritual ranks applied in Egypt. While giving his directives daily, Hiram exercised constant vigilance. He could tell the courageous from the lazy, the attentive and the negligent, the skilful and the clumsy. To fill the ravine did not need remarkable competence, but perfect organisation. Hiram also appointed foremen capable of making the teams of workers carry out his orders.

Some weeks later, Jerusalem had changed its appearance. The rock no longer dominated in grand isolation. It had become accessible by a wide slope that ended near the houses of the lower part of town. Everyone was proud of the result obtained, feeling that Solomon's dream could come true. The

167

proud rock became the humble platform of the future sanctuary.

Solomon had experienced no resistance. No one had failed to collaborate with the project. The people did not protest. Israel was in the grip of a magic enthusiasm that led it on towards a new horizon, resplendent and grandiose. From the surrounding regions came congratulatory messages. The peace that Solomon had so desired was consolidated every day. The non-aggression pact signed with Egypt, the presence of a Pharaoh's daughter at the court of Israel dissuaded agitators from acting.

Was an era of happiness beginning? Was the holy city really taking shape on Jerusalem's summit? A new faith reigned in the hearts of the people. If it had not been impious to venerate a man as an equal of God, Solomon would have been worshipped.

Hiram remained in the shadow, working without respite, allowing himself no rest or distraction. He was completely engrossed in his work. He needed to go yet further by training good workers, with the hope of turning them into the artisan elite that he would soon need. In this case, it was impossible to rely on the apprentices patiently educated by the geometers of Egyptian temples. Hiram was looking for strong, balanced and receptive characters. In a few months, he would need to apply a science that it took adepts several years to learn. It was the most worrying aspect of this mad enterprise: to trust the nascent talent of some of the workers, to establish a brotherhood of specialised fellow-artisans on the very site of their apprenticeship. Hiram would have dearly appreciated the precious help of other Master Masons! But this was a utopian expectation. The stone fraternity had taught him to deal with reality. To dream about illusory support was a waste of time.

The Master Mason finished composing a list comprising about fifty names. Those of the apprentices he would initiate in the knowledge of the laws regarding the creation of the temple, the handling of tools and the laying of blocks of stone.

He was rereading it when the echoes of a fight at the site's sole entrance resounded.

Someone was trying to force his way in.

Hiram rushed out of the Planning Workshop, greeted some workers who were resting and walked towards the guardian of the threshold who was warding off an intruder.

Barking marked the arrival of the Master Mason. Hiram recognised the yapping of his dog, which edged his way up to him, abandoning Caleb who was about to be manhandled by several workers. The calls for help uttered by the cripple were not in vain. Hiram came to his rescue just in time.

'Don't you know that this place is forbidden to lay people?'

'Let me speak to you, my prince! Even your dog has managed to get in . . .'

Caleb launched into a long tirade during which he complained of having been abandoned, of suffering from cold, of being incapable of maintaining himself, of sinking into poverty, of being cursed by Yahweh in person.

Interrupting the barrage of words, Hiram took him to a building whose door was under lock and key. He opened the door. Caleb saw a room twice as long as it was wide, lit by three windows with bars.

'If you wish to enter the site, you must undergo a trial. Right here and now.'

Caleb stepped back.

'My life . . . will it be at risk?'

'There is a danger,' admitted Hiram.

'Will you help me as your devoted servant?'

'The rule of the work site forbids it.'

'That trial . . . is it indispensable?'

'Yes, it is essential.'

Caleb came closer.

'I prefer to see nothing.'

'As you wish.'

Hiram blindfolded the eyes of the cripple.

'Don't move.'

The Master Mason entered the trial room. In the middle he put two cubic blocks one on top of the other. Then he set down on them a long and narrow wooden plank and came back with Caleb.

'Take my hand,' he advised. 'Do not be afraid. If you are brave, you will survive.'

Caleb shook all over.

His limp accentuated, he went forward. Suddenly he had the sensation he was climbing a steep and smooth slope. Hiram let go of him.

'I am frightened!' he shouted.

'Go on,' recommended Hiram. 'Don't walk back!'

Under the weight of the walker the plank tipped over. Unbalanced, Caleb screamed in desperation, sure he would break his neck.

Hiram caught the cripple before he reached the ground. He sat him down, put the stones and the plank away and removed the blindfold.

'You succeeded, now you belong to the brotherhood.'

Caleb was having trouble catching his breath.

'If there are other trials like these,' declared the cripple, 'I prefer to give up.'

'Do not worry. I will give you a precise mission.'

'Which?'

'You will be my eyes and my ears on the work site. You will circulate everywhere, you will observe and listen. You have an excellent memory. Do not be an informer. Forget about compliments, pay attention only to criticism and dissatisfaction.'

On the doorstep of the trial room, Anup waited for Hiram, waggling his tail as a sign of contentment. He jumped on his master. He would also know how to keep watch. Hiram was no longer completely alone. He could now rely on two overseers.

27

Upon Hiram's orders, Caleb contacted each worker mentioned in the list drawn up by the Master Mason. He transmitted a pass phrase to them, 'my strength is that of the Master', and convoked them to come to the trial room where they presented themselves in the evening. Hiram asked them to utter the pass phrase and formally embraced them. When they were gathered in the northeastern angle of the room, he explained what he expected of them. Not just work as good as that of their comrades, but also an initiation in the art of building that would be conveyed to them during the hours when the work site had become silent. The future adepts must swear to observe complete secrecy with regard to what they would see and hear. If that oath was ever broken the penalty would be death.

Three among them preferred to turn back and left the assembly. The others took the oath. The instruction started immediately. Caleb, wrapped warmly in a woollen blanket, guarded the exterior of the building. This would go on for several nights running, and as a special treat, Caleb would be given a jar of milk and fig bread, courtesy of Hiram. Anup would help him.

The workers sat down on the floor. Hiram gave them some ostraka[1] and some chalk. Patiently, he taught them to draw the

[1] slices of fine white limestone and potsherds.

171

signs of the brotherhood of builders, such as dots, straight lines, squares, rectangles . . . He taught them how to draw a perfect line with a steady hand. Then he made them aware that the human body was structured according to geometric proportions, proof it was the work of a divine architect. Thus, he allowed them to experience the eternal forms, created by the spirit and transcribed by human hand. Finally, he conveyed to them the first precepts of the rules of the builders: to work for the glory of the creative Principle, not to look for personal reward, to give priority to the interests of the brotherhood, to know how to keep quiet and respect the tools as if they were living beings.

During the consolidation of the path that led to the rock and its levelling, Hiram taught the men intensively. The neophytes, unequally gifted, gave nevertheless unanimous proof of their will to go forth on the path delineated by the Master Mason. The initial fear they felt had given way to a growing admiration of Hiram. The architect knew how to address each of his pupils in terms that were adapted to each in particular. Severe, intransigent, refusing to accept any slipping, he nevertheless showed them warmth as soon as a new step had been taken.

Two months later they had the feeling they lived in another world. They spoke another language, loved each other as companions who shared the same ideal, the same secrets, the same duties. Hiram had attained his first objective: to establish coherence at the heart of the small group destined to orient the other workers.

A decisive stage was imminent: the celebration of the apprenticeship rite. The ceremony took place on a night when the moon was full and lasted until dawn. Each neophyte, after a period of isolation, was put in the presence of a corner stone sculpted by the chisel of the Master and promised to continue the Work by humbly participating in the building of the temple. Completely naked, the apprentices were showered with purifying water. Then

Hiram made them contemplate the flame of a torch, which served to cauterise the wounds incurred during the taking of a blood oath.

When the Master Mason wrapped the leather loincloth around the hips of his apprentices, he gave them each a new name. Thus, it symbolised their rebirth into the future temple whose living stones they would become.

The adepts, drunk with fatigue and happiness, had fallen asleep. Caleb had gone back to his fresh straw bed, happy to see that this tiresome period of teaching had ended at last. Even Anup snoozed. The work site was deserted. It would only become animated when the first rays of the sun shone, when the stars would return to the immense body of Osiris' Widow, Isis, enveloping the world with an invisible light, with a crown of constellations.

Hiram greeted the guardian of the threshold and went out of the enclosure. He went along the tents where the temporary contingents of workmen lived, requisitioned to perform the chore duties. The empty silence would soon be followed by noisy agitation. The camp ended in a scrubland where some foxes ventured forth.

Before a dead tree stood a woman, wearing a long white dress, her black hair floating over her shoulders.

'I am the Queen of Israel,' said Nagsara. 'I was coming to visit your work site, Master Hiram.'

'Only this part is accessible, Majesty.'

'Why is there a fence, why are there so many secrets?'

'Our rule demands that it be so.'

'Are there never any exceptions?'

'None.'

'I have a secret too. But I am not as miserly as you.'

Through the pinkish blue of the beginning of the day, Hiram thought he saw a silhouette that hid behind a tent. Not hearing any noise, he concluded it was one of the last nocturnal spectres returning to the other world.

Nagsara came close to the Master Mason and uncovered her throat.

'Look,' she said. 'The gods have written your name in my flesh. Why? What mystery do you harbour to inflict this suffering on me?'

The letters shone as if the white skin of the Queen was lit by a fire that flowed through her veins. Hiram had only seen the young Nagsara during the ceremonies when the Pharaoh appeared in public surrounded by his family. Now, he saw a young woman, with a fragile charm, condemned as he was to live in exile, but living at close quarters with Solomon, the man who was becoming the equal of an Egyptian monarch. How could he not be troubled by this naked beauty standing in the nebulous morning light, by this unreal vision of a Queen talking of a miracle, forgetting her modesty?

Nagsara noticed that Hiram was disturbed. She hid her throat and put her hand on the Master Mason's chest.

'My fate is bound to yours. I need to clarify this enigma. How could you refuse to help me?'

'May the Gods preserve me from cowardice.'

Nagsara's palms were soft. Hiram would have liked this moment to linger, but the Queen moved away, suddenly aware of her daring.

'We will see each other again at the palace. Israel has many prophets and one of them will be able to unravel this mystery.'

The white silhouette seemed to dissolve in the cloud of sand stirred by the desert wind. Hiram closed his eyes. What did that apparition mean? Up until then, he had had to fight only against Solomon and against himself. The temple had invaded his soul, suppressing the outer world. Nagsara reminded him of his loves on the banks of the Nile, the boat outings on the canals, the walks in the papyrus forests, his passionate amorous encounters in the palm groves where tame monkeys jumped from tree to tree. His youth had been so ardent, but so very brief . . .

A terrible scream pulled him out of his reverie.

Hiding behind a tent, a man had jumped out and stabbed the Queen with a dagger. 'Die, you impious bitch!' he screamed in his delirium.

In a few short steps, Hiram arrived at the spot where the attack had taken place and overpowered the criminal effortlessly. A slim individual whom he struck down with a blow on the back of the neck. Blood covered the Queen's throat. With vacant eyes, she tried in vain to speak and then fainted. Hiram's powerful voice called out to the apprentices for help.

A sad procession passed in the street of Jerusalem heading towards Solomon's palace. Hiram carried in his arms a young, inanimate woman, incapable of containing the breath of life that was leaving her body.

He was followed by workmen who pushed before them an assassin who insulted them.

Solomon had just finished explaining to Sadoq the High Priest the new dispositions adopted to ensure the financing to the temple. He decreed a tax that compelled the priests, as well as the rest of the Hebrews, to offer a tenth egg laid by a chicken. In the realm that was divided into ten provinces, each would provide in turn to the needs of the work site.

Sadoq protested vehemently. He was the only one who could, given his rank, still resist Solomon.

'Why waste so much richness on building one more chapel? Yahweh was quite happy with the shelter we provided for him. Lack of restraint would displease him.'

'The temple is neither a chapel nor a royal whim,' objected Solomon. 'It will be our country's sacred centre. It will maintain God's presence on this land and peace among the State. The unity of Israel will be asserted around this sanctuary.'

'Could it be true,' said Sadoq ironically, 'that God lives here on earth?'

'Who would dare claim that the King of the Hebrews propagates such a heretical belief? The One that the sky cannot contain remains invisible to us, but His radiant presence can be perceptible. It will be His presence, not God Himself, that will inhabit that new abode.'

'Is that not the doctrine of the Egyptians?'

'Is it contrary to our faith, Sadoq? Would the unique God not become manifest in the work of the builders that He will crown with His light?'

The High Priest sulked. He had not reckoned that Solomon was so knowledgeable in theology. He pursued the combat on another terrain.

'The people will not accept to pay such heavy taxes. They will rebel.'

'The temple is the material expression of the spiritual order that reigns over our country,' indicated the sovereign. 'The heart of the people and that of the sanctuary will beat in unison. They will see what shape their labour has taken. They will know that each portion of the tax has become a temple stone, that the holy city has been rebuilt by Our Lord. The fields up to the Cedron will be consecrated to Him. Never again will they be ravaged or destroyed, for the mission of the temple is to propagate peace.'

'Will the army not lack funds?'

'Would a High Priest be meddling with military strategy now? Ours is a strong army. Our security is guaranteed. We no longer engage in ruinous wars. The temple will protect us.'

Having run out of arguments, Sadoq was about to refute Solomon's project categorically, when the King's secretary, Elihap, erupted into the throne room.

'Sire . . . a terrible tragedy . . .'

Hiram, holding Nagsara's assassin by the neck, threw him down on the paving stones.

'Here is the wretch that tried to kill the Queen of Israel.'

The man threw an imploring look in Sadoq's direction before covering his face with his hands. But Solomon had had time to recognise him.

'Is this criminal not a priest? Does he not belong to the ritualists?'

Sadoq did not deny it. His acolyte cried out.

'I am leaving, it is up to the King to do justice.'

Solomon stood up.

'The Queen . . .'

'Your doctors are trying to save her. I must go back to the work site.'

The King turned towards Sadoq.

'You are no longer in a position to voice any protests, High Priest. Perform your religious duties and watch your subordinates. Make sure they are people of integrity.'

Nagsara kissed Solomon's hands and pressed them into hers. It was very comforting to see him sitting by her bed while she convalesced. Each day, he spent at least two hours with her, contemplating her face with his deep blue eyes that contained all the beauty in the world. The Queen blessed her aggressor. Thanks to him, thanks to the wound he had inflicted on her, she enjoyed the presence of her master. She basked in the attention he paid her; his distress over her condition was even more precious than love.

She imagined thus the conniving tenderness of old couples who perceive each other's intentions without uttering a word. To listen to each other breathe, tasting the moment of communion that no fate could wrench away. If she fought not to give in to death, it was to prolong these days spent in idyllic closeness, so far removed from the dying chamber of a moribund.

Nagsara had no other ambition than to be resuscitated a thousand times in Solomon's heart. This is where her garden with its comforting shade was, where the sycamore flourished with branches covered in joyous birds, where the sun shone untouched by the devils of the night.

She loved the King more than life itself. She venerated him with the folly of her youth, she was drunk with a happiness that was as lively as the spring of a gazelle.

Nagsara had forgotten that the blade of the dagger had

struck precisely where Hiram's name was engraved in her flesh.

An eye for an eye, a tooth for a tooth, a hand for a hand, a foot for a foot, a burn for burn, an injury for an injury, a wound for a wound, a life for a life: such was the law of Israel. The priest who had tried to kill the Queen had to be sacrificed as an expiatory victim. Therefore, according to the sentence pronounced by Solomon, he was stoned before the whole court.

The High Priest Sadoq ignored the ordeal, his gaze was riveted on Solomon.

28

Sadoq was triumphant. He threw on the stone floor of the audience room about ten amulets representing stars, ibises symbolising the god Thot, fertility necklaces, magic eyes, silver serpents, hippopotamuses in lapis lazuli.

'This is what we found on Master Hiram's work site, King of Israel. These monstrous figurines prove that there are some idolaters among the workers. The guilty must be punished.'

Solomon understood only too well what was going on. Through the person of his Master Mason, it was the King the High Priest wished to attack.

'Would you dare name him, Sadoq?'

'Caleb, the cripple. Hiram's servant. The amulets were hidden in the straw of his bedding.'

'And who found these things?'

'I was warned by a worker who is Yahweh's faithful servant.'

'A denunciation . . .?'

'An act of bravery, your Majesty.'

'Does Caleb admit being the owner of the objects?'

'He has yet to stop insulting the priests who are guarding him.'

'Have the priests become policemen?'

'They watch over Israel's welfare. They demand that justice be done and that Yahweh's law be sovereign.'

*

A wooden throne gilded with gold leaf was carried to the entrance of the work site. Solomon sat on it surrounded by a cohort of priests. Sadoq had spread the news; pagans were employed in the construction of Yahweh's sanctuary, soiling the temple of the only God. Either that enterprise, now become Satan's, must be interrupted or severe punishments must be enforced. The priests demanded that the culprits be whipped with leather strips, that their feet and their hands be burned. The fanatics wanted to throw them from the top of the rock.

Solomon was in a dark mood. Sadoq was playing a destructive game and the result would be the abandoning of the project to which the King had devoted his life. By striking out Caleb, whether he was guilty or not, the guilty verdict would demean Hiram in the eyes of his workers. Every one would know Hiram had favoured an idolater. The architect would be tainted by scandal, Solomon ridiculed . . . those were the High Priest's aims and the King had no right to dodge the issue. He must do justice in view of the facts.

A disquieting rumour added to the King's worries. Hiram had refused guards free access to the work site. Banaias was rejoicing. To assault the work site, to destroy the fence, exterminate some wretches and humble the pride of the Master Mason would be exploits that would be the talk of Jerusalem for quite some time.

Solomon had been caught in a trap. Even if the brotherhood defended its rights, even though he was certain that Sadoq had set up a conspiracy, he could not tolerate that his authority be contested. Should the door of the work site not be opened, he would be forced to use violence.

A bitter taste filled Solomon's mouth. Why were human beings always locked in the past, why did they hold on to such superficial privileges, forgetting that the present celebration of divine grandeur was the condition for their salvation? Was it necessary to dwell on petty problems, on palace intrigues? Should he be resigned to tackling divisions in the provinces, internal quarrels, petty wars in which only suffering was the conqueror? Solomon grew conscious of the fragility of a throne that many thought was solid. Israel's priests plotted, trying to create a State within a State. A power the King wanted to dismantle by building a new temple, a new religious hierarchy, a renewed drive pushing his entire people towards the sacred. Sadoq, used to the subtleties of power, strengthened by the post he held, had concocted a stumbling block.

'In the name of the King, open!' ordered Banaias.

The guards had spread out on both sides of the work site's sole entrance. The guards raised their spears and the vindictiveness of the priests was fired. Sadoq smiled and thought that the destruction of that accursed building was well worth a few dead bodies. Israel would know the will of God and learn that a King, even if his name was Solomon, would not govern without the High Priest's consent.

The monarch hesitated in giving the go-ahead for the assault. It would destroy the meaning of his reign, and reduce him to a pathetic figure in the history of men. The summit would remain deserted, a hostile fortress, defying a young King who had believed in the Lord's protection. Solomon was sure that Hiram would not buckle under before danger. He would galvanise his workers into action and would rather entice them into senseless resistance than lose face.

Banaias looked at Solomon. The latter was condemned to intervene. To procrastinate would ruin his prestige.

The door to the work site opened slowly.

Hiram appeared naked from waist up, wearing a long red leather apron, with a heavy mallet in his right hand.

'Who dares trouble my work?'

'Do you not recognise me? I am the commander of the royal guard. I have come to arrest your impious servant.'

'Beyond this threshold you are nothing. On the work site only the law of the builders prevails.'

Banaias took his sword out of its sheath. The architect did not show the slightest fear. His fingers tightened around the mallet's handle.

'Caleb, the cripple, is accused of hiding blasphemous amulets. That crime is an insult to Yahweh. He deserves an exemplary punishment.'

'Who is accusing him?'

Sadoq nodded for a priest to present himself.

'I am,' he said harshly.

'You are not a worker. How did you enter my work site?'

The priest looked embarrassed.

'No matter,' said Sadoq.

'On the contrary,' said Hiram, 'how can you judge without knowing the full facts?'

'Speak, High Priest,' demanded Solomon.

'No one can doubt the word of a servant of Yahweh's. This priest managed to enter the work site and obtain the proof of the sacrilege. The architect is seeking to delay Solomon's sentence.'

'Lies,' said Hiram. 'No one goes further than the entrance to the work site without the consent of the guardian of the threshold.'

'Let him come before this assembly.'

'That would be useless,' protested the High Priest.

'Let him come forth,' stated Solomon.

The guardian of the threshold, an old man with a strong jaw, approached with hesitation.

'Did you let that priest in?' asked Hiram.

The guardian of the threshold bowed low before the Master Mason.

'I . . . I accepted the silver coin that he offered me. He did not stay long . . . It was last night . . .'

'What does it matter? The amulets exist!'

Hiram approached the throne.

'What judge could accept proof obtained by corruption?'

Sadoq intervened.

'Majesty, you are not going to listen . . .'

'That's enough,' concluded Solomon. 'The King of Israel will not soil the justice whose guardian he remains. This process cannot take place. Those who have tried to compromise me will regret it.'

The High Priest did not dare pronounce himself against the sovereign's judgement.

'These events are unfortunate. They will not occur again. Whoever walks into the work site, without Master Hiram's consent, will have his foot cut off.'

The King's word became law.

From the garden where she was resting, Nagsara heard the noises emanating from the lower part of town and from the immense tent encampment inhabited by hundreds of men enrolled to perform the chore duties. Out of danger, the Queen was recovering from her wounds. As her convalescence progressed, the King spaced out his visits. Life tasted more bitter than the suffering she had endured. The strength that returned to her body drove her master away. Together with the whole of Israel, Solomon thought only of the future temple, forgetting the love of a young Egyptian whose eyes were too passionate.

Nevertheless, Nagsara was sure passion was still alive in the King's heart. She would continue to fight against this ever more powerful rival, this sanctuary of a jealous God, who seemed to be envious of her. Nagsara, a foreigner and a woman of flesh and blood, stood her ground before the symbol of a Israel, a temple whose body was made of stone.

She had often interrogated the flame about her own destiny. But she had only discerned uncertain shadows, as if the goddess Hathor refused to hand her the key to her fate. The Queen would not give up.

She would not let Solomon become indifferent to her. Whatever the price, she would bind her King to her on this earth and beyond it.

29

The full moon of the spring equinox had opened, as it did each year, the Easter festivities. More than two hundred thousand men, who came from the provinces, had left their towns and villages to come to Jerusalem and catch a glimpse of the work site of the famous Master Hiram. Invading streets and alleys, the pilgrims looked briefly beyond the fortified walls and at David's palace. The rock, the new access path, the camp of tents and the fence that isolated the expert artisans from the outer world excited their curiosity.

A thousand and one rumours circulated. Each person knew more than his neighbour, they knew a part of the architect's secret plan, described the future building and the mysterious rites practised inside the enclosure. There was not a single onlooker who was not informed of Solomon's projects, not a wanderer who did not know one of Master Hiram's disciples who had revealed the keys to numerous enigmas. People forgot that Easter celebrated Moses' exploit of freeing his people from persecution, taking them out of Egypt. No one thought any longer of the exterminating angel's presence who punished the impious. The whole country seemed to identify with a temple, still invisible, the most beautiful and grandiose ever conceived by a King.

Prayers were given up to Yahweh. The lambs were sacrificed, their blood sprinkled on the doors of houses, smells of burned flesh filled the city with foul odours. 'Blessed be the name of the Lord, thanks be given for His kindness,' sang the faithful when it was time for the banquet, 'Glory be to the Lord, for we are his faithful servants!'

Queen Nagsara, still feeling weak, had not attended the beginning of the ceremonies. The more they proceeded, the less joyful they were.

Terrible news had spread with the speed of an Egyptian hare: Master Hiram had renounced building God's temple. In fact, Solomon presided alone over the festivities, when everyone expected the architect to be at the King's side. Hiram was sought all over. He was nowhere to be found. The work site was closed for Easter and the workers confirmed that he had not taken refuge in the Planning Room.

The radiant face of the High Priest, to whom Solomon paid homage according to custom, confirmed his worst fears. The populace and the nobility were aware of the hatred that Sadoq bore Master Hiram. No doubt he had managed to persuade him to leave. Not wanting to admit his defeat, Solomon feigned ignorance by being silent. The men who had come to perform the chore duty would be sent home, the artisans would return to their provinces, the fence would be brought down in a few months or it would rot *in situ*. The bare rock would continue to scoff at Jerusalem.

When the libation cups circulated, passing from hand to hand, there was no longer any doubt: Master Hiram had abandoned the work site, giving in to the menace of the priests. He had probably returned to Tyre.

The prophets, who had predicted no monarch would modify David's city, had been right.

The old order had triumphed.

Hiram, walking in a field that had whitened in time for harvest, tasted an ear of barley, crunching it. Not far from there, some peasants handled sickles, whose dented blades cut the high stems. The sheaf-makers knotted the bundles, leaving behind those that the poor would pick up as they could only search in the parts already harvested.

Anup bounded in front of Hiram, sniffing the ripe spring air. At the extremity of the field, the thrashing floor, which had been patiently packed down by the oxen, received the first ears. Placed on an elevated terrain exposed to the wind, it was visible from afar. Some peasants were preparing a cart with spikes for the thrashing, leaving behind a golden mass of grain, husks and straw. The winnowers were sharpening their pitchforks before throwing the mixture up in the air, trusting the breeze to do the sorting. The straw would fly away, on the thrashing floor the grain would pile up purified by the spirit of the wind. The farmers would store it under their roof, where it would be sheltered from the rain, beyond the reach of robbers, beasts or prowlers.

Preceded by his dog, the Master Mason went beyond the thrashing floor where the days were eternally the same. He crossed the garden full of wild flowers, on the edge of the small house where he had been living for several days. In the cellar, dug beside the house, he took a goatskin full of fresh water and some wine. Then, in the open oven, he grilled some wheat grains, prepared some cakes with fine flour perfumed with cumin seeds and some honey fritters. Anup ate and drank with voracity. Hiram sat beneath a fig tree to enjoy his meal.

In Jerusalem, the worst accusations must be circulating about him. He was probably seen as a coward and a runaway; as someone who had betrayed Solomon. Was he despised by the workers he abandoned? They must be feeling cruelly deceived, having held him in high esteem, like a father. The veneration that the Master Mason had inspired was turning into loathing. His reputation was forever damaged.

Anup barked, warning Hiram of the arrival of a peddler pulling a donkey laden with carpets, tunics and crockery. Almost bald, with lanky limbs and a raucous voice, the travelling merchant went from village to village.

'What might you be needing, Sire?'

'Go on your way,' said Hiram.

The peddler had a keen eye. If that man was not a client, he nevertheless needed his talents.

'I am also a barber, the best in Israel! I cut hair, I perfume it and trim beards. As far as you are concerned, I arrived in the nick of time. Tomorrow, you would no longer resemble a human being.'

Hiram smiled and put himself in the barber's skilful hands.

'Do you live alone here?'

'Silence is my only friend.'

The barber, for whom conversation was a favourite pastime, bit his tongue. He felt there was in this quiet man a dangerous force that it was best not to awaken. Therefore, he concentrated on the haircut.

'It's been a long time since my last visit to Jerusalem. What is going on in the capital?'

'A terrible scandal! The temple's architect has abandoned the work site. He has returned to Tyre, his homeland, for he was unable to draw up the plans according to Solomon's wishes. The King has given up his project. The priests are satisfied and even more powerful than before. Solomon is but a prisoner at their mercy.'

'What do you think of that Hiram?'

'He is a foreigner . . . Israel's destiny matters little to him. And then, a new temple . . . what purpose would it serve?'

The sun's setting gave way to a different kind of light as the stars began to appear. Hiram addressed an Egyptian prayer to the light enveloping the sanctity of dusk. He lit an oil lamp, whose orange shimmer mirrored the light of the sunset that coloured every house, forming a long chain that vanquished darkness. Sitting on the terrace of his temporary abode, the architect contemplated the Pole Star, one of the axes of the world, around which gyrated indefatigable planets. From the warm earth, a fragrance of thyme and wild flowers emanated. The peace that reigned was enveloped in a deep lapis lazuli blue that coloured the immense sky. How bitter Jerusalem must feel believing itself betrayed by a treacherous Master Mason!

Hiram tasted the sublime quiet of a dusk that nevertheless lacked the scintillating shimmer of the Nile, the majesty of the temple erected by his ancestors, the mystery of the desert where the pure lines of future monuments were set out. The temptation of a real flight took hold of Hiram's soul. It was the serene richness of these moments that he yearned for and not the relentless fight that had begun in Solomon's city. To lay down his tools, to forget his plans for the project, to take the road leading to Egypt, the land beloved of the gods . . .

Hiram crossed a small canal on which a small dam had been built. Inspired by methods devised by the Pharaohs, the Hebrew peasants had created a network of irrigation channels that had proved efficient against drought. It was here, at the frontier with Samaria, to the north of Jerusalem, at the confluence of the rivers Yabboq and Jordan, that the architect found what he was looking for. The mission entrusted to him by Solomon had to be carried out in the utmost secrecy. Therefore, the Master Mason had left on foot during the night, taking only his dog for company.

The priests rejoiced over Hiram's flight. This illusory victory calmed their spite and weakened their vigilance. Solomon preferred not to clash with Sadoq any longer. Hiram's plan for the project had reached a most delicate moment. The King had asked him to act with the greatest of discretion so his actions would not be thwarted by any ploy from the ecclesiastic caste.

The rough terrain Hiram was searching for was a copper mine mentioned in the old texts written by geographers. If offered, above all, a perfect place to cast bronze. The clay would provide excellent moulds. The workers would have abundant water. The wind would suffice to feed the fires of small furnaces whose usage would be reserved for specialised artisans. The bronze would run along sand channels to the cadence of hammers' beats. Who else but Hathor, Lady of the Turquoise, had taught the casters their art?

But the Master Mason encountered a problem: the land belonged to a peasant whose wife was the daughter of a priest pertaining to Sadoq's tribe. Any authoritarian injunction by the King would unleash the High Priest's anger and ensure the matter ended up in the Courts of Law thus delaying the work's progress. Hence, Hiram had decided to solve the problem by buying the land officially.

The peasant was working on his small plot. The smell of the lumps of earth gave off a heavy, reassuring and pleasing fragrance. He stopped as soon as he saw Hiram.

On a flat stone, the Master Mason laid a purse containing several silver coins and a contract. The sum was much higher than the land was worth.

The peasant calmly went to his farm and brought back beam scales with basalt weights. This most precious object allowed him to carry out the most difficult transactions with great efficiency. He read the contract drawn up in simple terms and weighed the silver coins, checking their validity. Satisfied, he took off his sandals and offered them to the buyer. From that point onwards, he would no longer tread the soil as its owner, land that had brought him such an unexpected fortune.

The peasant disappeared. Not a word had been uttered. Hiram had just acquired the site for the temple's foundries.

30

On the spot where Jacob had fought with the angel, hundreds of workers now handled moulds for metals, driving the huge bellows to fan the furnace flames. Considerable quantities of wood were delivered each week.

The first bronzes to be cast by sculptors under Hiram's supervision were of a couple of lions. Hiram watched over every stage of the casting of those animals that would adorn the temple access. They would watch over the causeways that came up from the Nile valley towards the secret sanctuaries.

The Master Mason travelled backwards and forwards between the foundries by the River Jordan and the quarries on the outskirts of Jerusalem. The beds to be quarried were marked by an Egyptian sign similar to the symbol of life, the ankh. Hiram had shown the apprentices how to extract blocks by digging furrows around them wide and deep enough for the wooden wedges then placed at regular intervals. The choice of the stone blocks was essential, for the building's very solidity would depend on them. Quarriers and stone-cutters, after at first mishandling the stones and ruining tools, now worked with more and more adroitness. They extracted the stone layer by layer, carving out the blocks without causing any shattering.

When the first columns made of copper and limestone were built, Hiram knew that his apprentices had assimilated the elementary precepts of the art of building. Thus, he called the best among them to meet in the Planning Workshop where he initiated them in the science of the brotherhood. It would allow them to erect walls on which they would divide the properly cut blocks harmoniously. Wearing white leather aprons, carefully cleaned after the day's work, the adepts swore that they would reveal nothing to the apprentices or to lay people of what they learned. By becoming repositories of an ancient wisdom that transformed linear lines into volume, they began to reign over the matter at the very heart of the spirit. In the trial room, always plunged in twilight, Hiram drew a double square. He joined two of its angles by a diagonal. Thus he demonstrated the space where the divine proportion was inscribed, the gold Number that Egyptian architects considered the most precious of treasures. Before the awe-struck eyes of the new companions, Hiram unfolded the world of the cube, the polyhedron, the spiral and that of the star of sages whose flamboyant points indicated the right route to voyagers lost in the darkness. He showed them how to solve the squaring of the circle, how to perceive the law of proportions without having to use calculations, how to handle the thirteen-knotted string, shaping it into a T-square or a compass. He conveyed the knowledge of life's eternal forms, inscribed in the universe. They would integrate all this into the body of the temple, ensuring it grew harmoniously.

After five days and five nights of tuition, the companions were filled with a knowledge that was beyond their understanding. Towards Master Hiram they felt a gratitude that no words could express. The fraternity that bound them to him was as brilliant as the summer sun.

The architect proceeded along his path step by step. To develop the work sites, to prepare the men, to plan the foundations of the building were stages he had to keep under control, whatever the circumstances. He hoped not to have been mistaken when he placed his trust in his companions.

Could he presume to understand the hearts of men as deeply as he did the stones of the temple?

The toilers brought in for the chore duties received payment at the end of a week's work. This did not apply to the companions or the apprentices, who had their salary bestowed upon them, inside the enclosure, in front of the closed door of the Planning Workshop, each feast of the new moon. The apprentices formed the first rank and the companions a second one. All stood in silence as one by one they presented themselves before Hiram and whispered in his ear the password corresponding to their grade. The Master Mason modified it several times a month, thus discouraging any attempt at fraud. He paid them in gold and silver coins, taken from coffers deposited at the work site by Solomon's personal guard.

Hiram made a point of fulfilling that task himself, so that no exaction or injustice was committed. In fact, each member of the Brotherhood received a different sum, corresponding to the quality and the intensity of the work carried out throughout the lunar month. Whoever considered they had been cheated had the right to protest to the architect.

When this ceremony was over, Hiram descended with a torch in his hand to the darkest spot of the quarry. There, he was carving out an underground room at the heart of the rock. He accepted no one's presence in that secret place though working himself to the point of exhaustion. Its purpose was known to him alone.

When would he be able to use it?

Nagsara put on a pale yellow dress, ornamented with a golden belt that drew attention to the slenderness of her waist. She had dyed her nails a light orange hue. On her feet, she wore white leather sandals with elegant straps and with soles made of palm tree bark. From the dress hung silk ribbons. On her wrists, the sovereign wore golden bracelets; on her fingers solid silver rings.

Thus adorned, the Queen of Israel left the palace at noon. Servants ran towards her, offering a sedan chair that she refused. She dismissed her personal guards, demanding she be left alone.

The sun dazzled her. She proceeded without haste up the ascending path that led to the barrier that blocked access to the wide road leading to the rock to all but the transport of materials. On that Sabbath, no one was working. An apprentice sculptor and a soldier appointed by Banaias, sitting against a block of limestone, prevented anyone from passing.

'Get out of the way,' ordered Nagsara.

The soldier and the apprentice stood up. The former recognised the Queen.

'Please forgive us, Majesty . . . It's impossible.'

'Would you be courting death for having offended your Queen?'

The apprentice ran off. The soldier gave in, seeing the determination of the Queen. How could orders issued by Solomon possibly apply to his spouse?

Nagsara discovered the vastness of the levelled platform. The rock had accepted that first stage in its domestication. But there were no traces of foundations, just the naked stone flattened by the light. Did the architect really intend to build a temple? Wasn't he deceiving Solomon by announcing wonders he was incapable of achieving? There had been the filling of the ravine, certainly, but was this within the capacity of any competent master mason? Doubt froze the heart of the young woman. Was her husband setting out on a path without issue, blinded by a pride that he mistook for divine will?

No matter. Solomon would act according to his desire. The object of Nagsara's desire was not Yahweh's sanctuary. She just wanted the King to be happy, his radiant face lighting the peaceful flow of the years she would spend by his side.

An Egyptian woman, instructed by the magi, did not remain passive before a contrary destiny. She changed its nature. To accept fatality would have been stupid and cowardly. Nagsara had to crush that temple before it came into existence. She would make Solomon forget this obsession, bring him back to her. By the enchantment of her body and the fervour of her passion she would know how to keep him there.

Going to the extreme tip of the rock, out opposite David's city, Nagsara contemplated the Cedron Valley to her right and the plains of Samaria to her left. The beauty of spring in Israel made her homesick for that time of year in Egypt. During that season, the young princess used to go on boat rides along the tamarisk-planted canals of Tanis. She steered the oar herself, playing at chasing families of ducks. In the evening, in the pavilions erected on the small islands, she listened to flute and harp concerts given by female court musicians.

Here, in this wilderness, nature's music sounded rough. Israel was too young a country, lacking that maturity brought by centuries of wisdom. The Hebrews had the enthusiasm of a people lacking experience. They still ignored the serene attitude of the old scribes with rounded bellies, unfolding on their knees the papyri where eternal words lived. The failure of Hiram's work site would teach them humility.

A block of stone, clearly jutting out above the void, caught the Queen's attention. It carried a quarry mark that looked like the sign of the Egyptian Cross of Life, no doubt the work of a labourer who had been in Egypt. One would have expected to find in its place Solomon's seal, two intercrossed triangles, ensuring the perennial duration of a work. The language of the Brotherhood was known only to its members, but they would be powerless before the magic rituals of a Queen.

Nagsara took off her rings and her bracelets. She placed them in front of her in a circle. Then she undid the laces of her sandals and undid her belt, making a second circumference that surrounded the first. Kneeling, she opened her arms and invoked the winds of the four cardinal points, calling on them to disintegrate the rock and condemn it to sterility. As an offering, she threw the jewels into the void. So as to seal the spell she had pronounced, she knotted her laces and her belt, creating a rope linking her thought to the goddess Sekhmet.

A vain exploit, if Solomon were to remain distant from her. Nagsara knew the price of her act. To the terrifying lioness, to Sekhmet avid for blood, she gave up several years of her existence. But would an old woman attract Solomon's love? Wasn't it best to have a brief but passionate life, consumed in the fire of a impassioned love?

Nagsara took off her yellow dress. She laid it on the magic rope. Naked before the sun, she would now shed her blood to seal the spell.

Her fingers caressed the silver-handled dagger that had been part of Tanis' treasure. She had imagined using it to defend herself from the assaults of a horrible King whom she detested . . . and yet it had become an instrument of love, to create an incandescent blood bond.

Nagsara could no longer bear to feel Hiram's name inscribed in her flesh. By piercing it with a blade, by transforming the letters into red tears, she was freeing herself of the horrendous curse that stopped Solomon from loving her.

She struck.

The dagger slipped and the blade slid over her skin, burning a trail. An ochre fog clouded the Queen's vision.

She heard her name. Someone was calling her from the other edge of the rock, begging her not to kill herself.

She still had time to be the victim that Solomon would dearly love. But she trembled. The mist grew thicker. A hand gripped her wrist and forced her to drop the weapon.

Hiram picked up the yellow dress and covered Nagsara. With his foot he kicked the rope into the abyss.

'No,' protested the Queen weakly. 'You don't have the right . . .'

'No one will prevent the birth of this temple. Only a celestial will could be stronger than mine. I will render the curses ineffectual.'

The Queen threw her head back, breathing in life renewed after brushing with death.

'Who are you, Master Hiram? Why do you engrave an Egyptian sign on the foundation stones of the temple?'

'You were not meant to see that mark, your Majesty.'

'As an architect, should you not face up to reality? What if you were a priest? What if you were deceiving Solomon . . .'

'Come, Majesty, these trials have exhausted you.'

'Do you refuse to answer me?'

'I am indifferent to what people think of me.'

Blood seeped through the fine yellow fabric. The mist that clouded the young woman's vision grew denser. She could no longer discern Hiram.

The chasm was so near, so attractive . . . By extracting the ultimate strength from her body, Nagsara needed to take but a few steps to put an end to all her anguish.

'You are an Egyptian,' reminded the Master Mason. 'Too kill yourself is forbidden. By acting thus you would destroy your soul and lose Solomon's love forever.'

'How . . . how dare you . . .'

Hiram supported the Queen and helped her walk.

'You need to see to your wound, Majesty.'

Contact with this man whose strength was so imposing troubled her. Her unease dissipated. The sun again shone through.

'I want to know, Master Mason, I want to know why . . .'

'We are the toys of the invisible. The rest is silence.'

Hiram escorted Nagsara back to the palace. A strange calm spread through her. The fire of the wound ceased, but the mystery remained unbearable. The architect seemed close and yet distant, tender and insensitive. What kind of magic did he possess?

31

Reluctantly, Solomon was forced to accede to the High Priest's request to convoke the Crown's council, bringing together Sadoq himself, General Banaias and his secretary, Elihap. Israel's sovereign felt his irritation grow while listening to the words uttered by the man of the cloth.

'I will tell you again, Majesty,' insisted Sadoq, 'Master Hiram is becoming a dangerous character. Without your knowledge he has gained control over thousands of workers.'

'Is the workforce not Jeroboam's responsibility?'

The High Priest became sarcastic.

'One more illusion! Even with the toilers, the prestige of your architect is immense. They obey Jeroboam, but they admire Hiram. Do you not know that he has created his own community, composed of apprentices and companions who are slave-like in their obedience? You yourself accepted the work site should be a law unto itself.'

'Is that a reproach, Sadoq?'

Elihap stopped taking notes. He approved Sadoq's remarks, but feared that his words had been too frontal.

The High Priest changed his tone.

'Master Hiram extends his empire day after day. Tomorrow he will govern an army larger than that led by Banaias.'

The general nodded. His surly air betrayed his discontent.

'A peaceful army,' enjoined Solomon.

'We are entitled to wonder, Majesty. They are armed with tools that many among them have learned to handle with dexterity. If their master ever decided to encourage rebellion . . . we have misjudged the influence of that Hiram. Is he not the most powerful man in Israel today?'

'You are offending the King, High Priest!'

Sadoq stood his ground.

'Why was that foreign architect not kept under closer scrutiny? Why grant him so many privileges? I speak in the interest of Israel and its sovereign. Is Hiram's prestige not a veritable insult?'

'The High Priest is right. I dislike this native of Tyre,' muttered Banaias.

Elihap still kept quiet, but Solomon knew him well enough to sense that his silence meant he was in agreement with the other two council members.

'You must act,' insisted Sadoq. 'Jeroboam would be an excellent architect.'

'He has only built stables and fortifications.'

'He is a faithful servant, whose nomination would be approved by the council.'

Sadoq was consumed by a dark passion, but his arguments held a certain coherence. Solomon admitted that enthusiasm had made him overlook certain dangers. Perhaps he had misconstrued Master Hiram's ambition. His desire to hold, given the nature of his post, the reins of Israel's economy. Perhaps he had in his own bosom fed a dragon that now prepared to devour him.

Noticing that the King was thinking about what had been said, Sadoq felt very pleased. He had played a dangerous game, but hoped for a happy outcome. Seeing that he still managed to influence Solomon, would he not be able to stop the building of the temple?

'The Crown's council does not govern Israel,' said Solomon at last, 'its role is to formulate proposals. It is down to the King to accept or reject them. With regard to Master

Hiram, he will remain the temple's architect and he answers only to me.'

Solomon spent the night thinking, omitting to visit Nagsara. The Queen, her wound now cured, suffered from a languidness that only the King's presence could heal. Sensitive to her fragile beauty, he accepted the warm shelter of her arms and the passion of her kisses. After the stormy meeting during which he had disavowed his counsellors, the pleasures of love seemed insipid and vain to the King. Therefore, he had retired to David's mortuary chamber, unentered since his death.

Solomon had forgotten the modest bed, the rough walls, the smell of desperation. Even his father's features disappeared under death's thick darkness. Nevertheless, was it not the place where he would meet the soul of the monarch? The King whom God had forbidden to carry out the Work? Should Solomon ask him to provide the necessary help from the world beyond?

Master Hiram was neither of a brother nor a friend. He no longer behaved like a servant, but like the leader of a brotherhood absorbing the life forces of Israel and threatening to lead them astray for his own benefit. Who but a mediocre King would have accepted seeing his throne weakened in this fashion? Despite his hatred, Sadoq's ideas made sense. If David had renounced the building of the temple, was it not because it would lead to an inevitable coup d'état by a horde of workers, who, guided by shrewd leaders, would become conscious of their power? The birth of the building was, nevertheless, linked to an underlying change in Israel, to the existence of a huge work site where every Hebrew would contribute his share.

Was the path followed by David perhaps dictated by wisdom? Should Solomon be content to reign over the present and neglect the future? Should he preserve tradition instead of upsetting the established order? How precious the presence of a father and a counsellor would have been. All around was the dead penumbra of a silent chamber, bearing the traces of death's agony.

Solomon put himself in God's hands. He prayed to Him with all the disquiet of a lost son seeking his home, with the despair of a beggar before whom doors close.

A little before dawn, when the hills became tinted with violet and orange hues, God spoke to Solomon.

He promised to give him a certain sign. The first being he met would give him the answer he required. At that time he would know if he should abandon the building of the temple.

The King left the funerary chamber and stalked the cold, deserted corridors of the old palace. He did not miss the sunlight, avid to know the message of the Lord of the Clouds. That first being, would it be a man, an animal, rain or wind? Would he need to question a stone or the dust of the path, address a bird or someone struck dumb?

An irresistible impulse made Solomon leave that place. Passing between the guards posted at the top of each side of the stairs leading to the square, he perceived a silhouette emerging from the last remnants of the darkness, walking towards the palace.

With his arms extended before him, the walker carried a chest that hid his face.

He must be Yahweh's envoy.

Solomon ran to meet him. The man stopped in the middle of the square and put the chest down.

Solomon recognised him despite the darkness that overshadowed his features.

'Master Hiram . . .'

'I require an audience, your Majesty . . .'

'At this hour?'

'I have just finished the plan of the building that will cover the rock. I must show it to you without delay.'

The architect opened the chest and took out the papyrus that measured about fifty metres and unrolled it over the pavement.

He did it carefully so that the sheets sewn together unfolded properly.

The light of the rising sun illuminated the gestures of the Master Mason, magnifying them as it increased.

It revealed a detailed plan. Inside a vast rectangular enclosure whose long sides were not parallel were set out the sites of a palace, a throne room, a colonnaded room, a treasury and a large temple. Each line was inscribed with the indication of a measurement. Each part of the plan was linked to the other architectural details by lines that formed a gigantic star.

Solomon felt a harmony that was both clear and stable. It was as if he contemplated a living being whose soul he perceived before it took the form of a body. The drawing was much more elaborate than that of a simple sketch. Here, there beat a geometric heart indifferent to human vicissitudes.

God had answered him.

For over an hour, until the first rays of the sun shone brilliantly, Solomon contemplated the plan of the work site. He read it with the eyes of a King, transposing the lines into stones and reckoning the volume. Could it be that that splendour had been created by human hand alone? Had Master Hiram not been inspired by the single God, even if he did not believe in Him?

The architect gave no explanations. Solomon did not stoop to ask for any. He summoned him to the palace for the beginning of the first wake.

Hiram arrived late. The cleaning of the tools and the inspection of the work site had required his presence. Solomon did not mention the offence. His guest refused food or drink.

'I am satisfied with your plan. You are, therefore, going to carry it out. Where do you propose to keep this precious document?'

'In the Planning Workshop.'

'That shed is no longer adequate for someone of your rank.

From now on, you will live in one of the wings of this palace. The work plan will be secure in the royal treasury.'

'I refuse.'

'Why?'

'Whatever relates to the work site shall remain there. The comfort I currently have is quite sufficient.'

Solomon was being defied in his own house. The work site plan was prodigious, but its author was acquiring a stature that surpassed his initial role. Master Hiram's attitude corroborated only too well the High Priest's suppositions.

'As you wish,' conceded Solomon.

In a village lost in the mountain of Ephraim, the heads of the tribes of Manasse and Ephraim, several priests who were traditionalists or friends of the deposed High Priest Abiathar, and some commanders of peasant militias listened to Jeroboam's speech. The red-haired giant, to whom Solomon had entrusted the organisation of the workforce, spoke passionately before an attentive assembly, hidden by the summit of a rocky hill, guarded by watchmen. The gift brought by Jeroboam had impressed his hosts: two golden calves, reminiscent of the famous feasts during which the Hebrews, far from Yahweh, had given in to forbidden pleasures.

'Do you wish to abandon the cult of the single God?' asked a priest.

'Since that unjust power favours the plans of a mad King, why continue to adore him? Yahweh led us into war in the old days. Today, our people are weak and feeble. The true Yahweh does not need a sumptuous temple. The Ark of the Covenant suffices for Him. He is a nomad, like you and me, and avid for victories! Solomon wants to achieve the religious unity of the realm, to become priest to a peaceful God whose world confidant will be the sovereign himself. Solomon is a Pharaoh, not a King of Israel. He will take away power from the tribal chiefs. He will eliminate Sadoq, just as he banished Abiathar. He will raise taxes, ruin the country to feed that accursed temple. We do not have the right to allow him free reign any longer.'

Jeroboam's words bred unease in the conscience of those present. The master of the workforce, to whom Solomon had refused the title of Master Mason, was reaping his revenge.

A servant took from a large barrel a mixture of fig and carob juice that he poured in some cups and offered to the members of the conspiracy.

'Do you wish to take Solomon's throne?' asked the chief of the Ephraim tribe.

Jeroboam lifted up his angular chin. At last, the real theme of this secret reunion was being addressed.

'Israel needs a strong and brave sovereign, not a poet and a coward. Solomon's peace is leading our country to destruction. Egypt will invade us at the first opportunity. Under my leadership, our soldiers will regain confidence and attack the empire of evil.'

When the debate started, Jeroboam was certain he had won the day. Who could fail to see in him a warrior capable of rallying his troops to the fight? The red-haired giant heartily breathed in the mountain air. This province, just like the others, would be his. He would possess that land and make it proud of his proverbial courage.

Deliberation was short.

The head of the Ephraim tribe came towards Jeroboam.

'We shall remain faithful to Solomon,' he announced. 'We shall forget your proposal.'

The plotters headed back down the paths that would take them to the plain. Jeroboam screamed with rage. With a kick he upturned the barrel, and as the juice spilled, reddening the soil, the red-haired giant cursed the cowards who had betrayed him.

32

Anup barked. Caleb called out to a crowd of apprentices and companions. They were all dismayed by the horrible discovery.

It was the sweeper who had alerted them. On the eve of the Sabbath, he had climbed on to the roof of the Planning Workshop, a mere plateau made of clay. Someone had broken through, gaining access to the building whose locked door gave an illusion of security.

Hiram, who had been inspecting the furnaces in Ezion-Geber for the last two days, was recalled to Jerusalem. No one had dared check the dimension of the disaster before his arrival.

The Master Mason put the key in the lock and went into the building that he had thought well protected. The tools, the papyri, the reed pens had disappeared. Livid, Hiram opened the chest where the work plan was kept. The latter had not been stolen.

A strange theft, in reality. Why had the essential been spared? The architect unfolded the precious papyrus, fearing it might have been damaged. His fears proved foundless. He asked the companions to build a new roof with a brick terrace on which a guard would henceforth keep watch.

Anup, pleased to see his master again, tried to tempt him into going for a walk, but Caleb interfered and asked to talk with him away from the work site. Despite his disability Caleb walked quickly, as if chased by a demon. The dog enjoyed the pace and plunged into a bush, emerging from a thicket, sensing the route to be followed. The two men walked for a long time in the countryside until they came to a narrow gorge pieced by a series of small grottoes where the flocks sheltered during the rainy season. Exhausted, Caleb sat down below a wild fig tree laden with huge fruits.

'I am too old for these long walks.'

'I had entrusted you with guarding the work site,' reminded Hiram. 'A theft was carried out. What have you learned?'

'Nothing, alas! That infamy was committed during the night. I was asleep, so was your dog. But I have been your eyes and your ears. Should I now really tell you what I have seen and heard?'

A close heat filled the rocky basin. There was no air. The cripple could no longer keep his secrets to himself.

'King David took refuge here during a palace rebellion. You would do well to do the same and forget about Solomon's temple. Look at these beautiful figs . . . There are plenty of these around here. If you bought me a farm, I would pick them, dry them in the sun and sell them at the markets. We would share the profits and enjoy a peaceful existence.'

Hiram's silence discouraged Caleb to go on in the same tone.

'You insist on building the temple, that's for sure . . . You might as well learn the truth! Among your workers, there are quite a few rascals, liars and idlers. I am even afraid that some apprentices may be associated with that clique. The buildings progress so very slowly . . . No one can foresee the end of the work. People are getting tired. There are murmurs that you are making no progress, that your projects are much too ambitious. The task is not well borne. Some of the companions think they are badly paid and that you do not recognise their merit. Tomorrow, you will be but a scapegoat. Be clear-minded. You are vilified and betrayed. You are less and less popular. Solomon's dream is floundering tempestuously.

Soon, it will be too late to flee. The country is once again succumbing to tribal warfare. No one will be able to avoid disaster. There will be a lot of deaths, countless ones. Leave, Master Hiram. Leave as quickly as possible.'

After nightfall, Hiram verified the boards of the fence one by one. He examined the terrain around the enclosure, looking for signs of the tunnel that the robbers might have dug to enter. He thought they might have used rope ladders.

No traces or signs were found.

'The men, Master Hiram,' murmured a voice behind. 'The solution is the men.'

The architect turned around and stood face to face with King Solomon. Thick clouds hid the new moon. The obscurity of the night concealed the sovereign and the Master Mason.

'You have forgotten that I reign over this country, Master Hiram. It was enough for me to bribe the guardian of the threshold, some supervisors, and to pay a very thin young boy. He broke through the roof of your workshop without any difficulty. What better way to prove to you that the work plan will only be safe under my protection, in my palace? Would you at last accept coming to reside near me?'

The moment has come, thought Hiram. It was Solomon himself who was forcing him to initiate this new stage he so feared. The Planning Workshop would be open to the companions, who would keep their tools and their aprons there and ensure it was guarded night and day.

'No, your Majesty. From now on I will reside in the quarry in direct contact with the stone. Therein lies the solution. Stone is truer than man. It does not cheat whoever shows it respect.'

Solomon did not try to dissuade Hiram. He had been wrong to try to break him with that demonstration of strength. On the one hand, he was sorry to see his ploy had failed. On the other, he was reassured that he had entrusted the temple to a master of such stature. Nevertheless, he was wary of that admiration that weakened him. He alone governed and he would have to go on governing alone. The happiness of Israel depended on it.

The architect worked several nights in a row to finish building the underground room accessible only by a narrow descending gallery. The entrance was guarded by Caleb and Anup. He had given it the proportions of a cube. At the end, there was a niche that reproduced the intermediary room of the great pyramid, a kind of staircase that leading to heaven that the adept had to climb. It went from the heart of the earth and from the centre of the stone, passing an infinite number of visible and invisible doors that took the adept closer to the divine light.

When the ceremony of payment took place, Hiram selected nine companions to whom he did not give salaries, asking them to wait for him. This unusual procedure provoked both fear and envy among their colleagues. What was happening? Were these men being condemned or promoted? Why them and not others?

The architect imposed silence.

Then he led the nine companions up to the grotto. The dog and the cripple formed a rearguard to make sure no one was following.

Following Hiram, each of the elected lowered their head and descended bent forward along the narrow passageway leading to the secret sanctuary lit only by a single torch. They formed a circle around the Master Mason who, removing a sliding and perfectly adjusted stone of his own creation, revealed the cubit and the cane with seven palms.

'Here are the instruments of the masters,' he revealed. 'With these you will calculate the measurements of the temple. I will teach you the Numbers which engender Nature at every moment and whose secret is conveyed by cut stone. Before this, however, you must die to the world.'

Some were reticent. They were all young men who did not have the slightest wish to die.

'Are any of you afraid?'

They each asked themselves if that was the case. Fear knotted their guts, but the desire to have new mysteries unveiled was stronger.

Hiram offered each companion a cup of wine.

'If you are worthy of mastering this knowledge, this drink will give you strength to face these trials. But if you have lied, if you have betrayed, if your word was not pure, you will die at once.'

Their hands trembled when they received the cup, but none of them refused it.

'Drink,' ordered Hiram.

With a knot in their throats, the companions obeyed. One of them felt a terrible burning in his chest. He thought that death had him in its grip. His colleagues remained standing. They looked at each other, happy to have passed the test.

'Lie down on the floor with your eyes on the stone vault,' Hiram took their aprons off and covered their faces with them.

'You no longer belong to the universe of ordinary men. Life and Death confront each other in you, so that death may die and life may live. Your past no longer exists. You belong to the future temple. You are servants of the Task. No other master can impose his law on you. By the rule of the Brotherhood of which I am trustee, I declare you born to Knowledge.'

Hiram touched the cane on the prostrate bodies. From head to foot, it became their axis around which their existence would henceforth unravel. The initiation that the architect had received he now passed on. He had himself experienced the power of that rule of the Master Mason in which the proportions that would create the temple as a living being were inscribed.

An agreeable torpor overcame the companions. It was not sleepiness, but a serene ecstasy illuminated by an orange sun that shone beyond the roof of the grotto. The latter was no longer a stone barrier, but a starry heaven illuminated with such brilliance that it seemed daylight. The adepts enjoyed a deep feeling of wellbeing. They had the impression of moving beyond themselves, delivered from the weight of their bodies. And they heard Hiram's voice revealing the secrets and the duties of the masters.

When they exited from that journey into brilliantly coloured space, the companions had taken on the age-old geometric tradition of the ancient builders and the youth of conquerors.

Hiram helped them up one after the other.

'The norm of Solomon's temple,' he indicated, 'will be the cubit that goes from my elbow to the extremity of my middle finger. You will calculate the proportions using it as a base.'

Hiram gave the new masters a reed measuring fifty-two centimetres that would be the key to the building of the edifice.

'Have we been through death?' asked one of the adepts.

'Personal ambition has been effaced in you. By my side and under my orders, you will act henceforth to transform matter into luminous stone. What has died in you is your mortal side, your selfishness, your smallness. From now on, you will fulfil the role of foremen and you will teach the companions and the apprentices. You will be supervising the work site, calling to work the men serving the chore if their aid proves necessary. I will spend most of my time here, so as to transform the linear plan into volume. During the first wake you will join me and together we will study the development of the building.'

The masters swore on their lives to preserve the secret that they shared.

Hiram's heart was full of joy. With these beings, animated with a new vision, and despite their small number and their inexperience, he would be able to direct efficiently hundreds of workers. Solomon had ventured into the craziest of adventures. He had not perceived the real difficulties it entailed. No doubt, he no longer believed in his dream himself. Nevertheless, Hiram and his brotherhood would make it happen.

33

The peasant woman pushed the handle, thus turning the upper wheel of the millstone on the lower one. For hours, she would repeat the same gesture to grind the wheat. Rubbing against one another, the stones gave off a plaintive noise. It was as if they suffered in their task to nourish dozens of bellies. If the humming of the millstones ever stopped, said the sages, it would be the end of the world. Weary, the peasant woman traded places with a young girl and went home, where she would weave tunics using the distaff and the spindle. A tenth of her production would be requisitioned by Solomon's tax collectors, in accordance with the King's edict. A very heavy toll for the population, but indispensable. To give in order to build the temple, wasn't that a way of ensuring a resurrection among the righteous?

A noise disturbed her. A metallic grinding sound repeated a thousand times over.

Frightened, she abandoned her work and went outside. In that mid-afternoon, a veil covered the sun. A veil whose terrifying nature the peasant woman identified. She screamed in terror, a sound soon followed by a concert of lamentations. Everywhere, work stopped, everywhere people recognised the plague that had fallen on Israel.

Thousands of pilgrim locusts darkened the sun. Flying in a compact blocks, they formed a grey sky, a mobile vault of several tons, the sum total of insects who weighed only a few grams. These monsters, with perpetually agitated antennae, swooped down on the cultivated fields. A locust ate its weight in food daily. Their swarms attacked even the sheep, whose wool they devoured.

Nothing would escape them. Guided by infallible instinct, they spotted fields and pastures, not sparing even an ear or a blade of grass. During the first assault, an old labourer had brandished a fork and killed dozens. But their acolytes bit him to the blood and fiercely set on him until he fled. During the reign of David two newborn babies had been devoured by locusts.

Hiram, who was examining the bases of the columns that the companions were polishing, felt the danger. The years during which the lion goddess had not been correctly invoked, clouds of locusts had threatened to spread famine in Egypt. Only a Pharaoh's magic was able to repel the invasion. For how many weeks would Israel be the victim of these pitiless aggressors? For how long would work on the site be interrupted? Men had not been able to hinder the progress of the Master Mason, but the locusts threatened to do so.

Queen Nagsara, who was resting in her garden, took refuge in her apartment. During the banquets given at the palace in Tanis, storytellers had evoked the year of the locusts. There was no escape, the only thing to do was to take refuge in the houses and hermetically seal all openings.

Solomon, from the height of David's palace, dominated by the rock, rolled up the papyrus on which he was writing a hymn to wisdom. Was the horrible cloud of insects a punishment sent by God or the devil's malediction? Did Yahweh condemn the King's desire? Were the powers of darkness trying to annihilate him? Solomon had the means of knowing it, by questioning Nagsara.

Time was short. The whole population would soon panic. They would blame Solomon for the cataclysm. The King would have to answer for it before God and before his subjects. The High Priest would accuse him of having brought

God's wrath upon Israel, by soiling with an impious building the rock that previous sovereigns had respected.

Nagsara bowed before her master. Just to see him made her unimaginably happy. The Egyptian woman's black eyes shone with fiery youth. Solomon was tender, but did not hide that he needed to consult her magic talents once more.

Nagsara acquiesced. She consulted the flame once again, relinquishing a few months of her existence by doing so. But what could be more satisfying than attending her master's request?

The answer of the invisible was unequivocal. Solomon held Nagsara in his arms for a long time, thus restoring energy to his wife's exhausted body. When she fell asleep, the King used his ruby. The magic stone would allow him to hear the voice of the elements. One of these forces would be sufficiently powerful to fight against the insects.

The countryside of Samaria and Judea had been abandoned. There was not a living soul in the village squares. Jerusalem itself was invaded by clusters of locusts that munched through the rare gardens. Solomon had been praying since the day before. Would his imploring reach the sky, would it be able to pierce the shield of insects that obscured the sun?

When the wind started blowing, lifting clouds of dust on the work site, Hiram was both full of hope and yet distraught. Had the King of Israel found a cure that was even worse than the plague? This violent, fiery breath was no other than that of the redoubtable khamsin.

The temperature rose unbearably. Just to breathe set the lungs on fire. But the khamsin drove the clouds of locusts north. The night that followed their departure was glacial. Numerous workers fell ill. Exhaustion befell those who were not suffering from pneumonia or tonsillitis.

Hiram made them ingest honey and distributed blankets. With the dawn, the scorching heat returned, taxing the bodies even more. An apprentice whose chest was torn by coughing seemed at death's door. The Master Mason, despite his robust constitution, started to feel the first signs of exhaustion. He forced himself to go from tent to tent, encouraging the workers. Fear penetrated his thoughts. Was the spectre of an epidemic emerging from hell, from what he called the valley of 'gehenna'?

While Hiram was talking to a foreman, pondering on whether to ease the work programme for the following weeks, some shouts of joy were heard. What incongruous event could possibly bring them about in these sad circumstances? Hiram went to the entrance of the camp.

Able-bodied or not, the workers and artisans acclaimed Solomon. Wearing his long purple robe with golden fringes, the sovereign inspired respect. The Master Mason broke the ranks of the King's admirers to come face to face with him.

'The wind has brought illness, Majesty. It is imprudent to venture on the work site.'

'The khamsin drove away the locusts. The fields will be saved, there will be food for everyone.'

'Who will be strong enough to work? Whoever spread that destructive breath, was he aware of what he was unleashing?'

'Only God can master the elements,' reminded Solomon. 'Do you doubt that?'

Hiram feigned not to notice Solomon's irony, although he was persuaded that the sovereign had intervened by practising magic.

'Do not expose yourself further,' recommended the architect.

'I have come to heal. Who knows better than I do the demons that wreck men's temples, rip skulls, inflame the eyes, pierce ears, gnaw the entrails, destroy hearts, impair kidneys or break legs? Kings learn how to fight against cramps, abscesses, pains, fevers and leprosy. Bring those who suffer to me.'

No one waited for the Master Mason's authorisation to do what the King had ordered. In no time at all, there was a queue of patients. Those who were most affected were brought by their comrades. On the back of the neck of each of them, Solomon laid his seal.

While he healed, whining and groans could be heard coming from beneath the earth; the demons exorcised by the King seemed to flee into the depths, distraught by the suffering they had caused. Solomon continued until nightfall.

The deep sleep of the peaceful pervaded the tents that night.

The King of Israel and the temple's architect stood facing each other. Like the Pharaoh of Egypt, Solomon had proved capable of relieving illness by the art of the thaumaturge.

'Wonderful victory, Majesty. But a dangerous venture.'

'Not at all, Master Hiram. Why not use the gift I received from my ancestors? Those who have benefited from the imposition of my seal will not know suffering or death during the building of Yahweh's sanctuary. The dangers have been averted. Work in peace.'

'You have weakened my authority. It was up to me to look after these men.'

'You are a builder, not a healer. It would be vain to believe that you would bring the work to completion single-handed. Your mastery of building techniques and of the Art of Planning is absolute. Once again, you are forgetting the men. They are not all able to equal you, or even to assist you. Your fire is too passionate. You are both hated and admired. Thus goes your destiny and you do nothing to alter it.'

'Only Kings have that power.'

'That is true,' recognised Solomon. 'I hope I have proved that you can count on my help. It can be even more effective, if you so desire.'

Hiram's dearest wish was to return promptly to Egypt, to the land of his ancestors. If ever there was someone incapable of helping him, it was Solomon.

'I ask nothing of you but that I control the work site for which I am responsible, Majesty. The rest is not my concern.'

'You are not a God. Illness and suffering prey on you. If you weaken, it will imperil the temple. Why not accept the imposition of my seal and thus protect yourself against attack by accursed forces.'

The stars scintillated in the sky. The insects had gone to spread desolation further afield. The sky was once again limpid and vast. In the silence of the night, a warm wind blew.

'Follow your path, Majesty. I will follow mine.'

'Do they not meet?'

'They cross while this work site is open, then they will diverge.'

'In Egypt, the Pharaoh grants life to those close to him, as well as health and strength. The same is true for me. Why refuse these gifts?'

'I am not one of your subjects, but a nomad who keeps his word. As soon as this edifice is built, it will be done and I will depart. I do not want to owe you anything. Govern your country, I will reign over my work site.'

Solomon did not insist. He had chastened the architect without dominating him.

'Do not forget that your work site is part of my kingdom.'

'Do not forget the men, Majesty. The apprentices, the companions and the masters are subject to one authority: mine. Without that hierarchy, the temple will not see the light of day.'

34

To smooth the passage of trolleys and sleighs bearing the cut stones, Hiram had some ancient houses knocked down, broadening streets that were too narrow. Breaking the labrynthine layout of the upper town, he had created a vast perspective that opened up onto Solomon's palace, dominating David's ancient city.

When the work was sufficiently advanced, the Master Mason guided the King and the Queen on to the site. The austere rock had changed enormously. A multitude of steps led to an esplanade. On the northern side there were the walls of the future treasury and on the eastern those of the throne and judgement rooms. One had to walk beyond the walls of the latter to discover the palace with its numerous rooms leading on to an open-air inner courtyard. The sovereigns contemplated the huge foundations and the five-metre-high blocks of stone polished like marble. Nagsara touched the stone and judged them as perfect as the granite sculpted by Egyptian sculptors. Hiram and his artisans had performed a truly prodigious work, combining solidity and refinement. The apartments of the King and his spouse were almost finished, although still being ornamented with wooden panelling. The cedar beams were set at a six-metre height, giving the sensation of a vast interior. According to tradition, Hiram had separated the King's bedroom from the Queen's, as well as their annexes, their water rooms, lavatories, offices, reception rooms and the entrance hall. To Solomon, the palace's northern wall seemed much thicker than the others. The Master Mason explained that that wall would be adjoining the temple and in its middle the Master Mason would open a door that would connect the King's house to the temple.

Solomon remain cold and reserved. He did not want to show the immense pride that filled him. Never had a King of Israel lived in such a splendid palace to which rooms reserved for banquets and concerts, concubines' quarters, those of the palace staff, servants and guards were still to be added. Hiram had conceived a plan that was as harmonious as it was comfortable.

'From next month onwards, we will come and live here,' decided Solomon.

'The noise of the neighbouring work site . . .' objected Nagsara.

'It will be pleasing to our ears. There will be no other abode for the King of Israel. Let the Master Mason speed up the conclusion of the main rooms.'

Hiram, smiling, bowed.

Solomon's wish was granted. The companions worked without respite on the interior of the palace, under Hiram's vigilant supervision. The masters oversaw the apprentices, the companions and the jobbers at Ezion-Geber and in Jerusalem, both in the foundries and in the quarries, so that the production was continual, especially of the quickly worn copper scissors, and the stones, cut and worked according to the Master Mason's instructions before being numbered and deposited in the warehouses. Jeroboam organised the workforce without complaint. Although his relationship with the masters was distant, he responded to their demands.

At the royal couple's request, Hiram's carpenters had turned out some beautiful furniture. Beds, throne, chairs, tables and chests were manufactured, using cedarwood, olive-wood and acacia. The majority was covered in gold leaf. The lighting would be supplied by torches of differing sizes supported by bronze pedestals, giving out a light that would vary according to their spacing. The ventilation was ensured by an ingenious placement of windows that were easily covered during cold weather.

Despite the insistence of the master of the palace, who was keen on protocol, Solomon had refused to agree to any inauguration before the consecration of the temple. In three years, Master Hiram had managed the easier of tasks, to build the royal palace. Admittedly, it was a brilliant achievement, but the ultimate goal still lay in the far distance.

When the Queen first took up residence in the wing of the palace that was destined for her, the King accepted her invitation for dinner. The young woman, who was entering her twentieth year, had dressed in the Egyptian fashion. She wore a transparent linen dress with shoulders straps, leaving the breasts uncovered, a gold necklace with carnelian stones and lapis lazuli, gold bracelets at her wrists and ankles. Her hair was arranged in plaits and perfumed, her lips reddened and her eyebrows tinted black. How seductive she was, that foreigner, whose eyes betrayed her passion! How she offered herself, with her gracious gestures and her feverish breath!

Solomon neglected dinner. He undressed her slowly and made love to her so passionately and with such tenderness that she vibrated with all her being, as a lyre under the fingers of an inspired musician.

When Nagsara fell asleep, satiated with pleasure, Solomon contemplated her. Naked, abandoned, she was harmonious despite the strange mark on her throat, those letters inscribed there magically spelling out Hiram's name.

Solomon's mouth tasted of ashes.

He could not lie to himself.

He no longer loved Nagsara.

Hiram unwillingly responded to the Queen's message asking him to come and examine her reception room. Busy with transport difficulties involving goods coming in from the quarries, the architect had little time to deal with the whims of a sovereign. From the moment of her arrival, the Queen had complained of the poor quality of certain wood panelling and the lack of finish to a chair with lattice work. Aghast, Hiram nevertheless carried out a thorough examination.

'Are you jesting with me, your Majesty? I can detect no fault.'

'And you, Master Hiram, why are you lying to me?'

A cold fury animated the eyes of the accused.

'I will not allow anyone to insult me in this manner. Your rank does not authorise you to be unjust.'

'If you are as innocent as you pretend to be, explain to me why the plan of this palace so closely resembles that of Tanis? Why are the techniques used so close to those of Egyptian architects? Why, inside these walls, do I feel I have returned to my country?'

Hiram sustained Nagsara's gaze, but remained silent.

'You have saved my life twice, yet I do not know who you are. A native of Tyre, so you say. I doubt it. You have lived in Egypt. Everything in you recalls the behaviour of my father's architects, those men with high foreheads, with a severe demeanour, who often seemed so far removed from the world. Confess, I order you.'

Hiram crossed his arms.

'I understand at last why your name has been engraved on my flesh. We belong to the same race, born of the same land. You are in exile, like me. The gods order me to approach you, as if you were the key to my happiness. But I love Solomon . . . He alone is my life. I want to destroy that inscription that binds our destinies, Master Hiram. I hate it and I detest you. There is but one solution to efface this curse that stops Solomon from feeling a growing passion for me: your departure. Leave Israel. The palace is finished. You have fulfilled your contract. As soon as you are far distant, your name will fade from my throat. My skin will be purified. You are the bad genie who destroys my happiness. Please leave, I beg of you. Leave, and I will not reveal what I have discovered.'

'I have nothing to fear from your revelations,' declared the architect. 'Your imaginings are unhealthy. I have taken an oath that I will build a temple and I will keep my word. Then I will leave.'

'How much longer . . .'

'Several years.'

'That is impossible! The curse will have killed Solomon's love!'

Nagsara threw herself at Hiram's feet.

'I am begging you . . . Do not make me suffer any longer. Return to your country.'

Hiram helped the Queen up.

'A word given cannot be retrieved, Majesty.'

'You really don't understand . . . That mark, your name . . . I cannot bear it any more.'

The architect turned his back on Nagsara, thus not seeing her pick up a dagger and dash at him. But he sensed the danger as a wild animal would.

With his forearms he staved off the attack, averting the weapon's trajectory.

Nagsara dropped the dagger and took several steps backwards.

'Leave Jerusalem or I will kill you,' she promised.

A winter wind had buffeted the rock for several days and nights. The royal couple nevertheless remained in their new palace, now decorated with earthenware objects. Some braziers gave off agreeable warmth.

Violent rains followed the wind. They caused landslides that surprised the cattle breeders used to leaving their flocks grazing the hilltops. Torrents and wadis filled up with a furious current that rushed down the slopes.

The tented camp of the workers residing in Jerusalem was flooded, as was another for the foundries on the banks of the River Jordan. Some men drowned. Among those assigned to corvée duties, the mandatory workforce, there were about one hundred victims. Jeroboam declared he was unable to cope with the disaster. He blamed Hiram for it. The Master Mason did not dodge the accusation. He organised aid with Solomon's help.

The tools and cut stones suffered damage. The main quarry had been inundated and would not be operational for weeks. The earth paths were flooded and impassable to vehicles. Some regions had been cut off.

Sadoq and the priests prophesied the works would be discontinued. Among the populace, people murmured against Master Hiram. The enthusiasm of the first years was waning fast. The temple was becoming a utopian objective. The rock was now occupied by the royal palace. Solomon had stated his prestige. What more could he wish for?

Assisted by the masters, Hiram lit campfires around which the workers gathered. The royal administration saw they lacked neither food nor clothes. The King and the Master Mason joined their efforts. Hiram's words were an efficient weapon; by his warmth and the strength of his conviction, he persuaded his Brotherhood that the work site would not be abandoned and that his plan would be carried through to the end.

Solomon made the same statement to the Crown's council. The people knew the King's will to be inflexible.

When the sun reappeared, the water receded. The work started again. None of the workers healed by Solomon's seal had perished. The return of clement weather was attributed to Solomon whose wisdom God had recognised.

35

Hiram's temperament darkened. That the beauty of the palace served Solomon's glory did not matter, but that building the temple was becoming more and more difficult, prolonging the duration of his exile, certainly did. The men who formed the mandatory workforce complained. Jeroboam voiced their protests: they deplored their miserable living conditions and blamed Hiram as the sole culprit. To calm the growing anger, Solomon had been forced to increase their pay, thus depleting his treasury faster than he would have wished.

Some apprentices had reached the rank of companions. But no companion had become a master. The nine workers elected by Hiram to become masters remained silent as to the secrets they held. To companies requesting promotions and a better salary, they replied that they did not have the power to decided. Only Hiram, if he so judged, could make a master of a companion. An impatient apprentice who had dared insult the Master Mason had been sent back to his village. People thought the punishment severe, but it was not contested.

Hiram allowed himself only one pleasure: country walks with his dog for a few hours a week. Then, he forgot his daily worries and dreamt of a lost freedom and Egyptian landscapes. He communed with the sun and with the air and felt detached from the labour that consumed his life. He fantasised about being a traveller on his way to his native country.

This time, the walk gave him no pleasure. It was like eating a meal without salt. The way the work plan was being carried out did not correspond to the architect's requirements. The resting periods were too long. The workers were becoming lax. Despite his dog's happy leaps and the splendour of nature ready for spring, he could not stop thinking about a new labour organisation. Tomorrow, he would double the number of team workers, recruiting from the men now performing their corvée duties.

Caleb, as usual on the eve of the Sabbath, cleaned the underground room where Master Hiram lived. He had filled the lamps with oil and put on a stone a plate of broad beans, round flat bread and figs. During the day of sacred rest, tradition bade people not to cook and to eat cold meals.

'This Sabbath again,' protested Hiram, who had just taken a bath.

The following day it was forbidden to wash.

'It's our most sacred tradition,' said the cripple. 'We observe it from generation to generation. Did God himself not rest on the seventh day after having completed his creation?'

'I have not finished mine. These idle days interfere with my work plan.'

Caleb thought that the Master Mason's attitude was inappropriate.

'We have to have a breathing space! Are you forgetting that the first man was born on the beginning of the first Sabbath? And that our people managed to flee Egypt on the day of the Sabbath? Not to respect it would be to give very serious offence. My prince, you're not thinking . . .'

'Sweep, Caleb.'

Helped by some workers, the carpenters laid a gigantic tree trunk down on to the ground. The pruning of the branches started immediately. Hiram gave out abrupt and precise orders. There was but an hour left before the beginning of the Sabbath. Jeroboam observed the sky. He waited impatiently for the moment when he would liberate the men from their mandatory duties.

With the first three stars appearing in the gathering dusk, the Sabbath began. The trumpet rang for the first time, enjoining workers to cease their toils. The jobbers yielded to the custom at once. When the second bell rang, the shopkeepers closed up their stalls. At the third ring, a lamp was lit in front of every house, a symbol of Divine presence manifest in the resting of souls. Soon, people would dine. On the menu there would be wine and spices, thrice blessed.

One of the carpenter companions, according to the rule established by Hiram, picked up the cut branches. The work site had to be clean at the end of each day's work.

Furious, Jeroboam picked up a stone and threw it at the companion's head. The latter fell. His blood reddened the earth.

'He violated the Sabbath,' screamed the red-haired giant. 'He deserved to die!'

The workers came between their chief and Hiram.

In the families, prayers for peace were being said.

Solomon had not agreed to summon his tribunal, despite Hiram's insistence. According to several witnesses, the unfortunate victim had committed such a grave sin that divine wrath immediately struck him down. Jeroboam had only acted as Yahweh's agent. Who would have dared punish him?

Before the King, the architect did not repress his rage.

'Religious feasts, sacred rests, inflexible rites . . . in your eyes, do these justify the assassination of an innocent man?'

'He was guilty,' replied Solomon. 'The Sabbath is the sacred moment when God prepares anew, in his rest, the creation of the world. It precedes the Law of Israel and justifies it. Whoever does not respect it knows what he is courting.'

'That companion was obeying the rule of the work site.'

'They could not possibly run contrary to those of Israel. You are responsible for this tragedy, Master Hiram.'

*

The architect walked the deserted alleys on the banks of the River Jordan. The furnaces were cold, having been turned off for a week. Duties had been suspended and the workers, confined to their tents, played dice. On Jerusalem's rock, the activity of the builders had ceased. The royal palace rested enthroned, splendid and quiet.

The accusation made by Jeroboam had been duly registered by the secretary, Elihap, and would result in a trial. Had Master Hiram, in the eyes of faithful believers, despised the Sabbath and trampled on Israel's most sacred values? Wasn't he guiltier than the companion who had been stoned?

The High Priest had supported Jeroboam's complaint in such a way that Solomon was forced to preside over a court of justice. How could one doubt the outcome? Hiram had closed the work sites. He had announced to the masters that their great enterprise would fail. Once the Master Mason was condemned, neither apprentices nor companions would accept another authority. But the architect demanded no rebellion trouble the order imposed by Solomon.

The entrance to the underground room was guarded by Caleb and Anup, that of the Planning Workshop by the masters. Hiram had retired to the solitude they offered, these places he had learned to love, usually animated by shouts, songs and cheers. Their emptiness felt strange.

Only the hammering of tools made them beautiful. Without it, there were but the signs of man's suffering, in the effort to attain perfection.

Hiram did not accept this reversal of fortune. A Master that had come from the House of Life became unworthy of his task in renouncing the Work. Whatever the circumstances and the obstacles, he held himself responsible. He had been stupid, incapable of dodging Solomon's wiles. The King, now that the palace had been completed, had found a way of getting rid of a cumbersome architect.

Change his destiny . . . yes, an Egyptian adept, initiated in the mysteries, had that capacity. He used that immortal spiritual strength which no earthly event could affect. He oriented the mirror of his being differently so that the sun's rays would strike at a different angle. Thus, the course of an existence was modified. But Hiram would not desert the path that had been set before him despite his will. Beyond the order of the Pharaoh and Solomon's will, there was the challenge that Hiram had put to himself. He wanted to build the temple and to endow it with the wisdom that had been transmitted to him and to prove his art in the middle of adverse conditions.

If the ritual of the Sabbath and the intervention of despicable characters reduced him to impotence, and even perhaps to definitive silence, at least they would not have the satisfaction of seeing him flee.

Hiram was preparing himself to appear before Solomon's tribunal when Caleb, joyful, brought him a lamb.

'Look, my prince! It is still warm . . . it has just died. It is God who offers it to us. I need you to brand it with red ink in a place that is not easily discernible.'

'And why?'

'This is a gift from heaven, I am telling you. Brand it. I will take care of the rest. Just make sure you stay alive.'

Caleb refused any explanation. His wish granted, he ran to a destination known only to himself, pressing the dead animal in his arms as if it were a priceless treasure.

Solomon held court in David's old palace. To receive Hiram within the new legal venue was impossible. Legally, the place would only exist after the inauguration of the temple.

The temple . . . Who would build it after the architect's condemnation? How would the Brotherhood that had granted him its trust behave? But Hiram had broken the law. Solomon could not absolve him without denying the very sacred order that gave Israel its life. Was it not the same in the country of wisdom, in that Egypt where divine law, embodied by the goddess Maat, was the intangible basis of civilisation?

The King was compelled to judge and punish an exceptional Master Mason without whom Yahweh's sanctuary would remain but a project. The law of Israel that he had to preserve forced him to destroy the work that would give his reign meaning. A prisoner to his own station, the implacable adversary of him who should have been his friend, Solomon felt that wisdom had abandoned him. In what desert, in what inaccessible ravine had it taken refuge? Why was wisdom avoiding him in this way? Was it not becoming more and more distant from Jerusalem every second, to return to the land of the Pharaohs?

The High Priest was about to vanquish the King. Once Hiram was out of the way, Solomon would take refuge in his palace on the rock, believing he ruled over a people from whom he would become increasingly estranged.

Beside the throne sat Sadoq. Dressed in his ritual vestments, the High Priest ostentatiously held the scroll containing the law. He would recall the importance of the Sabbath. In the name of respect for religion, he would demand Hiram be stoned, guilty of sacrilege and subversion. Solomon would be forbidden to grant any clemency. The architect would pay with his life for the death of a companion who had erred by obeying his orders.

Sadoq had convoked civil and religious dignitaries. They made up the large audience animated by a desire for vengeance against a foreign Master Mason; a man who had invariably despised them. For once, wisdom would not come to the rescue of his royal patron.

Hiram walked towards the judgement room. He was not thinking of the trial's obvious verdict, but of the companion who had been executed before his eyes.

The Master Mason was dressed in a white robe. On his chest, he wore a gold pectoral. In this right hand, he carried the rod symbolising his authority over the Brotherhood.

The master of the palace, with the key on his shoulder, introduced the accused to the courtroom.

As soon as Hiram entered, astonished sighs rose from the audience. Sadoq's expression changed. Pale and tight-lipped, he understood the architect would benefit from supernatural grace. Like himself, all those present saw a materialisation take place in Hiram's very person. He became the master builder of all origins carrying his powerful rod, a mythical figure known to everyone in the room.

Solomon, radiant, realised that wisdom had not abandoned him.

'Take a good look at that architect,' he ordered. 'No one can judge him. It is he who holds the rod with which the builder who comes from the heavens measures the future temple. Master Hiram puts Yahweh's word into action. He possesses the tool for the creation of the temple.'

Filling the threshold with his presence, the architect upheld the prophetic rod. Everyone bowed, with the exception of Solomon.

36

Solomon reread Elihap's reports, filled with rows of numbers. The sums did not lie. The coffers were being emptied faster than had been foreseen. In less than a year, the royal treasure would have dried up and the temple was far from complete. Would the people rebel on learning this?

The one person who would not hesitate to divide the country and encourage the old factions had to be contained. The occasion that presented itself was a gift from God. It found Solomon heading to the capital where the High Priest had just celebrated morning service. Sadoq was surprised. The King had never come to visit him in such a way. Had he finally understood that sovereignty was not exercised without sharing and that he should vow allegiance to the clergy?

The monarch sat on a stone stool. Sadoq sat at his right.

'Do you know the duties of a High Priest well?'

'Of course, your Majesty.'

'You have not, therefore, married a widow?'

'Certainly not!'

'Nor a divorced woman?'

'Majesty . . .'

'Nor an ex-prostitute?'

'Majesty, you very well know that I am a widower and that I have not taken another woman.'

'Indeed, Sadoq. You have not cut the corners of your beard?'

'God forbid! That would be an unforgivable fault.'

'As sinful as drinking wine before the services?'

Sadoq began to worry.

'Would the purpose of this visit be to speak to me about the rituals regarding my position?'

'One in particular. Do you ignore that you are forbidden to eat a dead animal that has not been slain by the knife of the sacrificer?'

'To ignore that would be one of the gravest transgressions.'

'Yesterday, you ate impure lamb.'

'That is impossible, Majesty!'

'I have proof and a witness. You have been imprudent.'

The King did not quote Caleb, the cripple, who had tricked the High Priest after having taken care to inform Solomon.

Sadoq lowered his head. The monarch did not make such accusations lightly. The High Priest risked being dismissed in the most infamous way, the reputation of his lineage forever soiled.

'I will grant you mercy on condition you remain confined to this chapel and that you do not utter another word against Master Hiram. Stop opposing the building of the temple.'

On the rock, masters and companions had once again taken up work, guided by the master plan unrolled on the floor of a new workshop built specifically to house it. The masters deciphered the dimensions inscribed by Master Hiram who each morning revealed the proportions, allowing the workers to proceed from a linear perspective to volume, from abstraction to reality.

As the architect was leaving the underground room for good to go and live on the work site to sleep near the Master Plan, Solomon requested his presence at the palace.

Young servants with lithe bodies brought cups of fresh wine and melting dates.

The architect refused to sit down.

'It is no time for socialising, your Majesty. Too much work has been delayed.'

'It will be even more so should you refuse to listen.'

'Are there new obstacles?'

'The temple is a vast work. The economy of Israel is at its service. The effort made by the people willingly corresponds to the vastness of this enterprise and all the hope it inspires. Nevertheless . . .'

'Nevertheless,' said Hiram, 'the months go by quickly and the royal treasury is running out of resources.'

Solomon had counted on the architect's shrewdness. The future of the sanctuary would depend on his decision.

'A King,' continued the Master Mason,' cannot stoop to ask for the help of a servant. Especially if that King has the reputation of being a sage. You have been too ambitious, your Majesty. Israel has proved insufficiently rich to transform that rock into God's abode.'

Solomon felt like killing Hiram, to choke his pride and his arrogance. The sovereign would go no further down the path of humiliation.

'I only love what is monumental,' confessed Hiram. 'Your adventure has become my own. I will again intervene with the Queen of Sheba's Prime Minister. Let the fields of Israel produce great quantities of wheat and you will once again obtain gold.'

When Sheba's gold arrived at the port of Ezion-Gaber, sailors, soldiers and dockers acclaimed Solomon's name. Had he not obtained the favours of the Queen who had inexhaustible treasures? Had he not convinced her to treat Israel like a privileged ally? Many sovereigns had failed in this endeavour. It was clear that Solomon's success was due to his keeping wisdom at his side. Did it not inspire his thoughts and dictate his behaviour?

Master Hiram kept quiet about his intervention, leaving the laurels to Solomon.

The new debt contracted by the King of Israel made him sullen. The Master Mason never ceded an inch. Nevertheless, he could have taken more evident advantage of the prestige he enjoyed. The priests had stopped attacking him. The populace was afraid of the architect. Certain high-placed civil servants wished to see him named general superintendent. But Hiram never came to the palace. He buried himself in the temple's work site.

That attitude intrigued Solomon. He did not believe the architect had no interest in human affairs. At the head of a strict hierarchy, surrounded by a government of masters who proclaimed their absolute fidelity, Hiram played an ever more remarkable role at the heart of the Hebrew State.

If the construction of the temple was slow, if the work had suffered delays, was it not due to the Master Mason's will? Had the latter not chosen to exchange his knowledge as a builder against such growing power that he would be considered Solomon's indispensable counsellor?

Nagsara's arrival did nothing to lighten the King's mood. For over a month now, he had not visited her. The pleasure he needed he obtained from his concubines, who were silent and docile.

The young Queen, with a jealous and exclusive temperament, would not be able to bear such a situation for much longer. To listen to her recriminations would be unbearable for Solomon. Would she force him to reject her?

Nagsara smiled, radiant. She sat the King's feet, tenderly coiling herself around his legs.

'My love is as vast as the sea,' she confessed. 'My desire to make you happy is as boundless as the waves. The happiness that you expect from me I can give you tenfold.'

'You mean . . .'

'I am carrying your child, my love.'

Solomon picked the Queen up and took her in his arms. The children born of concubines would be but princes without dynastic role. The son of the Queen of Israel would be his legitimate successor, the child conceived by a King of Israel and a Pharaoh's daughter. Thanks to him, the peace policy would last. To this child, Solomon would convey his experience, his vision and his magic. He would teach him to reign and would bestow on him a solid, illustrious and prosperous throne and open up the path of a brilliant empire for him.

An empire in which two fellow countries, Israel and Egypt, would share the world between them.

More than ever, a great temple was necessary. Thus Solomon's fame and that of his son would echo down the centuries.

Hiram was working late with the masters. The building was taking shape in their spirit. Its proportions came alive in the hands of the artisans and exaltation filled their hearts. The Master Mason tried to calm them down and asked them to avoid being impulsive, which would in turn result in vices of construction. He demanded they work slowly and prudently. He insisted on the slightest detail, rectifying projects that seemed perfect.

When the masters were so tired they could not keep their eyes open, he gave them leave to rest. While Caleb cleaned the workshop, the architect perched out on the end of the rock. With his dog crouching at his feet, he meditated in the quiet of the night.

Why had he offered to help Solomon? If the financing of the temple had been interrupted, Hiram would have left Israel and returned to Egypt, but he had fallen in love with his work. The sanctuary would not be Yahweh's but his very own. He would leave the imprint of his signature on it alongside the genius of ancient Egypt. He would transcribe eternal wisdom, endowing it with a new form.

Hiram had become involved. He served neither man nor King, but a being made of stone to whom he offered his science and his life. The Brotherhood was proving obedient and efficient. Constituted slowly over the years, it would have been able to rival one of those powerful State guilds that the

House of Life produced to build the abode of the gods. Almost unconsciously, Hiram had behaved like an architect from Tanis or Karnak, appointed by the Pharaoh to carry out an ambitious building project.

The Pharaoh . . . why did Solomon resemble him so?

37

The northern reaches of the lower quarters of the old town were a den for passing travellers, a haunt for small crooks and dealers. Respecting their own laws, they were careful not to violate Solomon's. Therefore, the royal police avoided the sordid, foul-smelling streets, where at dawn a few corpses were sometimes left lying around for a patrol to make discreetly disappear.

Solomon had refused to raze the miserable enclave to the ground. He preferred to maintain it as a focal point for grievances, rather than spread such evil forces throughout Jerusalem. In this way, he could control them with a minimum of effort.

Elihap, his secretary, did not feel safe there. His head covered by a brown veil, dressed in a dusty tunic, he managed to look like the regulars of the ill-reputed neighbourhood. Thanks to the precise information given by Jeroboam, he found the hovel easily. There the man in charge of the conscript workers waited. He pushed open a worm-eaten door and went down an eroded staircase full of moss, and arrived in a dimly lit basement where the red-haired giant bade him welcome.

'Welcome, Elihap. You were right to trust me.'

'Why did you ask me to come here?'

'I have acted on the orders of one who wants to save Israel.'

Taking hold of a torch whose smoke blackened the

basement's damp ceiling, Jeroboam lit the dark reaches of the room to reveal a thin character with a beard whose corners went uncut.

'Sadoq, is that you . . .'

'You're not a friend, Elihap,' said Sadoq. 'But although you were born in Egypt you have nevertheless become one of us. I know that you no longer approve of King Solomon's decisions. Like us, you have to watch over the happiness of the people that the King is putting in peril.'

Elihap was afraid. Despite himself, he found he was involved in a plot in which he was forced to participate. Jeroboam would not let him leave that basement alive were he to oppose the High Priest's plans. The secretary felt guilty about betraying a King who had saved him from misfortune before going on to promote him to an enviable position. Despite the risk, he should have defended Solomon, showing the dissidents that they were mistaken, convincing them to remain faithful to the King. But Elihap was not a fighter. He had only one life. His powerful protector would certainly give in in the face of adversity and the growing opposition to his policies. Did the secretary have the duty to prepare the future, his future? Was Sadoq not right to intervene in this troubled period during which the monarch saw his power weakened by a foreign Master Mason? Was Hiram not also seeking to dethrone Solomon, to impose the reign of his Brotherhood? Not to oppose this would have been criminal.

'I approve of your plans,' declared Elihap.

The High Priest embraced Solomon's secretary, granting him thus the most significant sign of friendship.

'You are a brave man,' said Sadoq. 'With your help, we will rebuild Israel.'

'What is Banaias' position?'

'The general is a simple man. He knows only how to handle the sword. Our plans must remain secret, our faces unreadable. To let him into our project too early would be a mistake, but he is with us and will obey us when the time comes.'

Jeroboam was jubilant. A glorious path was opening up before him. Soon, he would be King of Israel and head of its armies. Old Banaias would be sent to a provincial residence to see out his remaining days. Sadoq would become a recluse in David's old chapel. Elihap would be condemned for high treason. Jeroboam would then have absolute power and assemble the largest army Israel had ever seen. He would conquer Tyre and Byblos, before attacking the marshes of the Egyptian Delta, overcoming the Pharaoh's troops to enter victoriously the proud city of Tanis.

Thanks to Elihap, he would get to know Solomon's administration as if he himself governed the State. To spy on the King from the very heart of his palace would prevent him being caught unawares. The last obstacle to overcome: Hiram and his Brotherhood.

'How do you plan to act?' asked Elihap.

'You will keep us informed as to Solomon's intentions,' answer Sadoq.

'Watch his relationship with Hiram,' added Jeroboam. 'We want to break their baleful alliance.'

'Their alliance . . .' repeated the secretary, doubtful. 'Is that the right word? Sometimes, I have the feeling that they are as close as blood brothers and that nothing will ever come between them. It is no doubt an illusion. Solomon detests Hiram. His reputation puts him into the shade. When the temple is complete, how will the King be rid of him? Despite the rumours that are circulating and that must be fostered by Hiram himself, everyone knows that the Master Mason will not leave Jerusalem after having concluded his masterpiece. His prestige will be at least equal to Solomon's and he will want to enjoy it.'

'This is why we are going to prevent the birth of that useless sanctuary,' stated Sadoq. 'Solomon will be grateful to us.'

'He will hate us for ruining the project that is to symbolise his reign,' objected Elihap.

'That monarch is a tyrant and he is quite mad,' judged Jeroboam. 'He no longer deserves to rule Israel.'

'Prevent the building of the temple . . . Who would be capable of such a feat?'

'Me,' answered Jeroboam.

Two conscript workers approached the entrance of the work site, bent over. Only a Brotherhood member could go in. The foundations of the temple were almost finished and Hiram admitted no outsiders. Those taking part in carrying out the plan had sworn their trust to the Master Mason and to keep what they would see and hear secret. Their initiation in the Mysteries of Planning would allow them to handle the stones lovingly and place them correctly within the fabric of the building.

Hiram reported regularly on the development of the work, but refused to reveal the techniques used. More and more cantankerous, the architect spaced out his brief encounters with the monarch. The work required his constant presence on the rock, where, behind high fences, the sanctuary grew.

The workers remained stationary. The entrance of the sanctuary was watched over by two threshold guardians, one on the inside, the other on the outside. To reach that point had been easy. Paid by Jeroboam, the soldiers usually blocking off the path leading to the rock had to grant access to messengers from the man organising the conscripts' duties. The rest of the expedition would be harder. Were Hiram's workers carrying out their surveillance rounds? Were watchers posted behind the large blocks piled up near the entrance?

In the blue of the dawn, they watched. The guardian of the threshold, sitting with his legs crossed and crouched over, seemed fast asleep. Detecting nothing unusual, Jeroboam's envoys stood up. One of them approached the sentinel. The other, lagging behind, had given him a torch lit with coals contained in a firebox.

Surprised by the glimmer, the guardian woke up.

'Who are you, friend?'

'A worker who requires to be received on the temple's work site.'

'Go on your way. Master Hiram is not hiring anyone else.'

'I was told the contrary.'

'You were misinformed.'

'This is quite a pretentious Brotherhood . . . Those who harbour secrets are either cowards or plotters.'

'Go away or I will take my stick to you!'

'Take this for your punishment.'

Handling the torch as if it were a sword, the worker lunged and set fire to the guardian's garments. While the unfortunate man rolled around in pain and called for help, the two conscript workers ran away.

News of the attack spread like wild fire. Seriously burned, the guardian of the threshold had been healed at the palace by Solomon himself. The King's magnetism, the balms from Saïs – the city of Egyptian doctors – and poultices made of figs would heal him. Despite investigations carried out by the master of the palace and by the secretary, the two assassins had not been found.

Hiram had firmly opposed the idea of a string of armed guards around the work site. Despite the risks, the members of the Brotherhood would continue to take care of their own security themselves.

The King enacted a decree announcing the immediate stoning of whoever harmed a master, a companion or an apprentice. No one was allowed to venture up on to the rock without a pass, a wooden tablet stamped with Solomon's seal.

The people murmured. Everyone thought that the monarch's dependence on Hiram was growing and reaching alarming proportions. Didn't the King meet all the Master Mason's demands? Was he perhaps becoming a mere puppet in his hands? In fact, Solomon was digging deep into his treasure to finance construction works that were becoming increasingly expensive. Hiram rejected stones with even the slightest defect, knocking down columns whose shaft curve did not have the correct proportions, pulling down walls that did not meet his exacting standards.

To the King's despair, he worked as if he had the whole of eternity to complete his task.

On a cloudless, windless night, Hiram gathered all the members of the Brotherhood. In silence, the builders observed the Master Mason. With the help of a cedar stick pierced at the top by a surveyor's rod, he pointed at the Pole Star. His outstretched arm thus became the cubit of the stars. The foundations were impregnated with the inalterable light from the north. Endowed with life, the stones were no longer subject to the wear and tear of time.

That night, the wine flowed freely on the work site. The artisans shared their certainties and hopes. They were conscious of taking part in a grandiose adventure. Just to listen to Hiram, so close to them as to be almost fraternal and yet so distant due to his science, gave them unending energy. Next morning, forgetting headaches and the need to sleep, they would continue to place the well-measured course stones, to use the drills with flint points, to rough-hew the stones.

The companions polished them with dolerite compounds, ensuring the finish with copper scissors on which the workers pounded with wooden mallets. Quickly spent, the blades were resharpened and the tools replaced.

An order from Hiram interrupted the song of the scissors. The artisans gathered around him. The Master Mason climbed on the highest stone course, which formed a step in relation to the plinth of the temple. At his feet lay several beams. He picked up one and placed it vertically, held up by three pine tree jambs. Then he elevated the second beam and attached it perpendicularly to the first, so that it pivoted from bottom to top. Afterwards he suspended a third beam and fixed it. He tied some ropes. Two masters raised a block and suspended it at the end of the beam close to the axis. The seven other masters pulled on the ropes, creating a counterweight that allowed Master Hiram to suspend, without great effort, a block to the height of the next level to be attained. It sufficed to use a supplementary beam, some levers and slipways to be able to glide the heaviest stones quite safely and then to place them in position with great precision. Thus, before the approving eyes of the Brotherhood, Hiram had just revealed one of the leverage procedures used by the builders of the great Egyptian pyramids.

38

Hiram rolled up the papyrus containing the temple's plan. Carrying it in his arms, he went as far as the end of the rock where the Holy of Holies was to be built. Then he set fire to the sewn-together leaves.

The architect no longer needed a plan. The flames consumed the key proportions and the measurements would remain only in his memory. The building had become the flesh of the Master Mason, his very substance. He would not make any mistakes when guiding the masters and the companions in enacting his designs. Henceforth, the temple would speak through him. The desire to create it burned within him like an insatiable passion. To continue to live, Hiram had to build.

In the orange light that rose towards the night sky, the architect could make out other flames in the distance. Someone, far away, had lit another fire, a strange response to the sacrifice performed by the Master Mason. Hiram, intrigued, left the work site and went along the walls of the palace. The Gihon Spring and the Kidron Valley dominated the city of David. Hiram spotted the place where fire mingled with black and foul-smelling smoke.

Passing through the barrier formed by Solomon's soldiers, Hiram walked up to the edge of this deep and isolated valley. There was a bunch of beggars crouching there who did not seem bothered about the smell of burning flesh.

'Do not go there, Sire,' recommended one of them. 'It's the

Gehenna, Jerusalem's dumping ground. Even thugs like us do not dare venture there.'

'In the old days, innocent people were killed in that place to assuage Moloch's rage. Today, rubbish is piled up along with animal carcasses. The old demons still hover around . . .'

'At night,' said a third beggar, 'spectres devour anyone who enters the charnel house.'

The beggars were not speaking in jest and Hiram took their warning seriously. But an irresistible force impelled him to explore the Gehenna. Despite the lamentation of those poor wretches, he went forward.

It was indeed like going into hell. Filthy debris and mouldy litter offended the eye and one's sense of smell. The architect stepped over a pile of bones. There was a fire shining at the bottom of that valley of despair whose horror forbade human presence. Nevertheless, by the flames, with a singed face, stood a man in rags who laughed dementedly.

'Impure!' he screamed, seeing Hiram. 'You are unclean, only I am pure!'

The madman had his face and hands covered in tattoos representing Moloch and demons with bloody mouths.

'Do not go any further! You don't have the right!'

The shimmer had for a second lit a massive form covered in detritus. The architect stepped nearer.

'Stop! Only a pure being can touch that stone!'

Lost in the heart of the Gehenna, lying on the soil, was a huge block of pink granite. Hiram remembered his masters' teaching. Was this not the stone that had fallen from heaven, the treasure offered to the artisans by the Architect who created men, so that they may build God's sanctuary?

The possessed man stood up. Suddenly his delirium calmed down.

'Do not touch that block, Master Mason! No force, from below or from above, can lift it.'

Hiram did not listen to the entreaties. When his hand touched the granite polished to perfection, he knew that that masterpiece had come from Egypt. Only an adept from the House of Life could have thus polished that black and pink surface.

'Forget that,' exhorted the possessed one. 'Go away. Keep out of this place! Otherwise your work will be destroyed!'

The madman's scream rang in the sky. With a leap, he threw himself into the fire. His rags caught fire, his hairs became torches. He died laughing.

Terrified, Hiram nevertheless felt a terrific joy.

He had just discovered the temple's cornerstone.

After about one hundred men doing their conscript duties had opened a path in the litter strewn in the Gehenna and cleaned the block of its coating of filth, Hiram and the masters tried in vain to move it. It was first necessary to dig deep into the earth and then build solid hoisting mechanisms.

Solomon, accompanied by General Banaias and his secretary, Elihap, came to admire the marvel. He too touched it with respect.

'How do you intend to use this block?'

'As the foundation of the Holy of Holies,' answered Hiram. 'On condition that I can manoeuvre it.'

Solomon turned towards the West, closed his right hand on the ruby and lifted his head towards heaven.

'Where men fail, the elements succeed. Do you feel the power of the wind, Master Hiram?'

A strong wind started blowing, harsher than the Khamsin. It shook the bodies to the point of making them waver.

'I know the spirit of the wind,' continued Solomon. 'I know where it forms, in the immensity of the universe, near the banks of the algae sea. That wind was the one that, obeying the voice of God, opened up the waters of the Red Sea to let my people pass. Today, its strength will be greater still. It will lift up the stone.'

Unbridled, the force of the tempest made Elihap and Banaias take shelter. Solomon stayed upright, as if he could not feel the hurling wind. His gaze met Hiram's when the block of stone moaned, as if it were being ripped out of its shroud. The architect did not hesitate any longer. With a gesture, he ordered the masters to imprison the stone with ropes. One of them went to call the companions. With the aid of that wind gushing from the root of the cosmos and after spilling milk down the towpath, the Brotherhood ensured the cornerstone of the temple slid towards its destination.

Whereas Jerusalem celebrated the feast of the Hasartha[1] when the people ate blessed bread and commemorated the giving of the Divine Law to Moses, Hiram finished choosing the imposing cypress tree trunks that would cover the floor of the temple. Then he verified the perfect state of the olive trees, chosen one by one in the countryside. Those trees, suffused with the sun's energy, twelve metres high and at least four hundred years old, would provide the *prima materia* for the symbolic sculptures that would decorate the sanctuary. The stones cut in the quarries, deposited on granite plinths, formed an imposing cortege, waiting to be inserted in the construction.

The crucial stage was about to begin. For several days, no one had heard the song of scissors, mallets, scrapers or polishers. The iron clanging did not break the work site's silence; meanwhile masters and companions received from the Master Mason the necessary secrets to transpose to space linear print inscribed on the master plan.

Before an enthralled audience, the storytellers proposed one hundred explanations, each more fabulous than the previous, to justify that absence of noise. First of all, thanks to Solomon's intervention, the demons had ceased to undo nightly the work of the builders. Then, by order of the King, these made their amends by participating in the building. Paying homage to Solomon's wisdom, those hostile forces had accepted to help the artisans. Issued from the earth, from the

[1]Pentacost

waters, from the air, from the plains and the ravines, from the forests and the deserts, emerging from the metals hidden in the depths of the earth, from the sap of the trees, from the lightning of the tempests, from the waves of the sea or from the perfume of the flowers, the demons bowed before Solomon who marked them with his seal. Therefore, they carried the blocks and the trunks, the gold and the bronze, gliding them along above the ground. But the most inspired of the storytellers was even better-informed: it was a sea eagle whose vast wings reached from East to West, from South to North, who had brought Solomon a magic stone extracted from the mountain of the setting sun. The King had given it to Hiram, enveloping it in a precious fabric placed inside a gold box. It sufficed for the Master Mason to draw a line on the rock of the quarry and place the talisman on it: the stone cut itself off. All the quarrymen had to do was to carry the blocks to the work site. To adjust them one to the other, there was no need for a polisher: thanks to the gifts of the eagle, they assembled with such exactitude that no joints were necessary.

'We have failed,' concluded Sadoq. 'Solomon and Hiram have never been stronger.'

Meeting the basement in the lower town, far from curious ears, Elihap and Jeroboam were disgruntled. According to the secretary's report, the works of the temple, after five years of detailed preparation, now progressed at surprising speed. Once the foundations were finished and the first stone course had been laid, the cornerstone of the Holy of Holies put in its place, the sanctuary grew according to a new rhythm. As for the King's palace, it grew more beautiful every day. The audience room was decorated. Tomorrow, the Treasury would be built.

The people rejoiced. The effort required by Solomon seemed light. As wisdom inspired the King and lived in his heart, why not trust him completely? What he had promised, he was about to deliver. The proud rock, whose haughtiness had been mastered by Hiram's Brotherhood, had become the servant of God's temple where the light of peace would shine.

'Those wretched artisans are fearless,' complained Jeroboam. 'The attack against the guardian of the threshold should have caused them to disband. What if we tried again?'

'It's no use,' objected Elihap. 'Master Hiram takes away their fear. They are ready to die for him and will not give in to any threats.'

Furious, the red-haired giant hit the damp wall with his fist.

'In that case we must do away with that architect!'

'Far too dangerous,' considered the High Priest. 'He is protected by the masters and the companions. Solomon's inquest would soon find us out. By attacking Master Hiram, we would lose our lives.'

'Must we, therefore, abandon the fight and become resigned to see Master Hiram and Solomon triumph?'

'Of course not, we can still use cunning. Is it not true, Elihap, that some apprentices complain of low salaries?'

'That is quite true,' answered the secretary. 'They want to become companions. But Master Hiram does not plan on granting any promotions.'

'Let us disrupt the Brotherhood,' proposed Saoq.

'Those men have taken an oath,' reminded Elihap. 'They will not betray their master.'

'Every individual has a price,' said Jeroboam. 'Let us be ready to pay it.'

39

On the first day of the feast of the shearing of the lambs and the consecration of the flocks at the beginning of the summer, Hiram gave the Brotherhood artisans a day off. They took part in the banquet organised by the peasants, who still could not get any answers to their many questions on the progress of the work.

The architect did not participate in any festivity. He went walking in the countryside, far from the villages, accompanied by his dog.

In front of the entrance to the work site stood Caleb, furious to have been nominated guardian of the external threshold. The hours seemed to drag on forever! Who would dare ask him to pass, when more than a hundred soldiers, with Master Hiram's consent, were supervising the site until the return of the Brotherhood? The cripple hated solitude. Especially when he was missing the opportunity of eating as much as he could and getting drunk on fresh wine. No one opposed the building of the temple any longer. Each citizen waited impatiently to contemplate its splendour. Caleb would have been more useful filling cups than watching an empty space, sitting in the thin shadow of the work site entrance.

He was first astounded and then frightened to see striding towards him a tall man, coiffed with a golden diadem and dressed in a white robe with a golden hem.

Recognising King Solomon, Caleb started shaking.

'No one . . . No one can enter without knowing the password!' he declared in a trembling voice.

The King smiled.

'My seal gives me access to all the worlds. If you oppose me, I will transform you into a wild beast or a headless demon.'

Caleb knelt before Solomon.

'Sire . . . I have received orders!'

'Are you a member of the Brotherhood?'

'A little . . . only a little. But I do not know anything important!'

'In that case, you will forget that I came. Hold your tongue and get out of my way.'

Did the temple not pertain to the King of Israel? That he saw it sooner than expected, what matter? Even though a cripple, Caleb liked the human form that God had given him. To confront Solomon's magic powers would have been madness. Therefore, he obeyed without delay.

Once over the threshold, Solomon progressed slowly through Hiram's domain. Hidden by the enclosure, the walls of the temple were made of brick covered in wood panelling. The lower part, composed of three courses of cut stones, surmounted by rows of cedar beams, functioned as connection points and ensured the coherence of the whole right up to the summit. Cedarwood beams, linked to the wall by diagonal master beams, formed a strong roof that would bear the weight of terraces. The construction gave an impression of grace and serenity. The architect had known how to convey, in the lines of the building, the most secret of Solomon's thoughts, his ardent desire for the peace he wanted to reign over the world.

It was impossible to go inside, for planks and blocks of limestone barred entry. Frustrated, the King ventured into the part of the work site where the tools were kept and where Hiram's workshop was. The silence of a place usually so animated made him feel imbued by a strange wellbeing. He had the feeling of collaborating in the work of the sculptors, of perceiving the beauty of their gestures, of sitting near them during their evening rest. In the absence of the artisans, their spirit continued to transform matter as if the work went on alone beyond men.

The Planning Workshop . . . That part of his realm was forbidden to him. In this modest building, the sanctuary of Yahweh was being conceived. Solomon could not resist the temptation to push on the door.

It opened.

On the threshold there was a miniature door made of granite. On the jamb, an inscription read, 'You who think you are wise, continue to seek wisdom.' On the ceiling, five-pointed stars alternated with winged suns. On the floor was a thirteen-knot string surrounded by a silver rectangle. In the angles of the room, there were jars and pots containing T-squares, cubits and papyri covered in geometric signs. On the end wall, a second inscription: 'Don't burden yourself with earthly goods; where your steps are taking you, if you are one of the just, you will lack nothing.'

Solomon meditated for a long time in the interior of the workshop. Hiram had made fun of him, wanting to teach him a lesson. By designating Caleb as a guardian, the Master Mason knew the cripple would present no obstacles to the curiosity that would necessarily draw the King to the deserted workshop. Words and objects had been set out ready for the eyes of any indiscreet visitor.

The vanity of a tyrant would have been cruelly wounded, but Solomon came through the trial finding a feeling of belonging to a Brotherhood that, instead of demeaning him, exalted within him his love of wisdom.

He too would have loved to handle the tools, live within the warmth of a fraternity, attach himself to the perfection of a finished work.

But he was the King, and no other than himself could walk the path that God had drawn.

*

A son was the crowning glory of old men. It was like a young olive tree called to grow under a luminous sky. It was an arrow in the hands of a hero. It was the reward of the sage. Indeed, a son heralded a blessing.

The Queen of Israel was about to give birth to Solomon's son, helped by several midwives who had placed her on the birthing chair. The King imagined the delicious moment when he would hold in his arms the small body. The newborn infant would be bathed and scrubbed with salt, enveloped in swaddling bands before being shown by Solomon to a large crowd who would cheer. The monarch thought dreamily of the circumcision ceremony. The priest would perform the removal of the prepuce with precision and would put on the wound a poultice of oil, cumin and wine. The father would take his son on his lap and, calming the pain with his magnetism, he would speak to him of his future as crown heir. He would teach him that to be indulgent towards one's child bode no good. Folly and ruin would prey on the one whose father did not guide him towards heaven.

Nagsara's cries disturbed Solomon. The young woman suffered because of God's punishment, a sentence that would weigh on human birth to the end of time.

Then came the delivery.

A midwife presented the newborn to Solomon.

The King rejected it.

Nagsara had not given him a son, but a daughter.

The mother, considered impure, had to remain in isolation for eight days. She was forbidden to leave her room.

Nagsara could not stop crying. How could she be forgiven? By giving Solomon a son, she would have reconquered her spouse's heart. That little girl, that her mother had not even wanted to see, insulted the magnificence of the King of Israel.

When Solomon consented to visit her, Nagsara begged his forgiveness.

'Let us forget this misfortune, my master! I swear to you that I will conceive a son!'

'I have other worries. Rest, Nagsara. You are exhausted.'

'No, I feel strong. I want to get up and serve you.'

'No follies. Give yourself up to your servants' care.'

'It is your care that I need.'

Solomon remained distant.

'The country's administration requires my constant attention.'

The throat of the young woman tightened. She refused to believe in the decline that awaited her.

'When will I see you again?'

'I don't know.'

'What do you mean? Are you rejecting me?'

'You are a Pharaoh's daughter and my wife, by your presence Siamun linked Egypt's destiny to that of Israel. I will not break that union, nor ours. I will never reject you.'

A hint of hope lit up a very dark sky. Nagsara became passionate.

'So, your love has not died . . . allow me to stay by your side. I will be quiet, more impalpable than a shadow, more transparent than a ray of sun, sweeter than the autumn breeze.'

Solomon stretched out his hands to Nagsara who kissed them passionately.

'I do not have the right to lie to you, Nagsara. I have loved you, but that flame died. Passion went away like a horse seduced by the open spaces. Like my father's, my desire goes from hill to valley, from slopes to summits. No woman will imprison it.'

'I will vanquish my rivals! I will tear them up with my nails and will throw them to rot in the refuse of Gehenna!'

'Appease that fever, my wife. Hate does not nourish love.'

'All that matters to me is your affection. All my strength will be geared to conquer it.'

'You will have all my respect, forever.'

'That will not suffice, it never will.'

Solomon moved away. How much he would have loved to feel the same passion as the young Egyptian! But what human being could compete with the temple? It was the one thing that filled the King's heart, the only love he felt. Pleasure was only passing exaltation and a distraction for the body. The temple absorbed the whole being of the King of Israel.

When he left the room, the Queen, despite her weakness, decided to consult the flame. How many years of her existence would it steal from her this time, to tell her the truth?

At the end of her clairvoyant session, Nagsara fainted. She remained unconscious for several hours.

Upon waking, she knew.

It was not the face of a rival that she had perceived within the bluish orange shimmer of the supernatural flame, but a gigantic monument dominating an overjoyed city.

Nagsara saw Jerusalem's temple, Solomon's temple.

Thus, Yahweh's sanctuary killed all of Solomon's tenderness for the woman who was offering him her life.

How could she fight a being made of stone which, day after day, became more powerful, if not by striking the one that made it grow, Hiram, the architect?

It was to the goddess Sekhmet that Nagsara would turn. She who was the terrifying one, the destructive force, the propagator of illness.

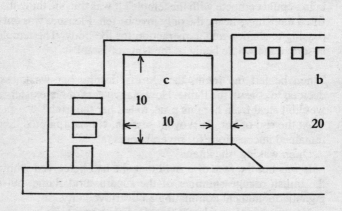

c *Debîr* – Holy of Holies ▬▬ b *Hêkal* – Sacri

(Measurements expressed :

40

'The temple is finished,' declared Hiram. 'My Brotherhood has been working on this masterpiece for more than six years. I offer it unto you this day, King of Israel.'

Solomon stood up and descended the steps of his throne and faced the architect.

'May God protect his servants. Guide me to His abode, Master Hiram.'

Side by side, the two men left the palace, crossing a large courtyard bathed in an ardent sun before penetrating the sacred area via a passage that linked the King's house with Yahweh's.

They stopped before two bronze columns, ten metres high, bearing bronze capitals both ornamented with pomegranates.

'Those columns are hollow,' indicated Hiram, 'and they do not support anything other than the fruits containing creation's thousand and one riches.'

The Master Mason thought of the tree that had sheltered Osiris' corpse. He had resurrected and vanquished death. To those who approached the sanctuary, as in Egypt, the two columns, analogous to the obelisks that preceded the entrance pylon, would announce to the world the obligatory death of appearances symbolised by the passage through the vertical trunk, to be reborn in the shape of a pomegranate, before bursting like a ripe fruit in the wonderment of the sacred.

Solomon approached the right column and marked it with his seal.

'God will establish his throne here forever more,' he declared. 'That is why I name you *Jakin*[1].' Then he did the same with the left column.

'In the strength of God, may the King rejoice! That is why I name you *Booz*[2].'

For the monarch, the two columns rising to heaven were like the Tree of Life, whose splendour lit up the universe. He had dreamed it and it had come true. By his genius, Hiram rendered possible the return to Paradise, to the blessed place that existed before the Fall and prior to sin.

Beyond that frontier, there was a vestibule measuring ten metres wide and five metres long, empty of all objects. The walls were adorned with sculpted flowers, with palms and winged lions gilded in gold shining in the bright light. Hiram had thus emulated the room of an Egyptian temple that preceded the secret sanctuary.

'This place will be called the *ulam*, "The One that is in front",' decided Solomon. 'Here the priests will purify themselves.'

This narthex was closed off by a wooden partition. In the middle, there was a heavy door in cypress wood that the King pushed open.

He discovered a large room, twenty metres long, ten metres wide and fifteen metres high. Windows with stone bars admitted a dim light. As Solomon's eyes adapted, he noticed the walls covered in cedarwood panelling, gold flower garlands and palms. On the lintel, there was a triangle. The floor was covered with wooden cypress parquet.

Hiram had placed five gold chandeliers to the left and five to the right of the entrance. On either side of the centre stood a gold altar and a bronze table. Thus he had crossed the middle

[1] Ritual wordplay on the term 'establish, erect.'
[2] Ritual wordplay on the term 'strength'.

room and the offering room, where the Egyptian Pharaoh held the ritual ceremonies.

Solomon took off his shoes.

'Whoever enters this place, the *hêkal*, will walk barefoot. On the altar, incense and perfume will be laid out so that God may partake of them daily, thus nourishing himself on the subtle essence of matter. On the table, the offering of twelve breads will be laid out.'

At the heart of the Holy of Holies was a chandelier with seven branches[1] whose light symbolised the essence of the mystery of spiritual life.

Solomon went from surprise to surprise. Not only had Hiram created the perfect temple, but a spirit spoke through the King, dictating the words that named the parts of the building.

He stood still by the curtain that separated the *hêkal* from the final room of the temple.

'Is it immersed in darkness?'

'No light penetrates it,' answered Hiram, who had taken inspiration from the *naos*, the secret site where the Pharaoh communed with the divinity.

Did the Scriptures not reveal that Yahweh demanded He reside in total darkness? Solomon lifted the veil. Hiram prevented it from falling again. The monarch could thus contemplate the inside of that enormous ten-metre-long stone cube without windows.

'Here is the *debîr*,' he murmured, 'the sacred room.'

The walls of the Holy of Holies were covered with gold from Sheba, forever invisible to the profane. Only the King or his delegate the High Priest could enter the sacred place.

The floor was clearly elevated in relation to that of the other rooms, according to the Egyptian canon that established that

---

[1] During the sack of Jerusalem, the legionaries of the Roman Emperor Titus considered this chandelier as the prize item of the pillage. It symbolised the mystery of the universe and the knowledge of its laws.

the earthly floor should rise towards heaven and the celestial roof should be inclined towards the earth.

Beneath that space had been placed the gigantic block of granite that had fallen from heaven.

'Here the Ark of the Covenant will be kept,' decided Solomon, 'the reliquary that maintains the presence of God among His people.'

The King turned towards Hiram.

'Leave me alone now.'

The curtain fell.

Immersed in the darkness of the Holy of Holies, Solomon relished the peace of the Lord. In that moment of wholeness, at the heart of the silence and seclusion that the invisible light of God demanded, the monarch felt he had reached the culmination of his reign. What he had hoped for, not for himself, but for the glory of the One God, had become reality. At the end of the path, there was that implacable and serene void. From now on, this was where Solomon would come to invoke wisdom.

When he left the temple, the King was dazzled by the sun. What he saw so astonished him that he thought he was hallucinating.

On the forecourt, not yet paved, stood two winged creatures with human heads, five metres high. Made of olive tree wood, covered in gold, they resembled the sphinxes that guarded the alleys leading to the Egyptian temples. Master Hiram had however endowed them with Solomon's features.

'Here is the masterpiece of the masters,' said Hiram.

Solomon scrutinised the amazing sculptures. Not a fault tainted their magnificence. Who else but the Lord of the Heavens could contemplate these angels that the Scriptures called Cherubim?

'Let them be placed in the Holy of Holies,' decided Solomon, 'and may they disappear from human sight. Their wings will protect the Ark of the Covenant. They will incarnate the breath of God. In their flight, they will carry the souls of the just.'

The King again admired the two columns, travelling down the middle of the temple in his mind.

'Can we proceed with the inauguration, Master Hiram?'

'The forecourt and the annexes are not finished.'

'Are they so necessary?'

'Don't you think they are indispensable? Without them the temple would be incomplete.'

Salomon calmed his impatience. Master Hiram was right.

'Furthermore,' added the architect, 'there is another task, a unique one, which I would like to begin. All the Brotherhood will work on it, helped by the foundry workers.'

'For how long?'

'A few months, if you give me your full support.'

'How could it be otherwise, Master Hiram? If words could express . . .'

The King stopped. To thank the architect for having fulfilled his contract would have been demeaning. A monarch did not have the right to express a feeling of gratitude to his servant, even if he was a Master Mason. Solomon would have liked to manifest his friendship for this cantankerous architect and share with him his worries and his hopes, but his rank forbade it.

Sitting between the columns, Hiram watched the sunset. Exhausted, the members of the Brotherhood rested before again starting work. This final phase would be very dangerous. The architect would take all necessary precautions to avoid putting the lives of his artisans at risk. He had to make a sacrifice in order to succeed, but this would require help. To see any one of his work companions perish was unbearable to him. Nevertheless, it was impossible to relinquish the idea that had grown within him. To crown the temple and to purify himself of the superhuman effort carried out during his long years of exile, his vision must be translated into form.

Hiram regretted that his meeting with Solomon in the temple's forecourt had been cut short. He would have liked to express out loud the admiration he felt for a king so devoted to God, to manifest a friendship born of so many trials. But Solomon reigned over Israel, and he ruled over his Brotherhood. The monarch had not handled the tools, spilt his sweat or scratched his hands. He would never be that Brother both in pain and in joy. What they had carried out, the King and himself, was larger than both and did not bring them together.

With the last rays of the sunset, Hiram wandered around the work site. In a few days, he would dismantle the Planning Workshop. The work and the labour of the builders would be erased from History. The edifice they had created no longer belonged to them.

The foot of the Master Mason hit a limestone fragment hiding a hole. Forced from his shelter, a black scorpion ran away, looking for another hiding place.

The scorpion of the goddess Selket, the divinity that choked the throat, stopped the air from passing and prepared the onset of death . . . Was the killer with the dark coating an omen? What demise could he be announcing?

41

'I demand a death sentence,' said Sadoq.

'Why such severity?' asked Solomon, astonished.

'Because your spouse is guilty of practising black magic. Several priests saw her paying homage to false divinities, lighting a candle in full daylight and pronouncing incantations before falling into an impious trance. In Yahweh's name and before the Law of Israel, I request that this be an exemplary court case. No one is above justice.'

Sadoq was not feigning anger. Apart from the hatred he bore the Egyptian, there was a High Priest's demanding faith.

'Are your witnesses ready to testify before me?'

'They are, your Majesty.'

'The accusation will, therefore, be formulated.'

Solomon knew that the populace murmured. At the city gates, where the markets were held and where the daily workers were hired, the faithful, scandalised by the Queen's behaviour, demanded she be punished. The conversations on the subject were animated, tongues wagged. When Yahweh was about to enjoy the most beautiful temple ever built, how was it possible for a foreigner to defy Him with pagan rites?

If wisdom assisted Solomon in his enterprises, was he not harmed by the presence of a she-devil by his side? Was Nagsara not responsible for all the ills that plagued the elderly, for the premature death of newborn babies, for the drought by the Khamsin wind, for poor harvests and for harsh winters?

Was she not hand-in-glove with the demons of the night and the clouds of insects? The judgement of the people had already been declared: Nagsara, the Egyptian, should disappear.

The Planning Workshop had been dismantled. The forecourt was taken up with the workers laying the pavement. Master Hiram once again went back to live in the underground room, accompanied by his dog and Caleb. The cripple, who did not like the atmosphere of the temple's site, devoted himself exclusively to his tasks. He now had the opportunity to shine again by preparing excellent dishes that the architect appreciated almost as much as Anup.

By using fragments of limestone that he mashed between his fingers after using them, effacing any trace of his work, Hiram drew plan after plan, ceaselessly improving the working drawing of the *magnum opus* that was to be built on the sacred space and make Solomon's temple famous for centuries to come.

Caleb served Hiram grilled lamb cooked with rosemary. Despite the disapproval of the cook, the dog was given a good portion.

'Is there a chance that the Queen might be condemned?'

'Solomon does not have a choice,' answered Caleb. 'There are numerous witnesses, tongues wag, the Egyptian has been practising black magic for too long.'

'What sentence might she incur?'

'Stoning.'

'How can she defend herself?'

Caleb thought it out while sipping a cup of wine.

'There might be a way . . . a very old ritual . . .'

'Which one?'

'The trial of the bitter water. The accused has to drink a horrible mixture composed of dust, animal excrements and plant refuse. If she vomits, her guilt is proven. The punishment is inflicted immediately. If not, she is judged innocent.'

'Perfect.'

The cripple frowned.

'Perfect? What does that mean? The execution of a woman would make you happy? That is not like you.'

The architect remained silent.

The Queen of Israel, informed by Solomon's secretary that she must appear before the royal court accused of practising black magic, remained a recluse in her apartments in the new palace. She had not been able to reconquer her husband. The goddess Sekhmet had not had time to rescue her. Although she had exhausted herself in consulting the flame, Nagsara had not found a way of destroying Hiram and sending him to the nether world. That realm which, sentenced by the man she loved, she would soon enter.

Nagsara did not want to die. She possessed sufficient strength to continue fighting, enough magic power to vanquish the whole of Israel. Her imprudence ruined any chance she might have. To this disaster was added the humiliation of having to see him whom she most detested, the architect of the temple. Through Caleb, he had asked for an audience. First, she thought of refusing and then had thought better of it. Was it not the opportunity to kill evil by plucking it out at the root?

When Master Hiram entered, Nagsara tightened the grip on the dagger she had hidden in a fold of her dress.

'Do you come to persecute me further?'

'I have come to help you, Majesty. I know the cruel destiny that may await you. As soon as the accusation is formulated, demand the trial of the bitter water.'

Hiram described it in detail to the Queen.

'Why should I obey you?'

'To save your life.'

'Strange solicitude.'

'I find injustice unbearable. You are accused only because you are Egyptian.'

'What do you know about it?'

She approached the Master Mason.

'I have practised magic and I will go on doing so. I want Solomon to love me. If my behaviour shocks you, condemn me, like the others!'

She could draw the weapon, strike, strike again . . . Simple gestures, sudden, precise, and she would be free of the demon that prevented her happiness.

'I repeat, Majesty, I have come to help and not to judge you.'

'I do not understand . . .'

'Pour into the bitter cup the potion of purple aloe contained in this flask. This tincture will stop you vomiting.'

Disoriented, Nagsara threw the dagger on the floor. Hiram did not even look at the weapon that was meant to kill him.

'May the gods protect you, your Majesty.'

The Queen listened without protesting to the accusations formulated by Sadoq. She looked in vain for a smile on Solomon's lips, a glimmer of warmth in his eyes. He remained cold and distant, content to preside over Yahweh's court.

Sadoq called the witnesses for the prosecution.

The Queen did not contradict them. After their statements, she demanded the bitter water trial. The High Priest, certain of the result, made no objection. Before drinking, her back turned to the court, Nagsara poured the antidote. Fear took hold of her. Had Hiram given her poison to speed her death and avoid her lapidation? Had he played the most terrible trick on her?

She gulped the mixture down.

An atrocious taste invaded her mouth. Fire burned her entrails.

But she did not vomit. After greeting Solomon, she passed before Sadoq with her head held high.

While the people acclaimed Nagsara, judged innocent by God's will, the High Priest gathered his allies, Elihap and Jeroboam. After this new failure, Sadoq felt like giving up.

The fight was too unequal. He too believed now that wisdom inspired Solomon's thoughts and acts. Whoever stood against him was defeated. Did reason not recommend the High Priest be content to fulfil his function and serve his King faithfully?

'I have excellent news,' said Jeroboam effusively. 'Several apprentices are very disgruntled with their lot. Master Hiram treats them like slaves. He imposes ever more work and refuses to raise their pay. Their lodgings are filthy hovels.'

'Are you not responsible for that?' asked Elihap, astonished.

'Yes,' admitted Jeroboam happily. 'But I convinced a group of discontented workers that I was only following Master Hiram's orders and that he despised the apprentices. A rumour is spreading in the Brotherhood. The architect intends to create an extraordinary masterpiece that would crown the temple. To accomplish it, he needs all to collaborate, even the casters from Ezion-Geber. If we foment a rebellion among the apprentices, we will ensure his failure and his fall will engender Solomon's.'

Sadoq shuddered. The hatred that Jeroboam felt for the King made him jump to conclusions. But to weaken the Brotherhood and Master Hiram would indeed be a considerable result.

'Have you paid those men?'

'Some apprentices refused, others accepted . . . In time, I will buy them all and Master Hiram will think he reigns over a Brotherhood that belongs to us.'

Sadoq remained sceptical. The companions and masters would know how to explain that a few mediocre members would not affect the coherence of the group. Master Hiram's prestige was too deeply rooted to be tainted by some malfeasant insect bites.

'Can you embezzle a part of Solomon's treasure?' Jeroboam asked Elihap. 'The better we pay, the more partisans we will have.'

'That may not be necessary.'

The red-haired giant grew angry.

'Would you be against my plan?'

'Fate will fulfil it by ensnaring Master Hiram in a curse.'

'I have another piece of good news. In the lower part of town, a worker has just died of dysentery.'

42

Summer made people's throats dry. The scorching heat exhausted the most robust organisms. Five workers had fallen ill with dysentery. More than one hundred had been affected. Clouds of mosquitoes, coming from marshes close to the River Jordan, had invaded Jerusalem. Dust, swirling in the scalding winds, penetrated people's eyes, causing numerous eye infections.

The doctors were unable to produce sufficient quantities of eye drops made with antimony. To those whose guts were tortured by demons, they prescribed herbal teas made with rosemary, rue, and juice extracted from palm roots.

About twenty apprentices asked to see Master Hiram. Anup growled. Caleb answered that the architect was working on the plan for his masterpiece and that he would summon them soon. But at the insistence of their leader, Caleb consented to disturb Hiram.

The latter left his work and went to see his apprentices. His angry face imposed silence on the workers' ranks.

'What does this mean? Would you have forgotten our hierarchy? Do you not know that you must address your requests to the master in charge of your guidance?'

The leader, a young man of about twenty years of age with frail shoulders, knelt before the Master Mason and threw several silver coins on the floor.

'Only you can intervene. Some men are trying to bribe us,

we will resist. But why should we live in such sordid quarters? Are we considered to be sick animals?'

'Is it not Jeroboam who is in charge of your lodgings?'

'He says he is following your orders. We would prefer to live in the tents. He has made us move, invoking your authority.'

Thus, even inside the Brotherhood, Hiram's name could be used for evil purposes. The brotherhood that he had built up was turning out to be quite fragile.

'Take me to your lodgings. I want to see them for myself.'

Hiram was shocked when he found out the truth. The apprentices had been stationed in the low houses, without air or light. The walls were mouldy and full of red holes where there were masses of cockroaches. The ones who were ill were lying on filthy straw mats.

'Leave these hovels immediately,' ordered Hiram, 'and return to the tented camp.'

When the Master Mason tried to leave the capital by its main gate to return with haste to Jerusalem's temple, he was faced with a vociferous crowd of workers. Some were calling for a strike. They complained of insufficient salaries, late payments and unhealthy food.

Hiram plunged into the middle of the group. He let them scream themselves out. No one dared touch him. The rebellion calmed. When the clamour died down, the architect spoke.

'Your claims are just,' he recognised. 'Where is your leader?'

'Jeroboam is travelling in the provinces,' answered an old man. 'You are our leader! You are responsible for our misfortune.'

Tension immediately went up again. Some insults were heard.

'Those who slander their master are unworthy of the work they are entrusted with,' said Hiram. 'You do not belong to my Brotherhood, but to the workforce that Jeroboam is in charge of. I will not address you but the King. As Master Mason, I will obtain that which must be granted to you. If any of you doubts my promise, let him throw a stone in my face.'

The circle of workers opened up.

One of them shouted: 'Glory to Master Hiram!' followed by hundreds of others.

'If I have called a meeting of the Crown Council,' explained Solomon, 'it is to examine an important document that I have just received.'

All Jerusalem was talking about Jeroboam's dismissal, requested and obtained by Master Hiram, who was in turn nominated head of the labour force. The power of the architect grew even further. After he had granted the demands of the workers, his popularity was almost equal to Solomon's. The council members were convinced that the King had summoned them to study this dangerous situation. But that was the least of the King's concerns.

'Here is the letter that I have received,' said the King. *'To my Brother Solomon, the powerful King of Israel, from his Sister, the Queen of Sheba. The trees that grow in my country were planted on the third day, in the purity of creation before humanity's birth. The rivers that irrigate my lands spring from Paradise. The natives of Sheba do not know war or how to handle the sword. It is as a messenger of peace that I am writing to you. I have sent you my gold, for you wished to build a temple. Today, I would like to contemplate it, to know to what end the riches of Sheba have served. Will my Brother invite me to visit his court?'*

Sadoq, Elihap and Banaias were astounded. Solomon was definitely blessedly fortunate. Never had the Queen of Sheba left her country. And lo and behold, she proposed to enlighten Jerusalem, the son of David's city, with her presence!

'May that woman bow before you first,' demanded the suspicious General Banaias. 'She forgets that all sovereigns on earth must pay homage to your wisdom. If she refuses, my army will be unleashed on her.'

Solomon pacified the warrior.

'Let us welcome the peace that she is offering. Her voyage will be a homage to Yahweh.'

'Be wary of that woman,' recommended Sadoq. 'If that Queen purifies herself in the rivers of Paradise, if she nourishes herself on the fruits of trees born before the Fall and sin ever existed, if her riches are the most abundant, would her wisdom not surpass yours?'

'I will take the risk,' indicated Solomon. 'Do you have other objections to the arrival of the Queen of Sheba?'

The three members of the Council remained silent.

'There is only one other person that I must consult. Be ready to write an answer, Elihap.'

Solomon met with Master Hiram just before his departure for Ezion-Geber. The two men walked side by side on the large paved road linking Jerusalem to Samaria.

'Yahweh is rewarding us with a miracle: the approaching visit of the Queen of Sheba. The Crown Council has given its approval. What is your view on the matter, Master Hiram?'

'You are the ruler of Israel, Majesty.'

'Do you wish the Queen to be present for the inauguration of the temple?'

'As I see it, it would be a mistake. That moment is reserved for a dialogue between the King and his God. No foreign monarch should disturb it.'

'A wise precaution,' recognised Solomon. 'For when would the Queen's arrival be scheduled?'

'When the temple has been inaugurated, when the palace and the annex buildings are finished. Then the King of Israel will be able to show a completed work.'

'How long will that take, Master Hiram?'

'In a year, Majesty.'

Jeroboam gave vent to his rage. His post as head of labour was lost, he resumed his post as manager of Jerusalem's stables.

The apprentices had simulated a betrayal to warn Hiram of the plot that was being woven against him. The attempt at fomenting rebellion. Hiram had used the incident to his advantage.

The architect seemed as untouchable as the King. A divine protection benefited both men.

'You should be satisfied with your fate,' observed Elihap. 'While demanding your dismissal for incompetence, he nevertheless appealed for clemency for you.'

'I have been ridiculed in the eyes of a flock of sheep that I commanded yesterday!' roared the red-haired giant. 'Me, the future King of this country, I am reduced to being a mocked servant!'

'Let us renounce this plotting. Fate is not favourable to us.'

'There is one last chance,' judged Sadoq. 'Jeroboam's idea was excellent, but we used it badly. The apprentices are too devoted to Hiram.'

'Do you intend to corrupt the masters?' said the ex-labour head ironically. 'They would die for Hiram!'

'I'm thinking of the companions. Let us give up the idea of using corruption and let's consider ambition. Among them there are some who ardently desire to become masters, discover the password that will open the door to the great mysteries. First of all, we have to weaken Hiram's prestige. Let us make his masterpiece fail. Then, let us persuade two or three companions to force that bad architect to deliver the secrets of the mastery. Thus, the heart of the Brotherhood will be destroyed. Finally, we prove that Solomon is a weakling, who compromises Israel's security and betrays Yahweh's law.'

Elihap, despite the fear he was feeling which made it difficult for him to breathe, dared not protest.

Hopeful again, Jeroboam smoothed his hair. The High Priest was a remarkable spirit, but dangerous. Once Solomon had been deposed, to eliminate Sadoq would be vital.

*

The land of Sheba lived in peace and happiness. The vast forests, where monkeys leaped, ornamented the summit of the hills between which rivers flowed with jasmine on their banks. The plains were full of giant gardenias where hundreds of birds nested, with their brilliant red, green and yellow plumage.

When the sun rose, Balkis, the Queen of Sheba, appeared on the upper balcony of her temple. It was decorated with sphinxes and stelae dedicated to the Egyptian goddess Hathor. She admired the suspended gardens crowned with olive trees that were hundreds of years old. Legend had it that they had been planted by the God Thoth himself during one of his trips to Sheba.

Opening her arms to the rising sun, the Queen addressed a long prayer to it, a tribute for all the blessings granted her country and her people. Today as yesterday, the mountains produced gold. Specialists would harvest incense, different types of cinnamon; some fishermen would dive for pearls.

These splendours would be taken to the palace where the Queen would call for the blessings of the sun and of the moon to be bestowed on them.

A silver hoopoe bird landed on the terrace's stone parapet. Was it an omen that a messenger from Israel was about to arrive? In fact, the Prime Minister soon came to see Balkis with a letter.

She read it with joy.

'I will come,' she murmured, 'in a year, Solomon, I will come to Jerusalem.'

43

Inspired by the purification basins situated in the forecourt of Egyptian temples, Hiram had conceived the project of a monumental bronze basin that he was now ready to create on the banks of the River Jordan. The masters, upon looking at the plans, had termed the architect's masterpiece, the 'sea of bronze'. They feared the technical difficulties, almost insurmountable, that the casters would have to face.

Brick walls had been erected around a gigantic mould dug in the sand. It would receive the molten bronze issued from the open mouth of various furnaces.

Hiram was disquieted. The enterprise promised to be perilous. Multiple channels allowed for the deviation of the river of fire if an accident occurred. But the precautions taken did not reassure the Master Mason. Of all those who would work on the site he asked that they should interrupt work at the first sign of danger. He was even tempted to leave his creation in the realm of dreams, but the enthusiasm of the masters was such that he agreed not go back on his plans.

Hiram verified one of the scaffolds placed around the future 'sea of bronze'. He examined at length the furnace placed under it, and made the workers repeat ten times the gestures they would have to make. Everything seemed in order. The stimulus of critical moments quickened the hearts.

According to the casters' tradition, the work started when the stars became visible. During the night, the slightest anomaly would be immediately spotted. The eye would be able to follow the meanders of the fire.

That was the moment chosen by Jeroboam and two men on chore duties to act. The surveillance of the work site had relaxed and obscurity favoured their intention. They fissured the main mould in several places.

Hiram raised his right hand. From the summit of the brick towers the metal poured into the channels that would lead it into the furnace. The molten red metal broke the darkness, illuminating the waters of the river and the surrounding countryside. The flabbergasted artisans had the impression that a fractured sun had burst out of the depths of the earth, a light from the nether world nourished by the flames of hell. The incandescent river seemed to flow from a forbidden world governed by unknown laws.

The ignited flow became inflated, threatening to burst out of its channels. But the caster managed to regulate it and keep it within bounds. Hiram and the masters themselves broke the terracotta stoppers blocking the passages heading in the direction of the furnace.

When all the channels were filled by that metallic lava, their network formed a fiery landscape irrigated by a hundred rivers converging towards an insatiable central mouth. Fascinated, the artisans watched the metal casting fill the cavities of the 'sea of bronze'. Smiles flashed across faces reddened by the heat. The masterpiece was taking shape.

Suddenly, the burning liquid overflowed out of one of the channels, threatening to set a wood scaffolding on fire.

'The fire jars!' screamed the Master Mason.

On the top of the tower, several casters used long poles with attached jars at their extremity. They plunged them into the metal torrent whose mass and flux they managed to reduce. The operation was carried out so quickly that no damage was inflicted on the vast bowl. The excess bronze poured into the earth where it fizzled out.

Hiram made sure that none of the workers had been wounded. He breathed a sigh of relief. The casting began to take place, starting to trace the immense circle of the 'sea of bronze' and giving shape to the massive forms of the twelve bulls that would uphold it.

A scream of terror pierced his heart.

'The mould! The mould is bursting!'

The caster who had just observed the fissure was sprinkled with a furious jet of lava that had escaped its container. With his face and chest turned to carbon, he died on the spot.

Everywhere on its course, the river of fire tried to overflow its banks. A few minutes more and the 'sea of bronze' would be born.

A companion rushed towards Hiram.

'Master, you must stop the casting, if it overflows everything will be destroyed and there will be dozens dead.'

'If we intervene too early, it will be worse.'

The mould cracked even more, but the bronze was solidifying. The companion, thinking the Master Mason had lost his mind and that he was only concerned with his masterpiece, forgetting his Brothers, climbed to the summit of one of the log towers containing thousands of litres of water. Crazed with terror, he liberated the flood.

While the casting continued to make the mould whine, the burning surface, in contact with the water, was transformed into a geyser. A rain of fire fell on the workers who ran away screaming. Many of them fell near the scaffolds, which soon caught fire.

Solomon admired the creation of Master Hiram. The 'sea of bronze', still fuming, emerged sound from the night of suffering and misfortune during which it was engendered. From the moment the disaster was announced, the King had left Jerusalem for the foundries on the banks of the River Jordan. More than fifty workers had died. About one hundred were horribly burned. But the 'sea of bronze' had gone through the trial victorious. Born in the spirit of genius, the purification basin with twelve bulls was henceforth part of the greatest marvels fashioned by human hand.

In the middle of that scenery of devastation stood a monument of stunning beauty.

'Where is Master Hiram?' asked the King to the foundry supervisor.

'No one knows. He organised assistance to the wounded, then he disappeared.'

'Let the masterpiece be carried to the temple's forecourt. See that nothing damages it.'

Solomon ordered a squad of soldiers from his personal guard should stay on the work site. No soldier was allowed to accompany him. It was up to him, exclusively, to find the architect.

He walked along the river and reached a barrier of reeds. He was convinced that Master Hiram, cruelly wounded by the death of those he governed, had sought refuge in the most remote solitude. Pushing aside the vegetal curtain, Solomon ventured into a hostile universe where some small carnivorous animals attacked bird's nests. Some broken stems proved to the monarch that the Master Mason had taken that path. When he was an adolescent, the King had hunted in these recondite places where he loved dreaming of wisdom.

When he reached the top of the hill of red earth dominating the hibiscus lake, a tiny surface of water surrounded by sweet-smelling plants, Solomon saw Hiram. Naked, he was washing, scrubbing his skin with natron.

The King made some twigs crackle, Hiram raised his head, saw the intruder, but did not modify the rhythm of his gestures. Once his ablutions were finished, he donned a white and red tunic and then sat by the side of the lake. Solomon joined him and sat by his side.

'It is an immense victory, Master Hiram. The "sea of bronze" is prodigious.'

'The most horrendous of my defeats. Men have died because of me.'

276

'You're wrong. I am convinced that there was sabotage. We will prove it and punish the culprits.'

'I should have foreseen it and thwarted their trap.'

'You are but a man. Why burden your shoulders with every misfortune?'

'That work site was mine and the disaster is my responsibility.'

'You are too proud. Has your masterpiece not become a reality?'

'Its price is too high. No creation justifies the loss of human lives. I loved those men. They were my Brothers. In my eyes, I am forever unworthy. The "sea of bronze" has rendered me impure. Nothing will efface that blemish.'

'As far as I am concerned, you have accomplished your aim. You have nothing to reproach yourself for. But you should not have lied to me.'

The architect turned his head for a moment.

'You are circumcised,' continued Solomon. 'If you were a Hebrew, it would be the visible mark on your flesh of the alliance with God. The men from Tyre are not circumcised. And you are neither a Hebrew nor a native from Tyre. With the exception of my people, only high-ranking Egyptians practise that sacred rite. You have hidden your origins from me. How can I possibly have allowed an Egyptian to build Yahweh's temple? I should kill you with my bare hands. Did you not hide in the sanctuary's wall some pagan secret that changes its nature?'

'Are you not seeking wisdom, Majesty? Do you not know that wisdom is the light at the heart of Egyptian temples? In that land, I was educated by the sons of the pyramid builders. They formed my sprit. Amon or Yahweh . . . the name of the Single Principle may vary, but that does not change its essence. Wisdom is light, not doctrine. Nothing tarnishes it. Whoever venerates it from dawn may find it sitting at his doorstep in the evening. I hope God has granted me the blessing to remain faithful to the teachings of the ancestors and allowed me not to betray you.'

'I prefer wisdom to the sceptre and the throne,' said Solomon. 'I prefer it to wealth. No treasure can compare with it. All the gold of Sheba is but a grain of sand compared to it. I prefer it to beauty and health. It was wisdom that taught me the science of government, the laws of the this world, the hidden nature of the elements, the language of the stars, the power of the spirits, the virtues of plants. But it escapes, it runs far away . . . Have you captured it within the stones of the temple, Master Hiram? How could I have let an Egyptian guide the workers of my realm? Is that not the error of an unworthy King?'

'I did not know your people or your land. I have learned to love them.'

'But you are still Egyptian.'

'What separates us, Majesty?'

'The event that will be celebrated on the occasion of the inauguration of the temple: the exodus of the Hebrews out of Egypt, the deliverance of my people oppressed by yours.'

'You know as well as I do that it did not happen the way you are evoking. The Hebrews manufactured bricks in Egypt. They received a salary for their work. No one reduced them to any miserable condition. Slavery has never existed in Egypt. It is contrary to cosmic law, whose son and guarantor the Pharaoh is before his subjects. Moses held a high position in his court. If he left Egypt to found Israel, it was with the acquiescence of the Pharaoh he served.'

'That secret, Master Hiram, neither you nor I should broadcast. No one is yet ready to hear it. The memory of my people has been fed on the tale contained in the holy book. It is the foundation of our history. It is too late to modify it.'

'I do not believe you, Majesty. By the temple erected on the rock of Jerusalem, you have decided to establish a new pact between God and Israel that will be a new alliance between Egypt and Israel. Disunited, neither country will know peace.'

Hiram read Solomon's soul, Solomon saw into Hiram's.

They did not confess this to each other, fearing to break the magic bond that united them.

Solomon knew that the Master Mason would not forgive himself for the deaths of his workers. Hiram knew that the King would blame him for having concealed his Egyptian origin. But the secret they shared made them Brothers in spirit.

'The temple is God's flesh,' said Hiram. 'The King is the one that makes it live. You are the sole mediator between your people and Yahweh. The only one, your Majesty.'

44

Before Solomon's departure, Hiram undertook to return to the work site. He had promised the King not to abandon the temple, to watch over the installation of the 'sea of bronze' and to finish the forecourt. But he also demanded he be left alone in the desert for three days and three nights. He felt the need to distance himself from any contact and to look inside himself for renewed clarity.

The Master Mason came across groups of a kind of marmot that ran at the slightest alert. He heard the laughter of the hyenas and the plaintive cry of the jackals. He saw wolves and wild pigs, bathed in an ardent sun, walked in the ochre sand and slept beneath rocks forgotten by the One who had created the desert. What was the presence that emanated from the immensity of that landscape like a column of incense, if not that of the Creator?

Hiram loved the silence, the vast emptiness crushed by heat, the abnegation of a land that had renounced fertility to make place for and welcome in the invisible perfection of being.

Nothing escaped the desert. The Master Mason offered up the death of his work companions. He buried the memory of them in the sanctity of that red evening, entrusted their souls to the spirit of the wind that would take them to the end of the universe, near the primordial source where darkness had not yet been born.

When he was about to take the track returning to Jordan, he

saw a red and white tent assembled on top of a dusty hill.

He immediately understood. The hour had come. The joy he ought to feel, instead tore him up.

Hiram penetrated the tent. A nomad, dressed as a Bedouin, was sitting there, cross-legged like a scribe. The short, pointed beard meant he was of the Semitic race. About fifty years of age, with questioning eyes, he offered his guest a cup of fresh water with some vinegar.

'Welcome, my guest. May I offer you shelter until the salt you will eat has exited your belly.'

Hiram accepted the salt of the earth, presented on an alabaster dish.

'How did you find me in this desert?'

'I have been in the region for over a month. Your coming was announced at the foundries. From the hills, I watched the birth of your masterpiece and I have not let you out of my sight. From afar, I saw Solomon come to you, then I followed you, respecting your retreat. Before you return into the world, I have to speak with you.'

'More than seven years after my departure from Egypt . . . Is it the Pharaoh who sends you?'

'Of course, Master Horemheb. Only the Pharaoh and myself know about this mission. Did you not expect a sign from the King of Egypt, as soon as your task was finished?'

Hiram took his head in his hands, like an exhausted traveller at the end of a long voyage. He had dreamt of this moment for seven long years. He had conceived it as a deliverance, a happiness with a taste of honey, a sun with benevolent rays. But there had been the drama of the 'sea of bronze' and the meeting with Solomon, near the lake lost in the high vegetation. The architect wished to return to Egypt, but he no longer had the right to leave Israel. To render assistance to Solomon, help him consolidate his throne and peace, finish the temple that would bless his people. Those were the duties he had to fulfil.

'Are you satisfied with your creation, Master Horemheb?'

'What architect would be unless he were to wish to place the dry tree of vanity in the centre of his garden? That temple could have been larger and nobler . . . But I had only the surface of the rock to work with.'

'Did you inscribe on those walls the wisdom of our ancestors?'

'Egypt is the heart of Solomon's sanctuary. Whoever can read Karnak will decipher Jerusalem. Whoever can read Yahweh's temple will know the mysteries and the science of the House of Life.'

'You have been the Pharaoh's faithful servant. For that, you deserve honours and distinctions. But the happiness of Egypt seems to rule otherwise . . .'

'What do you mean?'

'The Pharaoh hopes to see you return near him. He would have named you head of all of the King's works. Alas, Lybia's ambitions are rekindled. Siamun fears an attempted invasion. How will Israel behave? Will Solomon be an ally? Only you, given the knowledge you have of this country and of its King, would be able to warn us if ever there was treason. That is why the Pharaoh requests you prolong your sacrifice.'

Hiram drank the water with vinegar. Who would have dared discuss a Pharaoh's orders? Siamun did not give him a choice. When would he see Egypt again? Would another seven years in exile be inflicted on him?

Only the wind of the desert knew the answer.

That day would remain unique in the history of men. For the feast of the temple's inauguration, the streets of Jerusalem had filled with exuberant crowds. The villages seemed deserted. No Hebrew wanted to miss this most exceptional event. When Solomon announced the birth of Yahweh's sanctuary, Israel would be reborn, elevated to the rank of a powerful State, able to clamour to the heavens its faith and its hopes.

To circulate in the small streets was almost impossible, for the masses of pedestrians were becoming compact.

Everywhere there were priests dressed in white robes. The chieftains of the tribes of Israel, preceded by a cohort of servants, were sitting imposingly at the foot of the rock.

Not an inch of the slope going from the city of David to Solomon's temple was free of people. Everyone admired the enclosure wall, and its three rows of cut stones. When would the doors open? They were guarded by Solomon's soldiers and gave access to the esplanade that was the aim of the pilgrimage of thousands of believers.

That day would be commemorated as the most glorious in Israel's adventure. The one when the nomad God had finally found His peaceful abode. His sanctuary would be the place for the sacrifice linking the earth to heaven. The other divinities and the other cults would be abolished, vanquished by the formidable power of the One God.

Solomon put on Hiram a purple coat.

'Here is the insignia of dignity that you should wear on the day the temple is completed.'

'Will it ever be finished, Majesty?'

'Time has stopped on the threshold of the temple, Master Hiram. It surpasses its creator.'

The two men were alone in the forecourt. To the East was a sublime portico, with its triple alignment of more than two hundred columns. Through them one could discern the shapes of the Kidron valley and the green hills filled with sunshine.

'I want to forget everything that is the past,' declared Solomon. 'One hour spent here is worth a thousand days in paradise.'

With pain in his heart, the architect contemplated the site that would soon no longer be his. The majestic forecourt had an altar in the centre, to the left of which was the 'sea of bronze' supported by twelve bronze bulls, three on each cardinal point. The gigantic bowl evoked the sacred lake at Tanis, where at dawn the priests purified themselves before taking some water that was used to bless the food offered to the gods. The 'sea of bronze' had a rim sculpted with petals. It symbolised the lotus born of the primordial waters over which the sun of the first morning had risen. Around it there were ten basins each of a thousand litres. They were deposited on chariots that the priests would move according to ritual needs. The liquid necessary to clean the sacrificial beasts would be drawn from them.

Solomon opened the doors to the enclosure himself. Sadoq and several priests carried the Ark of the Covenant slowly inside. The tables of the Law left forever the ancient city of David. They would henceforth reside in the Holy of Holies of Solomon's temple.

The High Priest bowed before the King, who approached the Ark and touched it with veneration. He remembered the blessed day when, dreaming of an impossible peace, he had performed the same gesture. The divine law had granted him his most ardent desire. He closed his eyes, dreamed of a world where men would have abolished war and hatred, where their gaze would always be directed towards the temple so as to acquire wisdom.

'Help me, Master Hiram.'

The architect lifted up the rear supports of the Ark, the King the front. The weight, despite being considerable, seemed light to them. They passed together between the two columns, crossed the vestibules and then the *hekâl* where the altar of the perfumes was, the tables of the blessed breads and the ten gold candlesticks. Finally, they penetrated into the *debîr* where side by side the Cherubim kept watch; the latter stood at half the height of the Holy of Holies; the outer side of their wings reached the lateral walls, the extremity of the inside of the wings formed a dome under which the Ark of the Covenant was placed.

The Master Mason left.

Solomon presented the first offering of incense to the Ark. In the perfumed cloud, the divine presence was revealed. The

King felt enveloped by a warm light. The golden eyes of the Cherubim shone.

Solomon appeared before the people. Raising his hands, with palms turned towards heaven, he entrusted the temple to Yahweh. Thousands of faithful knelt, tears in their eyes.

'May God bless His sanctuary and the faithful! Thus, they will renew their alliance with Him. Thus, He will be merciful and give us His help to fight the power of darkness. May the Lord be with us as he was with our ancestors. May he not abandon us. May He open our hearts to Him, so that we walk His path. Yahweh, God of Israel, there is no God like Thee, in the heavens or on earth. You Who are faithful to Your pact. May Your eyes contemplate this temple day and night and this site where Your name lives.'

As the acclamations rose up to the King, he was over-whelmed with anguish. Would God really live among men on earth? If the heavens were too narrow to contain Him, what of the temple of Jerusalem?

Two smiles appeased Solomon.

The first, that of Hiram, magnificent in his purple coat before the 'sea of bronze'.

The second, that of Queen Nagsara, in full regalia, to the left of the High Priest, standing slightly behind him.

Both expressed joy and pride. Reassured, Solomon went up the steps of the high altar, placed at a height of ten metres, at the end of the forecourt.

The Master Mason, the High Priest and the Queen com-posed a triangle whose centre was the King of Israel. Around them were the priests. The guards threw open the large doors to the enclosure, leaving the way open for the pilgrims who invaded the esplanade.

Absolute silence reigned. All eyes were fixed on Solomon lighting the fire of the Holocaust, the spectators watching the ritual that celebrated the 'first time' held their breath. The flame that would not die out seemed to reach up to heaven.

Carrying a lamb in his arms, a priest approached the King; he slit the animal's throat, whose blood flowed along the rivulets ending at the four corners of the altar. The cinders would fall through a horizontal grid.

Upon a sign given by Solomon, trumpets rang, liberating the altar to a multitude of celebrants who came to sacrifice the animals that would be eaten during the gigantic banquet. More than twenty thousand oxen and a hundred thousand lambs would be immolated for the glory of God.

Solomon had succeeded. The temple was born. A Master Mason inspired by genius, Hiram, had given form to the insane project of a monarch in love with the absolute.

Solomon cried with joy, immobile and alone, in the Holy of Holies.

Hiram, crushed by the weight of exile and the death of his Brothers, cut himself off in the cavern in the company of his dog.

Queen Nagsara, alone, in her magnificent chamber in the palace, cried over her lost love.

Caleb, the crippled, drunk with gaiety and wine, celebrated at the table of the wealthy who sang the glory of Solomon, the wise King, and of Hiram, the Master Mason.

45

From the moment of its inauguration, the temple became the heart of Jerusalem.

People came to wander around the esplanade, talk and even conclude business transactions. It was forbidden to strike the pavement with a stick. People had to go barefoot or with spotlessly clean sandals. Priests, who were permanently in evidence around the temple, made sure no monies passed hands on the site.

Sadoq was more than content to move into the lodgings that, upon Solomon's orders, Master Hiram had built for the priests. A large wooden gallery, along the temple walls, led to well lit and well aired small rooms. There the direct subordinates of the High Priest were housed. They were in charge of organising the work of the fifteen thousand priests who daily officiated at the temple. To consecrate a priest who would then become part of one of the twenty-four classes of priests who looked after the holy site required a purifying bath in the morning and a clean white linen robe, then the sacrifice of three animals, among which was a bull. Candidates were given clothes and abundant food according to their function. The attribution of the different functions in the temple was determined by drawing lots, a procedure supervised by the High Priest. The burning of the incense was highly prized and desired as that task gave the right to eat oxen meat and drink excellent-quality wine.

Solomon bestowed on Sadoq an unequalled stature. Placed at the head of a powerful administration, the High Priest benefited from incomparable honour. Was he not becoming the richest person in the realm after the King?

Yet, the High Priest did not fall into the traps set by the Solomon. The King had believed that he could distract his vigilance by showering him with benefits. This had not made him forget the only reality that mattered: in the monarch's hands were concentrated both political and religious power. Despite the prestige he enjoyed, Sadoq was but a subordinate whom the master of Israel could dispose of at any moment.

As the temple was there and it satisfied the people, he may as well preserve it. That is, as long as the trio he still hated, who were leading Israel to its perdition, were eliminated: an ambitious Master Mason, an impious Queen and an omnipotent King.

The tool shack, planted on the edge of the field under an old fig tree, was large enough to shelter three peasants. At the end of a morning full of warm colours, it harboured the High Priest Sadoq, Jeroboam and Elihap.

'The inquest on the accident that took place at the foundry is going ahead, arrests will be made, the guilty will talk. If the name of Jeroboam is mentioned too often . . .'

The ex-head of work duties had left Jerusalem discreetly wearing a peasant smock, imitated by Elihap. As for Sadoq, he had left behind his magnificent robes, adopting a simple brown robe fastened at the waist by a wide belt.

'Let us not despair,' recommended Jeroboam. 'Solomon trusts Hiram to ensure the support of a solid Brotherhood that brings Hebrew and foreign workers together. But this is far from being as stable as they both might believe.'

'Have you bought their trust?' asked the High Priest.

'Almost. Several companions are very displeased with the way Hiram treats them. Three among them, a Syrian mason, a Phoenician carpenter and a Hebrew blacksmith, asked for promotion and were refused. Let us encourage them to find out the password of the masters and discover their secrets. In exchange for our support, they will convey them to us. Then the architect's power will be broken, putting the King in a difficult situation.'

'You can count on me to go further,' assured Sadoq. 'Get rid of Hiram and I will banish Solomon from the throne.'

Elihap did not know if he should associate himself with this new plot. But he was too afraid of his accomplices to object.

What remained of man after his passage on this earth? A luminous trace, a shadow, an emotion . . . Did they too go into the nether region where silence reigned, so distant from this world that even Yahweh's rage, thundering like a thousand tempests, could not reach them?

Thinking thus, Hiram watched the sunrise on the temple's forecourt, disturbed by his dark thoughts. Death flew around him like a night bird resisting the daylight reborn.

When the trumpets rang, the doors of the sanctuary opened and the first prayers were offered up to Yahweh. Sadoq proceeded to make the sacrifice at dawn. Blood flowed and the flesh of the lamb sizzled. The smoke drifted north, foretelling rainy days.

Joy had left Hiram. He disliked playing the role of a spy. To create a temple so as to shape ancient wisdom into a new form was worthy of the House of Life. To betray a King for whom he felt admiration and friendship repulsed him. To debase himself in his own eyes would be unbearable. Hiram had recurring dreams in which he was surrounded by menacing shapes . . . Were they warnings from the world beyond?

'You are very pensive, Master Hiram.'

'Your Majesty? You . . .'

'Sometimes I feel lonely, as you do, and then I come here just before sunrise to contemplate your work. God brought me the support of an architect of genius, perhaps even that of a friend. Would you be a messenger of that wisdom I seek everywhere?'

'No, Majesty, just a simple artisan.'

'An Egyptian Master Mason,' rectified Solomon. 'A man educated by sages and different from other men.'

'A man for whom the return to his country is come, Majesty. My work here is now really finished. The "sea of bronze" has been installed. No stone in this temple will shift for centuries. Free me from my charge, Majesty. I need your approval.'

'You are proud and fierce, Master Hiram, but you know how to deal with men and guide them.'

'Only when the purpose is to build, to govern is your business, not mine.'

'When do you intend to go on your way?'

'As soon as this last conversation ends, alone and without escort. In Egypt, I will sojourn for a long time in the desert. Perhaps it will purify me.'

'You deserve important rewards. A veritable treasure would hardly be sufficient.'

'I wish for nothing, Majesty.'

'And what about the members of your Brotherhood? What will become of them after your departure? You organised gigantic work sites, undertook great projects, hired and trained hundred of artisans, thousands of jobbers, structured an entire society. Who will it obey, if you are no longer its master?'

'Their King, your Majesty.'

'No, Master Hiram. I still need you. Each year great riches arrive in Jerusalem. The work of the provinces, commerce, distant expeditions have brought me more than twenty-three tons of precious metals. The richest sovereigns send me gifts. Thanks to the temple, Israel has become a great nation blessed with fortune. With the gold of Sheba, you will manufacture two hundred normal-size shields and three hundred smaller ones. My elite guard will show the first to the people on the occasion of the great festivities. The smaller will constitute the basic treasure that will be housed in a construction you will build. The rest of the gold will be hidden under the ground of the Holy of Holies. It would be used if my country undergoes a poverty-stricken period. It is my will, Master Hiram.'

The architect went to work passionately on this new enterprise. Masters, companions and apprentices were happy to continue their adventure under the orders of the one they loved. After having submitted a model to the King, Hiram surrounded the temple on three sides with buildings. These had three floors and were linked by hatch doors. The floors diminished as they went up. They would house the riches of the realm.

Along the road leading into town the most massive of these constructions would be erected. The House of the Forest of Lebanon. Inside this imposing fifty-metre-long, twenty-five-metre-wide and fifteen-metre-high Treasure, Hiram had planned a profusion of cedar trunks that would support the ceiling. At the summit would be a network of beams made from the branches of around sixty trees.

More than a year went by, during which enthusiastic community work was undertaken. It reaped its most beautiful fruit during an unusual autumn. The harvests of olives and grapes were exceptionally abundant that year. In the fields the labourers goading the oxen that pulled the plough admired the elegant silhouette of the House of the Forest of Lebanon. That vision consoled them in a labour rendered arduous by the aridity of a rocky soil where thistles thrived.

The New Year, marked by the feast of the Great Pardon, was preceded by a time of repentance during which Israel ritually expiated its sins. During the autumn convocation, a time when the whole nation implored God to grant them His mercy, all activities were forbidden on penalty of death. Severe fasting was obligatory.

On that unique occasion, Solomon authorised the High Priest to enter the Holy of Holies to purify it of the soiling from the year then ending. To mark the occasion he performed the sacrifice of a bull and a goat, mixing their blood. Announced by the blasting sound of trumpets, a procession headed towards the temple. The chants sanctified the countryside, where kneeling labourers heard the voices of their ancestors, reminding them that only the Lord made the earth fertile.

Around Jerusalem, tents and huts sprang up everywhere. Thousands of pilgrims came to reside in them, as well as citizens leaving their homes for the duration of the Feast of the Tabernacles that took place after that of the Great Pardon. Thus was commemorated the eternal wandering of man in this world. Thus was evoked the exile of a race torn between nomads and settlers.

Beside Solomon, in the temple's forecourt, Hiram listened to the choir of the priests chanting about the finding of the primordial stone that had been used as the cornerstone of the temple. He, the finder and architect, felt excluded. Towards what angle of the universe would his life be oriented from now on? Egypt refused him and Israel imprisoned him.

'The goat!' cried an officiating priest. 'Here is the scapegoat that will take upon it our impurities and our sins!'

The High Priest, helped by two assistants, led a superb animal, rebellious and undisciplined, to the foot of the central altar.

'Lord,' prayed Sadoq, 'your people have sinned. They committed crimes and violated Your Law. Grant them Your forgiveness. Be merciful. Banish this animal into the desert. Guide it to a precipice where it will die for the expiation of our sins. May it perish in solitude. Let no one come to its rescue.'

Sadoq moved away. A priest whipped the back of the goat and it bounded forward.

The animal stopped about a metre from Hiram. The eyes of the Master Mason and the condemned beast crossed. The former read no distress in the eyes of the latter. Only a pride that no misfortune could extinguish. The goat lifted its head, exhaled a sigh that came from deep within it and rushed to its death.

Caleb ate overcooked bread and fresh cheese. Anup begged for food, which the cripple gave him sparingly, whereas Hiram was engrossed with his work on new plans.

'You never rest then . . .'

'The Queen of Sheba is on her way to Jerusalem. Solomon demands that the capital should be even more beautiful. My artisans should accomplish miracles.'

'Even God takes rest.'

'He is not Solomon's servant.'

'Has the King become your best friend?'

Hiram put down his reed pen and stared at Caleb.

'Is that a reproach?'

The cripple lowered his eyes and concentrated on his bowl.

'No one can be a King's friend. A great part of the population admires and respects you. What monarch would bear the presence of a rival for long? You have been very lucky. The temple is finished and you are still alive. You should take advantage of it to go on your way.'

The Master Mason drew a red line on the papyrus. His hand acted with a precision and a rapidity that almost frightened Caleb. Did a spirit not drive it?

'You have always been a prophet of doom, my dear Caleb, but it has not come to pass. Thanks to my Brotherhood, Israel is a rich and magnificent country. Would it be fair that I abandon those who have built the temple and the palace? Would I not be behaving like a coward?'

Caleb was no longer hungry. He put the bowl on the floor and the dog licked it happily.

'The hunter does not miss the same prey twice. Solomon will kill you, Master Hiram.'

'Here is my New Year's gift,' said Solomon to Nagsara.

On the floor of the Queen's apartment, the servants unfolded a huge emerald-green silk carpet embroidered with gold thread. In the Eastern corner of the room, they set down an ivory throne; in the Southern, a bed made of purple fabric; in the Northern angle, a gold table laid with gold crockery; and in the Western corner, jars of oil, goatskins filled with wine and vessels full of honey.

The Queen contemplated the one she loved with a passion that her reclusion made all the more ardent. For more than seven years Solomon had not aged, no sign of wrinkles marred his fine features, now framed by a jet-black beard that added to his natural authority.

'Many thanks for your kindness, Majesty. But these are not the treasures I need. I suffer, my heart is wounded. The goddess Hathor no longer answers my prayers. Each night I question the flame, and it no longer answers me. Deprived of your gaze, I no longer have a future. You are too wise, too perfect, too far from common humanity. Would you not consent, like your father David of whom the courtiers speak with such tenderness, to succumb to weaknesses, to forget the State to worry about the distress of a mere woman?'

Solomon left the palace quarters reserved for the Queen. It was not she who occupied his thoughts, but Hiram.

Up until now, he had rejected the rumours about his Master Mason. He had not taken into account the warnings and the slander, for friendship should not harbour doubt. But a venomous feeling had started to burn in his soul. Hiram perhaps was another man, ambitious, a monarch hiding his real name. Solomon did not have the right to turn a blind eye, even though his lucidity might destroy this most precious friendship.

Suddenly, he felt like abandoning Israel to its fate and ordering the wind to make it disappear in the immensities of the sky.

THIRD PART

I am black, but I am beautiful, daughters of Jerusalem . . .
Tell me, you my heart loves
where you will take the flock to graze,
where you will take it to rest at noon
So that I may no longer err as a vagabond?

Song of Songs, first poem

46

From Israel's frontier to Jerusalem, the Queen of Sheba passed between the two rows of peasants who presented her with their most precious objects; they acclaimed the visitor coming from the richest country in the world. In the vicinity of the capital, Solomon had covered the road with pearls and diamonds. From the height of a nacelle, on the back of a white elephant who obeyed her slightest order, Balkis discovered the Promised Land.

A mesmerising beauty, her black eyes accentuated by green eye shadow, with a smiling mouth, a supple body barely veiled in a linen dress tinted with murex purple, her neck ornamented with a lapis lazuli collar, gold bracelets worn on wrists and ankles, the Queen of Sheba inspired awe and respect. To a charm that bewitched the driest of hearts, she added the power of a spirit as lively as the mountain eagle.

A shawl made of byssus on her shoulders, Balkis was at the head of a parade of elephants, camels and horses laden with gold, precious stones, silks and spices. They were driven by more than one thousand black natives from Sheba. Their Queen had a copper-coloured skin, like a Southern Egyptian woman. At the end of the cortege, there were heavy chariots laden with flasks containing myrrh, nard, lily, jasmine, rose and cinnamon.

Before Jerusalem's large gate sat Solomon, on a gold throne placed in the centre of a crystal platform that reflected the transparent autumn sky. Around the King stood dignitaries dressed in silk ornamented with coloured bands and woollen belts knotted several times around the waist. The priests' attire, enhanced with tassels, was of a hyacinth blue. Sadoq, upon the sovereign's request, was dressed in full regalia, although he remained hostile to the coming of a Queen who adored pagan divinities.

May she be able to teach me a power mightier than my power, thought Solomon, a wisdom greater than my wisdom, may she help me consolidate the peace that is the key to the happiness of nations. The King was thinking of Nagsara, whose presence had allowed him to initiate the work for peace, when the scent of the aromatic plant nard announced the arrival of Balkis.

The midday sun bathed the nacelle perched on the white elephant. The Queen of Sheba sat up. She wore a purple crown. In front of the pachyderm, servants waved fans to dissipate the cloud of perfume embalming the cortege.

Solomon stood up as soon as the impressive mount stopped. Sadoq, outraged by the impudence of that foreigner who thus dared to dominate the master of Israel, turned sideways.

'Queen of the wealthy country of Sheba, be my guest and that of my people.'

The elephant knelt. Two natives of Sheba helped their Queen dismount. She paused a few metres distant from Solomon.

'The universe celebrates your power, King Solomon. I come from a paradise built by architects who have sculpted mountains, brought water through channels and fertilised the desert. My ancestors dug lakes, planted trees and rendered the steppes green. To honour you with a sample of my realm, I brought a thousand gifts. When I saw the road leading to your capital, paved with pearls and diamonds, I was ashamed. Was it not better to throw in the streams the miserable riches of Sheba? All opulence becomes poverty before you.'

'My palace awaits you.'

'I cannot accept your invitation, Majesty. Tomorrow is the day of the Sabbath. A foreigner should not disturb Yahweh's cult. Before the stars shine, my retinue will have put up tents on the border of the Kidron Valley.'

Solomon, enchanted by the melodious voice of a Queen so familiar with Israel's customs, gave in to her wishes. How could he have heard, amid the concert of acclamations welcoming the Queen of Sheba, the cries of his spouse, Nagsara, forlorn in the luxurious palace she hated?

At the first rays of the rising sun, the Queen of Sheba mounted a white horse and entered Jerusalem. A silent crowd admired her. The most humble of wanderers felt that the fate of Israel was being played out in that solemn moment. The High Priest, who had not been consulted, was still angry. In private, he threatened the foreigner with divine wrath. Some women deplored the sinister fate that had befallen Nagsara. Everyone noticed the strange absence of Hiram, the Master Mason.

As soon as she dismounted, at the beginning of the sloping path leading to the temple, Balkis greeted the sun. Her prayer scandalised the cohort of priests. But Solomon did not reprehend the Queen of Sheba who, in a very sober light green dress, was even more resplendent than the day before. He requested that she take a seat by his side on the sedan chair of gilded wood that Hiram's carpenters had created. Balkis wore short hair, of a brilliant black and as fine as her eyelashes. Her features, as graceful as a doe, had the tenderness of doves and the freshness of lilies.

'What is the real reason for your coming?'

'To see the temple, whose perfection is sung by all peoples, to discover the country governed by a monarch whose penetrating spirit is famous and whose words are known as wise. Blessed are your women, blessed are your servants who are perpetually near you. Blessed is the God who placed you on the throne of Israel.'

'Those words are too flattering.'

'Has Yahweh not endowed Solomon with an intelligence as vast as the sand by the sea? Is your wisdom not more glorious than that of all the sons of Levant?'

'No one possesses wisdom.'

'Do not be so modest. Your reputation has travelled beyond Israel's frontiers.'

Solomon was suspicious. Did the Queen of Sheba intend to ask him to solve one of her famous riddles that ridiculed the wisest men and ruined the most established reputation? Whoever did not come up with the solution was dishonoured.

'I have, nevertheless, a reproach to make to you.'

'Which one?' asked the King, astonished.

'There are rumours that you command demons, that you understand the language of animal and plants. Would you have access to forbidden kingdoms?'

'Is there a realm forbidden for the one who seeks wisdom?' Balkis smiled.

'Jerusalem is a splendid town,' she said softly.

'The earth is a circle surrounded by water,' revealed Solomon. 'It is the architect of the worlds who has created it. At the centre, he placed Israel. And at the centre of Israel, the rock of Jerusalem where his spirit incarnated, an invisible presence that nourishes the souls of the just.'

The Queen of Sheba paid attention, drinking the words of the King like honey.

'Your marriage with the Pharaoh Siamun's daughter created a great hubbub. Why is she not by your side?'

'It is not the custom. She is only the first of my wives. You will see her at the banquet that will be held in your honour.'

Solomon offered Balkis his arm, helping her to climb down from the sedan chair. Together they proceeded up the steps leading to the esplanade where priests and courtiers paid homage to her. The Queen of Sheba discovered the judgement room, the House of the Forest of Lebanon, the colonnade opening out on to the Kidron valley, the palace and the temple.

She filled her eyes with these marvels. Balkis' beauty, enhanced by the simplicity of her clothes, fascinated Solomon's court. The perfection of the construction, surpassing those of the buildings in Sheba, made the Queen speechless with admiration.

'Who is the author of these masterpieces?'

'Master Hiram.'

'I would like to meet him.'

Solomon ordered his secretary to go and fetch the architect.

'Here I am,' replied the grave voice of Master Hiram, standing on the roof of the judgement room.

Balkis raised her eyes towards him. Despite approaching his fortieth year, the Master Mason had preserved his robust stature. His wide forehead, bearing deep wrinkles, bore the characteristic traits of a fierce character. His appearance had disturbed the group. Dominating Solomon and the Queen of Sheba, he conveyed a serene majesty that some found offensive.

The Queen of Sheba could not take her eyes off him. Like Solomon, she knew how to penetrate forbidden realms, where she dialogued with invisible forces. By the power of her thought, Balkis saw through human beings, going to the depths of their soul.

Solomon had the stature of a great King and the intelligence of those chosen by God. Hiram resembled him, but he burned with a different fire, darker, more tormented. Together, the two men rendered each other capable of the most amazing achievements. Separated, they would suffer the cruellest fate. But neither was fully conscious of this.

'Are you not aware that this day was meant to be a holiday?' asked Elihap, irritated.

'The Sabbath was yesterday,' answered Hiram. 'Today, my workers will feast in honour of your majesties. As for me, I have to work, this roof has to be finished.'

Elihap turned to Solomon, hoping for his support. But it was Balkis who intervened.

'Why not assemble your workers, Master Hiram? Should you not associate them with this moment of peace when two great realms meet in harmony?'

Hiram had never seen such a beautiful woman. The elegance of her silhouette and her fine features rivalled those of the prettiest Egyptians. Her lips smiled, yet her eyes betrayed grave thoughts. In her, the joy of a woman in love mingled with the serious stance of a Queen.

Hiram had sworn to himself that he would never use the powers he possessed. But Balkis was submitting him to a test that he must not fail. Giving into an impulse that came from his deepest self, he raised his arms, forming two T-squares, in a gesture that Egyptians called the *ka*.

For a few long minutes, he remained thus, immobile, similar to a man in vigil immobilised by the sun.

Irritated, Solomon took this for a senseless attitude. How could the architect convoke his workers who were dispersed both in the town and the countryside? The King felt like interrupting this charade. But Balkis stared insistently at Hiram.

Suddenly, a murmur rose from the crowd at the entrance of the forecourt. The courtiers bumped into one another, making room for the masters and companions who, in an aggressive positioning, surrounded the esplanade. By the surrounding alleys came hundreds of apprentices, followed by jobbers, stonecutters, quarrymen, masons, carpenters, joiners, foundry men, blacksmiths, who walked towards the temple, responding to the Master Mason's call.

They formed a silent and peaceful army whose power seemed evident. In less than an hour, Hiram had assembled thousands of men who, obeying a sign, placed themselves under his orders with more zeal and discipline than experienced soldiers.

The courtiers were frightened. Solomon remained impassive. Thanks to the Queen of Sheba, he now knew the limits of his power: he did not reign alone over Israel.

The architect crossed his arms on his chest.

'Your wish is granted,' he said to the Queen of Sheba.

'Take good care of yourself, Master Hiram,' murmured Balkis.

47

The soft autumn wind blew. It brought small white clouds over Jerusalem, announcing the end of the very hot weather. It was time for numerous groups of youngsters to camp in the vineyards, under fig and olive trees planted among the vine stock yet to be pruned. The most experienced taught the novices how to handle the pruning knife to cut huge bunches of red grapes bursting with sunshine. Usually, there was no hurry; this time, the most robust filled straw baskets quickly and hurried to empty them into a cellar where youths pressed grapes with their feet.

The master of the palace had requested quantities of fresh wine destined for the banquets offered by Solomon to the Queen of Sheba. He had put up numerous tables; all the courtiers wished to be presented at the reception. Directing a cohort of cooks and cupbearers, he ran from one place to the other, afraid of not being on time.

His attention was, nevertheless, drawn by the strange attitude of the secretary, who was going to his office hugging the walls. The master of the palace barred his way.

'What's happening, Elihap?'

'Nothing . . . some papyri to file.'

'The secretary lied badly.

'With these festivities, I am in a hurry,' indicated the pot-bellied secretary. 'Are you worried? Why?'

Elihap pressed on his chest a crushed document.

'Show me.'

'No . . .'

'Some secrets are too heavy to carry alone.'

Elihap's fear was so evident that he did not resist when the master of the palace grabbed the papyrus.

Reading it disoriented him.

'Warn the King immediately, Elihap.'

Solomon was getting ready when his secretary asked for an audience. Importuned, he acquiesced.

'Be brief.'

'Majesty . . . It is about a report.'

'Is it so important?'

'I'm afraid so.'

The King's curiosity was awakened.

'Speak.'

'The conclusions of the inquest are definitive. It was men who worked under Jeroboam who sabotaged the installations of the "sea of bronze". They are guilty of the death of dozens of workers.'

'Jeroboam . . . Let that report be kept secret. If it is divulged, I hold you responsible.'

Elihap bowed.

Solomon and the Queen of Sheba presided over a sumptuous banquet. Nagsara did not attend, for she was ensconced in her room with a high fever. Master Hiram was busy working with his best artisans to finish the judgement room.

'This meal is a sacred act,' said Solomon before the food was shared. 'May it be offered to God, as God offered it to our father Abraham under the oak tree of Mamre.'

Some chariots had brought to the palace barley, wheat, olives, melons, figs, grapes, pomegranates, almonds, pistachios, blackberries, carob pods, honey from bees, honey made from grapes and dates, served with grilled bread and meats. The wine, whose manufacture had been revealed by

God to Noah, flowed abundantly. Ceramic cups welcomed the warmly coloured red beverage contained in jars or in goatskins.

The King presented Balkis with rare myrrh from the thorny plants that grew in the sinister region of the Ghor whose arid landscape produced the most precious perfumes.

Poets read magnificent verses, glorifying the beauty of Israel and the virtues of her children. Solomon feared the Queen of Sheba would choose this moment to ask him to solve a riddle. But Balkis was content to savour the delicacies and to answer the admiring looks of the guests with smiles.

Jeroboam took off the hood that covered his head. He had cut off his beard, dyed his hair black, and disguised the scar on his forehead with make-up.

'I have run great risk coming here, Majesty.'

'You did not have a choice,' said Nagsara, harshly. 'A subject cannot discuss the order of his Queen.'

The colossus laughed.

'I no longer have King or Queen . . . This palace will no longer see me bowing before its authority.'

'Why are you so bitter?'

'What is the reason for this secret meeting?'

Nagsara, through Elihap, had convoked the man that the secretary of the King already considered a renegade and a rebel.

In the wing of the palace occupied by the Queen there was only an old blind man who spent his time sleeping. The other servants were serving at the banquet table.

The Egyptian was afraid of herself. From Jeroboam there emanated the violence of a primitive being, stubborn, capable of taking his hatred to extremes. But she could no longer go back. Her happiness would be conquered at the price of a terrible act.

'I need you, Jeroboam.'

The angular chin of the man who had once been the

commander of work duties was held high. The Queen of Israel was humiliating herself before him.

'I am listening, your Majesty.'

'Do you wish to be wealthy?'

'Tomorrow, Solomon will have me arrested. Riches will not save me.'

'What is it that you want?'

'A letter written by your hand to be received by your father, the Pharaoh. To flee to Egypt is the only chance I have of saving my life.'

Nagsara took a reed pen and wrote some columns of hieroglyphs on a very expensive papyrus.

'There you are, Jeroboam. Thanks to this message your wish will come true.'

'What service must I render you?'

The eyes of the Queen became animated with a disquieting glimmer.

'Kill the Queen of Sheba.'

The seven silver trumpets that announced the beginning of the daily ritual rang. The Queen of Sheba presented herself on the part of the forecourt reserved for pagans. Sadoq and the priests felt sure she would go no further. Only a true believer had the right to go beyond that point.

Radiant in her gold and crimson dress, Balkis stood still.

Solomon approached her. He offered her his hand and guided her into the part of the forecourt reserved for women. Scandalised, several priests looked away. When the King of Israel and the Queen of Sheba crossed Israel's sacred forecourt, Sadoq, revolted by so much impudence, went up to the main altar on which were laid out cakes made of fine flour, kneaded olive oil, breads, a mixture of incense, onyx, galbanum, and the thigh of an oxen. He preferred to concentrate on the celebration of the cult and not witness the violation of traditional customs. When a fly soiled the meat, the High Priest knew tragedy was about to strike. No insect had, until now, ever rendered impure a meal consecrated to the Lord.

Turning, he saw Balkis and Solomon going into the forecourt reserved for the priests . . .

Sadoq lit the sacrificial fire and prostrated himself giving praise to Yahweh. The temple musicians fulfilled their role. The eldest blew into the ram's horn, recalling the sound that Moses had heard when he climbed the mountain of Revelation. Then the harpists, the oblique flute players, those who played the cithara, lyres, tambourines enjoined.

The smoke of the offering and the music of the rites rose up to the clouds. Sadoq came down from the altar.

'King of Israel, I am firmly opposed to this violation of the Law. We are here on the forecourt of the priests and no other . . .'

'May everyone leave the sacred site,' ordered Solomon. 'I want to be alone with the Queen of Sheba.'

Controlling his rage, the High Priest obeyed. Balkis appreciated the deep homage that Solomon was paying her. She had the temple to herself, Master Hiram's masterpiece, under the warm sun. Thinking the light was too bright, the Queen of Sheba, with a melodious voice, pronounced the name of several birds, which, coming out of the clouds, darkened the sun. A hoopoe landed on her left shoulder. Yahweh's temple was full of the flapping of wings, the joyous flights and crystal-clear songs.

'Would you happen to speak the language of the birds?' asked Solomon.

'They give us a little coolness, Majesty. Do the souls of the just not incarnate in these fragile creatures, who are nourished by light and inhabit the heavens?'

Solomon no longer saw the blue sky. He forgot the temple's forecourt. He drowned in the gaze of that woman come from distant lands where the breathing of mountains was transformed into gold. An unknown feeling filled the heart of the King of Israel, a feeling that endowed him with eternal youth and the desire of a bounding torrent.

The hoopoe flew away. The stones of the temple were enveloped in a golden light born in the dawn of time.

Jeroboam could not have dreamed of a better occasion. The Queen of Sheba descended, alone, the steps of the priests' forecourt. Solomon was not following her, seemingly under a spell whose force he was slowly becoming aware of.

The Queen walked slowly, taking her time to admire the architecture born of Master Hiram's genius. The priests had left the temple, at Solomon's request.

When Balkis turned the corner at the angle of the House of the Forest of Lebanon, Jeroboam, invisible, would strike.

Solomon finally decided to follow the Queen, but he felt as if he was imprisoned in a vice. As if Balkis had imposed a distance between herself and the King that he could not transgress. The young woman entered the passage between the judgement room and the royal Treasury.

Jeroboam jumped out holding the leather string with which he would strangle the Queen of Sheba.

Balkis did not tremble. She knew immediately that the man with his head hidden under a hood wished to kill her. She stared at him without fear and again called numerous birds.

Jeroboam stepped forward but clashed with an invisible barrier. Furious, he managed to go around it. He was very near Balkis when he felt the first beak on his head. After the hoopoe came some crows, jays, magpies, buzzards whose sharp beaks plunged into his skin. With blood running down his face, Jeroboam ran away.

48

Face to face in the vestibule of Yahweh's temple, Solomon and the High Priest confronted each other openly. Sadoq would not back away. His faith had been insulted, he did not accept the sovereign's behaviour. Conscious of the risk he was taking, he nevertheless wanted to be worthy of the habit he wore.

'The Queen of Sheba is a magician, Majesty. She commands birds. By acting thus on the forecourt of our Lord's sanctuary, she is defiling Him and humiliating us. That your spouse does not belong to our race is a grave enough offence to Yahweh. That you should authorise a heretic, coming from a debauched country, to behave in such a way is a sin that Israel will pay for with blood and tears. Banish her and repent. Implore God's mercy. Otherwise, misfortune will befall your people.'

The King remained calm, showing the serenity that seduced spirits and appeased the anguished.

'You play your role well, Sadoq, but the High Priest does not govern the realm, thank God. The Lord is happy to inhabit the universe of the temple, and what happens beyond the forecourts and the enclosure is of no concern to Him. As King of Israel, it is my duty to marry the earth with heaven. God has sent us the Queen of Sheba. It was her gold that allowed the building of this temple. May she stay among us for a long time. Her presence is the most precious contribution to the peace we

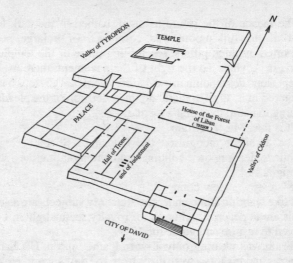

have enjoyed for almost ten years now. We must continue to build it. Pray for Israel, Sadoq, and let me reign.'

Is a King who is blind with love still capable of governing? wondered Sadoq.

The masters and the companions had left the work site of the throne's portico; that was where Solomon's tribunal was installed, adjoined to the large room destined for the reception of ambassadors. Hiram remained alone, dedicated to his task. A dark feeling intimated he should not waste a second. The need to create became so intense that he was no longer able to rest. From the floor to the ceiling, cedarwood panelling made the tribunal solemn and austere. The architect was himself working on the sculpture of the ivory and gold throne. Each armrest had the shape of a lion.

It was well into the night when he put down the mallets and scissors. He would sleep for two or three hours sheltered beneath the great colonnade and would return to open the work site at the first rays of dawn.

The façade of the future tribunal, bathed in the dark blue light of the full moon, was composed of a large porch supported by thick pillars, resembling those of the temple of Osiris in Abydos. To the right of the pavement, there was an abrupt slope descending towards Jerusalem. Large steps had to be carved in it, so as to facilitate the ascension of the pleaders, coming to claim the King's justice.

'It is late, Master Hiram.'

The architect recognised the Queen of Sheba's elegant silhouette, leaning on a column and contemplating the sun of the night.

'Majesty . . . How come . . .'

'I like walking alone under the stars. My subjects are asleep. Souls are at peace. The burden of royalty seems lighter. I ask heaven to inspire and guide me.'

Hiram was wearing only a worn leather apron. His hands, his arms and his torso were dirty from the day's work. No one could have told him apart from a simple worker, if he had not had that haughty stance of a man used to commanding.

'Where do you come from, Master Hiram? What is your homeland?'

'My homeland is this work site. I go from one finished work to another that has to be finished.'

'Where did you learn your art?'

'In the desert, looking at the stones and at the sand. They are eternal materials.'

'Only an Egyptian can express himself in this way. But Solomon could not have accepted an Egyptian build Yahweh's temple!'

Hiram kept his counsel. He felt trapped. To dialogue with matter was familiar to him. To answer the questions of this woman endowed with an agile spirit was a difficult trial, though to listen to her voice was a delicious pleasure.

'It is because of you, Master Hiram, that I have endeavoured to make this long voyage. Your friend, my Prime Minister, belongs to your Brotherhood of Architects. He insisted that my gold contribute to the building of the temple. I wanted to see it.'

'Are you disappointed?'

'On the contrary. I have also discovered a great King.'

'Are you not the heir of an ancient wisdom? Would you be planning an alliance, or things worse, with a shepherd's son, the leader of a rebellious people without tradition?'

The Queen of Sheba looked at the Master Mason, astounded.

'What surprising rage! Are you not aware that Israel is no longer a sickly nation? The tradition that is still lacked, did you yourself not provide it in building this temple? Would you be jealous of Solomon?'

Hiram banged a pillar with his fist and disappeared, abandoning the Queen of Sheba to the moonlight, her admirable body visible through her linen dress in the bluish shimmer of the night.

For the whole night, Hiram sculpted. A fever had taken hold of him. He carved a block of granite, giving it the shape of Balkis, a woman of shadows and of light, a distant goddess that had come to haunt the human world. An apparition from the world beyond. Too close to be forgotten. He modelled the round breasts, the slender hips, the flat belly, the long legs. His hand did not tremble. It brought into existence the beauty hidden in the stone, creating a queen he could caress and who belonged exclusively to him.

In the morning, he destroyed his work.

Solomon went up the six steps leading to the royal throne. He sat on the gold seat, resting his forearms on the ivory armrests.

He observed the gathered crowd, large and silent. In the first row were Sadoq and the priests, behind them the dignitaries of the realm. To the left of the throne, at the bottom of the platform, stood the master of the palace; to the right, Elihap, equipped with writing board and several reed pens. Thanks to the cedar panelling, the room of the tribunal resembled an oratory, where no voice would give in to passion.

Solomon presided over his first court case in the building erected by Master Hiram. The architect was making last-minute improvements to the House of the Forest of Lebanon; he was providing it with caches to house gold shields.

'We have to pronounce sentence on the unworthy behaviour of the former labour master, Jeroboam. He is accused of desertion and crime. He has not answered the summons of the secretary. Does anyone among you know where he is hiding?'

General Banaias asked to speak.

'I do, Majesty. I have just received a report that leaves us without any doubt of Jeroboam's villainy. He has taken refuge in the Egyptian court. Our law knows only one punishment for assassins and traitors: death.'

Nagsara was crying. Hot childish tears cascaded, impossible to contain. Her miserable plot had failed. The Queen of Sheba continued to conquer Solomon's heart. Tomorrow, she would reign over Israel forever, relegating the King's Egyptian spouse to despair and shame.

Nagsara felt no resentment for Solomon. He had fallen prey to a magician, born in an accursed land, who had come to Yahweh's country to spread misfortune. A victim of malevolent forces, her spouse had been blinded by Balkis' bewitching wiles.

The Egyptian would not renounce.

In her was awakened the pride of a race that had built pyramids and temples, fertilised the desert, exalted wisdom at the heart of human institutions. In her was the nobility of a lineage of Queens who had known how to govern the most powerful State in the world.

Nagsara went up to the roof of her wing of the palace. She put down a lamp whose wick she lit. The flame rose up into the luminous air.

316

With the point of a sharp stiletto, she dug into her flesh where the name of Hiram was engraved. For a few days now, she had the impression it was vanishing. When her blood gushed out, the Queen of Israel caught it in her hands before plunging them into the flame.

'My life for her death,' she implored.

49

The fresh water ran through the gardens planted with bay trees, sycamores and tamarisks. In the green valleys of Judea and Samaria, the perfume of the lilies and mandrakes embalmed the breeze twirling in the clarity of a warm afternoon.

'Do you like this house, Balkis?'

Solomon led the Queen of Sheba to the threshold of a wooden palace, with balustrades filled with vases full of flowers and windows closed off by crimson curtains. On the roof, doves cooed.

'I sojourned here for several months when I was a child. I spent happy moments in this place and I promised myself I would not return before tasting real happiness.'

'That of having finished the temple?'

'That of having met you, Balkis.'

The Queen of Sheba avoided Solomon's eyes and moved towards an olive tree. She took a stick and hit the branches. On the floor fell large ripe olives that she tasted.

'I learned to extract olive oil with a small millstone, behind the house,' added the King. 'It was my favourite game.'

Solomon removed the beams closing the country villa.

'I am thirsty,' said Balkis.

The King looked for a cup, cleaned it and filled it with fresh water at the well. The Queen dropped its contents on the earth.

'You, whose reputation for wisdom is legend, could you

present this cup to me filled with water that does not come from heaven or earth?'

Solomon remained calm. With accomplished mastery, Balkis had chosen this restful moment to assail Solomon and ask him to solve an enigma. The King's breathing remained unaltered. He sat on the coping of the well, and thought without jarring his calm.

It was by contemplating the two fiery horses that had pulled his chariot that he perceived the solution. Detaching one of them, he mounted it and galloped off into the countryside. Returning to the villa, he placed the cup along the horse's flank and filled it with drops of sweat.

The Queen of Sheba opened her right hand to reveal an emerald.

'Observe this precious stone, King of Israel. It is pierced by twelve almost invisible spirals. Are your fingers deft enough to pass a thread through it?'

Solomon held the treasure. No artisan, no matter how skilful, had the slightest chance of succeeding. Pressing the stone to his chest, he took a dry stone path leading down to an orchard. Often, meditating under a tree had brought him replies to the most difficult questions. He passed among the olive trees, brushed the trunk of a sycamore and discovered the saviour towards which his instinct had taken him: a superb mulberry tree whose leaves presented two different sides, with ramified veins.

After having carefully chosen the place to put the emerald, he went back to meet Balkis.

'I have entrusted it to the silkworm who will rewind his thread in the twelve spirals and will recreate the zodiac inscribed in the stone. Were you not asking me, in such a way, to always respect the teachings of the cosmos?'

The Queen smiled.

'Your reputation was therefore not usurped. Truly, great is your wisdom.'

Solomon's semblance darkened.

'Verily, a poor wisdom indeed! I have observed nature as the humblest of peasants. My science is immense, say those who are naïve. It is but an accumulation of heavy knowledge that weighs like a full goatskin. That science does not bring happiness or wisdom. It is like a sky, heavy and low. Too much knowledge causes pain and sadness; to increase it ceaselessly leads to madness. Who can unveil the laws of creation? What sage will come to know God beyond form, beyond even the light in which He hides? I am not a sage, Balkis. I have written treaties on the secrets of plants, of minerals, of the animals and the stones. None knows better than I do the word of the winds or the messages of the underground spirits. In centuries to come, magicians will use the Key of Solomon to open the door to nature's mysteries. Thanks to that key they will partake of my power. But all that is but vanity. What else could I still desire? Is it not said that I have the greatest powers within my reach? Is it not recognised that I practise the art of healing and of assuaging the sufferings of the soul? People admire my success and the realisation of my plans. From those false riches, nothing will remain. They are but an illusion. I am not a sage, Balkis, but I need your love.'

The hoopoe came out of the clouds and came to rest on the shoulder of the Queen of Sheba. In its song, the young woman recognised the words of a very ancient poem depicting the emotion of a woman in love: 'before the breeze of the evening blows and darkness falls, go to the mountain of myrrh, to the hill of incense. There he awaits you and will make you lose your senses.'

No man was more handsome than Solomon, none had such presence. Humiliated, torn by torments he was not able to share, he maintained the nobility of a monarch that the tempests shook without destroying. What Balkis was feeling surpassed the admiration a Queen felt for a King. She longed to run to him, to snuggle up in his arms, to abandon herself . . . Why did destiny forbid her from behaving like a woman drunk with passion?

'You are the descendant of the illustrious Sem, father of both the Hebrews and the Arabs,' reminded Solomon. 'If you consent to marriage, we will recreate the lost unity. We will forever obliterate the spectre of war.'

'A grave mistake,' she objected. 'The kingdom we would form would arouse too much envy. Our neighbours would rally to destroy it. And which one of us would accept submission to the other? Don't dream, Solomon. You don't have the right.'

'I dreamed of peace, Balkis, and it came about. I dreamed of the temple and it was built. I dreamed of love, and you came. Why refuse hope?'

'Sheba is so far away . . .'

'I beg you to think it over.'

Balkis was on the point of giving in when she saw on the road an ochre cloud of dust. A horseman belonging to the King's guard appeared. Out of breath, addressing King Solomon, he spoke hurriedly.

'Forgive me, Majesty . . . Your mother is dying.'

According to her wishes, Solomon had not seen Bathsheba since the day she decided to leave the court to retire to a vast palace near the Sea of Galilee where David had loved her, for a whole summer forgetting the demands of power.

On her deathbed, Bathsheba was lulled by passionate memories in which the poet monarch enchanted her with his poems.

When Solomon approached her bed and knelt to kiss his mother's hand, death again assailed the old lady.

'Here you are, my son . . . before going to the realm of shadows, I would like to speak to you for the last time.'

'Why these sombre thoughts?'

'A Queen must know when her death is come, accept it as a benevolent friend. But my heart is bleeding because of you.'

'What pain have I caused you?'

'Are you not neglecting the woman who loves you? Are you not seeking pleasures that turn only to sadness?'

'I only desire peace, Mother.'

'The Queen of Sheba will not reinforce it. Nagsara brought it to you. It is a grave mistake to ignore her. Go, now. I must prepare. Be just, Solomon. Be worthy of your father.'

Balkis had chosen to spend the night at the villa. The sun had risen when someone knocked. The young woman rushed to open, hoping to see Solomon, of whom she had dreamt the whole night. But it was only a red-headed green woodpecker, who flew away swiftly.

Disappointed, she walked barefoot in the dew, enjoying the morning light and the song of the birds. Would she continue to refuse Solomon's proposal for long? By marrying the King of Israel, she would cause Sheba to lose its autonomy. Would acting thus be treason of her ancestral lands? Did Solomon's love deserve such sacrifice?

Seeing some women drawing water, she returned to the house and placed a jar on her shoulder. Dressed in a simple tunic, she joined them. Suspicious at first, they were won over by Balkis' smile and agreed to talk to her. As she was alone, without companion, she could only be a servant.

The Queen listened to their complaints regarding the hard work in the fields, the violence of the Khamsin and a fortune-teller's prediction that heralded a glacial winter.

'What is happening in Jerusalem?' she asked. 'Is a foreigner still receiving the court's homage?'

'The Queen of Sheba . . . It is said that she has conquered Solomon's heart.'

'Would a wedding be on the cards?'

'That would be calamity,' stated a peasant. 'Solomon's wife is Nagsara, the Egyptian, no one else! The people have accepted her. If the King is a sage, he will not give in to a moment's desire.'

'It is said that she is very beautiful,' declared her companion. 'Our King is such a seductive man . . .'

322

'He can have a taste of love's pleasures, but Solomon must respect his marriage!'

'Would the union with Sheba's sovereign not promote peace?' asked Balkis.

'That is an illusion,' judged the most vehement of the peasant women. 'Thanks to the Pharaoh's daughter, Egypt and Israel live in harmony. Sheba will bring only misfortune. Solomon would do better to worry about the architect from Tyre.'

'Why is that?'

'With his army of workers, that Hiram is the true master of the country. He can create anything, build anything. He even looks like a prince and the demons lend him a hand.'

'What should Solomon do?'

'The King must get rid of him! Otherwise, because of Hiram, he will lose his throne. In our country, there is not the room for two Kings.'

With her jar full, Balkis wandered the nearby orchard, then sat beneath a fig tree. The sweetness of the fruit on her tongue, the freshness of its shadow, the tenderness of the air . . . Israel resembled paradise. A paradise whose Queen she would not be.

50

Violent winds blew in from the East, casting the pestiferous odours of a holocaust over Jerusalem. Incense and burned flesh combined for an abominable smell. A cold spell hit Israel; numerous priests, obliged to walk barefoot on the forecourt floors, fell ill. Colds and dysentery kept them from the cult whose organisation left a lot to be desired.

Solomon stayed in his palace. He had not granted audiences for a week. When the Queen of Sheba announced her irrevocable decision not to marry him, he had immured himself in silence, refusing even to see Sadoq and Elihap.

The last lodgings for the priests were finished. Hiram had given orders to remove the scaffolding and clean the façades. The sacred site of Jerusalem, on the rock domesticated by the architect, now shone in its final splendour.

How could it gladden Solomon's heart, when he had suffered his first ever failure and the most painful of defeats?

From Ezion-Geber on the banks of the Jordan, Hiram went from one work site to another. As the great works in Jerusalem were finished, he assigned new functions to the worker corporations that answered to him. He had made the Brotherhood's organisation where there had been anarchy. At the head of each artisan profession, he placed a worker in charge of reporting on their activities to the council of the masters. In a few years, Israel would be a new Egypt. Carpenters and stonecutters would rebuild villages, erect new temples and make towns magnificent.

Anup followed his master everywhere, whereas Caleb kept order in the grotto where Hiram persisted in living, refusing any other residence. It was there that he granted himself a few hours rest between trips. The cripple had opened a path to the neighbouring spring, hidden by chaotic vegetation, where bushes, jasmine climbers and young palm trees mingled. It was Solomon himself who, at the beginning of his reign, had found that water spring thanks his father's water-diving rod.

The architect came to wash there every morning.

He did not expect to meet the Queen of Sheba, naked, gracefully splashing water on herself, glistening in the sun.

'Don't run away, Master Hiram. Would the sight of a naked woman frighten you? In Egypt, do not naked women play musical instruments during banquets?'

The architect retraced his steps and leaned against a palm tree.

'Your place is not here.'

'Why should a Queen not converse with the most powerful man in this country?'

'Who dares . . .?

'The people, Master Hiram. Its voice is something one should hear.'

'I know only those of my workers. To govern is not my profession.'

'Would you be that jealous of Solomon?'

'Do not marry him, your Majesty.'

The Queen left the water and dried herself with a white cloth and unhurriedly dressed in a light tunic.

'Do not marry him, your Majesty.'

Hiram had not ceased looking at her for a second. Neither had she tried to avoid his eyes.

'I will not marry Solomon,' she revealed. 'But that does not stop me loving him.'

'You do not love him. He intrigues you. He fascinates you, like the mountain lion. He will suffocate you.'

'Our natures are similar. I have nothing to fear from the King of Israel.'

'I must go, your Majesty.'

'Why run away again? Why take refuge in a work that no longer satisfies your aspirations?'

Balkis took some water into her right hand.

'Do you hear it flow between my fingers? Do you think about your destiny, a destiny being drained in this country and that would be reinvigorated in Sheba?'

'Why so many questions?'

Balkis watched him retreat. For a second time he escaped her.

When the sky turned dark blue, covered in stars, Nagsara went to the foot of the rock. Her head covered by a veil, barefoot, she resembled the servants who carried out the water chores.

Anguish oppressed her. Would Master Hiram reply to her invitation? Had the cripple given him her message? Above her, the sacred site crushed her with its imposing mass. How much Israel's capital had changed! The city of David had become Solomon's domain. No one thought of challenging the prestige of the King, equal to that of the Pharaoh. God had given His people an exceptional guide, whose memory would be even more glorious than that of Moses.

Nagsara might have been happy if he had given her a little love, like a wild animal coming back to its den after a long day's hunting. She would have accepted, always, to be his consenting prey, living only for the hope brought by a fleeting gaze. By forgetting her, Solomon destroyed her very being. That accursed Balkis had used magic artifices that the daughter of the Pharaoh could not succeed in countering.

She saw Hiram climbing a steep path. He too had covered his face in disguise although hardly able to disguise his imposing frame and commanding stance. Along with

Solomon, he was the only man who impressed Nagsara to the point of making her shudder. He did not possess the King's solar beauty, but his severity and his power made him as seductive.

'Here I am, Queen of Israel.'

'I need you, Master Hiram.'

The architect noticed the Queen's emotion. Her voice trembled. When the moonlight lit her features, he saw she had lost a lot of weight.

'Help me save Solomon. He must be delivered from the evil spell of the woman from Sheba. You are Egyptian, I am certain of it. We belong to the same race. The Nile is both our father and our mother. On this foreign land where fate condemns me to live, you are my only support. That is why your name is engraved on my throat.'

In an unreasonable impulse, Nagsara snuggled against the Master Mason's chest.

'Hold me . . . I am cold and I am so tired, so very tired . . . I simply want to be loved. Why does Solomon not understand?'

'The King will not marry Balkis,' revealed Hiram.

The young Egyptian felt warmer already. How well she felt, protected thus! How she would have loved that that chest, those arms, that face had belonged to the man she adored.

'That woman must be banished. She brings desolation. The oracle of the flame warned me. Be the instrument of my vengeance.'

'What are you asking of me?'

'That you should convince Solomon to send her back to Sheba.'

'Is that not childish?'

'You are the secret master of this country. If your workers strike, the King will be forced to obey you.'

'My workers only stop working when they are no longer able to carry out their task correctly. A strike is like a war. It must not be used for any blackmail.'

'So, you must kill Balkis.'

Nagsara moved away from the embrace. In her cry, the hatred accumulated through many sleepless nights had been expressed.

'My hands are made to build, not to kill. What you are asking is folly.'

'You too, you detest me . . .'

Nagsara collapsed against the rock. In the dark night that engulfed her, what help could Hiram have brought?

After an exchange of diplomatic correspondence, on Solomon's orders Elihap had made use of winter to take the road to Egypt so as to solve the problem posed by the sojourn of the traitor Jeroboam at the Pharaoh's court. If the alliance concluded between Egypt and Israel was not to be jeopardised, given the presence of Nagsara in Jerusalem, custom would demand an enemy of Solomon be extradited by Siamun and vice versa.

Elihap realised that the peace established by David's son was no illusion. Moving with just a small escort, he passed peaceful and happy towns and villages, where artisans belonging to Hiram's Brotherhood restored old houses and built new ones. Up to the border, Solomon's secretary saw a country that was peaceful and prosperous. He was taken under the protection of a detachment of the Egyptian army to the magnificent town of Tanis, lined with canals amidst gardens and parks where the villas of the nobility were established.

Elihap was struck by the silence that reigned in the streets. The Egyptians had the reputation of being a lively and laughing people. In the markets, people were debating hard. Normally, the city streets were filled with chariots. But Tanis seemed inert, as if emptied of its inhabitants.

The corridors of the palace were deserted. Not even a group of courtiers conversing. An attendant ushered Elihap into the Vizier's vast office, whose openwork windows gave out onto ponds with water lilies. The Egyptian Prime Minister was a tall and authoritarian man. A small black moustache did not attenuate the severity of his face.

'Forgive us for this mediocre welcome, but this is a dark time for us. The Pharaoh is gravely ill.'

'Are you afraid it might prove fatal?'

'The best doctors are at the King's bedside. They have not lost hope.'

'No doubt you must feel my visit untimely.'

'Not at all. But you will understand that many matters, even though important, will have to wait. Nevertheless, nothing stops us from talking about them.'

'The case of Jeroboam . . .'

'He is presently living in a town situated in the Delta. Our two countries are allies. Hebrew citizens who respect our law can circulate freely in Egypt.'

Solomon's secretary felt that luck was on his side. Siamun's succession promised to be difficult. Many murmured the name of a Libyan who, once on the throne, would think only of breaking off the peace treaty to favour Solomon's enemies. Banished, Jeroboam would perhaps be an important character in Egypt's future court. Elihap had to play his cards on several levels. Success seemed probable on condition he eliminate a dangerous adversary that he would never manage to integrate in his strategy.

'May I wish, in the name of the King of Israel, that his brother the Pharaoh enjoys a swift recovery. In regard to Jeroboam, we know how to show patience and will await for Siamun's decision.'

This attitude reassured the Vizier. Siamun's soul would soon cross the threshold to the world beyond. No medicine would be able to save him. In the shadow, the Libyan prepared for his demise. His partisans were numerous and resolute. Jeroboam, who nourished his hatred for Solomon, had already met with him. As he was not forced to expel him, the Vizier played for the time necessary to evaluate the new situation that would become clearer over the following months.

'Solomon's wisdom is worthy of praise,' he recognised. 'Egypt will be grateful for his tolerance.'

'A major worry saddens us,' revealed Elihap.

'What is that?'

'The fact that the Master Mason, Hiram of Tyre, who built the temple, has far too much influence. The members of his Brotherhood are everywhere in Israel and they obey only Hiram. Solomon is irritated by it. But how can he act against the builder of Yahweh's temple? I would like to know your government's position with regard to Master Hiram.'

The Vizier, who was there to be the Pharaoh's eyes and ears, knew Hiram was none other than the Egyptian architect Horemheb, who came from the House of Life. He had been asking himself for a long time now why he had remained in Israel after the end of work on the rock of Jerusalem. Only Siamun knew that secret.

'We do not have to take any stand on the fate of a foreign architect,' said the Vizier.

'He speaks against Egypt with vehemence,' indicated Elihap, indignant. 'He frequently proclaims his hatred for the Pharaoh, to the point Solomon was forced to bid him be silent.'

Thus, concluded the Vizier, the ex-Horemheb had really become Hiram. Seduced by the advantages of his position, he had forgotten his place of birth and betrayed his origins. As every renegade, he had become the fierce adversary of the land that had cherished him.

'Solomon is an indulgent king,' assured Elihap. 'His dignitaries will have to defend him from excessive kindness, especially with regard to Master Hiram. Would Egypt be offended by this?'

'I will say it again: we do not have to concern ourselves with a foreign architect.'

51

The retinue of the Queen of Sheba had settled in a field full of flowers facing Jerusalem. Hiram's artisans had built kiosks and pavilions in light materials, erecting an elegant wooden palace for the Queen.

Dozing under a fig tree, Balkis dreamed of a love as strong as death, of such a fiery passion that even the most vivacious waters would not extinguish it. The Queen had not slept for days. By announcing her decision to Solomon, she thought she would be relieved of an unbearable weight. She found that, on the contrary, she felt even more burdened. But how could she give up Hiram, the Master Mason whose true nature was that of a King? How could she possibly abandon Solomon, that King who would make a slave out of her?

Irritated with herself, she went into a garden where, between pomegranate trees, a vine had been planted. The most delicate displays of mother nature's abundance no longer gave her happiness. She walked around aimlessly, hoping for a sign, a promise. Suddenly, she stopped. She thought she'd heard a chariot approach. Was it her lover coming to see her, leaping over hills like a young fawn? Was he hiding behind the wall, hidden by the vine?

'Stay!' she shouted. 'Do not go away!'

The chariot had stopped. Was Solomon making a mistake coming here and confessing to Balkis that he could not get her out of his mind?

Christian Jacq

The Queen of Sheba was as beautiful as a luminous spring day. Her light yellow dress showed off her naked shoulders and underlined her breasts. A red belt emphasised the slenderness of her waist. Solomon was frightened, afraid of becoming even more bewitched.

'Stay,' she implored, 'I will dance for you.'

Her naked feet drew a spiral in which her body twirled slowly, as a leaf fluttering around a branch it has just left. Balkis drew invisible curves, creating a silent rhythm that matched the murmur of the flowers.

Solomon rushed towards her and took her in his arms.

'I love you, Balkis . . . Your lips are like honey, your dress is perfumed. You are like an enclosed garden, an untamed spring, a scented reed, like the water that fertilises gardens . . . Your love is more intoxicating than wine, the aroma of your skin is the most exquisite of miracles . . .'

The eyes of the Queen filled with hope. Solomon knew then that she no longer played with her passion. At the end of a tender kiss, he obliged her tenderly to bend backwards and laid her on the short grass warmed by the sun. He undressed her slowly with a delicate and precise hand. Their eyes remained locked in a loving trance. As love set their beings on fire, a hoopoe landed on the top of the pomegranate tree, protecting them from a forgotten world.

'You no longer need me,' stated the cripple.

'I had entrusted you with a mission,' reminded Hiram.

'It is accomplished,' estimated Caleb. 'The temple and the palace are finished. I have no one to supervise on the rock. You run from one work site to another. I am alone in this damp grotto.'

'It is very dry and rather comfortable.'

'It is bad for a man to sleep alone in a household, even one as miserable as this one. He will fall victim to a female demon. I want to escape that unfortunate fate.'

'In what way?'

Embarrassed, the cripple busied himself with the cooking pot where some vegetables boiled.

'Happy is the husband of a good wife,' declared the cripple. 'The number of his days will double. A strong woman gladdens her husband's life and ensures he will enjoy the fruition of many peaceful years. Such a woman is the best of fortunes. It is the Lord that grants such happiness to the true believer . . . even poor, the husband of such a spouse is happy. The grace of an honest woman fulfils her husband. She preserves the vitality of his bones, she keeps him young into his old age.'

Hiram tasted the broth.

'Would that beautiful speech mean that you propose to get married?'

The cripple became sullen.

'Perhaps . . . I mean, certainly. With a servant, hard-working and frugal.'

'The one you banished when we arrived in Jerusalem?'

Amazed, Caleb looked at Hiram as if he were a devil from the depths of the earth.

'How do you know?'

'Simple deduction. Are you sure you will be happy?'

The architect filled a bowl that he gave his dog, who lapped up the broth with delight.

'Of course. I do not have a dowry to offer her. But she is pleased to have me.'

'Where will you go?'

'To a village situated in Samaria where her parents have a farm.'

'Are you not afraid that that will mean a lot of work?'

'It is preferable to the slow death you inflict on me here.'

'Am I that cruel?'

'I do not like the atmosphere of this town any longer; remaining your servant has become risky.'

'Are you not exaggerating?'

'You are a great man, Master Hiram, but you are not a good

judge of imminent danger. Your power will eventually trouble Solomon. He will be without mercy.'

'Your prophecies do not often come about.'

'If you were sensible, you would leave with me.'

'Would you really abandon me, Caleb?'

With his back to Hiram, the cripple dried a tear.

'She is making me do it, Master Hiram, please understand.'

'You used to be my friend.'

Caleb was no longer hungry.

'I am rushing to meet her. If I stayed any longer, I would no longer have the courage to leave.'

The steps of the cripple became heavy. Hiram was tempted to hold him back, but what right did he have to intervene in the fate of a man who sought happiness elsewhere? The architect regretted not having conversed with him more, not having initiated him into the mysteries of Planning. These were now but vain thoughts. The cripple was already on his way down the path, leading a donkey loaded with his meagre goods.

A damp snout caressed Hiram's hand. His dog was thanking him for an excellent meal. In his eyes there was a love as limpid as a mountain spring.

When they saw Nagsara appear in the central alley of their camp, the Queen of Sheba's servants hurried to warn her. They had heard the rumours, they know Solomon's wife bore Balkis a fierce hatred.

Preceded by two soldiers and followed by several women servants, Nagsara was dressed in full regalia with a coat closed by a gold fibula. In her hair a turquoise diadem shone. Out of habit, she invested her visit with an official character.

Balkis was having lunch on the terrace of her wooden palace. A servant was perfuming her hair. Another was pouring fresh wine into a cup. The visit of the Queen of Israel seemed to please her immensely. She stood up and bowed.

'What a lovely surprise, your Majesty. Forgive my clothes.

If you had let me know, I would have welcomed you with the homage due to your rank.'

'Let us forget the protocol, please.'

'Can I invite you to my table?'

'I am neither hungry nor thirsty.'

'Let us speak under the fig tree. I believe it symbolises peace in Israel.'

The two Queens descended a gentle slope leading to the orchard. How frail Nagsara seemed, almost fragile! The woman from Sheba proposed the Egyptian remove her coat and her diadem. She refused dryly. Balkis sat down by the tree. Nagsara remained standing.

'Go back to your country,' she demanded. 'Your presence is pernicious.'

'Your voice trembles,' observed Balkis. 'You are exhausted. Why not rest by my side?'

'Because I detest you!'

'I do not believe you. You suffer, you are unhappy and you know I am not responsible.'

Nagsara's soul was filled with anguish. She had prepared for a violent confrontation, for such a sharp quarrel that she would have used all her strength to destroy the enemy. She would have fought. Nagsara would have grabbed Balkis by the throat and tightened her grip until . . . But the Queen of Sheba welcomed her with the kindness of a sister, without aggression. Her smile disarmed her and her sweetness beguiled her.

'I will not marry Solomon,' declared Balkis. 'He has loved me, it is true, like one of his concubines. What does this ephemeral passion matter to you who are the Queen of Israel. The one who guarantees peace between Egypt and your country. Show yourself worthy of your station, Nagsara. Your role is very important.'

The Egyptian burst into tears, covering her face with a part of her coat. Balkis stood up and took her tenderly by the shoulders.

'Sit down near me.'

Broken, Nagsara obeyed. Balkis took off her diadem, dried her tears and split a fig.

'We are women and we are Queens. That is the only reality. Solomon is the man of the Lord of the Clouds. No terrestrial love will bind his heart. Keep in the treasure of your memory the happy moments you have lived with him. I will do the same. Solomon is beyond this time and this country, Nagsara; he lives in a space that we do not know, in the company of angels and demons who help him build his nation.'

'Not to be loved by him is unbearable to me.'

'Who could bear it? Every woman, and you more than any other, would wish to keep him in the rays of her passion. But none will succeed.'

'You? Would you renounce?'

The eyes of Nagsara cried with hope. The Queen of Israel was but a little girl, lost in the meanderings of her folly. Balkis understood that it would be useless to try and reason with her. She had no reason for living other than her belief in Solomon's love reconquered.

'Yes, I renounce,' said Balkis gravely. 'Do not see me as a rival any longer.'

'Will you stay long in Jerusalem?'

'Perhaps a month. I must see the King again so as to ascertain our diplomatic and commercial conventions.'

Nagsara was once again suspicious.

'You . . . you will no longer tempt him?'

'Have no fear.'

The Egyptian felt she was caught in a turmoil. She felt veneration for the one she should have hated. But Balkis was giving her back her stolen happiness. Thus, the flame had vanquished. By offering it her life and her youth, Nagsara had distanced the Queen of Sheba. What did it matter that she felt her days bounding away like the desert gazelle, no one could prevent her from reconquering Solomon any longer.

52

The last rains of the winter had filled the streams and made the prairies green. Judea, Samaria and Galilee were covered in flowers playing a concert with the colours blue, pink, red, yellow and white. In the transparent air there floated wild perfumes, carriers of the earth's resurrection.

Israel became resplendent. The country enjoyed a quiet happiness that it had never known in the past. Each lauded Solomon's wisdom, God's chosen one. Each admired the dedicated work of the Brotherhood of Master Hiram who, continuing to travel from one village to another, continually inaugurated new sites. With his college composed of nine masters, he directed a peaceful army who built houses, farms, foundries, boats, chariots, opened quarries and renovated town-planning. Possessed by a frenetic creative drive, the Master Mason prolonged the impulse engendered by the building of the temple and gave it a formidable impetus.

Jerusalem, the magnificent, provoked the jealousy of other nations. Enthroned on the rock, dominating its provinces, Yahweh's temple and the King's palace stated the grandeur of the Hebrew State.

Solomon left his apartments, crossed the open-air court, took the passage that led to the forecourt the priests were leaving after the morning's sacrifice. The smell of the incense impregnated the stones. Sitting on the steps leading up to the temple, Master Hiram had responded to the King's summons.

'We have not spoken in a long while.'

'I am rarely in Jerusalem, your Majesty.'

'Is my capital no longer enough for you?'

'I have some projects to propose. It would be advisable to develop the lower part of town, and abolish the insalubrious alleys, create more places that provide shade.'

The sun, as fierce as a ram, already beat down with an intense heat.

'Let us go into the temple's vestibule.'

Hiram showed some reticence.

'My presence in that edifice might shock the priests.'

'You built it, is that not so? I am still master of this country. Every one of my subjects owes me allegiance.'

Solomon was not aggressive. He spoke with that pleasant assurance that disarmed his adversaries. The architect felt the monarch had decided to submit him to a harsh trial. He detected some reproaches in his voice.

The two men, under the indignant gaze of some priests, went up the stairs separating them from the two columns. Hiram admired the pomegranates that decorated the capitals. He had almost forgotten their splendour. When he passed between *Jakin* and *Booz*, the architect felt pride. To these stones he had entrusted a part of his being. To this temple he had given the very best of his talent.

In the interior of the temple, coolness and silence reigned. The empty room discouraged human passions. Solomon had hoped that the place would be appeasing and would remove his wish to speak with Hiram. But Yahweh did not grant him that blessing. What the King's heart had conceived, his tongue must express.

'My people are happy, Master Hiram. Israel enjoys the peace of the Lord. Nevertheless, I have reinforced the army. Siamun is dying. I fear that a Libyan might ascend to Egypt's throne. I will know how to ward off that external danger. There is another, more serious threat against which people believe I am impotent. You, the architect of this temple.'

Hiram, with his arms crossed, observed stone slabs on the roof with perfect joints that rivalled those of Karnak.

'What threat do I pose?'

'Your Brotherhood and its mysteries are detrimental to me.'

'In what way?'

'I do not control it. You are its only master. Would you agree to put it in my hands and subject it to my sovereignty?'

Hiram walked along the wall of the vestibule. The artisans had carried out the plan to the ultimate detail. The temple lived, breathed. The Art of Planning had transformed inert blocks of stones into living matter.

'No, your Majesty.'

'In that case, you have to dismantle it.'

Hiram confronted Solomon.

'I am the most despicable of ingenious men. I thought you felt friendship for me.'

'You are not mistaken. But a King cannot allow another power that opposes his inside his own country.'

'It is not my intention,' protested Hiram.

'That is irrelevant. Only reality matters.'

'Do you not understand that I am building this country in Egypt's image? By the work carried out, thanks to my Brotherhood, you have become Israel's Pharaoh.'

'I am aware of that, but you have acted outside my royal authority. Your Brotherhood has developed without my knowledge. Tomorrow, you will be intoxicated by power and you will succumb to it.'

'You misjudge my nature, Majesty.'

'I must protect you against yourself.'

'If you were not a King . . .'

'Would you feel like hitting me to assuage your fury? Think about it, Master Hiram. You know I am right. If you have worked for the grandeur of my realm, hand me the keys to your Brotherhood.'

'Never.'

Hiram left the temple, incapable of containing himself any longer. Solomon had foreseen that reaction. To twist the knife in the wound was indispensable. By opposing the man he admired most, the King saved Israel.

Hiram had but one recourse. Leave the country and return to Egypt as soon as possible. His blood boiled in his veins. To be so near his goal and fail because of a monarch who had become a tyrant . . . The first thing to do was to disperse masters, companions and apprentices, so they might escape Solomon's vindictiveness.

Before the entry of the grotto was a red and white tent. One of its sides was drawn up. Sitting on a folding chair was the Pharaoh's envoy.

'Your dog did not stop barking while I settled.'

'Where is he?'

'Behind me, asleep. He understood that I was a friend.'

'What mission has been entrusted to you?'

'None. I act of my own intent. Siamun is dying. The Pharaoh can no longer protect you.'

Anup came out of the tent and asked to be stroked.

'Protect me?'

'The Vizier and the high administration consider you a traitor. Do not return to Egypt. You would be arrested and condemned. We will not see each other again. I do not want to judge you. I hold you in the greatest esteem.'

Stunned, Hiram watched the Egypt envoy strike his tent, fold it, put it on the back of his camel and depart.

A pariah . . . that was what the architect of Yahweh's temple was reduced to. Israel banished him, Egypt refused him. His native land and his adopted country both rejected him. The desire that he had managed to stifle burst within him like a spring storm when it fills the dry wadis with torrents of water.

Hiram and Balkis crossed the famous gardens of Jericho, near the mouth of the Jordan. With winter bringing colder weather to Israel, that part of paradise preserved a pleasant mildness. Spring arrived earlier here. The fruit ripened quickly, taking on splendid forms containing abundant juice. In that city of palm trees, where the tree trunks exuded balm, the Master Mason, who had been silent during the whole journey from

Jerusalem, at last spoke to the Queen of Sheba.

'This is a splendid country.'

'Thanks to you I am discovering it, Hiram.'

'It is in the image of a happy love and full of promise.'

Balkis remembered the arrival of Hiram at dawn mounted on a brownish-red stallion with a fiery temperament. Without saying a word, he had shown the Queen a black horse. Without hesitating, she had mounted the animal, galloping off in the architect's wake. Together they had become drunk with speed and perfumed air. Together they had reached that Eden.

'Will we sojourn here?' asked the Queen.

'I am too old to dream. Let us go further.'

The horses headed towards the Dead Sea. Once they passed the alder barrier, the Queen and the architect penetrated a heavy atmosphere where breathing became difficult. They met a desolate landscape, almost deprived of life. Unbearable, a white light hit the naked rocks bordering an immense expanse of water into which some meagre wadis meandered. Here and there were crusts of salt and crystal cones.

'No one can breathe in this desolate landscape,' commented Hiram. 'Neither animal, or vegetable . . . only a myriad of mosquitoes that bite the skin.'

Balkis dismounted. She entered the turquoise water that seemed oily. She tried to bathe in it despite the smell of decomposed minerals that offended her nostrils. But her body was repulsed. It was impossible to swim.

'That sea sinks into the earth,' said Hiram. 'Like the mountains that surround it, this sea repudiates human presence. A door to hell . . .'

'Why did you bring me here?'

'This is what I have undergone for months now, Majesty. Today my decision is taken. I want to know the gardens of paradise.'

'Have you chosen?'

'To leave for Sheba, and build other temples there, other palaces: that is my wish.'

Suddenly in Balkis' eyes that desolate landscape became radiant. In the turquoise colour of the Dead Sea, she seemed to see Sheba's green hills, its gold mountains, the basins full of flowers of the capital of her land. Thus, her perseverance had triumphed. She had managed to seduce Hiram, that inaccessible man, too proud to accept love. And inexpressible joy then transported the Queen of Sheba to the river of her childhood whose banks were planted with tamarisks. There her woman's body had awoken to pleasure. The Master Mason delivered her from the past, from the time that made souls weary, and made her carefree and happy.

Shadows still prevented her from believing in that miracle.

'Would you abandon your Brotherhood?'

'That would be shameful and despicable. Many companions will follow me. As to the masters, I will show them how to take over from me; they will disperse. The Art of Planning will be transmitted.'

Balkis approached Hiram.

'For me, you would accept the dissolution of your work . . .'

'That temple is but a temple. What my hands have built, other hands will destroy. Only tomorrow's work matters.'

'Could it be that your friendship with Solomon is over?'

'I have already left that land.'

The lips of the Queen of Sheba brushed against Hiram's. Her breasts filled, her eyes filled with tears.

'Not here and not now,' implored Hiram. 'When we are in Sheba, my Queen.'

After the Master Mason's departure, Balkis stayed for a long time on the shore of the Dead Sea. She inscribed in her memory that mineral and hostile universe where her existence had been enveloped in a cloak made of hope and marvel. Hiram was making the supreme sacrifice by abandoning his masterpiece to a King who had not understood the grandeur of his architect. What could be a clearer proof of demented passion?

Soon, in Sheba, the Queen would unite with Hiram.

53

In the grotto where he had initiated them, Hiram gathered the nine masters who were at the head of the professions that composed the Brotherhood. On an unrolled papyrus, he drew the symbols that would bond them forever by mysteries only they knew. To the wisest, he entrusted his T-square and revealed the secrets of the cubit, the relationship between proportions that, beyond any calculations, would allow him to build the most ambitious buildings.

Hiram bared the arm of the one he had chosen as his successor. On his inner arm, on the bend of the elbow, he pressed a seal containing the T-square with unequal branches and the rule of the Master Masons.

'In you is incarnated the truth contained in Planning. Your forearm will henceforth be the measure whence the keys to creation will derive. Only the masters are to learn this.'

Then, Hiram established the chart of duties that his disciples must follow. He required that they take a new oath, demanding that they promise to admit into their midst only a companion who had passed the harshest trials. He asked them to leave Israel with the best artisans, as soon as the first signs of oppression became manifest.

'None of us is worthy of being your successor,' objected one of the masters. 'Each one of us knows this, you above all. Why deceive us into believing otherwise?'

'Go on working according to the laws that you have learned.

Be assured that I will never abandon you, even if large distances seem to separate us.'

Many of those rough men, used to suffering and pain, wept. One of them demanded that Hiram promise to return. 'How could the Brotherhood remain united in the absence of him who gave it a soul?'

'No man owns wisdom,' answered Hiram. 'It is the practice of our art that will make accomplished men out of you. Forget yourselves and think only about transmitting your experience. For my part, I have decided to conquer a new world. When temples shall be erected in the greatest countries in the world, there will be no more frontiers between souls.'

Knowing their enterprise was bound to fail, the masters gave up trying to hold Hiram back. They agreed the Master Mason had to escape Solomon's wrath first. The King was disturbed by the growing power of the Brotherhood. Then, the latter would prepare the arrival of the architect in an Eastern country, where he would again become the master of all the professional corporations.

The feast of the autumn had gathered together the entire nation, communing in the cult of Yahweh and of Solomon. The people had gone up to the sacred rock, under the guidance of the priests, reciting the psalms and singing the hymns composed by the King. The luckiest and the cleverest had managed to reach the forecourt, where thousands of faithful were crowded.

A surprise awaited the dignitaries during the celebration of the banquet offered by the palace: the presence of Queen Nagsara beside Solomon. Wearing the most precious jewels, made up carefully to disguise her thinness, the Egyptian seemed to blossom. During the meal, she smiled and conversed with a gaiety that she had not shown for years. She was gratified to hear the praise addressed to the sovereign. Nagsara took an interest in the rumour that told of the possible decline of Master Hiram, and seemed pleased to hear of the

Queen of Sheba's probable departure. The latter had not been invited to attend the festivities.

At the end of the banquet, Nagsara asked Solomon to accompany her to her apartments. On the threshold of her bedroom, she begged him to enter. The King resisted. Had they not been separated for several months now? He gave in in the face of the Egyptian's insistence. When she made way for him, he discovered with wonder a carpet of lilies and jasmine.

'Here is the garden where I once again wish to enjoy your love.'

Nagsara took off her diadem and knelt before Solomon, kissing his hands. The night before, she had contemplated the flame until it penetrated her pupils and burned her past torments. The young woman was possessed of a devouring force that deprived her of any freedom. Only Solomon's love could liberate her.

The Egyptian, with the tips of her pearly fingernails, made the shoulder straps of her linen dress slowly fall. Tenderly, Solomon interrupted her gesture.

'I beg you . . . Let me offer myself to you!'

Solomon perceived the presence of the demon that tortured his wife.

'You have gone too far down the path of darkness, Nagsara.'

'No, my master! I am certain that I have not . . . Your caresses will chew it away, your kisses will destroy it.'

'You're wrong. My love has died. Even if it were as vast as the Nile's flood, it would not spare you the torment that you have chosen for yourself.'

The King prayed to the Lord of the Clouds. Would he not grant him a new desire for that adoring spouse, a new fire for this moving woman? But Yahweh remained silent. Solomon looked at Nagsara with compassion. When his hands rested on the forehead of the Egyptian, they conveyed the warmth that put an end to the gravest maladies.

'Love me . . .'

'I love you, Nagsara, as a father loves his daughter.'

*

At the far end of a tavern of the suburbs of Jerusalem, three men talked quietly. The Syrian mason, bearded and pot-bellied, imposed his loquacious manner on the Phoenician carpenter, a small wily man with a thin black moustache, and on the Hebrew blacksmith, an old white-haired artisan who did not express himself very well. They were all companions belonging to Hiram's Brotherhood, although they deplored the strict application of the hierarchy that they judged excessive, the authoritarianism of the Master Mason, the demanding work.

'We should have become masters a long time ago, I know my profession perfectly well, I could teach it to any Brother. Hiram's behaviour is unjustifiable.'

'I have never protested,' added the carpenter. 'This time is too much.'

'I agree completely,' added the blacksmith. 'I had thought Hiram would be an exceptional master. By not recognising our merits he has proved the contrary. He is a stateless nomad.'

'Does he not come from Tyre?'

'He has too much knowledge. His methods and his teachings resemble those of an Egyptian architect.'

'Solomon should not have employed him!'

'That is not our concern,' interrupted the Syrian mason. 'Hiram possesses the ancient secrets that endow the masters with power and fortune. We have obeyed him for several years, he owes us a promotion to masters.'

'That is true,' admitted the blacksmith. 'How can we get him to admit it?'

'Let us speak to him and try to convince him.'

'What if he refuses to listen to us?'

'Then, we will have to resort to force. Hiram is but a man, he will give in.'

'Impossible,' objected the carpenter. 'We shall be severely punished by Solomon.'

The Syrian smiled.

'Certainly not. I have had a long meeting with Sadoq, the High Priest. He told me that the friendship between the King and the architect is strained. Solomon wants control over the Brotherhood. To see Hiram in difficulty will please him. When we become masters, we shall certainly manage to convince our colleagues to get rid of that pretentious architect and put us under the authority of the King of Israel.'

The Phoenician and the Hebrews were convinced by the parlance of the mason. Their fate was cast.

At the end of the autumnal festivities, the believers left Jerusalem and went back to the provinces. Master Hiram convoked all the members of the Brotherhood to meet on the banks of the Jordan, in the solitude of a wild landscape. Thousands of workers gathered there. Their number had increased with a speed that was as surprising as it was disturbing. The majority were but jobbers assigned by the apprentices to do specific tasks. With a brief speech, the architect recommended they have patience and courage. If they knew how to show humility and respect, they would gain access to the first mysteries of the Brotherhood.

Those young men cheered the Master Mason spontaneously. Many among them would, nevertheless, fail. But Hiram's voice endowed each one with the desire to succeed.

Once the jobbers dispersed, the Master Mason shared the bread with the masters, the companions and the apprentices. Some wine was poured into the cups that toasted the glory of the Art of Planning. The Syrian mason, the Phoenician carpenter and the Hebrew blacksmith stood out by the over-zealous way in which they served the masters, in particular, Hiram. They made sure that he, as leader of the Brotherhood, did not lack roast meat or round flat honeyed bread.

At the end of the banquet the architect addressed the group. He recounted the works carried out by the Brotherhood, starting with Yahweh's temple and Solomon's palace, then evoking the work sites, the foundries, the workshops where his

347

Brothers had learned to master matter making it reveal its most hidden beauty. Together, they adorned Israel with its first group of buildings. Other conquests would come.

During the pleasant autumn evening, Hiram's words became graver, he announced that the nine masters would exercise new responsibilities. They would choose by unanimous vote the companions who would be initiated in the great mysteries during the new spring moon.

The feast of the Brotherhood was coming to an end. Master Hiram gave the kiss of peace to each of its members. When he presented himself before the Master Mason, the Syrian mason could not resist asking him the question that obsessed him.

'Am I among the elected companions?'

The look the Master Mason gave him expressed such wrath that the Syrian was frightened and stepped back.

'Those words will long exclude you from the small circle of future masters. Be content to exercise your profession with rectitude. If you are worthy of the supreme mysteries of our Brotherhood, the masters will become aware of it. Forget your ambition, it will lead you to your downfall.'

Like his brothers, the Syrian bowed and received Master Hiram's embrace.

54

Preceded by the soldiers of the royal guard, Solomon descended from his palace to the Queen of Sheba's tent encampment. Forewarned by an onlooker, a crowd gathered along the road the King took, acclaiming him with an enthusiasm that left him indifferent. Balkis' invitation worried him. Her master of ceremonies had invited the King on her behalf for a meal during which the Queen would offer him one of the rarest treasures. What could lie behind such an unusual ritual?

Inside the royal tent, red and green silk cushions had been arranged. Languid, almost abandoned, Balkis savoured vermilion grapes. Numerous places had been set for guests, but none was occupied.

The entrance drape was lowered by the master of ceremonies.

'Welcome, King of Israel, please recline and partake of these delicacies.'

On the central table there were roast meats, steam-cooked with aromatic herbs in terracotta receptacles, pastries and fruits.

'Your Judean wine is delicious. Nevertheless, it does not possess the fruity flavour of that produced in Sheba. I shall have some jars left. Would you like to taste them?'

'Have you elected me your wine taster?'

'That is a severe comment. I have known you in more charming moods.'

'What fabulous treasure do you wish to present me with?'

Balkis stood up gracefully and placed the bunch of grapes on a silver platter. In her eyes, the pleasure of defying a monarch with such immense power was mingled with the despair of a failure.

'My departure, Solomon. Its value is inestimable. It will give you back serenity and the love of your spouse.'

A slight wrinkle marred the King's forehead.

'Do you believe you can destroy passion with distance?'

'It is not the woman in me that you love, but the Queen. From her you hoped to obtain an alliance that would reinforce the peace you have devoted your life to. I will sign that treaty. That victory is yours.'

Solomon poured some wine into two gold cups. Balkis accepted the one he presented to her.

'If you became Queen of Israel, we would reign over an immense empire.'

'You would reign, Solomon. You and you alone. I would be forced to bow before your decisions and obey you. I accept neither your customs nor your religion. My own satisfy me completely. I accept the alliance, but I reject dependence. To be forever loved by you would fulfil me, but to grow old as a slave at your side, never.'

Balkis sat down. Solomon did as she, taking her hands in his.

'You do not trust me.'

'Would I be worthy of my station if I were to give in to such a temptation? Drink, Solomon. Drink to our last meeting. Far from each other, we will commune in harmony. Together, we would have destroyed each other.'

'I refuse. A cup will await you in my palace. It is to our love that you will drink! When the night is full of stars and torches lighten our silk-decorated bedroom, your heart will open.'

Solomon thought the Queen weakened. But her voice remained firm.

'There is a time to laugh and a time to cry, a time to love and a time to remember, a time to live and a time to die. When you shall celebrate the sacrifice at dawn, I shall be gone forever.'

Solomon was sure that Balkis loved him. But he also knew that she would not go back on her decision.

'Tell me the truth. At least accept sharing your secret with me.'

The Queen hesitated.

'It would make you suffer.'

'I prefer suffering to doubt.'

Balkis turned away. She no longer had the courage to look at the King whose strength was so reassuring.

'I am pregnant with your child. It will be a son. I will name him Menelik and he will be one of the sacred ancestors of my race. Goodbye, King Solomon.'

Deserted, the tribunal room was silent in the dark. When Sadoq entered, torch in hand, he first discerned the wood panelling, then Solomon sitting on his throne. For a moment, he feared the King had been transformed into a statue.

'Majesty, I have looked for you everywhere.'

'Do not importune me, High Priest.'

'Forgive my insistence . . . It is a matter of the utmost importance.'

Was there anything more important than the loss of the woman he loved, who was carrying in her breast the son borne of his desire? Solomon had prayed to Yahweh to make him slide slowly into the void and into forgetfulness. He had dreamed of becoming incorporated into the throne of justice, transformed into stone, out of reach of both joy and pain.

'Will you allow me to speak, Majesty?' asked Sadoq, surprised by the monarch's state of inertia.

Indifferent, Solomon raised his right hand with lassitude. The High Priest interpreted the gesture as an assent.

'Your Master Mason betrays you.'

Solomon's countenance became sombre.

'In what way?'

'The inquest carried out by trustworthy priests has not yet reached clear conclusions, but it seems probably the architect is preparing to sell the secrets of his Brotherhood to Israel's enemies.'

Overwhelmed, the King wedged himself into his throne.

'He has refused to hand them over to me . . . What can I do? Hiram will leave.'

'There are rumours that he will not depart alone.'

Solomon leaned forward, intrigued.

'What rumour?'

'Some say that the Queen of Sheba has employed him.'

Balkis and Hiram . . . How could Yahweh allow that unseemly mismatch? Why so cruelly offend the King of Israel, the faithful servant of God. What had he done to offend Him?

'I thought, Majesty, that it would be timely to call the Master Mason to order and to admonish him severely. He owes you his fortune and his glory. It is to Israel that he owes allegiance. The man is proud and rebellious, but he will bend before your authority. Would you authorise me to take the necessary measures?'

Solomon could no longer act directly. Summoning the Queen of Sheba about Hiram would have been humiliating. The King was well aware that Sadoq was happy to gain his revenge. But had the architect not brought it upon himself by his unworthy behaviour? Tired, wounded, exhausted by an unjust suffering that distanced him from wisdom, the King accepted the proposal of the High Priest who, this time, seemed to be serving the realm's higher interests.

In front of the grotto, Hiram himself carried out the payment of the companions and apprentices. For the last time, he gave those men the salary corresponding to the effort they had provided. He knew them all, their merits, and had known how to conquer their esteem. As usual, the ceremony took place in silence.

Once the last man was gone, the Master Mason fed his dog.

Anup fell asleep immediately after his meal. Hiram went up to the temple. He wanted to contemplate the work to which he had dedicated so many years of his life, those stones where, according to the mission he had been entrusted with, he had incarnated the wisdom of Egypt in a new form.

At dawn, Balkis would depart for Sheba. Some days later, after having given his successor the final instruction, Hiram would follow. There, under the protection of the golden mountains, they would love each other. In his mind, the architect was already building a palace with a thousand apertures, terraces full of flowers, lakes for leisure, a temple flooded with sunlight. He would rebuild Sheba in resplendent light. He would dedicate its monuments to his Brothers who had died on the banks of the River Jordan, victims of Jeroboam's treason and his own lack of foresight. How could he expiate that fault that still haunted his memory, if not by creating again and again?

The forecourts were deserted. The priests rested. The thin crescent of the new moon dispensed a shimmering light. The Master Mason remembered the work site, the Planning Workshop, the correct gestures at the right moment, the enthusiasm of the artisans, the fire that animated both hands and hearts, the communion that effaced the fatigue and the disappointments. Perhaps he preferred those hours of anguish and hope to the finished work, the exaltation of the unknown task to the built walls and the finished rooms. But his preferences did not matter. His role was to bring the work to completion, without benefiting from the fruits of his labour.

Hiram saw a glimmer of light to the west of the Tyropeon Valley. Someone had just hurriedly blown out a torch. Intrigued, the architect walked towards the place where he had seen the flame.

A man was standing in the shadows.

'Who are you?'

'A companion from the Brotherhood.'

Hiram, used to the darkness, recognised the Hebrew blacksmith. His white hair shone in the night.

'What are you doing here?'

'I wanted to speak with you.'

'You should address the master in charge of your instruction.'

'I no longer need his teaching. I am worthy of being initiated into the great mysteries. Give me the password of the masters and initiate me into the secret of their powers.'

'Have you lost your mind? I would never agree to such a request.'

'Not even at the cost of your life?'

The blacksmith brandished a hammer. The architect did not draw back.

'Hand me that tool,' demanded the architect. 'Go back to the banks of the River Jordan, resume work and I will forget this folly.'

Although failing in words, hesitant, the Hebrew nevertheless gave vent to his rage.

'The password.'

Hiram put out his hand. The companion hit him on the head. Blood gushed out. Blinded, Hiram stumbled northward. He bumped into the Syrian mason.

'I too am a companion. Give us the password. We have a right to it.'

'Never!' exclaimed Hiram. 'What demons have possessed you . . .'

'Quickly, Master Hiram. I have lost patience.'

The Master Mason tried to distance himself, but his aggressor, bearded and corpulent, plunged a pair of scissors into his left flank.

The blacksmith and the mason, stunned by their own boldness, regrouped. They dared not follow their victim. Hiram, despite his wounds, managed to flee westwards. But the Phoenician carpenter emerged from the shadows and barred his way.

'Do not be so obstinate. Give us the password and swear you will not pass any sanction against us.'

Menacing, the little man with a thin black moustache held a heavy iron compass in his left hand.

'Go away,' ordered Hiram in a weak voice.

'That's enough obstinacy!' shouted the Phoenician angrily. 'The password!'

'I would rather die.'

'If you desire it, here it is!'

Furious, the carpenter plunged the compass point into the heart of the Master Mason.

'Why, Solomon, why?' murmured Hiram, slumping on to his back.

His corpse covered three pavement stones of the forecourt. The assassins contemplated it for a long time. Each blamed the other two for the murder.

'Let us not abandon the corpse here.'

Taking off their aprons they tied them together and created a shroud in which they wrapped the architect's body.

'How heavy he is,' complained the Phoenician.

'Let's take the path,' recommended the Syrian. 'We must hurry, someone might see us.'

Balkis had brought forward the time of her departure. Consulting a golden mirror where the radiance of the great goddess of Sheba was hidden, she had heard the oracle bidding her to leave Israel in the middle of the night.

A storm broke when the Queen's white elephant left the tented camp. Balkis managed to calm the animal, which was frightened by a succession of bolts of lightning, followed by heavy rain. When the pachyderm, despite the violent wind, adopted the rhythmic step that would dictate the pace of the caravan of the retinue of the Queen of Sheba, Balkis felt relieved.

She was finally escaping Solomon's influence. At the end of a long voyage, she would go to the highest balcony in her palace and would stare at the Orient, from whence would come Hiram, the man with whom she would unite her life.

The rain was so abundant that the waters of the Kidron were already swollen in the riverbed. The elephant crossed the muddy torrents. When the last native of Sheba stepped on to the other bank, the waters had already effaced the ford.

The night was so black and tormented that Balkis could not see, on the slopes of the Kidron Valley, three men reaching a hillock where they set down their burden. There, they hurriedly dug a pit into which they threw the corpse of the Master Mason. The Syrian and the Phoenician quickly bolted. The Hebrew, struck with remorse, wanted to honour the deceased. He broke off a low branch of an acacia tree and planted it in the earth covering the remains.

Balkis, on her way to Sheba, the happy country where gold was abundant, had passed right by the martyred body of the Master Mason.

55

Solomon galloped across the plain of Jerusalem. Barely touching the soil with its hooves shod with gold, his horse seemed to fly. Fleeing from his palace and the cup filled with a wine that the Queen of Sheba would never drink, the King had ridden up and down the countryside for days, hoping to get away from the pain that oppressed him.

He could not bear Balkis' absence. With her departure, gone was the promise of a happiness as warm as a summer lake. That woman would have shown him a new path to wisdom. United with her, they would have formed a couple capable of bringing peace to the whole universe.

When a black shadow surrounded the midday sun, Solomon thought his sight was failing. The phenomenon lasted but a few seconds. The King then realised that someone dear to him had just died. Although the celestial body recovered its brightness, Solomon spurred his mount and made his way speedily towards his capital.

The High Priest welcomed him on the threshold of the palace.

'Your wife has died,' revealed Sadoq. 'She never ceased asking for you, to her final breath.'

Nagsara was lying on a bed of jasmine and lilies. Her hands were folded over her throat, where the name of Hiram had been engraved but was now effaced.

Solomon kissed the Pharaoh's daughter on the forehead.

*

'Convoke my Master Mason,' ordered Solomon. 'How many times must I repeat it?'

'He has disappeared,' confessed Elihap.

'Ask General Banaias to help you.'

'We have found his dog, Anup. He let himself die of hunger in the grotto.'

'Hurry, I want to see Hiram immediately.'

The secretary bowed and left Solomon's office hurriedly. That very night, he brought to the palace some peasants who lived near the Kidron Valley. One of them stated he had seen three members of Hiram's Brotherhood carrying a heavy load the night of the storm that had devastated fields and houses. Questioned by Solomon, he took back his words and asked for a cup of water. He and his companions washed their hands, repeated the same formula: 'Our hands have not drawn blood and our eyes have not seen anything.' Thus, they ritually acquitted themselves of any possible crime.

The following day, the King received the nine masters who directed the Brotherhood. They revealed to him that three companions had boasted to them about their abominable deed, hoping that Hiram's successor would be grateful to them for having done away with a despot. Had they not acted with the protection of the King?

'This is infamy!' protested the King. 'Where are those men?'

'Disappointed by our refusal to make masters of them, they have fled,' said the spokesman for the nine masters. 'Hiram has been assassinated. We wish to recover his body.'

'I can help you.'

'You are not a member of our Brotherhood, your Majesty.'

'Do not make a King beseech you. Homage I do owe to a genius who was my friend.'

The nine masters followed Solomon who, when he left the sacred esplanade, took the steepest path leading to the Kidron Valley. His vision was haunted by the image of the Master Mason wearing the honorary purple coat at the inauguration of the temple. The vibrations of the sceptre held by the King pointed them in the right direction.

What crime had he, Solomon, committed by consenting that Sadoq should punish Hiram? Without wanting to admit it to himself, had he not betrayed the architect? By his cowardice had he not condemned to death the only man he had ever envied?

When they approached the hillock, the sceptre became red-hot.

'It is here,' said one of the masters. 'Look at the upturned earth and the acacia.'

Hiram's Brothers dug and extricated the body. The face of the Master Mason was peaceful, almost smiling. His own blood had become like a crimson coat. The masters formed a circle around the corpse and in silence celebrated the memory of the leader of the Brotherhood.

'Master Hiram will rest in the foundations of his temple,' decided Solomon, 'under the Holy of Holies.'

Pale blotches on the skin of the sick left no room for doubt. Leprosy was spreading through the lower quarters of Jerusalem. Relentlessly, it would eat away at peoples' bodies. Most Brotherhood members, on the order of the nine masters, had taken to the roads leading out to the neighbouring countries.

In the villages and small towns, the organisation set up by Hiram was broken up. The last apprentices were driven away. Some inexperienced artisans took over the workshops and turned them into shops. What good would a Brotherhood of builders be in a country where all the major projects had been completed?

Solomon did not oppose the destruction of the community created by Hiram. Who else would have been capable of overseeing it?

Succumbing to the supplication of his people, the King again turned to the power of his magic ring to appease the winds that brought in the plague. Once the invocation was over, the precious ring fell down on to the pavement of the temple's forecourt and shattered. The epidemic was, nevertheless, stalled.

The winter that followed the murder of the Master Mason was, according to the memory of the elders, the most rigorous ever. Snow fell for days, covering even the plains of Samaria and Judea. The mountain slopes had become glaciers. Yahweh's cult was reduced to short ceremonies, for the violent wind that blew on Jerusalem's rock prevented the priests from lighting the sacrificial fire. Icicles whipped their faces, frosted rains attacked the altars. To circulate in the capital's streets proved difficult. The inhabitants thought only of huddling around an oven or a brazier in their homes. The *Qadim*[1] coming from the East blew in gusts over Solomon's city and whipped up storms on the Sea of Galilee.

Sadoq, who made a point of rendering homage to Yahweh, died suddenly of an embolism at the foot of the high altar. He was hastily buried. The King did not appoint another High Priest. When General Banaias departed, in his turn, for the valleys of the next world, the monarch was content with a small army corps.

Balkis had departed, Hiram had been murdered, Nagsara consumed by despair, who could Solomon confide in? The three beings he had loved had gone from Israel. As if the peace earned by the King had touched neither their hearts nor their souls, as if a curse weighed down on the Promised Land.

Wisdom had abandoned him. He had not known how to love the Pharaoh's daughter. By betraying Hiram, he had deprived himself of the only man who would never have betrayed him. By not succeeding in preventing the Queen of Sheba from departing, he had proved unable to gain the love of his betters.

Solomon became drunk on the world and its follies.

[1] Wind that can be as violent as the Khamsin.

Each night a banquet was celebrated, filling the palaces with dances, songs, and drunken jokes. The guests were gorged with roasted meat and there was an abundance of wine to quench their thirst. Only the best vintages of the East were served. Foreign diplomats praised the King's hospitality and his exotic court. Shapely young women would sit on the knees of any willing man, awakening his desire by taking off their clothes as the banquets unfolded, transforming them into orgies where caresses and kisses complemented the delicacies. The accomplished courtesans were joined by young virgins who further excited the lust of the guests and added to the prestige of Solomon's feasts.

Thus, for a time, the King no longer fulfilled his role as judge. He had abandoned the realm's government to a cohort of civil servants directed by Elihap. A serious, conscientious worker, the secretary of the King stood in admirably for his sovereign, asking his advice only on the most delicate matters. With his agreement, he had increased the number of soldiers as soon as the Libyan Sheshonq ascended to Egypt's throne after the death of Siamun. Jeroboam had immediately encouraged the new Pharaoh to prepare to make war on Israel, but the Libyan showed prudence, afraid of suffering a serious defeat. He preferred to maintain the status quo.

The numerous wives of the King, originating from various countries, requested temples and altars to worship their favourite divinities. Solomon at first refused. Then, when all refused him their favours, in a veritable conspiracy, he gave in. On the summits of hills, at the foot of the valleys, in towns and villages, pagan sanctuaries were erected where Solomon's wives came to pray. Even the remotest sites where the Ark of the Covenant had sojourned were not spared, those where the Patriarchs had heard Yahweh's voice. At the nascent spring of rivers, on the seashores, on the outer reaches of the desert, obscure idols were venerated, sheltered in earth huts, in wooden buildings, enthroned in porticos or in alleys composed by monstrous animals.

Solomon no longer believed in Yahweh. He prayed to each of these foreign divinities, hoping that one of them would grant him the rest that he was unable to find in pleasure and drunken revelry. The people protested in silence. Solomon violated the law of the one and only God, but the country remained rich and prosperous, rooted in a lasting peace, fountain of all blessings. But Solomon was a king who mastered the spirits. He had more knowledge than any other man alive. He had inspired the most beautiful words, recited by the most famous bards, at the courts of the most illustrious sovereigns. His wisdom was admired by the most powerful monarchs and in the end it guaranteed Israel's happiness.

As he grew older, Solomon recovered the reins of his realm. After having inebriated himself with pleasure, it was with work that he occupied his every moment. With Elihap relegated to playing a secondary role once again, the monarch examined each document, received every civil servant, settled all administrative details. The clarity of his intelligence ensured numerous improvements to the management of the provinces and to the trade with foreign countries. The treasury became richer. Each Hebrew had enough to eat. Every birth was welcomed as a blessing in families that celebrated the festivals with fervour and thanked the Lord for living under the authority of this most benevolent of sovereigns.

The ageless King had become an old man, yet his beauty remained unaltered. On his features there was but one hardly visible wrinkle. The peace had been preserved, the people were happy, the country respected. Solomon had not failed in his role as monarch. When pronouncing judgement, he had not wronged any of his subjects.

Solomon was alone. He had neither children, friends nor counsellors. No one understood him. No one tried to divine the mystery of his heart. The King no longer rebelled against Yahweh. He no longer prayed to any divinity. Despair was his daily bread. The just, the villains, men and beasts, did they not make their way into the same void? Did they not emerge from stardust to return to the dust of the earth?

The one whose wisdom was praised had come to an insurmountable wall: divine creation. He had not deciphered any of its mysteries. Henceforth, he knew that no one would be able to. It all was but vanity.

As spring blossomed, Solomon understood it would be his last. He went out of the palace and made his way to the temple that he had not entered for years. Alone, in the Holy of Holies, he did not hear the voice of God but saw into the future.

Peace would be broken and the tribes of Israel would again tear at each other; armies, avid for blood, would ravage the country; Yahweh's sanctuary would be ransacked and destroyed. A future where the Promised Land would be governed by the weak, implementing the most miserable of policies, geared to sate but their lowest instincts. A future during which the people would no longer rest under the fig and the olive tree, enjoying the fair weather. Solomon knew then that as soon as he died his work would be destroyed. Nothing would survive him.

The King put down his crown and his sceptre, took off his coat embroidered with gold thread. He set off down the path leading to the Kidron Valley and left in the direction of the desert. On his way, he broke a branch and made himself a cane. The young sun burned his forehead. Soon his feet hurt. But he walked and walked, like the humblest of pilgrims.

Solomon had decided to proceed alone, until he received a sign from God. Was he not now certain that success and failure were but vanity, as were joy and suffering? For him, there was but the past already vanishing dimly into a broken horizon. For his people, there were still years of plenitude and serenity that would leave their mark on Israel's memory. Perhaps, in a time so distant the King's thought could not foresee, this would be the seed for a new era of peace.

The hills of Jerusalem were no longer visible. The temple had disappeared. Although he had little strength left, Solomon went forth on his way. He had no aim, no reason to fight, if not that passionate quest for an unattainable wisdom that he would so have loved to glimpse, if not conquer.

When his heart failed, the old sovereign stopped at the foot of an acacia tree in full bloom. God had not spoken to him, but, in the clarity of spring, he saw the contours of an immense face as broad as the earth, as high as the sky, Master Hiram's semblance, grave and smiling, imbued with tranquil wisdom.

The Master Mason forgave him his betrayal. He waited for Solomon on the other side of death. The King leaned against the acacia tree and fell asleep surrounded by light.

Notes

Solomon was the contemporary of the Pharaoh Siamun, 'the son of Amon', the beloved of Maat. Siamun, who belonged to the twenty-first Egyptian dynasty, reigned from 980 to 960BC. His capital was established at Tanis, on the Delta. Vanquished by the Philistines, he understood, like Solomon, that a durable peace could not be secured in the Near East without a real alliance between Egypt and Israel. For that period, see Alberto R. Green, *Solomon and Siamun: A Synchronism between Early Dynastic Israel and the Twenty-First Dynasty of Egypt, Journal of Biblical Literature*, 97 (1978), pp 353–67.

Solomon was a true pharaoh. He was inspired by the Egyptian monarchy to govern Israel. See in particular M. Gavillet, *L'Evocation du roi dans la littérature royale égyptienne comparée à celles des Psaumes royaux et spécialement: le rapport roi-Dieu dans ces deux littératures, Bulletin de la Société d'Egyptologie de Genève* 5 (1981), pp. 3–14 and 6 (1982), pp. 3–17; A. Malamat, *Das davidsche und salomishche Königreich and seine Beziehungen zu Ägypten und Syrien. Wien, Osterreichishe Akademie der Wissenschaften, Phil.-hist. Klasse, Sitz.* 407.

On the close parallel between the pyramid built by Zoser and Solomon's temple, two monuments which correspond to a desire of creating religious unity in a country, see J.A.

Wainwright, *Zoser's Pyramid and Solomon's Temple, The Expository Times*, Edinburgh 91 (1979–1980), pp. 137–140.

Here are, expressed in cubits, the main measurements of Solomon's Temple:
The two columns: height – 18 cubits.
Capitals of the columns: 5 cubits.
Width of the temple: 20 cubits
Length of the *ulam* (the vestibule): 10 cubits
Length of the *hêkal* (the sacristy): 40 cubits
Length of the *debîr* (the Holy of Holies): 20 cubits

On the daughter of the pharaoh Siamun who became Solomon's wife, see M. Gorg, *Pharaos Tochter in Jerusalem oder: Adams Schuld und Evas Unschuld, Bamberger Universitäts zeitung,* Bamberg 5 (1983), pp. 4–7 and *Die 'Sünde' Salamos, Biblische Notizen*, Bamberg, Heft 16 (1981), pp. 42–59. The author shows that the Pharaoh's daughter introduced the cult of the serpent goddess Renenutet, simultaneously a goddess of fertility and of nourishment.

On the influence of Egypt on the architecture and administration at the time of Solomon, see G. W. Ahlstrom, *Royal Administration and National Religion in Ancient Palestine*, Leiden, 1982; H. Cazelles, *Administration salomonienne et terminologie administrative égyptienne, compts rendus du groupe linguistique d'études chamito-sémitiques*, 17 (1972–73), 1980, pp. 23–25.

On the Egyptian origin of numerous texts attributed to Solomon, see O. Ploger, *Sprüche Salomos (Proverbia)*, Neukirchen-Vluyn, 1984.

Several Arab authors note that the natives of Sheba, who worshipped the sun, travelled to Egypt on pilgrimages to the Great Pyramid. They believed that the pyramids of the Giza plateau were consecrated to the stars and planets. Sab, the son of Hermes, after whom their people was named, was buried there.

About a possible link between the famous queen-pharaoh Hatchepsut and the Queen of Sheba, see Eva Danelius, *The Identification of the Biblical 'Queen of Sheba' with Hatshepsut, Kronos*, Glassboro, New Jersey 1, no 3 (1976), pp. 3–18 and no 4 (1976), pp. 9–24. On the legend of the Queen of Sheba and the historical and archæological context, W. Daum, *Die Königin von Saba. Kunst, Legende und Archäologie zwischen Morgenland und Abendland*. Stuttgart und Zürich, 1988.

Bibliography used for translation

E.A. Wallis Budge, *The Dwellers on the Nile, The Life, History, Religion and Literature of the Ancient Egyptians*, Dover Publications, Inc., New York, 1977. Unabridged republication of the work originally published by The Religious Tract Society, London, 1926, under the title *The Dwellers on the Nile: Chapter of the Life, History, Religion and Literature of the Ancient Egyptians*.

Donald B. Redord, *Egypt, Canaan, and Israel in Ancient Times*, Princeton University Press, Princeton, New Jersey, 1992

The Archaeology of Society in the Holy Land, edited by Thomas E. Levy, Facts on File, Inc., New York, 1995

Margaret A. Murray, *The Splendour that was Egypt*, Sidgwick & Jackson, London, revised edition 1964

Manfred Lurker, *The Gods and Symbols of Ancient Egypt*, Thames and Hudson Ltd., London, 1974